The Suicide Society

Book Three

Kill It to Death

A Novel by

William Brennan Knight

Published by Altron Services
Copyright © 2019 by William Brennan Knight

Printed in the United States of America
First Printing, 2019
ISBN 978-1-7339698-1-9
Published by Altron Services

www.authorwbk.com

To Mike D: A best friend for an entire lifetime, but more importantly, a brother to an only child. Thanks for always looking out for me.

Books in the Suicide Society Series:

Chapter One

Mr. Cox sat motionless in his 18th century Jacobean chair, staring blankly at a wall in his stateroom in the underground bunker in Desolation. While he appeared distracted, his mind worked furiously to repair the substantial damage Zach Randall and Jarad Anston inflicted in the consummate psychokinetic battle they waged just two days ago.

Millions of individual thought-control tendrils were severed, and several of the main hubs were obliterated in an assault that penetrated nearly every lobe of Cox' unbalanced mind. Perhaps the most maddening aspect of the whole affair was that Randall, Anston, the whore and another interloper managed to escape.

While Mr. Cox was successful in defending himself from further attacks, he remained too stunned and weakened in the aftermath to stop them. His subordinates found themselves paralyzed in a morass of self-loathing and confusion as the filaments of his control further weakened.

The only balm that soothed his wounded psyche was the knowledge that he defeated them, although Mr. Cox conceded the brilliance of their plan. While he focused his efforts on destroying Randall, Anston emerged from the murky shadows of conscious concealment and unleashed the collective telepathic power of their entire group on him.

As improbable as it seemed, Mr. Cox was utterly unprepared for the assault. Either the beneficiary of blind luck or purposeful intervention, one of the increasingly frequent but unsettling time resets occurred immediately after Anston launched his attack. Fortunately, only Mr. Cox was aware of the reboot, and Anston was caught completely off guard as the Benefactor preempted the assault in the new reality. In the aftermath and confusion that followed, the interloper, the one named "Marshall," appeared out of nowhere and combined his own abilities with Anston's, which allowed the foursome to escape. The sequence of events remained somewhat muddled, and Mr. Cox imagined it would take time and further healing to sort it all out.

As he focused on improving the efficacy of the global network, the Benefactor heard someone calling his name in the distance, prompting him to retreat from the noosphere and reenter the present reality. He opened his eyes to find his most senior lieutenants, Xavier Watts and Alfonse Delgado, standing in front of him along with the rapscallion computer genius, Alan Ziminski.

"Benefactor, are you well?" asked Delgado.

"I continue to improve, thank you. Are you here to provide a progress report? Is everything still on schedule?" asked Mr. Cox.

"Yes, our plan is unfolding exactly as we expected," said Watts.

Xavier Watts was the senior member of the staff, having joined Mr. Cox nearly twenty years ago.

"Good, very good. Nonetheless, something doesn't *feel* right to me," said the Benefactor. "Have we apprehended the rogues, Alfonse?"

Delgado looked down at his shoes. "Unfortunately, no. We have not been able to locate them."

Mr. Cox looked up and conveyed a sense of anger his subordinates had learned to fear. "How were four defenseless people able to leave the premises unscathed? Where was our security? What about the loyalists? The town is full of those who serve me."

"Benefactor, when you were, ah, incapacitated during the confrontation with your enemies, much of your control vanished. We felt—lost in a quagmire of uncertainty. We found it difficult to think straight while the fear and confusion gripped us."

"And the townspeople, what was their excuse? Most of them are not worth the effort to place under direct mind control, yet they fear me. Why didn't they stop them?"

"The townspeople? Are you kidding me?" Ziminski scoffed at the notion. "They hate you. They probably helped them escape."

"Alan!" snapped Watts. "Do you know who you're talking to? Give the Benefactor the respect he deserves."

"No, no, it's fine, Xavier. Alan has his place in the organization, at least until someone more talented comes along."

Ziminski looked up, and when he spoke, his voice trembled. "Why do you hate me? Why do you hate your own son?"

3

"I have no intention of discussing this with you today, Alan. You couldn't possibly share my DNA. I can only create perfection, and you are clearly not that." Turning to Delgado, he changed the subject. "As head of security, I expect you to find these people. Our plans will not be entirely secure until they are apprehended and destroyed."

"Yes, Benefactor," replied Delgado. The corners of Watts' mouth turned up almost imperceptibly. He derived enjoyment from Delgado's discomfort.

"Tell me about the aftermath of the explosion in Chicago, Xavier."

"Certainly, Benefactor. It is glorious. As you are aware, this was the third nuclear detonation in a twenty-for-hour period. That it occurred on American soil has amplified the effect, and as such, the peripheral damage is far greater than the other two blasts. The world's governments are reeling in confusion and panic. They can't determine the cause, let alone the solution."

"Excellent, excellent. Have we implemented the next part of the plan?"

"Yes," answered Watts. "We have operatives in governments and the media who are spreading our planted rumor that we have negotiated a respite in the attacks. They believe that if we reveal the identity of the terrorists to anyone, the perpetrators will immediately set off another bomb. It is only by our grace and persuasiveness they are holding back as they empower us to find a solution that prevents another detonation." Watts paused and reveled in the Benefactor's obvious delight before continuing.

"Already there is a groundswell of support on the streets of many major cities across the world demanding that our conglomerate replace their current leadership. Our people are delivering goods and services to the masses in exchange for their loyalty. As previously planned, we are now working under the banner of the global organization."

"You mean, Humans United for Global Equality, correct? The HUGE conglomerate. I came up with that. Clever, isn't it?" said Mr. Cox with obvious pride. "Are these efforts yielding results?"

"In fact, they have. We are well organized in South America and Africa. Already, the countries of Zambia, Botswana, Uruguay and Paraguay are revolting and attempting to overthrow their fragile governments. We have people in those countries who are prepared to fill any power vacuum."

"Wonderful. Your news pleases me, Xavier. How are the plans for our transfer to the future capital city coming along?"

Watts grabbed a set of blueprints and unrolled them across the table. "We will be ready to complete the move within a week. The new command center is operational, and the renovation on your quarters is nearly complete. We are in the process of moving key international personnel to the new location."

"And all seven buildings are secure?"

"Yes, the entire complex, Benefactor."

"Well, then I suppose the plan couldn't be unfolding any better for us. Is there anything else? I have many things I must attend to."

Delgado and Ziminski briefly talked over each other. Alan looked at Delgado with disgust and turned back to the Benefactor. "I hate to break the vibe, but there are problems. Whatever happened between you and those other mind control freaks has really fucked up

5

the network. There's an open revolt in New England, and Europe's a mess. I had to threaten some regional managers with death if they don't get their people back in line. We've missed a bunch of payments. A couple of these shitheads actually took the money and kept it. It's bad. What the fuck is going on?"

The Benefactor sighed. "Alan, you know I detest profanity, so please speak in an acceptable vernacular."

"Sorry," said Ziminski, but his tone belied the apology.

"I know we have some—issues, and there have been—situations requiring attention. I have dealt with the most serious problems, and we should see immediate improvement. This small disruption may provide us with an excellent opportunity to identify promising management recruits who are not receiving my assistance but still demonstrate their loyalty."

"Sure, I'll make a list of the ones who are toeing the line."

"Yes, Alan, you do that. And you have my permission to eliminate the offenders and replace them with people who remained true to our cause."

"I'll start right away," replied Ziminski, who seemed to interpret the assignment as the Benefactor's way of displaying affection.

"Delgado, you appear tense. Do you have something for me? Be brief, there is much to accomplish."

"Benefactor, a man waits outside. He's not on the dignitary list and showed up out of nowhere. We can't determine how he got here, or how he was able to circumvent our security."

"What does he want?"

"He says he has vital information that can only be relayed directly to you."

"Bah," said Mr. Cox. "Send him away. Apparently, our present location is compromised. It's a good thing we'll be moving soon."

Delgado shook his head. "I don't think this location is compromised at all. He found out some other way and is very insistent. If you were hesitant to see him, he said to tell you he knows the location of the 'Suicide Society', whatever that means."

Mr. Cox froze. He hadn't shared the Suicide Society's name with anyone. Whoever this intruder was, he somehow acquired privileged information no one except the Benefactor himself possessed. Could it be another ruse from Anston and his minions?

Talking to him directly is a risk, but do I really have another choice? Mr. Cox could fuse the visitor's mind if he showed the slightest bit of subterfuge or hostility.

"Fine. Go ahead and send him in."

Delgado left momentarily, returning a short time later with the guest following at a respectable distance. Mr. Cox regarded him for a moment. He was tall, muscular and wore a pair of faded blue jeans and a skin-tight black t-shirt. His hair was long and blond, and a dyed blue streak ran through the middle of his hairline from the pronounced widows peak to the last shock that lay on his back. He wore an almost imperceptible smirk and radiated an arrogant self-confidence.

"Well, well," he said. "The great Mr. Cox. This is an honor indeed."

Cox smiled widely, revealing his perfectly straight and unnaturally white teeth. "I'm afraid you have me at a disadvantage, my friend. Who are you?"

"My name is Lars."

"And a surname?" Mr. Cox used a sweeping gesture to encourage his guest to sit.

"Lars will do," the man said while taking the seat opposite the Benefactor.

"I see. Well, Lars, what do I owe the pleasure?"

Lars leaned in and spoke quietly. "It's simple, really. I can perform a service you desperately need."

The Benefactor let out a single laugh. "I highly doubt that. There's little I cannot accomplish on my own. What did you have in mind?"

"I imagine you would like to eliminate the Suicide Society."

"Who the fuck is this *Suicide Society?*" asked Ziminski as he scratched at a bulbous pimple on the side of his nose.

"Ah, please leave us," Mr. Cox said to no one specifically. "I want to talk to Lars alone."

"Of course," said Watts, who bowed before turning toward the door. Delgado followed suit while Alan waited while picking his nose before finally slinking away under the glare of the Benefactor.

"So, Lars, a man of 'mystery'." Mr. Cox raised his arms and made a quotation gesture as he said the word, *mystery*. "How did you learn about the Suicide Society? They go to great lengths to keep their existence a secret. For that matter, how were you able to find our refuge?"

8

Lars unlocked his hands from behind his head and folded them on the table. The smug smirk never wavered. "I know many things about you and your business. That said, I can help you achieve your goal of eliminating the Suicide Society. I may not enjoy working with you, but we have a common purpose."

"You don't seem to understand. There are no secrets you can keep from me. Again, I want you to share your knowledge of the Suicide Society."

Lars merely shook his head without responding.

Instantly, the Benefactor released a ribbon of dark energy designed to simultaneously probe for answers and punish with pain. Yet, he discovered nothing of relevance in Lars' brain as the tendril dissipated harmlessly into the ionosphere. The sensation was odd and unexpected. Unlike his entanglements with Randall and Anston, Mr. Cox felt no resistance or counter attack. Instead, Lars harmlessly parried his mental thrust. With rising anger, the Benefactor mustered an even more ambitious attack, but the result was essentially the same. Only this time Lars' smile widened.

"Are you done yet?"

"Who — what are you?"

"As I said, it doesn't matter, but I'm glad we got that out of the way so we can get down to business."

"You do not understand who you are dealing with," said Mr. Cox. "So far, my efforts have been mild. If I strike with the total of my power…"

"Hopefully, we won't need to find out." Lars leaned back and slid down in his chair. "It might not make any difference, anyway. Where I come from, we learn certain disciplines that allow us to deflect telepathic and telekinetic attacks. You can try again if you like, but the result will probably be the same."

Mr. Cox drummed his fingers on the table. "I'll reserve that option for another time if it becomes necessary. For now, let's discuss exactly what you want."

"I told you, I want you to succeed. It's that simple. You were extremely lucky everything unfolded the way it did. In the old reality, it's entirely possible they could have diffused the bomb, so we were both very fortunate. It seems you received a second chance. Don't blow it."

"What exactly is your idea of 'helping'?"

"The Suicide Society remains a major threat to everything you want to achieve. They must be neutralized. I'll need access to your best people and your data systems as well."

"And once you destroy them, what will you want then?"

"You'll know when the time comes. For now, I'm only interested in eliminating the threat the Society presents."

Mr. Cox stroked his chin as he pondered the proposition. "I will need to think on this. You are another rogue; an unanticipated potential threat to my plans, and I don't know your true motives. It isn't as though I *need* you. I am perfectly capable of dealing with the Suicide Society myself."

"Really? Then where are they right now?"

"I—I'm not entirely sure. I've been busy tending to other business."

Lars stood up and straightened his shirt. "I know exactly where they are. Let me take seven men and give me an aircraft, and I'll eliminate them."

Mr. Cox smiled condescendingly. "I will consider your offer but make no guarantees."

"Think quickly. I don't expect they'll stay in one place for long," he said.

"Fine, fine, now leave me. I have much work to attend to."

"Of course, Benefactor." Lars rose, bowed and started toward the door at a moderate pace, but his sarcastic grin never wavered.

With the room empty, Mr. Cox shook his head in bewilderment and poured himself a small snifter of Chianti. *Who is this mysterious Lars? Why would he be here, and more importantly, who sent him?*

While sipping his beverage, the Benefactor made his way over to a stone façade blended to look as though it was part of a natural exterior wall. He put his hand on the edge of one of the stones and felt around until he found a button recessed in a small indentation. After he pressed it, a square section of faux rock opened to reveal a reinforced vault sunk into the granite itself. He looked into an optical laser that ran a retinal scan, and the locking mechanism clicked as the safe opened.

Briefly inspecting the contents, he took out a box adorned with priceless rubies, diamonds, sapphires and emeralds. He lifted the lid slowly, allowing the pulsating yellow energy that emanated from the interior of the container to wash over him. The power of the Third Orb of Gehenna was immeasurable, and Mr. Cox reached down and took the sphere out with both hands before holding it high over his head. He closed his eyes and drifted into an abyss of thick, dark energy that consumed him. His reservoirs of power grew as the color of the orb's light changed from yellow to deep red.

The veins on the Benefactor's neck bulged as he strained to absorb the massive quantity of light energy the orb emitted. He stumbled around the room while

11

moaning and muttering, trying to maintain control of a power that was utterly uncontrollable. When he reached the limits of his tolerance, he carefully placed the orb back into the lead-lined box and secured it inside the vault. After closing the door and replacing the fake veneer, he slumped back into his chair, taking several deep breaths.

The day was long and difficult. The damaged global network still needed his attention, but the momentum of the movement would buy him more than enough time to complete the restoration.

He closed his eyes and drifted into the infinite store of his replenished energy. It felt alive, and a tingling sensation crawled through his insides and over his skin, leaving him refreshed and electrified. Floating through the realm of the subconscious, he traveled at speeds that defied relativity, looking down at the various continents and countries that would soon join his confederation. The sense of change was strong, and the planet was transforming as its essence grew darker. The world was bending to his will, and its inhabitants would soon serve him.

A distant rapping sound became more pronounced, and Mr. Cox was forced to disconnect from the beauty of the world's malevolent wickedness. He returned to his stateroom and opened his eyes, taking a deep breath.

"Yes, come in."

The door opened and Xavier Watts entered. "Benefactor, I am sorry to disturb you, but matters are becoming pressing in what's left of the media. Our organization is a major topic of discussion as we gain more converts every day. They want to talk to the leader of HUGE, and I'm uncomfortable letting that incompetent who used to work for a national news network represent us. What are your wishes?"

Mr. Cox remained seated in his chair without turning around. "It is time for you to assume more responsibility, Xavier. I have given this some thought, and I want you to become the titular leader of the organization. It is important that I remain in the background, at least for now."

Watts stood in stunned silence. His mouth opened several times, but no words were forthcoming.

"Congratulations, Xavier, I have promoted you. Unless you are turning it down, of course."

Watts could hardly shake off the stunning shock of the moment. "Naturally, Benefactor, I am honored," he stammered.

"Is there anything else? We have a very busy day tomorrow. I need my rest."

"No—no, of course not. Good evening, Benefactor."

Chapter Two

Thanks to a warning they received from a mysterious sickly old man who somehow found their hidden lair in Portales, the Suicide Society prepared for an imminent assault.

With a sense of urgency, the overseers moved from their underground shelter, shredding documents, removing personal effects and safeguarding items of historical significance. The telepathic guardians were locked in a battle for survival after their plan to topple the psychotic telepath, Mr. Cox, failed.

They left the compound as a group, reaching ground level and scurrying through the abandoned textile factory toward the exit. Zach Randall peeked out the door, but the main street that ran through the center of town was no longer deserted. There were a few cars at Kirby's Food Mart, and he saw a couple of guys in tee shirts and jeans getting out of a pickup truck and walking into the local auto parts store.

Jarad Anston gathered the eight Suicide Society members and Sarah around him and began distributing bundles of crisp twenty-dollar bills to each of them.

"These straps have two-thousand dollars in them. I'll give each of you ten-thousand when we arrive at our destination. That should be sufficient to cover basic expenses if we get separated."

"But Speaker Anston, our families..." said the one named Rogelio Francisco, a man with olive skin, dark hair and hazel-green eyes. He spoke with a distinct Spanish accent.

Jarad nodded. "Of course. All of us want to contact our families. Perhaps we can purchase prepaid phones and use them to call our loved ones and tell them to find safe harbor. We can't go home; that would be too dangerous."

No one said a word as they looked at their leader with apprehension and concern. "Look, I feel your fear as you feel mine. This won't be easy for any of us."

"I have a daughter who means everything to me," said Randall. "I am devastated by all of this too. But Jarad, uh, Speaker Anston is right, we have to leave this place and travel to a more secure location." Zach glanced at the corpse lying on the floor, a look of dread permanently etched on his lifeless face.

"We must leave immediately, there's no time to waste. We'll meet you at the airport. Hurry!" Jarad looked at the group one last time with obvious concern and a bit of sadness.

Zach sensed his friend's guilt over the failed attempt to defeat Mr. Cox, even though the forces in play were much bigger than Anston could have imagined. Like the rest of the Suicide Society, he had to be wondering if the barriers protecting this resilient and formidable foe were insurmountable.

15

Jarad waited outside for the rest of the group to follow. He hesitated for only a moment before making his way to one of two black Lincoln Navigators parked near the building. Marshall and Sarah got into the back while Zach slid behind the wheel.

"Hurry, start the car. I think they're all in shock, and I'm afraid they won't leave until we do," said Anston.

Zach turned the key, and the engine roared to life, which seemed to trigger a sense of awareness in the group and snapped them out of a collective fog. The other six got into the second Navigator, and both vehicles drove slowly down Main Street. The next few days, weeks or even months would be difficult, especially for those who came from other countries. Zach didn't know how long they would have to remain in America, but with a possible traitor in their midst, they couldn't leave until there was a resolution to this horrific affair.

The short trip to the airport was relatively pedestrian. They passed an old Ford pickup and a late model Nissan SUV, but a man soaked with sweat in the truck and a lady with her children in the Nissan presented no threat. After pulling into the parking lot, they checked in and returned the vehicles to Sid Parkly, who was the airport manager as well as the flight director, rental car clerk and whatever job needed to be done at that moment.

The group hung out near the counter as Sid verified the manifest.

"Okay, you're set." He smiled, handed the paperwork to Anston and politely held open the door that led to the aircraft.

16

They stood in a circle for a moment, and then Jarad reached out and hugged Aminah Conteh, an attractive, svelte thirty-something woman from Kenya. She returned the hug and patted Jarad on the back. As if on cue, everyone started hugging one another, and tears of joy and appreciation began to flow. One by one, they passed Jarad and embraced him as he returned the warm gesture.

The display of obvious affection and emotion was difficult and awkward for Marshall, who was only beginning to explore the nature of his own feelings. His unfamiliarity with these strangers made it even more uncomfortable, and he shuddered at the thought of actually touching them.

Out of nowhere, an overseer named Jacques Franco grabbed him and hugged him tightly. Marshall's back stiffened, and he knew the other man noticed because he let go immediately. The group was very sensitive to a disruption in the energy that defined mood, and the exchange of hugs stopped instantly. Marshall realized they were all staring at him, even if they weren't looking in his direction.

"Friends, we must give Marshall some space and time to understand us and integrate. He's been thrust into these circumstances through no fault of his own, and he's just discovering his abilities." Jarad smiled and nodded at Marshall.

"Of course," said Yasin Antar, a tall Arabic looking man distinguished by a thick mane of black curly hair. "We apologize. How insensitive of us. Everyone was new to this group at one time, so it can be a bit overwhelming. After a while, the gift will feel more natural."

Marshall forced a smile because he suspected it was the appropriate response. The situation seemed like it was about to become even more awkward when old Sid Parkly ambled in and mercifully broke the tension.

"You're set to go. You can board the plane now." Jarad smiled and handed Sid a handful of bills, which the old man counted carefully. He nodded and waved them out onto the scorching pavement where they climbed the air stairs up to the cabin entryway.

After boarding, they took their seats on the luxurious Hawker 900XP. Anston sat next to Marshall, and they directly faced Sarah and Zach. Rogelio and Sasha took the seats in the next row, and the others sat on the bench toward the rear of the plane. The pilot taxied smoothly down the runway, throttled the engines up and gained speed until the nose tilted upward, signaling they were airborne.

After completing a long, sweeping banked turn toward the west, the plane started following a flight plan that would take them to Phoenix's Sky Harbor in less than two hours.

Anston leaned over the convenience table and motioned for Randall to do the same. The steady whine of the engines drowned out their conversation from those sitting nearby.

"I want to talk in words, not thoughts, Zach." Anston apparently wanted to avoid the potential for psychic eavesdropping. "There's no way I can truly express my regret for deceiving you as I did."

Randall reassuringly squeezed his friend's shoulder. "You don't need to apologize. The element of surprise was critical."

"I know, but…"

"No, there wasn't any other way. How else could you defeat Cox?"

"That's just it. According to Marshall, we *did* defeat Cox," said Anston. "It wasn't supposed to end this way. Someone — it's like I can almost remember what he looks like — diffused the bomb, and the world was saved. But this reality… It all feels wrong."

Zach nodded. "Yes, I sense it too. The energy has an undercurrent that's contaminated and corrupted." Randall lowered his head. "But what are we going to do now? According to the old man who came to warn us, we have a traitor in our midst… He talked about the future and — and he seemed to know Marshall."

"I know. I can't help but wonder if he's told us everything," Anston shifted his eyes in Marshall's direction.

"Where are we going, Jarad?"

Anston glanced in both directions to ensure no one was listening. "We need to stay together; that much I know. There's a second sanctuary on this continent near the North Verde Valley region of Arizona. Only the Speaker is trusted with knowledge of its location, and no one has visited it for many decades."

"Everything related to psychokinetic energy seems to center around the Southwest," said Randall. "Why is that?"

Anston raised his eyebrows as though he was deciding how much information he wanted to share. "It's simple, really," he said. "It's Sedona."

Randall tilted his head and frowned. "I don't understand."

"Sedona is the epicenter for telepathic and telekinetic activity here on earth. Our abilities are magnified by the spirituality that radiates from the sacred red rocks in that place. There's a magnetic resonance that can't be explained by science, but there is no question it exists. We always have at least one member in the area monitoring the purity of the harmonics and frequencies that reverberate in every living organism."

"I see. No wonder our forbearers decided to locate the primary sanctuary there." Zach leaned back and looked over at Sarah, whose eyes were closed. He slid his hand inside hers and smiled when her fingers tightened around his own.

***

Two Mercedes SUVs drove fast into Portales and pulled up to the shuttered textile factory. The door to the first vehicle opened, and an athletic man with long blond hair stepped out. He wore a tight tee shirt that hugged his torso and accentuated toned muscles. His jet-black Ray-ban sunglasses hid his eyes but set off his deep, rich tan. The jeans were skin tight, hitched together by a custom designed Colt Ford belt buckle and accented by Lucchese boots. He took off his Stetson for a moment, which revealed a dark blue streak that ran through the middle of his thick mane.

The doors to the two SUVs closed and several others clad identically in black jeans and t-shirts followed. When the support team finished assembling, their leader turned to face them.

"Okay, remember to do your job. My understanding is that these guys are capable of some weird mind shit. You stay low and keep your weapons hot." On his order, the men extracted magazines and snapped them into place. In a single motion, they pulled the slides and chambered the bullets. The seven-trained professionals standing with their leader were ready to rumble.

"Lars," said a man behind the leader's left shoulder. "Are there multiple entry points? The plans are pretty skinny. I only saw one way to get underground, and that's in an elevator. Not good."

Lars turned to the group and smiled, slowly removing his sunglasses. "Cold feet, Snash? You're getting paid. No one stuck a gun up your ass."

"I know, I get it," replied the one named "Snash", who had the sheen of multiple layers of dried sweat. "But I don't like this one, boss."

Lars moved with the swiftness of a cheetah. His hand was crushing Snash's windpipe before the victim even knew he was being choked. "You signed up for the job, and you're going to do it. It's the biggest payday you'll ever get, so don't fuck it up, got it?"

Snash shook his head vigorously, and Lars loosened his grip. After slapping him gently twice in the face, Lars said, "That's better. Anyone else?"

Collectively, they looked at the ground.

"Okay then, let's go in as planned. There's got to be another way out of there, anyway. We'll find it when we get inside. Timmy and Bosh, you get the point."

The two designated point men approached the door cautiously and stood to either side. One of them stepped forward, and with significant force, kicked at the old wooden slab. Due to age and warping, the brittle wood gave way after the second strike, revealing a solid plate of sheer steel behind it.

"As I suspected," said Lars while smiling slowly. "Steel door probably about six inches thick." He turned to one of the men standing behind him. "Baxter, tell me you can open this thing. If Jinks has to use C-4, it'll wake the neighborhood."

Baxter smiled and reached inside his backpack, pulling out a set of odd shaped tools from inside a leather pouch. He took a mechanical-only key card and inserted it into the keyway. After insuring it was set, he attached a device that caused the key to start vibrating, adjusting it periodically until it reached a preset frequency. Several seconds later, the mechanical motor in the cylinder turned and lifted the locking element. The tumbler subsequently disengaged, and the door sprung open.

Lars clapped Baxter on the back. "I knew there was a reason I kept you around." The safecracker smiled while Jinks looked dejected as he put two lumps of C4 back into his utility pack.

Two men rushed through the open door as a second team took up a position behind them. Lars came in last, surveilling his surroundings and making a quick threat assessment. Convinced the factory was abandoned, he turned on the lights and located an elevator against a far wall.

The doors opened immediately after Timmy on the lead team pushed the lighted button. The squad piled into the small cabin and descended to the lower level. The point men left the elevator and laser-painted a variety of potential hostile targets as they swung their automatic weapons from side to side. The other men moved cautiously forward while evaluating their surroundings.

Timmy and Bosh worked their way through the complex, poking into corners, nooks, crannies and anywhere else someone might try to hide. A few minutes into the search, they discovered the body of the dead old man. By now, his face and features had melted into a shiny, sticky lump of blood, bone and scabs. While his clothes seemed unaffected, something ate away at his skin and eyes, and only black, ominous holes appeared where the sockets used to be. Chunks of unidentifiable organic material had fallen off, and raw, angry lesions covered his head, arms and areas of exposed flesh.

"We got a dead one here. Disgusting. It's clear otherwise, boss," said Bosh.

Lars led the rest of the squad out of the elevator and into the large area leading to the conference room. "Over there," he said while pointing at a far wall. "That's a service door that wasn't on the schematic. If the power gets cut, that's how we'll get out to street level."

He looked down at the corpse and grimaced slightly while some of his men turned away. This was a hardened crew that Lars hired out of Mr. Cox' inventory at a premium price, and they experienced nearly every gruesome way a human being could be mutilated and killed. It looked like whoever slaughtered this poor sap wanted him to endure an especially painful death.

Lars cursed silently as he looked around the room. These miscreant freaks were supposed to be here at this exact time. The extermination was scripted, and Lars hated it when an operation didn't go as planned. He shook his head slowly. Once again, history demonstrated it was a very unreliable partner. Fluctuations in the time line were always the wild card, especially now when such a major change had just transpired.

"Okay, there's nothing here for us. Snash, take a sample of that guy's goo for DNA analysis. Gerard and Sam, check the other rooms for anything important."

Wrinkling his nose, Snash reached down with a gloved hand and grabbed a chunk of jelly from the corpse's face. A long string of blood and mucus stuck to the burned epidermis, and Snash had to separate it as he placed the specimen in a plastic bag.

"Ugh, that's repulsive," he said.

His companions chuckled for a moment, but then Lars cocked his head and motioned for silence.

Click

The sound was faint, but unmistakably familiar. Lars turned and began running from the conference room. "Bomb!" he shouted.

The explosion unleashed a deafening fury, and the concussive force created huge cracks in the walls and floors of the conference room, data room and the four connected bedrooms. Furniture, decorations and small appliances were ripped apart, sending jagged pieces of shrapnel on unpredictable pathways. The familiar heat and wind of a plastic explosive washed over Lars while the fireball expanded rapidly in search of oxygen.

The mayhem lasted only a few seconds, but Lars knew that he would recall the scene in such detail that his mind would try and convince him it had taken hours. The aftermath of the explosion brought a strange calm and a sickening feeling in the pit of his stomach. He stumbled to his feet and found Baxter and Jinks with only minor injuries. After retrieving their weapons, they approached the abandoned main room while trying to silence the loud ringing in their ears.

After scavenging through the rubble, they eventually found the other five who weren't so lucky. Debris covered Snash, Timmy and Bosh, and they lay semi-conscious and bleeding. With extensive battlefield experience, Lars decided Bosh had a chance to live, but Timmy and Snash were dead men. Timmy's arm dangled from the socket as blood pumped freely from a huge gash in his stomach. A piece of shrapnel severed one of Snash's major arteries, and he gasped for breath while pressing on the gushing, bubbling wound. Gerard and Sam, who were at the epicenter of the explosion, were mangled beyond recognition and obviously dead.

Lars coughed and choked on the dust that clogged his nose and burned his throat. He motioned for the survivors to grab Bosh, and they made their way back to the elevator. The power was dead, so Lars felt his way along the wall until he reached the service door he hoped led to a hidden fire escape.

Fighting through air that was hot and thick, the survivors climbed up to the first floor with Bosh in tow. While the smoke, dust and debris made breathing almost impossible, the battered squad was able to reach street level where the escape route was hidden under a non-functioning transformer box. Lars released a latch on either side and pushed the box away, gulping fresh air as he helped his men out of the shaft.

The size of the explosion would soon attract the state police, and Lars didn't want to answer any awkward questions. He instructed Jinks to get one of the SUVs, and they pulled the back seat down and placed Bosh's prone body inside before piling in. Baxter ran over to the other SUV, keys in hand.

No one spoke until they were clear of the town.

"What the hell happened, Lars?"

"They knew we were coming. I'm not sure how, but they knew we were coming."

"And they got away?"

"They may have got away for now, but they'll be dead soon enough. I swear, they'll be dead soon enough." Lars gritted his teeth, screamed and pounded the dashboard.

Chapter Three

Zach took her hand, and together they walked through a field of high grass swaying in the cool breeze of a warm mid-October day. The air smelled sweet with blooming flowers, a delicious combination of peonies, roses and asters. They looked at each other, and he silently slid his arm around her waist and pulled her close. Her smile widened, and she didn't resist.

They moved through the field and came upon a bubbling stream that flowed rapidly over rock outcroppings. The gently sloped banks were crowded with colorful vegetation, but they eventually found a grass-covered clearing nearby. Sarah placed a blanket on the ground and spread it out, setting a picnic basket — Zach couldn't remember them bringing one — in the middle. They sat down together and reclined. He felt her pressing up against the length of his body, and he closed his eyes and drew in a deep breath of fresh air.

With tenderness, he reached out to pull her closer but felt the ground shake for just a moment. Zach sat upright and looked around, but Sarah had somehow fallen into the water and was fighting against a strong current. She moved her lips as a look of terror crossed her face, but no words escaped. He got to his feet and ran toward her, but the ground shook again, this time with much greater force. What was happening?

Zach opened his eyes and looked quickly around the cabin as his mind struggled to process the receding nightmare and current reality. The seatbelt restraint caused pain as it pressed uncomfortably into his body, pinning him against the side of the plane. Amidst the screams and cries of anguish, it finally registered that the jet was plunging downward in free fall.

On the other side of the table, Sasha was pushed up against the back of the seat, and although she had unlocked her restraint, she couldn't gain enough leverage to fight against the g-force. Clearly, only those facing toward the cockpit had a chance to reach the door. As his hand felt the smooth surface of the safety belt buckle, Zach worked his fingers in behind the mechanism. A loud snap cut through the background noise as the latch released, and the hasp whipsawed around, missing Jarad Anston's face by a couple of inches.

Once he was free, inertia threw Zach forward with force, and he crashed into the wall that separated the cockpit from the cabin. The impact was sudden and jarring, and he clutched his shoulder and tried to clear his head. As he looked at the faces of his companions, he didn't need to be a transcendent to feel the terror and fear that permeated through the small space.

Fighting the extreme forces of gravity and rising nausea, Zach reached up and grabbed the handle to the cockpit door. He got enough of a grip that he was able to pull himself up into a standing position but couldn't move freely. Still, he was close enough to sense the pilot's neural activity since he was sitting just a few feet away. The man controlling the aircraft was a roiling mess of utter confusion and confliction. Without hesitation, Zach entered his mind and rifled through recent memories until he came upon images of large payments received from a murky, mysterious organization.

The pilot's name was John Simmons, and he was given a million dollars to serve as a contingency. According to the plan, he would probably make the flight back to Sky Harbor alone. However, if this group boarded the plane, he was expected to crash it. His family would receive an additional five million as compensation for his death. If he failed to follow through, they would torture and kill his wife and two children.

The pilot sensed the invasion into his mind and panicked, throttling the engines up higher and increasing the descent of the dive. In less than twenty seconds, there would be no chance for recovery. Zach fought against the intensifying g-forces and twisted his body around to face his companions.

We have less than fifteen seconds. I need you all to channel your mental energy through me. Give me your strength; give me your essence. We must meld together.

Zach felt an immediate infusion of psychic power coursing through his body, sending a jolt of current into his mind that energized and vastly expanded his capabilities. He experienced detailed sounds and sights from people on the ground almost four miles below. For an instant, he was tempted to explore the limits of this extraordinary power, but the dire circumstances brought him quickly to his senses.

A single stream of invisible telepathic energy less than the diameter of an electron pierced the shielding of the cabin door and penetrated directly into the brain of the pilot. A shrill, agonizing scream came from inside the cockpit that momentarily drowned out the loud drone of the engines. The shrieking continued for several seconds, eventually morphing into a full wail of pain and anguish. After a few seconds, the cries stopped suddenly and silence ensued, followed by loud, incoherent babbling and muted sobs.

Continuing to concentrate the collective power of the overseers, Zach sent several instructions through the established connection.

29

"No, no, no," the pilot pleaded. "They'll kill my family. You don't understand; they will kill my family." Against his will, he throttled back the power, leveled the wings and pulled the nose back above the horizon before adding thrust to regain altitude. Slowly, the jet reached equilibrium and eventually started to climb. Firmly in control of the pilot's mind, Zach accessed his knowledge of inflight procedures. He forced the pilot to execute maneuvers to correct the spiral stall, experiencing only feeble mental resistance and pushing it aside like a flimsy curtain.

With the crisis averted and the plane flying smoothly again, Zach looked back at his friends. They were trying to recover, but the terror was still fresh, and the cabin was an absolute mess. At least three people purged, and several mixtures of vomit created colorful slimy strings that hung from the ceiling and cascaded down over the seats and passengers. Sasha suffered the worst of it as a huge clump of spew clung to her blouse, and based on the seating arrangement, it probably came courtesy of Jacques.

Zach instructed the captain to engage the autopilot and open the cockpit door. The man stumbled out and faced the passengers with tears running down his cheeks and eyes that were bloodshot and puffy.

"I'm sorry," he said, "but my family is going to be killed if I land with you alive. I must crash this plane."

Zach broke the connection with the group and turned his attention to the pilot. "Who told you they would kill your family?"

"I don't know who they are. The leader has long blond hair with a blue streak in it. He is mean and persuasive. They offered me a lot of money to take the job when you chartered the plane. This wasn't supposed to happen. You should already be dead."

When he looked up, his anguished expression had not abated. With hands pressed against the sides of his head he squeezed tightly. "You're in my brain, and you're making me do things against my will. How are you doing that? For the love of God, please stop." The pilot pounded his temples with the bottom of his palms. Zach immediately intervened and soothed the distressed areas of the man's amygdala. Subsequently, the pilot's hands dropped, and a look of contentment washed over him, almost as though he had taken anti-anxiety medication.

Randall turned back to Anston, whose face finally regained some color. "Someone compromised the sanctuary in Portales, just as the old man predicted."

Anston nodded. Along with the rest of the group, he experienced the pilot's thoughts and actions exactly as Zach had. "So, we know the messenger, whoever he might be, was telling us the truth, at least about this incident."

Zach turned back to the pilot and gave him a series of instructions to ensure the plane arrived safely in Phoenix. The man robotically moved back to the captain's chair and took over the controls. He groaned and cried out every time he made an adjustment, but the plane kept flying smoothly at a cruising altitude of 30,000 feet.

Zach moved from the cabin to the cockpit and took the co-pilot's seat. His incursion into the pilot's mind revealed a trove of personal details. "John, why did you take the money? You must have made a good living as a pilot. Are you in some kind of trouble?" While trying his best to avoid invading the man's privacy, Zach retrieved a variety of deeply entangled memories he wanted to understand.

Simmons lowered his head and nodded slowly. "I don't know how you're able to do that. Who are you people anyway? My head feels like it's going to explode. They told me there was no chance you would ever board the plane. They told me I would be flying alone."

31

"I wish I could help you, John, but they're going to know you've landed the plane."

"Please, don't kill me."

"Please? You would have killed us all. I have some sympathy, but there isn't much I can do unless you work with me."

"It's not just me; it's my family. Can I at least talk to them?"

Zach paused and considered the request. "I'll let you make a phone call. One phone call to your wife to say goodbye, but I want it on speaker phone."

"Thank you," the pilot whispered. He pulled a satellite phone from his pocket, pressed a single stud and waited for a connection. By the third ring, someone answered.

"Daddy!" the voice of a small girl sounded excited.

"Hi, pumpkin. Can you get mommy for me?"

"I miss you, Daddy. When are you coming home?"

"I don't know for sure, Chrissy. But it'll be soon. Please get Mommy, sweetheart."

"She's not here... I'm watching the dinosaur show. Grrrrr...."

"Chrissy, get mommy... now!" Sensing her father's anger, the little girl dropped the phone and ran from the room. In the distance, Zach heard her call for her mother. In a few seconds, a new voice spoke.

"Hello, John? Where are you?"

"I'm getting ready to land in Phoenix. Margie, I need you to listen carefully. Take Chrissy and the baby and leave the house immediately. Don't go to your parents. You need to get far away. Get on a flight to Michigan and go to your cousin's place."

"John, what are you talking about? What's going on there? You're scaring me."

"Look, Margie, there's no time. For God's sake don't call the police, please. Just get out of town as soon as possible."

"John… I."

"I can't tell you anymore. I love you."

"What's wrong? …John?" He pushed the button to end the call. Tears ran freely as he disengaged the autopilot and turned to Zach. "We're going to be landing soon. You better strap yourself in. Thank you for letting me make that call."

Zach grabbed his shoulder harness and prepared for the descent, but just as he settled in, the cabin door opened, and Marshall leaned in.

"Don't land at Sky Harbor."

Zach turned around in his chair. "Why?"

"Wouldn't they have someone at the airport to make sure the plane crashed? There's also something else, but I don't know for sure. It's hard to explain, but I think it would be better to land at a different place, preferably an abandoned airport."

The pilot raised his eyebrows and shook his head. "There's no way. We're entering controlled airspace. I don't have permission…"

"I'm very serious, Mr. Randall."

Zach held Marshall's gaze for a long moment before turning to the pilot. "John, do you know any abandoned airports that will keep us out of controlled air space and off the grid?"

The pilot looked at Randall; his eyes were wide, and the corners of his lips turned down. "That's just crazy. I can't do that. There's a flight plan… My license — I can't."

"Look, John, if you know a place, you point the plane in that direction and go there now. I can make you do it if you won't cooperate. And besides, I assume you want to live."

"What? What do you mean?"

"You understand we'll all probably die if you land this plane at Sky Harbor. You told us air traffic control is falling

33

apart. If you stay away from the city, we may be able to disappear, and we'll all have a fighting chance. If they're waiting for us, they're waiting for you."

The pilot considered Randall's words for a moment and then turned off the transponder as he grabbed the yoke and executed a turn that took the plane out of its original flight path and redirected it to the west.

"We'll be off the grid soon, and we'll represent a threat to every plane that's in the sky. Please keep your eyes open for any aircraft you see in the distance. It'll be the ones above us or below us that would most likely cause a collision. We'll be entirely on visual."

"Where are we going?" asked Zach.

"We're going to an abandoned airstrip between Quartzite and Wickenburg in a town called Salome. The strip is old and unpaved, but I think it's useable."

Fortunately, the actual flight time was only about half an hour, and the sky was clear and free of clouds. Throughout the unscheduled change in flight path, the pilot didn't receive any communications from the control tower at Sky Harbor, which was unprecedented. The usual chatter was minimal, and it seemed only a few traffic controllers were left to struggle with the commercial flights still in the air. As he received updates, Zach could only wonder what was happening on the ground in the major cities.

Skirting the controlled airspace, the plane began a slow descent towards the abandoned airfield. Zach could see several runways in the distance, but as they approached, the obvious lack of maintenance was evident. Clumps of desert vegetation disrupted the surface, and he wondered if the pilot had the skill to dodge the creosote bushes and small Palo Verde trees that poked through the cracks in the aged asphalt.

"I'll use the north-south runway. It's not as long, but it's in a lot better shape."

After positioning the aircraft, he initiated landing procedures. As the details at ground level grew sharper, Zach thought the runway was flat enough, but the asphalt was thin and cracked in many places, and the bushes were too high. One wrong move and they could lose a wing or the landing gear, not to mention the chances of a tire blowing out.

The plane touched down with a series of small screeches, but the impact wasn't as severe as Zach feared. The pilot had full control of the plane, and he expertly massaged the controls as he applied the brakes. Gently rolling to the eastern half of the runway, he avoided most of the dense vegetation as the smaller bushes smacked the front and sides of the fuselage. After several tense moments, the jet rolled to a stop intact and its passengers unharmed.

The pilot let out a deep sigh and looked at Zach while rolling his eyes. He stood up and walked into the cabin as Randall followed. The expressions of fear and doubt on the faces of his companions mirrored his own thoughts and emotions. Marshall looked particularly distressed, and Zach wondered how he was coping with having so many others inside his mind.

Jarad was the first to get out of his seat, and he clapped Zach on the shoulder. "Well done," he said.

The pilot released the forward stairs, and one by one, the overseers left the plane and stood on the runway staring at the expanse of desert in all directions. One reason Simmons selected this particular airstrip was its proximity to the center of the small town of Salome.

Zach looked around, scanning the abandoned terminal for signs of trouble. From where he was standing, he could see a restaurant, hotel and grocery store. Since it was a scorching July day in the desert, he knew they needed to get out of the heat. Standing next to him, Jarad was also looking around, but he seemed to be focused on a large sign several blocks away that read, Al Shield's Salvage Yard.

They walked as a group toward Route-60, leading to the restaurant and hotel. A single pickup truck pulled over to the shoulder of the road, and the driver rested his arm on the doorframe as he leaned out the window, sizing up the strange scene unfolding before him. Jarad headed in that direction since it was obvious the guy wasn't leaving until he talked to them.

Within shouting distance, the driver yelled, "What the hell you doin' here? Did you crash, or do you have shit for brains? We ain't had a plane land here since…" He stopped talking, removed his sweat-stained ball cap and scratched his head.

Anston answered while continuing to walk forward. "No, we didn't crash, but you know, it's a mess out there. We couldn't land at Sky Harbor, and all the municipals are too crowded. We were running out of fuel, and this was the only place left to land." He shrugged as he made a sweeping gesture with extended arms.

The man grabbed the support on the pickup and looked off in the distance. "Well, okay, I guess. Should I call the highway patrol or something? Does anybody need an ambulance?"

"No," said Anston, "we're all fine, and the police are busy enough with real emergencies. We'll just walk over to the restaurant and get something to eat and make some phone calls."

"Yeah, okay, that sounds good — I guess." The driver scratched his head again as though he was conflicted. He seemed to know someone should be notified but really didn't want to get involved. After a long moment, he slammed the cap back on his head, put his truck in gear, and drove off.

Anston led the group as they walked toward the hotel, called the "Westward Inn." Inside, the lobby was decades old, but relatively clean, and he approached the front desk, ringing the bell as the others loitered near the door. After some moments, a short geriatric man with wispy white hair and a shuffling gait wandered out to the counter and eyed everyone suspiciously.

"You must be the people who landed in the plane," he said to Anston matter-of-factly.

"Yes, we are. Can we have ten rooms please?"

The old man's eyes lit up. "Ten rooms? Yes sir!" He paused a moment. "Can I see a credit card please?"

Anston reached into his wallet, but Marshall walked up swiftly and grabbed him from behind. "No credit cards, Mr., uh, Speaker Anston. Pay with cash."

Anston looked puzzled but nodded. He turned around and leaned over the counter, motioning for the aged desk clerk to come close. When they were within a few inches of each other, he said, "My name is Tom White. And who do I have the pleasure?"

"Name's Gus," the man said in an equally quiet voice.

"Look, Gus, as you can see, I kind of have a problem. I can't let the FAA find out I've been here, so I can't use my credit card if you know what I mean."

"I see…"

"So, how much do you charge for a room?"

"Uh, seventy-nine per night plus tax and fees?" It sounded more like a question than a statement.

"Okay. As long as you'll let me pay in cash, how about if I give you $200 per night per room, plus tax and fees of course?"

"Up front?" Gus tried to act cool, but the beads of sweat that formed on his brow and lip betrayed him. "Say, you're not running drugs or guns, are you?"

"Yes, I'll give you the money up front, and no, we aren't running contraband. You're welcome to search the plane."

The old man straightened up, and his eyes opened even wider. "Well then, yes, sir. Let me get you all checked in and give you your room keys..."

Chapter Four

Wanda sat on the gymnasium floor with a blanket pulled up around her, staring blankly at the far wall across the basketball court. A sign hung from the rafters that read, *Home of the Grenadiers: Mid Suburban League Champions, 1994.* Cots and bedrolls dotted the floor, squeezed together with no more than a few inches between them. The incessant wailing of infants and the moaning of afflicted adults drove her to the point of madness. If she wasn't medicated, she most certainly would be in the throes of a massive nervous breakdown.

She glanced over at Wallace lying next to her. The left side of his face was a deep crimson color, and blisters bubbled up around his eye, ear and down the length of his cheek and neck. While a burn suit covered the rest of his body, she had no doubt the damage was consistent through every limb and appendage.

The fates had favored her, and he drew the loser's hand. She was the lucky one; he was not. Wallace devised a complex set of formulas based on the two previous blasts and confirmed alterations in the timeline. Coupled with their friend Iglar's prescient list, Wallace predicted the nuclear bomb would explode in

Chicago, and he insisted on going there to try to stop the catastrophe. Reluctantly, and despite the promise she made to Marshall, Wanda went along with him.

Unfortunately, Wallace's calculations were close, but not close enough. They split up to cover a larger area, and they were both about a mile away from ground zero when the bomb went off. Those outside the blast radius weren't subject to instant incineration, but unfortunately, were still inside the radiation zone.

That's where luck came into play. The bomb detonated as Wanda took a shortcut through an underground parking garage on a people mover near the Merchel Energy building. The thick layers of reinforced concrete and steel embedded in the earth provided protection from the blast, particularly the lethal gamma rays that bombarded the immediate area. Hunkered down in the corner of the structure, Wanda absorbed a dose of radiation equivalent to only about five x-rays.

Wallace was walking at street level when the bomb exploded. He was on his way to inspect a Lutheran church when he heard the ear shattering sound and subsequently felt the thirty-miles-per hour blast wind. An invisible deadly cocktail that included Strontium 90, Cesium 137, Iodine 131, plutonium 239, gamma rays and a host of other radioactive isotopes bombarded his exposed flesh. The effects were immediate, and Wallace crumpled to the ground as if his skin was being burned off his body by a blowtorch. More importantly, he absorbed 600 rems, a dose that would ultimately prove lethal.

The radionuclides started to dissipate almost immediately, and within hours of the initial attack, the radiation levels in the parking garage where Wanda remained hidden subsided to safe levels. Crouched down in a corner with knees drawn up tightly to her chest, she rocked back and forth and cried in soft sobs that echoed through the empty garage. Afraid and unable to fully comprehend what had happened, she remained paralyzed with fear. Sirens blared from every direction, which only elevated the confusion in her mind.

After sitting and cowering for what might have been minutes, hours or days, Wanda noticed people streaming out of the Merchel Energy Building, running through the tunnel to their vehicles. Cars started whizzing by her, and the sound of roaring engines and screeching tires proved too much to handle, so she covered her ears and screamed.

"Miss, miss, are you okay? Wanda looked up at a stranger standing over her. Still dazed, she struggled to speak. The crushing noise remained, and there was no way to block it out.

"Are you alright," he repeated with more emphasis and higher volume.

"No, no, I'm not alright at all," she replied.

"Well, I think the parking garage may have saved your life, but you've got to get out of here. Night is coming, and I can't imagine what's going to happen."

He helped her up and led her over to his car. Carefully placing her inside, he got in and started the engine. After breathing a sigh of relief, he drove up the winding driveway to ground level.

"Everyone worried that the EMP might ruin the electronics in the vehicles, but it looks like most are turning over. Maybe the garage shielded them..." He paused and looked over at Wanda. "Are you staying around here?"

"Wallace!" She sat up in the seat with a start. "We have to get Wallace."

He looked at her and shook his head. "I — I don't have time to look for someone else."

"Please, he can't be more than a few blocks away."

Obviously shaken, he said, "I'm sorry, but there's no way."

They exited onto Madison Avenue and began traveling west. Naturally, everyone had the same intent to get as far from the city as possible.

Traffic moved slowly since the entire stop light network was out, and every intersection effectively became a game of commuter chicken. The electricity was off as well, and dazed pedestrians lay on the sidewalks and streets while others wandered like zombies as they tried to process what had just happened.

While they were stalled at Madison and Damon Avenue, Wanda suddenly yelled, "Stop the car! It's Wallace." Before the good Samaritan could react, she opened the door, jumped out, and started running toward him, dodging traffic until she reached the other side of the street. Her friend appeared dazed as he sat up against a metal storefront security gate.

"Wallace, it's me... Wallace!" Leaning down, she saw the ragged burn marks that covered his face, hands and clothing. He looked over at her and smiled slightly before his eyes fluttered and closed.

"Wallace, you have to get up."

"I can't," he mumbled.

"You have to. Now get up." She grabbed him by the shirt and assertively began to pull, slapping him once out of frustration, which caused him to howl in pain and regain a semblance of consciousness. "Okay, okay," he said in a slurred voice.

Wincing as he rose, she gripped his right arm and pulled him back out into traffic. Fortunately, the snarl hadn't abated, and she was able to maneuver between the gridlocked cars and get him into the back seat just before the other vehicles started moving again.

"Wow," the driver said. "I'd like to know the name of the woman so brave she would risk her life to save a friend."

For just a moment, Wanda paused and smiled. Rarely had anyone paid her such a compliment. "I'm Wanda Parsens, and I'm very grateful to you."

"You're welcome, Wanda Parsens. My name is Mateo Reyes."

It took nearly an hour to move less than a mile, but shortly thereafter, law enforcement and the National Guard arrived like a scene out of an alien invasion movie. Mateo wasn't able to make it to the freeway as the police and guardsmen started directing vehicles off the main roadways and into parking lots, side streets and onto the sidewalk itself. Eventually, they were forced to abandon his car but were fortunate enough to find refuge in the back of an M1078 FMTV stake bed truck, crowded with other victims of the disaster. The three Guardsmen assigned to the vehicle were in a hurry to leave the area, and once the bed was filled, they closed the gate and moved down Damon with the intent of intersecting with the Eisenhower freeway.

Benches lined the floor of the truck, but the lack of covering left the passengers exposed to the elements. The sky was a dark, dull gray, the result of the soot and dirt thrown into the air by the explosion's fireball and the storm system it conjured up during the last hour. Everyone with a rudimentary knowledge of nuclear fission bombs prayed it wouldn't rain because each droplet would bring radioactive fallout down with it.

Wanda sat on a bench that gave her an unobstructed view of the surrounding chaos through gaps in the metal slats. She saw people huddled on their porches and standing in business entryways looking frightened, shocked and confused. Three youths pushed an old man to the ground, and they kicked and punched him until a Guardsman shouted a warning and pointed his gun. The anarchists scattered, leaving the man lying in the street clutching his bleeding face in his hands. His eyes bulged wide in confusion, and he started to call out for his wife in desperate tones. "Celia... Help me, Celia, I'm hurt bad..."

Movement down Damon slowed to a crawl, and the truck driver honked his horn repeatedly while the violence seemed to escalate as they approached the freeway. Wanda heard wild talk of zombies and stories of nuclear holocaust that became more exaggerated as they passed from person to person. A rock from an angry bystander hit a passenger in the back, and the woman let out a cry and fell onto someone sitting at her feet.

A hail of semi-automatic weapons fire sent everyone in the truck diving for cover, and those in the road scurried to get out of harm's way. The soldier continued yelling as the truck lurched forward, and the threat of more gunfire scattered the crowd, leaving only the floaters, who stared down the soldiers and mumbled obscenities with malice and hate.

At the freeway entrance, a neighborhood mob gathered and blocked off the ramp by parking cars in front of it. Wanda looked over as a man who appeared to be in his mid-twenties, dressed in a ragged, white sleeveless t-shirt, held up his hands and waved the truck down. As he approached, Wanda could see a handgun tucked into the belt of his pants.

"Yo, bro, what's going on, man?" he said as he continued walking toward the truck with attitude. His gang crouched behind nearby parked cars but watched their leader intently and seemed ready for a fight. The truck slowed until it stopped about twenty feet away from the menacing figure. He kept moving forward, only this time more slowly.

The truck's doors opened, and two Guardsmen stepped out onto the pavement while the third remained in the cab. "Stop right there, sir. You and your friends are impeding a military vehicle. It's a violation of the UCMJ, which supersedes civilian codes during a time of martial law. I'm ordering you to move those cars."

The man looked agitated, and he shrugged his shoulders several times before glancing back at the mob. "I'm just trying to get some information, Holmes. A nuclear bomb exploded, man. We're probably all gonna die, anyway. Word on the street is this is the big one. The Russians and Chinese have nuked the whole country. Is that right, ese?"

"Sir, I'm not at liberty to discuss anything related to the bombing. Now, please follow my instructions and

45

remove the cars." The Guardsman raised his weapon high enough to convey his message.

The mob leader lifted his hands. "Okay, okay, don't get crazy on me, man. We're just trying to survive out here. These goddamn floaters are everywhere. They're like cannibals, man. We saw one of them feeding on a dead guy two streets over."

"There'll be more transports to take you from the city. Stay in your houses until they come for you."

"Yeah, and watch our hair and teeth fall out and shit like that. Anyway, good luck getting through; the freeway is a mess." He began walking back to join his gang, but Wanda could see he pulled the gun out of his waistband.

The taller guardsman got back into the vehicle as the other one climbed into the bed with the refugees. He stepped around the people sitting on the floor and took a position where he could set his rifle on the roof of the truck. While not exactly aiming at the assembled mob, his body language delivered the threat.

The vehicle lumbered slowly toward the freeway entrance, and the two cars blocking it backed up to create a pathway just big enough for the truck to slip through. The tension was palpable as they drove past the barricade, but it seemed like they were going to make it out of a tense situation. Yet, when an angry and frightened teenager pulled out a 9mm Ruger and took a single shot, a strained situation turned into a volatile crisis.

The bullet was meant for the guardsman but instead struck one of the metal stakes surrounding the truck bed. It ricocheted harmlessly away but caused the people riding in the back to panic, scream and duck for cover. The projectile left a pronounced dent in the steel slat, but one inch higher and it would have hit a portly Asian woman square in the face. She looked around anxiously, unaware of how close she came to instant death.

The guardsman in the bed was taking no chances. He grabbed his weapon, pulled the bolt and turned in the direction of the gunshot. A three-second spray of bullets fired over the heads of the crowd was enough to get their attention, and the result was nearly instantaneous. Handguns appeared from seemingly every belt or holster in the crowd, and they trained their sights on the soldiers. Meanwhile, the other two guardsmen exited the truck and hid behind the doors, automatic weapons drawn and ready.

"Your call." The soldier in charge yelled out to the mob leader. "But if you make a bad decision, a lot of people are going to die here today."

The tattooed man muttered and shook his head in frustration. "We're dead anyway, man. We're *all* off the grid now. Now *you're* gonna know what it's like soon."

"Not necessarily. This was a small nuke, probably hid in a suitcase. You all may die in the chaos, but it's unlikely you'll die from the fallout... What's your name?"

The gang leader lowered his gun a bit, and his facial expression softened slightly. "They call me Paco... Paco Rabinowitz."

"Well, Paco, my name's Jim Thompson, and I don't think either one of us wants to die today. Back off and let us through, and that'll be the end of it."

Paco considered the proposal for a moment as he scratched his whiskers with the barrel of his gun. After a few moments, he carefully put the weapon back into his belt and turned to the rest of the gang. "Let them through. Anyone else who shoots answers to me, man."

Jim Thompson and the other guardsmen got back into the truck, and after starting the engine, they rolled past the mob and onto the freeway entrance.

As expected, the highway was backed up for miles as frightened residents tried to flee the city in hope that the outlying areas were safer. Yet, despite their efforts, finding sanctuary would prove impossible. The rock that held back the landslide of societal chaos was plucked out, and the destruction of a functioning society that began in downtown Chicago was quickly rippling outward.

Law enforcement officials dispatched personnel from every city, district and suburban jurisdiction, and they accompanied National Guard units from Donnelly, General Jones Armory, Midway Armory, Northwest Armory and North Riverside to priority areas throughout the city, including ground zero. In all, about 50,000 in uniform were charged with containing a catastrophe that instantly affected ten-million people.

Fortunately for Wanda, Wallace and Mateo, keeping freeway traffic open was one of the priorities established by the Department of Homeland Security, which now coordinated the entire effort. They directed cars off the highway to keep one lane clear for military, police, rescue and emergency vehicles. Even with those efforts, the trip was a painful series of starts, stops and gridlock. Nearly seven hours later, the truck would arrive in Elk Grove Village, which was far enough away from the blast to provide respite from the gamma radiation. At least that's what the local officials hoped.

As she continued to stare straight ahead in an almost trancelike state, Wanda couldn't help but ruminate on the effects of the explosion. For all the safeguards in place, the panic that ensued after the detonation of the five-kiloton bomb in Chicago was a firsthand graphic lesson in understanding the fragility of modern society. The casualties that resulted from the fireball, air blast and thermal radiation exceeded 26,000, which made it by far the worst catastrophe on U.S. soil. Past disasters would soon seem trivial by contrast.

The initial damage was bad enough, but the ensuing fallout carried inland by a prevailing wind spread a slow, insidious death wherever it fell. Within two days, 25,000 people died from radiation burns and exposure. Before the bomb completed its path of destruction, another 60,000 would die. However, the worst was yet to come.

Wanda forced herself to look at Wallace, whose condition was worsening. He developed deep, angry splotches on his face, arms and legs. She imagined his torso was even worse. Clumps of his jet-black hair fell out every time he touched his head, and when he rolled over, she noticed a brown, bloody stain on the back of his burn suit where it covered his anus.

A small yelp escaped her lips, and Mateo placed his hand on her shoulder.

"You did all you could."

She turned around and looked directly at him. "Where is the doctor? They haven't even attended to him."

"Wanda, they have a lot of people who need their help, and they're prioritizing based on survivability.

49

They're probably overwhelmed. I have no idea how many were hurt or injured during the blast, let alone the radiation. We'll have to wait."

"I won't wait," said Wanda, fighting against the fear and sense of isolation that overwhelmed her. She walked off in search of a doctor, leaving Mateo with Wallace.

A makeshift triage center occupied an area near the entrance to the gymnasium, but she found it nearly impossible to push through the crush of humanity that occupied every inch of floor space. The smell of fresh sweat in an infinite variety of disgusting odors made her retch, and it was all she could do to maintain her balance.

Buffeted around by a mass of people, Wanda found herself pinned against an outer wall. Trapped by an excessively heavy man soaked with perspiration, Wanda's clothes showed fresh wet marks where he kept pushing up against her. She looked down and saw his pants had fallen low enough to reveal his intergluteal cleft, and sweat glistened and collected in the crevice.

Just as she started to faint, the lights in the gym went out.

Chapter Five

Mr. Cox looked out over the Detroit skyline from his penthouse in what used to be the central building in the Renaissance Center complex. Seventy-three stories above ground level, he relished the first day in his new, plush accommodations. Hundreds, perhaps thousands of fires dotted the landscape, and he closed his eyes and allowed the thick waves of deep despair and misery to wash over him.

Since the detonation of the bomb in Chicago, the Benefactor spent much of his time in a state of pure ecstasy. He found it increasingly difficult to focus on business as the fragile underpinnings that held civilization together crumbled. The savagery that filled the void was utterly delicious and nearly impossible to ignore. In fact, in some respects, he neglected his responsibilities to indulge in the pleasure of witnessing the brutality first hand. As the mob mentality asserted itself, he had a virtual smorgasbord of brutal, heinous acts to choose from.

His favorite events involved families and neighbors turning on each other. Relationships that prospered for years plunged into the dark abyss of hate as tensions rose and survival concerns became paramount. The violence started in the inner cities first but fanned out across the suburbs throughout America and the world, aided by the fear of additional nuclear detonations.

Against this backdrop, Mr. Cox envisioned Detroit as the new capital of America and ultimately the world. The city was already broken long before the bomb in Chicago exploded, and the resulting chaos would only hasten its demise. A small push was enough to send the once prosperous metropolis into unimaginable anarchy and turmoil.

Even before he began his quest to become the ruler of a world empire, Mr. Cox liked to visit Detroit. The city was a fertile recruiting ground with a suicide rate far higher than the national average. Many of the Gehenna corporation's upper echelon personnel were recruited directly from the streets of the worst neighborhoods, including several of the most violent gang members who now occupied positions of great authority within the Benefactor's hierarchy.

While still looking out the window, Mr. Cox smiled. "Detroit is the perfect location for the global capital, don't you think?" He turned around and faced the men sitting at the conference table behind him.

"Yes, Benefactor, the decision to move to Detroit was brilliant," said Delgado with emphasis. He placed his elbows on the table with forearms raised, and his hands touched together at the fingertips. This gave him a pensive look that was complimented by his Brioni suit and Salvatore Feragamo tie.

"I think it fuckin' sucks," said Alan Ziminski, who still believed he was the Benefactor's son. His red hair grew noticeably darker over the past year, and it hung limply along the sides of his face. At first glance, it appeared as though Alan hadn't bathed or groomed in weeks. He slumped in the chair and stuffed cheese flavored corn puffs in his mouth, which coated his fingers with an orange residue he periodically licked off.

"I agree with Delgado," said Xavier Watts, the Benefactor's second in command. "Detroit is perfect. We can coordinate all of our operations from a central location with the infrastructure we'll need to govern." Watts was also a man who took his appearance seriously. From his black double-breasted Kiton suit to his Manhattan Richelieu, the man radiated confidence and power.

"*Govern?*" The Benefactor bristled, and his eyes glowed with the deep red color his subordinates knew signaled anger. "We will not govern; we will rule. The people will worship me. They will have no other choice."

"Of course," said Delgado.

"Yes, certainly. I stand corrected." added Watts.

The fourth man smirked but did not speak. However, Mr. Cox saw the small change in facial expression, and he looked over in that direction as the corner of his mouth turned noticeably down.

"Do you find something funny, Lars?"

Lars tilted his head back and shook his blond mane. Now that he was outed, his smile grew even wider. "No, no, please don't let me interrupt. In fact, you need a title of some sort. Perhaps, Emperor Cox?"

"Are you mocking me?" Mr. Cox' lips appeared to grow even thinner as they formed a sneer disguised as a smile.

Lars turned and looked at the Benefactor. "Of course not, Your Excellency. If I have offended you, please forgive me. I am only here to serve." His tone bordered on insubordinate.

Remaining motionless with a smile still on his face, Mr. Cox finally started to chuckle, which served as a signal to the others they should laugh as well. Delgado and Watts both laughed in a low key, measured way. Ziminski continued to eat Cheetos and looked bored.

"You amuse me, Lars. I hope your sense of humor does not prove to be your demise."

The laughter ended promptly. Lars turned toward Cox. He leaned in and stared directly, his penetrating blue eyes conveyed his seriousness. "You have my loyalty, Mr. Cox. The success of your mission is vital."

The Benefactor nodded and moved to his chair at the head of the table. "Mr. Watts, tell us where we stand with the different populations."

Watts tapped his tablet several times and cleared his throat. "As we predicted, the third detonation proved to be the tipping point. Our operatives achieved success in communicating through various media outlets around the world. The vast majority of them are aligned with us. The movement is growing exponentially, especially since we are the only organization capable of providing relief. We control the major supplies of foodstuffs from the United Nations, Red Cross and FEMA, and we use that leverage to create more converts."

"Excellent, Mr. Watts, that kind of tangible progress pleases me. Now, tell me, what progress have we made in negotiating with the major world governments?"

Watts shuffled through several documents until he found what he was looking for. "As you know, we have agents in key positions within every major government, and they're putting severe pressure on their leaders by undermining them whenever possible. So far, Kenya, Columbia and New Zealand have ceded control of their governments to our loyalists. There are many others at the breaking point."

"Give me a list of the top twenty countries most likely to fall. I will make sure it happens. They call us the 'Deep State'? Bah. Wait until they see what we have planned for them next."

"Certainly, Benefactor," said Watts.

"Alan, I want you to increase the disruption in those countries. I've had the mainframe transferred from Desolation, so you should have access to the full power of the system within the day. The new processors are much faster and contain architecture of my own design. You will be the first to experience its power. Focus on disrupting the humanitarian aid. I want their people to suffer."

Alan looked absently at the ceiling and then back at the Benefactor. "I'll try, but a lot of the interconnected global systems are crashing. We control most of the cloud, but hackers are having a field day overrunning the IOT. Secure facilities like NORAD with the nuclear codes and stuff are still kind of intact, but we're close to penetrating their firewalls. If they're ever going to be vulnerable, it'll be now."

"Then do it," said Cox. "Once we have the nuclear codes, we can blackmail those governments into surrender if they haven't submitted already."

"Well then, you should be happy to know I've got the nuke codes for Pakistan and India. They were easy to hack."

Mr. Cox' face lit up for just a moment. "Really? Please transfer the codes to Mr. Watts."

Ziminksi waited for some acknowledgment or praise for his accomplishment, but none was forthcoming. His eyes filled with tears, and he squeezed hard on a deep-rooted bulbous pustule until it burst and sprayed a bloody, yellow gunge on the conference table.

The Benefactor glanced at Ziminski with disdain and shook his head before returning to the matter at hand. "We have much work to do. I'll ensure those in power are — compelled to do our bidding. We will achieve our goals no matter the cost."

"Benefactor," said Watts in a soft voice. "I'm receiving inquiries from several governments regarding our claim that we have persuaded the 'terrorists' to delay detonating the next bomb. They want information and are threatening arrest if we don't give it to them."

Mr. Cox placed his palms flat on the table as his eyes again blazed. "You tell whoever is applying pressure that the terrorists will detonate the next bomb immediately if they learn we are being threatened by any enforcement arm of the government. Do you understand?"

"Yes, Benefactor, I will tell them," replied Watts meekly. "We're still having issues with the media.

They want more information on the HUGE conglomerate. How much detail should I reveal?"

Mr. Cox contemplated the question for several seconds. "We need positive press, Xavier. We want footage featuring our representatives giving food to the needy and other such nauseating drivel. Any media organization that wants to launch a serious investigation should be—discouraged. Do I make myself clear?"

Watts and Delgado nodded enthusiastically, but Lars appeared to fight an urge to laugh.

The Benefactor rose and walked back over to the window. "The meeting is dismissed. I have many places to visit. Thousands of people will try to commit suicide tonight, and I want to be there for each one of them. Everyone may leave, but I'd like to speak privately with Lars."

Hastily, Delgado and Watts got up from the table and left the room. Alan wasn't as motivated, and he appeared to hesitate for no other reason than to irritate the Benefactor.

"Alright, alright, I'm going." Ziminski gathered his tablet and scurried away as Mr. Cox and Lars stared ominously at one another.

"I accepted you because I wondered if you might have something unique to offer. I allowed you to become part of my tightly controlled inner sanctum, and for my generosity, I must endure your subtle insults?"

Lars leaned back in his chair and folded his hands. "Insults? I was being gracious. As I told you when I arrived here, you need me, and you'll continue to need me. So if I seem somewhat insubordinate, don't take it personally."

Mr. Cox' smile disappeared, and his eyes pulsed like red-hot coals, and his breathing became shallow. He walked over to Lars and bent down, sticking his face so close to the other man that their lips almost touched as he spoke.

"Do you understand that I can turn you into a doddering idiot in a fraction of a second? I might make your blood boil until it burns through your veins. I could create such physical and mental pain you would beg me to kill you to end your misery."

He paused to allow the gravity of his threats to sink in. When he pulled his face away, the smile returned. "You will never show such insubordination in front of my associates again. Do you understand me?"

"Of course... Benefactor," said Lars without looking directly at Mr. Cox. "But now let me tell you something. I know much more about you than you might suspect. You can't succeed without me, and I believe on some level you know that. I'll toe the line in front of your peons if that makes you happy. But don't underestimate me."

Mr. Cox seethed with anger, and he came precariously close to unleashing an attack against Lars that would evaporate his soul. Yet, something held him back, and it irritated him like a rash that wouldn't heal. Lars was mysterious and defiant; but he had unusual abilities that might prove useful.

I must find out how much he knows about me and where I came from.

"You took seven of my best men and only three returned. I hope their sacrifice wasn't in vain. Perhaps worse, you still haven't addressed the Suicide Society problem as you promised."

58

For the first time since they had met, Lars smile disappeared, and he gritted his teeth as he spoke. "Someone warned them ahead of time, and the place was rigged with explosives. I lost four men; there are no excuses. These mutants are dangerous and resourceful, and I should have been more careful. I was overconfident, and it cost lives."

"Well, what will you do about it?"

"It won't be easy to find them. Have you discovered anything useful that might help locate them?"

The Benefactor shook his head. "They have the ability to cast a protective shield that is undetectable, even to me."

"Then we'll wait until they make a mistake. It's inevitable. I will find them, and next time I'll be more prepared."

"Make sure you are," said Mr. Cox. "I can't afford to lose any more skilled mechanics."

Lars rose and walked to the door as Cox said, "I dismiss you."

After pressing a button on his intercom, Cox waited for a familiar voice to respond.

"Yes, boss. What do you need?"

"Hefe, bring me a snifter of Chianti. Watts will be on television in a few moments, and I want to watch him."

"Yes, boss, right away. Hefe will get it quick."

It couldn't have been more than a minute before the automatic door swung open, and Hefe walked inside carrying a fourteen-karat gold tray with a half full glass of Chianti and the balance of the bottle next to it. The small man with a grisly face placed the tray on a serving table and brought the glass over to Mr. Cox. With difficulty, he pushed an ottoman closer to the couch in case the overlord wanted to rest his feet.

Taking hold of the remote control on an end table, Hefe pushed the button, and a 12-foot screen slowly dropped down. He pushed another button and tuned to a broadcast station where a news anchor talked rapidly. A banner scrolled on the bottom part of the screen: *Up next: Mr. Xavier Watts from the HUGE conglomerate.*

"Anything else, boss? Can I massage your feet or rub your back?"

"No, Hefe, I'm fine. Moving everything to this new facility has been grueling, and I want to retire."

"Ok, boss. Have a good night." Hefe waddled out of the room with a smile on his face. The Benefactor was in a jovial mood, so it seemed Hefe would make it through the day without being kicked, burned or beaten.

Mr. Cox adjusted the sound just as Watts appeared on a split screen between the news anchor and himself.

"Good evening, I'm Bureen Carbol reporting from Gehenna corporate headquarters, formerly known as the Renaissance Center. We have Mr. Xavier Watts with us tonight. He is the Chairman of the organization called, 'Humans United for Global Equality', more commonly known as HUGE."

The reporter turned from the camera and faced Watts. "Thank you for joining us, Mr. Watts."

"Thank you, Bureen. It's a pleasure."

"Mr. Watts, what can you tell us about HUGE and its primary mission?"

"Of course, Bureen. The HUGE conglomerate is a loose confederation of the four largest global corporations uniting together to find practical solutions to complex problems."

"I see. Can you give us more specifics?"

"Well, I think the explanation speaks for itself. We live in tumultuous times, and governments don't seem to be able to provide the solutions we need. When leadership fails, we step in."

"Does the Gehenna corporation control HUGE, Mr. Watts?"

"While we may have a controlling interest, we always work in consort with our partners to help the local communities we serve achieve the most favorable result."

"But exactly how do you help, Mr. Watts?"

Watts leaned back in his chair and assumed a relaxed posture. "We help in a variety of ways, Bureen. This includes distributing food to the hungry, shelter to the homeless and warm clothing to the shivering. We make mortgage payments for people about to lose their homes and offer transportation to those who can't get to work. Politicians just talk; we act."

"Interesting. We're hearing in some regions of Africa and South America, your people have taken control of certain local and regional governments. Can you confirm this and tell us if your group is a political movement or perhaps an insurgency?"

Watts smiled comfortably. "We are neither. Our only goal is to provide help in these troubling times. In some places that may be as simple as giving hungry people food. In more severely affected locations, it may require us to fill a leadership vacuum."

"It's rumored you have an ongoing dialogue with the terrorists responsible for detonating the three nuclear bombs. Shouldn't you divulge this information to federal law enforcement?"

"There isn't much I can tell you about that, Bureen. It's obviously a sensitive matter. We want to avoid any further loss of life. We're cooperating with United Nations authorities, that is, what's left of them. That's all I can say right now."

"Mr. Watts, there are rumors of a shadowy figure who actually runs the HUGE group. Can you confirm or deny the existence of someone you report to?"

"HUGE is very transparent, Bureen. As I explained earlier, leadership is comprised of prominent members of the four largest global corporations, all of whom have demonstrated a commitment to improving humanity's quality of life issues. However, there are delicate situations we find ourselves in that limit the amount of information we can divulge regarding our leadership structure. At the appropriate time, everyone will know who we are."

"Mr. Watts, thank you for taking the time to talk with us tonight."

"My pleasure, Bureen."

Mr. Cox snapped off the video feed and sipped his Chianti. *Well played, Xavier. Well played indeed.* Mr. Cox sent his sentiments telepathically to Watts, who was just finishing up in the TV studio on the third floor. Watts paused for a moment as Cox's thoughts registered in his conscious mind. With a rehearsed smile, he straightened his tie and began preparations for the next interview.

In the heart of downtown Detroit, the din of the angry mobs in the streets was background noise pierced by the sound of sirens. The pillars were crumbling just as the Benefactor had promised many years ago. By the time Watts reached the lobby and a security detail escorted him to another building several blocks away, his smile faded, and the permanent omnipresent despair had returned.

Chapter Six

Anston, the pilot and the rest of the Suicide Society sat at a corner table inside the *Cheap Eats* diner in Salome. They ordered breakfast and kept the conversation to a minimum, which seemed appropriate under the circumstances. The place was packed with locals as the word spread about the landing at the abandoned airfield. Speculation ran rampant as the gossip covered everything from a drug run gone bad to a secret CIA mission.

The little bell on the door jingled, and Zach looked up to see a small man in a uniform enter the diner. The drab olive-green shirt, matching pants and wide-brimmed hat with the requisite shiny badge easily identified him as a local law enforcement official. He looked around the diner briefly, removed his dark tinted glasses and walked purposefully over to the table the overseers occupied. He did his best to convey a sense of confidence by maintaining a mildly disgusted expression, but Zach didn't need telepathic abilities to notice the cop was agitated and fearful.

Conceivably, this may have been the biggest incident in Salome since the airport closed.

"Morning," he said without smiling or changing his countenance. "I'm Officer Krener from the La Paz County Sheriff's office. Who's in charge here?"

"Good morning, officer. My name is Jarad Anston." He extended his hand, which the officer accepted and shook tepidly.

"Mr. Anston, it seems we have a — situation. Your jet landed at Pierce Airfield, which has been closed for nearly fifty years. I'm wondering why? Did you have an emergency?"

"Excuse me, officer. I'm John Simmons the pilot. I was forced to land here because of a near miss at Sky Harbor where I filed the flight plan. The skies are very dangerous. We had no choice."

The cop fingered the brim of his hat and shook his head. "I understand. I'm not sure if you heard, but there was another midair collision this morning over L.A. A 737 and an Airbus A380. I guess over 700 people died in the crash."

"That's terrible," the pilot replied. "I'm afraid there will be more tragedies if they don't get this situation calmed down."

"Look, if one of you can open the plane and let me take a look, I'll just write up a report, and you can do whatever you need to do. We've called the FAA a dozen times, but there's no answer. I guess there are forced landings going on everywhere."

"C'mon, John, let's show Officer Krener that were not drug runners." Zach smiled and got up from the table, motioning for the pilot to follow.

"Mr. Randall, I don't think…"

Randall raised his arm and extended his palm outward. "I know, Marshall."

Officer Krener shifted his gaze between the two men. The suspicious look returned to his face as he placed his hand on the butt end of his gun and followed Zach and Simmons out the door and into the parking lot. The buzz inside the diner resumed, only this time it was louder. The latest speculation centered on gun smuggling to arm Mexican rebels across the border in Hermosillo.

Once they reached the plane, Simmons activated the hatch release and lowered the stairs. Krener climbed inside and looked around the interior, opening all the overhead and closet doors. He tapped his fist against the frame of the plane at various points, probably just to make it seem like he knew what he was doing.

Satisfied there were no drugs, guns or other contraband onboard, he climbed back down the stairs and walked over to the cargo hold. Zach and Simmons already removed the few suitcases the overseers brought with them. After looking in the empty bay and opening a couple bags, Krener adjusted his hat and rejoined the others.

"Okay, everything looks good," he said. "I'm just going to write up a report and have you sign it. We'll email it over to the FAA and let them deal with it."

"I don't know, Officer Krener," said Zach. "That probably isn't the best idea."

"What do you mean?" Krener stopped writing but kept the pen in his hand. He looked up at Zach, only this time the suspicious look wasn't an act.

"I'm just saying it would probably be best for national security if you just forgot the whole thing, at least for a couple days."

"No, I ca—I can't do that. I—have a duty."

"Your first duty is to your country, isn't it officer?"

"Well, yes. Of course it is."

"If I told you that we were on a vital mission to thwart another, uh, 'catastrophe,' and our whereabouts must remain hidden, would you believe me?"

"I—I don't know. Another catastrophe? Do you mean you're trying to stop another nuclear bomb? Oh my God, is it here in Arizona?" The officer took a few steps back.

"I didn't say that. Still..." Zach looked down and kicked some rocks. "I'm asking you to forget this plane ever landed here."

"I don't know..." Krener shook his head.

"You want to help us, don't you, Officer Krener?"

Something compelled Krener to look directly into Randall's eyes, and once he did, he couldn't break the connection. "I want to help you. I do want to help you."

"And the best way you can help us is by reporting to your superiors that this was a false alarm. It was just an old crop duster that was off course and ran out of gas. Isn't that right, Officer Krener?"

"Yes, a crop duster. I'll report that to dispatch."

"You'll also tell the locals we're here on an important mission for the government, and everyone needs to help us by staying quiet."

"Yes, stay quiet. I'll tell everyone..."

"Good. Now we're going to go back to the diner, and you'll come in and get a cup of coffee while we leave, alright?"

"Yes, of course."

67

John the pilot shook his head as they walked back from the airstrip. "How do you do that?" he said quietly.

Randall smiled. "It's an acquired talent. You have to die first."

Officer Krener stood outside the diner and shook hands with Zach and Simmons. This served as enough of a public display that the patrons inside the restaurant could see the goodwill the officer was extending, and it seemed to put them at ease.

Zach sported a wide smile, nodding and making eye contact with several of the customers as he and the pilot made their way back to their table. Krener went to the breakfast bar and took the place of a patron who spilled his coffee as he moved to give the officer his seat.

"Everything is taken care of. The landing will not be reported."

"Good," said Anston. "I already paid the bill and left a generous tip, so it's time to walk up the street to the only place in town where we might be able to get a ride."

The table emptied, and the diner once again grew quiet as the strangers left the restaurant. Once they were out of the building, a crowd quickly gathered around Officer Krener as he recounted the talk with Randall, providing just enough detail to tantalize the locals with a tale of intrigue and national security. New theories and speculation raced through the diner and the entire town within a matter of hours, but the La Paz Sheriff's office didn't receive a single call inquiring about the incident. At least for a short time, Officer Otto Krener would be considered a local hero.

"I asked Krener about getting a vehicle. He said there isn't an actual car lot here, but there's a junk yard down a few blocks off of Avenue B. I saw the sign when we landed. He told me the guy who owns it fixes up junkers, and he might be able to give us a ride or sell us a car if the price is right."

"Okay, Zach, let's take a walk down there. The rest of you can return to the hotel. As soon as we have things settled, we'll come and pick you up."

"Wait a minute," said the pilot. "We've got an airplane sitting over there. There's a lot of fuel left. I can take you almost anyplace you want to go."

Anston shook his head. "Thanks, John, but no. We have to keep a low profile right now, and I suggest you do the same. You're certainly welcome to come along with us."

"Oh, no. I've got to get the plane out of here. My whole life's invested in that thing. Besides, I've got to make sure my family is safe. I'll bet my wife is worried sick about me."

Jarad smiled and stuck out his hand. "Thank you, John. It may not have started well, but you've made some friends."

The pilot smiled back. "I don't know who or what you people are, but I know your work is important." He reached into his pocket and pulled out a business card. "My personal cell number is on the card. If you're in trouble and I'm still alive, call me. I'll do everything I can to help."

Zach walked up and patted the pilot's shoulder reassuringly. "Be careful, and I'm sure you'll be fine. Good luck, John."

The rest of the overseers said their goodbyes, and the pilot turned and walked toward the airstrip where the Hawker 900XP sat at the end of the ancient runway.

"Alright, Zach and I are going to try and find a couple roadworthy vehicles. We'll meet you back at the hotel."

"Uh, I'd like to come with you, Mr., ah, Speaker Anston, if that's alright." Marshall looked at the rest of the group sheepishly for just a moment.

"Of course, Marshall. You might be an asset in negotiations."

They split up, and as Zach, Jarad and Marshall walked down Apache Street, they could hear the roar of the jet engines in the distance as they powered up. Shortly thereafter, the changing pitch of the sound and the Doppler Effect confirmed the plane was airborne.

Turning onto Avenue B, they walked another block until they came upon *Al Shield's Salvage Yard*. The collection and assortment of old car parts, household appliances and building materials spanned the entire length and breadth of the expansive lot. A ten-foot chain-link fence topped with razor wire surrounded the property, but the gate that faced Avenue B was open. Walking inside, they were drawn to a large sign attached to a beat-up trailer that simply said, *Office*.

A set of steps led to the landing, and Randall opened the door and went inside, enjoying the relief from the window-unit air conditioner. A large man in stained bib overhauls slid out of a chair behind a battered metal desk and came to the front of the trailer.

"Name's Al Shields," he said while thrusting out his hand. "How can I help you?"

"Hi, Al. I'm Zach Randall. This is Jarad Anston and Marshall Beiner." Zach grabbed the huge paw and shook heartily.

"Nice to make your acquaintance," Al said to no one in particular. Marshall was thankful he didn't have to shake the yard owner's filthy hand. "Say, aren't you the ones that landed the plane at Pierce? Hell of a thing."

"Yeah, that was us. The skies just aren't safe anymore," said Anston while walking forward. "Al, we've heard you have cars for sale. Is that true?"

Al pulled out a red handkerchief and mopped his forehead and the back of his neck. "No, we're a salvage yard. All our cars are junkers."

"What about those?" Anston pointed to an area at the far end of the yard. "Are they sound? I mean those SUVs or that van over there?"

"They run. I replaced everything that needed to be replaced. They're all good for another 50,000 miles."

"Do you think they would make it to Sedona?"

The junkyard operator wiped his brow again as he thought. "What's that, about three hours away? Yeah, the Suburban's in better shape than the Yukon, but all of 'em should make it. Why, you wanna buy one?"

Anston shook his head. "Not if we can avoid it. Filling out all the paperwork would take up too much time. We need a ride if we can get one."

"To Sedona?"

"Yes, Sedona."

"Man, I don't know, I'd have to close the shop for the day. How many people you need to haul?"

"Ten."

"Whoa, that's a convention. The suburban holds nine, but with me, that's eleven."

Anston glanced back at Jarad and Marshall. Only he was overweight, and Sasha, Sarah, Aminah and Wei were very thin. "We'll make it work," he said.

"Well… I'd need about $200 for gas." Al lifted his eyes and looked at the threesome sheepishly expecting an objection. When none was forthcoming, he continued, "And I'll need $200 for my time."

Anston looked at his companions and then turned back to Shields. "Ok, Al, here's what I'm going to do. For now, here's $500, and I'll give you another $500 when we arrive. If you forget we were ever here, I'll send another $1000 cash to this address in exactly two weeks."

The junkyard operator stumbled backwards before recovering his balance. He leaned over so that he was within inches of Anston. "Are you guys with — you know — the Company? I served in Iraq in logistics, so I know a little bit about this sort of stuff."

Anston looked to his left and right as though he was making sure no one was listening. He said softly, "Look, Al, you know I can't talk about these kinds of things. Suffice to say you'll be doing a great service to your country if you complete this miss — uh — trip."

Al stood up and walked to a corkboard where several sets of keys hung on the plastic tipped thumb tacks. "When are we leaving?"

"How about right now?"

"Okay, I'll gas up. I hear you're staying at the hotel, so I'll meet you out front in, say, fifteen minutes?"

"Thanks, Al. We'll see you then."

Since they didn't arrive with many personal effects, the overseers were ready to leave several minutes before Al pulled up in the Suburban. It was vintage, but the old SUV wasn't burning any oil, and the engine sounded strong. With some creative positioning, all ten people fit inside as the lithe bodies of Sasha, Yasin, Wei and Rogelio got into the back row while Zach, Sarah, Marshall and Jacques took the longer middle row. Jarad and Aminah sat up in the front passenger's seat next to Al.

They were barely on Route-60 before Anston signaled the group without speaking or turning around to face them. *It is important that we maintain silence throughout this trip. Do not engage in verbal conversation with the driver that goes beyond anything general. If you need something, convey it through telepathy. Do you understand?* He received eight affirmative replies.

Despite his best efforts, Al Shields was unable to draw any information of consequence out of the group. He tried virtually every angle, starting with the nuclear explosions and transitioning to the crime and rioting in the big cities.

"Yeah, I hear it's absolutely crazy in Chicago," he said. "Hear everything's fallin' apart. They can't even get news people into that place with all the radiation and everything. You heard anything 'bout that?"

"Not much more than you," said Anston.

"Yeah, pretty bad. It's even getting' bad out here. Phoenix is still kind of ok, but you don't want to be out at night if you know what I mean."

"Yes, Al. I know it's getting pretty bad."

"Probably pretty bad where you're all from, huh? Where did you say that was again?"

"Actually, I didn't say. But as you guessed, I'm from a big city."

Zach could hardly stifle a laugh at the driver's clumsy efforts to dupe Jarad into revealing something significant. What struck Randall as particularly humorous was Al's ego, which made him think he outwitted these dumb city people and took them to the cleaners on the price of the trip. Little did he know Anston was prepared to pay five times that much if necessary.

Fortunately, the journey down Route-60 was relatively uneventful. Somewhere just outside the junction of the sixty and I-17, Al's probing became annoying, and Zach introduced a thought suggesting he should remain quiet. Without knowing why, Al wouldn't say another word until they gassed up.

About two-thirds of the way through the trip, Sasha sent a message to the group that she needed to use the facilities. They were nearing the Cordes Lakes exit, and Jarad suggested to Al that he take it since there was a Fast Mart with restrooms, gas and food. Al agreed and pulled into the convenience store, which was only 100 feet or so off the interstate.

He parked next to the closest gas pump, and everyone got out, stretching briefly before walking towards the convenience store. Traffic at the gas station was unusually heavy, and Al had to wait behind four cars before he finally reached the pump. With great effort, he slid out of the vehicle and started to dispense the gas while Jacques stood next to him.

"Wow, they doubled the price," said Al while scratching his head and looking at the digital display as the price-per-gallon numbers changed right before his eyes. "What the hell's goin' on?" Then, turning to Jacques, "Hey, I'm gonna need more money for gas."

Jacques nodded and said, "Of course, we will make sure you are treated fairly. It's the panic. People are topping off their tanks, I think."

Aminah turned back toward Jacques and adjusted her headdress. "Jacques, do you want anything? Water, food? We still have almost an hour on the road."

"Ah, just get me a big bottled water and a smoky link, will you?"

She tilted her head to the side and her facial features scrunched up. "A smoky link? What is that? We don't have those in Kenya."

Jacques smiled. "Ask Zach or Sarah, one of them will know."

Jarad told the group to get whatever snacks and drinks they wanted for the rest of the trip, and he gave the cashier a $100 bill and asked him to run a tab. After using the restroom and paying for their food and drinks, they gathered together at the door and began walking back to the Suburban as a group. Just ahead at the island, Al was pumping gas while Jacques talked on his cell phone, pacing and gesturing animatedly.

Casually, the overseers had split up with Sasha, Liu, Yasin and Rogelio in front and Zach, Sarah, Jarad and Aminah just behind them. Marshall walked up ahead by himself feeling very alone. Something wasn't right, and he had a hollow feeling in the pit of his stomach. These people were strange, and he felt marginalized. He missed his friends, but they were all dead. Hayden,

Iglar, Kenny, Wallace and Wanda. Above all the others, he missed Wanda with a depth of despair that hurt.

He kicked at the dirt in the parking lot and looked up just as Al replaced the nozzle while Jacques continued talking on his cell phone. Marshall stopped cold.

"No, no!" he yelled, dropping his soda and pretzels as he ran towards Jacques. "Mr. Randall, Mr. Anston, we have to go. We have to go right now!" Marshall shouted the words as he continued a full-out sprint towards the Suburban.

"Marshall? What is it?" Zach reacted to Marshall's sudden action with alarm.

"The phone. He used his cell phone. We've got to leave right now."

"Marshall, Marshall... stop." Zach ran after Marshall who was closing in on Jacques. The sudden confusion caused the other trailing overseers to react in different ways. Yasin and Sasha also began running. Rogelio, Wei and Aminah walked faster while Jarad and Sarah stopped in the middle of the parking lot.

Jacques turned around just in time to avoid a collision, and he winced and stepped back. Marshall reached out and grabbed Jacques' cell phone and threw it to the ground, stomping on it repeatedly as Jacques stood and watched in stunned silence. When he was sure the unit was completely destroyed, Marshall looked back at Jacques, who continued to stare at his cell phone on the ground.

"I'm sorry," said Marshall, "but your cell phone is a risk to all of us."

"You idiot!" said Jacques as he emerged from his stupor. He looked up at Marshall with contempt. "Why would you do that? I ought to…"

Jacques stalked Marshall aggressively. "What is wrong with you? You're going to pay for doing that. I was talking with my wife." He balled his fists just as Zach stepped between the two.

"Jacques, stop it right now, or you'll be dealing with me. Let's give Marshall a chance to explain."

"I—I…" Marshall stepped backward shaking his head. His whole body felt like it was seizing up, and he began to shake uncontrollably. The muscles in his legs suddenly felt like jelly, and he fell to the hard pavement. He pulled his knees up, covered them with his arms and began to cry.

The other overseers moved quickly towards Marshall. What none of them noticed was the black Mercedes GLE that pulled into the convenience store parking lot and was moving slowly toward the group gathered around the man on the ground.

Chapter Seven

Absorbed in the unfolding conflict between Jacques and Marshall, Zach didn't notice the Mercedes SUV until the doors opened and five men dressed in identical tactical uniforms got out. Before he actually saw them, he felt the dark energy descend like a polar vortex blowing in from the north.

Zach looked down at Marshall, who was still trembling. "The cell phone, Mr. Randall. They tracked it. It gave us away."

"But how could they get here so quickly? How..." Zach didn't finish his sentence as the crack of the first bullet pierced the air. The assailants approached with guns drawn and obvious ill intent.

Instantaneously, Zach communicated with the group and instructed them to focus their psychokinetic energy through him. He experienced a surge through his body and a jolt stronger than a charged defibrillator. As the second bullet whizzed through the air, Zach thrust the sum of that energy toward the approaching group.

Without waiting to see the result, he reached down and grabbed Marshall by the arm and hauled him to his feet. *Run to the Suburban. I'll keep them at bay.*

After getting him upright, Zach passed Marshall off to Jacques, who slapped his own forehead in anguish over his stupidity. He pulled Marshall away from the live fire, and they crouched down and made their way along the side of the bank of gas pumps least exposed to the assailants.

Zach purposely manipulated the transition of time so it appeared to slow, which allowed his mind to examine each threat at a measured pace. He looked at Al, who was inside the Suburban fumbling with the keys. No doubt he planned to save himself, no matter that it left the overseers at the mercy of the assassins.

Wait.

Zach sent a strong command that froze Al in his seat. He took the key, put it in the ignition and started the engine but didn't pull away.

As he turned his attention to the attackers, Zach's mind identified the five targets. Three were on the ground clutching their heads and writhing from the intensely concentrated burst of lethal thought plasma unleashed upon them. They might survive, but their lives would be permanently altered. The damage to the neural networks, synaptic pathways and physical brain matter was severe, and they would be lucky to be able to feed themselves.

Two of the assailants continued forward. One looked as though he was in intense pain, but the other appeared only mildly affected. The more distressed of the two lunged but couldn't muster enough strength to raise his weapon. The other man shook as he tried to control his extremities but still managed to squeeze off another shot.

Zach was vaguely aware of Yasin and Sasha running behind him, following the same path Jacques and Marshall took to reach the SUV. Seconds later, Rogelio, Wei and Aminah arrived. The surviving assassin continued to move closer, less affected by the energy Zach thrust in his direction. As the intensity plateaued, Zach sensed the stream should have been even stronger. Was someone holding back?

The assailant moved his arm in a different direction and started to squeeze the trigger. As the stream focused and tightened, Zach concentrated everything on the man's prefrontal cortex. An agonized scream and series of grunts drifted across the parking lot as the lone remaining assassin fought to control his own motor reflexes. He grabbed his right hand with his left and pushed his arm over as his limbs struggled in opposition to each other.

The gun fired once more before he collapsed to the pavement, grabbing his affected arm and rolling around in obvious agony. At the moment the gunshot sounded, something inside Zach mentally snapped. The bright flash and loud bang in his head felt similar to the concussion he suffered playing high school football.

The surging sense of light-headedness continued for the next several moments. The sounds of commotion and screaming seemed both near and distant as his consciousness faded in and out. Maybe it was Sarah, but he couldn't be sure.

"Oh my God," someone said as they ran by. He raised his head from the pavement — somehow, he had fallen—and looked at Sasha, Yasin and several others running. His eyes moved ahead to a prone form lying on the pavement some fifty feet away. Sarah bent over the fallen victim and appeared to be screaming, but he couldn't really hear her. As he regained full consciousness, Zach instinctively knew it was Jarad.

Struggling to regain his footing, he stumbled over to the group gathered around their fallen leader. Anston was bleeding profusely from his abdomen, and the blood was blackish in color and spreading. Sarah placed her hand over the wound to create pressure, but the blood flow was so great it leaked freely through her fingers. The sense of dread transferred among them quickly.

As he walked up to his friend and mentor, Zach could hardly comprehend what was happening. The cerebral concussion he experienced resulted from Anston's telepathic energy violently severed from the collective. Jarad was blinking and still conscious but had a look of fear and confusion reserved for the dying. After pushing through the gathering, which now included a few bystanders, Zach leaned down and took his friend's hand and held it tightly.

"Don't worry, Jarad. You'll be fine. We'll get you to a hospital."

"No," Anston rasped. "Take them away now. You've got to save them."

"Jarad, I can't leave you…"

"No choice. You've got to go right now." He lifted his other arm and motioned for Zach to move in closer. "In my right pocket… a map to the location in Sedona and the key to the spiritual chest. Its contents are now in your care. Beware, they are powerful and dangerous but may be useful. Now go!"

81

"Jarad, I—I don't know what to do. What is the spiritual chest?"

"You are their leader now. They will look to you for guidance. Go before it's too late, and find the traitor…" Anston's words trailed off as his life force faded. The glimmering white light and energy that formed his essence rose up slowly from his body and made several passes through the air, pausing for a moment over the form of the assailant who fired the fatal shot.

The man was on his knees when Jarad's glistening energy enveloped him, and when the brilliant aura retreated, he fell back to the ground, either unconscious or dead. The light grew in intensity as it rose and spread out over the entire parking lot. Anston's essence shimmered with intensity so bright and vivid Zach wondered if the purity of the whiteness would burn his retinas. Like a perfect starburst fireworks display, his quintessence shot up towards the heavens before fading away completely.

The crushing loss crawled slowly through his body and soul with a savagery so brutal and primitive Zach wondered if he would ever recover. The deep sense of emptiness felt as though a part of him died. Tears welled up, and he cried while still clutching the cold, dead hand of his friend.

"Oh my God, Speaker Anston is dead," shrieked Sasha, who fell to her knees and sobbed, laying her head on his blood-soaked chest.

"This can't be real," said Rogelio. "It's like my heart is ripped open."

A bystander pulled out a phone. "Has anyone called 9-1-1?"

"I did," said Zach. He needed to buy time, so the circumstances justified the lie. By the time the regular patrons figured out that no one had called 9-1-1, hopefully, the overseers would be long gone.

Away from the group Jacques stood alone. "Was it my fault? Was it the cell phone call? How? How could they have known?"

Marshall moved away from the gathering and pointed a finger at Jacques. "They know everything. You people didn't experience it the way I did. Sixtus Maras was a Time Sculptor and explained it to me. They have access to historical records, so if they're looking for something specific, they just comb the data. I imagine they found records of your call in some obscure data base, and they sent those guys back here to the place and time you made the call."

Yasin separated himself from the group and walked aggressively toward Marshall with his finger pointed directly at him. "You *al'ahmaq*. Why didn't you tell us about this? We would have been able to avoid this situation."

Marshall put his hands up and backed away. "I wasn't sure about it, and I was afraid you all would laugh at me if I was wrong. That's why I suggested we pay cash for everything. But it was only conjecture; there was no way to know for sure until something confirmed it…" Marshall turned away and put his head in his hands.

Yasin looked over at him with obvious disgust. "Yeah, well I guess you have your confirmation."

Zach let Jarad's hand drop to the pavement, and he looked over in the direction of the two assailants, who were still motionless. He reached into Anston's pocket and pulled out the paper and the gold-plated keycard

Jarad told him about. After putting them inside his wallet, he stood up and faced the group as they looked up at him with somber and tear-stained faces. Every one of them seemed lost and directionless. Zach knew he must be decisive, or this could be the end of the Suicide Society.

We have to go now. I'm experiencing the same sense of loss and pain as all of you, but you also know this lifeless shell is not Jarad Anston. You saw his essence as I did, and he has traveled to his next reality. He would want us to address this threat and finish his work. We must get to the Suburban right now. Zach paused, but no one moved, so he sent a mild shock along with the message that seemed to jolt the group back to reality.

"Let's go," was all he needed to say out loud. Sarah stood up and looked at her bloody hand as Liu offered her a paper towel from a dispenser near the gas pumps. They followed Zach away from the body and over to the Suburban where Al Shields waited. Several bystanders exchanged puzzled glances as the group got into the SUV, but Zach tried to convince himself that no one would be thinking clearly enough to write down their license plate number.

Once inside, Zach scanned the seats behind him to make sure everyone was accounted for, but he quickly realized Marshall was missing. Without hesitation, he jumped out of the Suburban and hurried back towards Jarad's body, which by now had the attention of almost every patron in the store and parking lot. Several people talked on their cell phones, either relating recent events to loved ones or alerting the authorities. If the overseers didn't leave soon, they might have to contend with the police.

84

Randall walked at a brisk pace back into the convenience store. He looked inside, but Marshall was nowhere to be found. Identifying those with the gift was relatively easy, so he sent out a mental probe that instantly traced the troubled overseer to a place behind the building. Outside, near a dumpster and couched down against a dirty brick wall, Marshall sat in the fetal position shivering uncontrollably. Zach shook his head in frustration but then slid down and joined him.

"Marshall, what are you doing? We have to leave right now. It's not safe for any of us to stay here."

"I don't fit in, Mr. Randall. And now they think I caused Mr. Anston's death. So much death I've experienced since this all began. I've had enough."

Zach turned so he was looking directly into Marshall's eyes. "We need you. Don't you want to help us stop all of this? Isn't that why you got involved to begin with?"

"Yes, but I've failed at everything."

"No you haven't. You uncovered a huge part of the plot we were unaware of."

"But you have many people in your group who can project mentally. I can tell they're far more advanced than I am. You don't need me."

"Marshall, I need you more than anyone. You're the only one who actually knew a Time Sculptor, and you're the only one who experienced the time shifts."

Marshall looked up at Zach; the shivering had stopped. "Do you mean that?"

"Yes, for God's sake; I mean it completely. But we have to go, *please*."

With some further encouragement, Zach got Marshall to his feet and coaxed him across the parking lot and ultimately into the Suburban. Fortunately, the police hadn't arrived yet, and the assailants still lay on the pavement in various stages of recovery. Al started the engine and pulled out on the frontage road that took them to I-17 where they continued traveling north to Sedona.

Zach sat in the passenger's seat and periodically looked back at his beleaguered group. He shared their fear, confusion and exhaustion. While they did their best to hide it, their lack of confidence was obvious. Only Sarah smiled reassuringly, and her belief in him provided comfort, even if she wasn't an overseer.

The route they followed kept them out of Phoenix, which was in a state of gridlock as the riots grew in number and intensity. Even north of the city there were signs of panic as hastily packed cars and SUVs created heavy traffic delays. The herd mentality gripped the population as people desperately tried to escape the chaos consuming the city. Older cars, poorly prepared for long trips, broke down and sat on the shoulder at regular intervals.

Zach saw the faces of children looking lost as their parents bent over hot engines trying to troubleshoot problems beyond their capacity to repair. The heat was scorching, and the temperature approached 100 degrees. Clearly, many of these unfortunate travelers wouldn't make it through the day.

While Cordes Lakes was beyond the reach of the floaters, it was a prime location for road bandits who were becoming increasingly common along the major interstates. Since the state police were busy augmenting the city's forces, the interstates were virtually unpatrolled. The governor tried to bring in the National Guard, but the feds were paralyzed in Washington DC, and the troops spread so thin anarchy was taking a firm hold.

"How did you do it?" Al broke the silence and brought Zach out of his introspective musings.

"What?"

"How did you do that? You made me wait for you. I heard you in my mind telling me to wait, and I couldn't do anything about it no matter how hard I tried."

"Maybe you simply decided to do the right thing, Al. After all, if you left us there, we might not have made it out alive."

"No, that doesn't sound like something I would do. I woulda tried to save my hide for sure, but you wouldn't let me."

Zach was about to speak when he heard the loud roar of motorcycles approaching quickly. Al looked in the rear-view mirror and punched the accelerator. The Suburban growled and fought against its age and the weight of the passengers it carried. The vehicle gained speed, but the motorcycles quickly covered the ground between them. Once they reached the SUV, the leader slowed down and looked inside. Whether it was the age of the vehicle or the number of passengers, he chose to move on. As they sped up ahead, Zach estimated there must have been twenty bikes in the gang, and most of them freely toted shotguns or automatic weapons.

Looking back at Al, Zach said, "If someone could manipulate my mind as you suspect I did to you, I would probably cooperate with that person. Who knows what damage he might do to my brain."

"Like the guys in the parking lot?"

Zach's jaw muscles tightened, but he didn't reply.

Al tightened his grip on the wheel and knew better than to speak for the balance of the trip.

The lack of cerebral communication from the overseers was deafening in its absence. Usually, there was always some minor activity in the spatial-temporal plane, but Zach detected nothing but silence and defensive shielding from everyone except Marshall, who probably didn't know any better. The group psyche clearly needed to undergo a great deal of healing before the productive work could begin. He took a deep breath. Jarad Anston's shoes would be very hard to fill.

Just before the exit onto Route-260, Al slowed as there was some kind of incident involving a large group of people and vehicles on either side of the road directly ahead. As they grew closer, Zach saw it was the same motorcycle gang that passed them some time before. The bikes encircled a late model BMW SUV, and the bikers were spread out as some of them pointed their guns at a terrified family while others pawed through their possessions.

Clothes were strewn haphazardly on the ground, and a discarded, broken lock box lay on its side in a ditch. One biker carried a large gas can he used to fill the tanks of the parked bikes. Another inspected several gold coins, and a third was counting a short stack of money from the haul. The husband had a large gash on his forehead, and he held his wife with one arm and his two children with the other. The woman buried her face in his shoulder, and the children clung tightly to his leg.

The scene disgusted Zach, but he had to turn away. They couldn't afford a confrontation, especially right now. Even with the diminished capacity of law enforcement, murders were still prioritized. In all probability, the police already had an APB out for the Suburban.

After a few more miles traveling down the 260 and 89A, they reached Dry Creek Road, and Zach instructed Al to pull over.

"Your job is done, Al. We'll walk from here. You can drive on to Sedona and get some gas or just head back home."

Al looked briefly around the barren landscape. "Well, okay. But I don't see anything out here. What if you get lost?"

"Don't worry about it, we'll be fine." Zach reached into Jarad's bag and pulled out a stack of $100 bills with a band wrapped around it and a stamp that read *Five Thousand Dollars.*

Zach held out the cash. "Go ahead, Al, take it. You deserve it. We only ask that you forget everything you saw here today. Can you do that?"

Without hesitation, Al grabbed the money. "Damn straight I can forget. In fact, I'm starting to wonder why I'm here and how I got here."

Zach clapped Al on the shoulder, and the other overseers climbed out of the Suburban. After gathering their meager belongings and a few jugs of water, they began walking down Dry Creek Road as Al turned the vehicle around, waved, and drove away. They needed about an hour and a half to cover the four miles to Vultee Arch, which turned into a dirt road as the pavement ran out after a couple hundred feet. They hiked for another third of a mile deep into the mountains before Zach realized there was no actual path to follow from that point forward.

"There's nothing down here except rocks and holes. It doesn't look like anyone has ever been in this place," said Rogelio.

"This is where it says to go on Jarad's map. We'll have to trust him."

Zach traversed the treacherous terrain, leading the group even deeper into the woods through the heart of the mountains surrounding Sedona. He continued to reference the map Jarad gave him, and when they reached a large outcropping, he signaled for everyone to stop.

"It's over there," he pointed in the direction of a massive red rock formation. "It's at the base of the rock that looks like a goat." They paused for a moment to absorb the exquisite beauty of their surroundings.

"My God," said Yasin, "I feel it. There's a synchronicity here. The energy is thick and rich. It's absorbing me."

"I sense it too," said Sasha, as they all signaled their agreement.

"C'mon, let's go," said Zach as he walked toward the sheer face of the red mountain. When he reached the towering wall of sandstone stained with iron oxide, he closed his eyes and tuned into the energy. A steady hum reverberated in his mind. Not annoying but pleasant and soothing. He followed in that direction until it grew more intense and pronounced, guided by vibrations emanating from the contours of the rock. His hand traced the outline of something smooth and metallic. He opened his eyes and looked down at a lit numeric keypad. He pulled out the keycard he took off Jarad Antson's body and looked down at five numbers engraved into the metal.

"My friends," he said as a smile crept slowly across his lips, "we have found the sanctuary."

Chapter Eight

A collective gasp came from the packed auditorium as people tried to gain their bearings in the darkness. Wanda kept her back to the wall while the obese man continued to rub his sweat soaked stomach up against her. She reached out to push him away, but he was far too heavy, and he used the excuse of the crowd behind him to push up even closer.

Wanda's revulsion launched a panic attack, and she screamed. However, the sheer level of terror in the building drowned out her cries for help. When his meaty paw began stroking her leg, she acted out of survival instinct and thrust her head forward, sinking her teeth into a fleshy fold somewhere between his sagging pectorals and stomach.

The reaction from the sweaty molester was instantaneous, and he howled more from surprise than pain as he tried to push Wanda away. When she was sure his sexual urges no longer represented a threat, she relaxed her jaws, and he quickly retreated while grunting and using his girth to create a pathway that took him completely out of her personal space. Just as he disappeared into the crowd, the emergency generators kicked on and the lights returned.

Wanda took several deep breaths as her knees buckled briefly. After refocusing, she muscled her way through the mass of humanity standing between her and the triage area. The smell, touch and texture of so many human beings crammed together like cattle created a claustrophobic personal hell. If someone asked her to describe her worst nightmare, she was living it at this moment.

Yet, her determination to find help for Wallace was the only motivation she needed to set aside her fears, and with great effort, she reached a set of lunch tables arranged in a way to create separation between the treatment area and the rest of the gym.

"Excuse me... Excuse me," Wanda said as she tried to get someone's attention. A nurse or volunteer sat on the other side of the table filling out paperwork, aware that someone was there but purposely avoiding eye contact.

"I said, *excuse* me." Wanda reached across the table and grabbed the nurse's arm. Almost as though she considered it an assault, the woman recoiled, and her eyes flashed with anger as she pulled away with obvious indignation.

"Don't you touch me like that again, or I'll have you put in the holding area."

Wanda ignored the admonition. "I need help. My friend absorbed an extreme dose of radiation at the blast site. He desperately needs a doctor."

"You'll have to get in line." The admittance nurse pointed to the crowd of people in front of her in a line that was at least twenty-five deep. Wanda checked the other admittance stations, but the wait was just as long.

"You don't seem to understand. He's in critical condition and needs to see a doctor."

The admittance person dropped her pen and looked back up. "Do you have any idea how many shootings, stabbings, car accidents and other catastrophes we're dealing with? Someone taking a full dose doesn't stand a chance. I'm sorry to be blunt, but your friend is already dead, and our resources are better applied to others with at least some chance of survival." She looked back down at her paperwork and resumed writing.

Wanda stood for a moment as an indescribable rage built up inside her. "You bitch!" She drew her hand back and prepared to deliver a solid slap to the face when someone grabbed her arm from behind. She turned around and glared at the man until she realized it was Mateo.

"Wanda, stop," he said. "Your friend is dead... I'm sorry; he's dead."

Wanda felt as if someone had taken a baseball bat and hit her squarely in the solar plexus. She struggled to breathe, doubling over and clutching her stomach. Mateo grabbed her around the waist and tried to straighten her up,

"Are you going to be sick?"

The admittance representative swiveled in her chair and pulled something out of a box. She reached out to Mateo without looking at him and continued writing. "She's hyperventilating. Have her breathe into this."

Mateo took the bag, inflated it, and gave it to Wanda to put over her mouth and nose. Several deep breaths later, she pulled the bag away as her breathing returned to normal.

"I'll take that back, please. And you're welcome," said the nurse with more than a hint of sarcasm.

Wanda put the bag on the table and stared at the woman, but she never looked up.

"C'mon Wanda, let's go over to the bleacher area." Mateo gently took her arm and guided her back to their cots where they could at least enjoy a small degree of privacy. By the time they got there, Wallace was already gone, and Wanda looked up at Mateo with alarm.

"He died right after you left. They have people with body bags patrolling the floor. I tried to talk them into leaving him until you returned, but they wouldn't hear of it. I guess they're worried about infectious diseases. They put him in a bag and took him away. I'm so sorry."

"I—I can't believe all of this," Wanda said as she buried her head in her hands and cried. Mateo put his arm around her and pulled her close, but it didn't comfort her at all. The only one she wanted to be physically close to was Marshall, and he was probably dead too.

"What am I going to do?" she said in a whisper.

Mateo sighed. "Where are you from, Wanda?"

"Arizona. I live in the Phoenix area."

"So, you're a long way from home too. I'm from San Diego... You know, if you want, we can travel together. Phoenix is on my way, so it wouldn't be a problem."

Wanda looked up, wiped the tears from her face and shook her head. "Thank you, but I'll just take a flight back home. I'm sure the airports are backed up for days, so I better try to make a reservation." She pulled out her cell phone and stabbed a finger at the touch screen while Mateo waited patiently. A few moments later, she looked up and said, "There's no service here."

"Yes, I know. I asked around and I guess all the carriers are down. It probably wouldn't have mattered, anyway. Rumors are running rampant, and a couple guys told me all the flights are canceled because there were several horrible crashes."

"Panic. That's what's happening, isn't it?"

"I'm afraid so," he said. "That's why we need to get out of here right away. I imagine it's going to get very ugly when the food and water run out, and there's no guarantee that the National Guard can keep everything flowing." Just as he finished his sentence, someone screamed from across the gym. Commotion followed, and it sounded like a fight had broken out.

"How can we get out of here?" asked Wanda

"I overheard a few of the security guards talking. This high school is in the middle of a residential neighborhood. One of them said there's a bunch of cars parked in garages nearby. We need to break in and borrow a car."

Wanda looked at him and shook her head. "I can't do that. That's first-degree burglary and car theft."

Mateo leaned down and grasped both of Wanda's shoulders, looking at her directly. "Listen to me; there's no other way to get home. We can't fly, and we can't rent a car. I fear if we don't get out of here soon, we won't be getting out for a very long time if ever. This thing is smoldering outwards like a forest fire, and we're at the epicenter."

Wanda sat on the cot as she weighed her options. One bed over a mother held her three children, all under the age of five. They were crying, and she rocked a baby screaming out of primal fear. A man with a knife wound sat next to her holding a bandage to his abdomen. Two spaces over, a man and a woman with multiple facial lacerations paced the floor in a dumbfounded stupor. *Were they in an accident? Beaten by street thugs?*

All through the gymnasium, people looked around and fidgeted as the stink of fear-sweat filled the space. Human beings revert to their animal instincts in these situations. Even while they desperately wanted to believe they were safe in this protected environment, most sensed that staying here would bring more hardship and maybe death.

"Okay, but I'll only drive the car as far as necessary," she said. "If phone service comes back on, and we can make a plane reservation or rent a car, we leave the stolen one behind immediately."

"Fair enough. See that guy over there?" Mateo pointed to a relief worker in a short sleeve Polo shirt holding a clipboard and talking to one of the evacuees.

Wanda nodded her head.

"Those guys are registering people. We need to get out of here before they find us."

"Why?" she asked.

"Because I'm afraid if they have our names, it will be almost impossible to get away. I worked too close to ground zero."

"Alright then, what are we going to do?"

Mateo drew her in closer and whispered in her ear. "We'll escape during the daylight hours, so we can find the right house. I don't want to trigger any security

97

lights at night. That might attract a neighbor. See that exit at the rear of the gym?"

She nodded.

"Let's make our way over there."

Mateo led Wanda by the hand, pushing through the restless crowd while taking care to avoid the relief workers. As they approached the rear door, she could see two armed security soldiers standing on either side of the exit.

Mateo walked up to one of them and stuck out a hand while displaying a friendly smile. "Hi there. My name's Mateo Reyes. My friend and I have someone picking us up, so we need to leave."

The soldier looked at his partner and then back at Mateo. "Do you have an exit pass?"

"An exit pass? Why do I need one? This is America."

"You have to check out before you can leave." His tone left no doubt the issue wasn't negotiable.

"Check out? Why do I need to do that? We're ready to go right now."

The soldier moved his face slightly closer and bent down a couple inches. "I don't make the rules; I only enforce 'em. I have orders that nobody gets out of here without an exit pass."

"Where do I get one of those?"

"Up front." Of course, up front meant the furthermost location from where they stood near the triage area.

"C'mon, Wanda," said Mateo as he took her arm and led her back through the tightly packed crowd, which was becoming increasingly agitated. Cell phone communications were still out, and mothers were dealing with hungry children. The facilities were strained beyond capacity, and the stench from overflowing toilets grew more pungent by the minute.

As he tried to push his way through the throng of people, Mateo was shoved repeatedly in anger born of frustration, and both he and Wanda weathered numerous insults and menacing looks that conveyed ill intent. When they finally got to the front of the building, the administrative tables blocked off the entrance. The lines at these stations were far longer than at triage.

"We're not standing in these lines," said Mateo. He nudged his way forward until he was standing next to the first person waiting for service.

"I was wondering how I get an exit pass?" he said.

A small man with wire-rimmed glasses, bald head and a name tag that said "Earnest," looked up and diverted his attention away from the person he was processing. "The line starts back there."

Realizing the futility of arguing with a bureaucrat, Mateo gestured to Wanda and walked to the end of a line almost fifty people deep. After two grueling hours of standing and inching forward in an indoor environment that was growing hotter and more humid by the minute, they reached the table and stood motionless for some time. After a seeming eternity, the processor looked up and pushed his glasses back up the bridge of his nose with his index finger.

"What can I do for you?"

"We need an exit pass," said Mateo in a voice that conveyed his impatience.

"Okay, I'll need to see your registration papers."

"We don't have any registration papers."

"Then you'll have to get them. *That* line is over there." He pointed to the far wall in the distance where more lunch tables were set up for processing. A hand drawn sign attached to the wall said *Registration*. Lines at those tables were also painfully long.

"We don't have registration papers because we have no reason to register. Someone is picking us up, so we're good. We just need to get out of here." Mateo leaned over the table and shortened the distance between them.

"You can't leave without an exit permit," said the small man in a disinterested monotone.

"Look, Earnest. This is America, and we can go anywhere we want. Just give us the passes, and it'll make it easier on everyone."

Earnest's look of exasperation intensified. "Did you hear the governor has declared a state of emergency? Freedom of travel is restricted so rescue and military vehicles can get around, and there's a curfew. You're only allowed to leave shelters if you are part of law enforcement, the military or a doctor."

Mateo looked at Wanda and threw his hands in the air while shaking his head. She paused for a moment and then stepped up to the table. Staring directly at Earnest, she reached into her purse and pulled out her wallet. After rifling through a series of plastic photo windows, she took out an ID card and flashed it in front of him.

"I'm a doctor," she said matter-of-factly. "I hold a doctorate in particle physics from MIT. That's the Massachusetts Institute of Technology if you haven't heard of it."

"Yes, I've heard of it," said Earnest while smiling smugly. "But I meant medical doctor, not an academic doctor."

She leaned over and whispered, "I was coming back from assessing the radiation fallout when they picked me up and brought me here. Actually, I'm an expert in the field, and if you give us two passes, I'll give you information the public doesn't know that could save your life." She leaned back up and looked at him, raising her eyebrows and tilting her head slightly.

Earnest took off his glasses and rubbed the bridge of his nose. Wanda noticed his hand was trembling. Several people in the line behind her were growing restless and began to express their frustrations. In what seemed like a snap judgment, Earnest grabbed two green cards from the stack behind him and wrote something on both of them. He pushed the cards at Wanda and Mateo without looking up. "Here. Fill these out."

Without hesitation, they quickly wrote down the requisite information that included their names, addresses and phone numbers. Wanda looked at the bottom line where Earnest had filled in the words "nuclear scientist and radiation specialist" on each card next to the ID number. He handed them plastic clip-on holders and said, "Attach these to your shirts, and you should have no problem getting out."

With that, he looked expectantly at Wanda, and she leaned over and whispered in his ear. While the processor did his best to hide any reaction, his eyes widened, and he swallowed hard. When she stood back up, he turned toward her and shook his head as though he didn't want to believe what she had told him. Wanda gave an exaggerated nod in the affirmative and then grabbed Mateo's arm and walked away. Neither of them looked back, but if they had, they would have seen

Earnest the processor hastily filling out his own exit card.

"What the hell did you tell him?" said Mateo once they were out of earshot.

"I told him the jet stream was blowing the worst fallout directly towards this location, and he had less than four hours before he would take a lethal dose."

"Is that true?"

"No," she replied "But we needed the passes, didn't we?"

Mateo smiled and shook his head. "Clever girl," he muttered under his breath.

The main exits were intentionally locked down to discourage anyone with thoughts of departing. They moved toward one of the side doors that faced a major residential street, but it was also well guarded. Fights were breaking out throughout the building, and Wanda sensed that it would become more difficult to leave as the situation deteriorated.

Calmly, Mateo handed their exit passes to one of the guards. He asked them for additional identification, and once confirmed, he opened the door just wide enough for both of them to slip out.

After taking several deep breaths of fresh air, Wanda slumped against an exterior wall. The pent-up anxiety was almost too much to bear, and she reached into her purse and took out a prescription pill bottle. She hated to take medication because she felt it fouled up her thought processes, but in this case, it was preferable to uncontrollable fear. The pill went down with the last swallow of bottled water she kept from the disaster facility.

After a few minutes, Wanda felt better, and with Mateo's help, she got to her feet and looked out over an expansive field covered with rich, green grass. The road was off in the distance, maybe fifty or sixty yards away. On the other side, a row of houses stretched down the entire length of the street. Looking from side to side, she noticed the ongoing activity as homeowners packed their cars and SUVs with supplies and personal belongings.

Mateo crossed the wide grass field and motioned for Wanda to follow. The weather was bleak, overcast and humid, and the smell of moisture wicking from the long grass was thick and pungent. Looking over her shoulder, she could see the long line of refugees waiting to get processed so they could enter the facility. In these circumstances, people yearned for order even if it wasn't in their best interest.

A ditch separating the two sides of the road forced them to go down about a block until they reached a crosswalk. As they passed a father and two children coming from the other side, Wanda noticed the man's hand creep slowly down to his pocket, and he pulled the children close until they reached the other side.

Trying their best to look inconspicuous, Wanda watched Mateo as he evaluated the position of the houses and checked to see how many were occupied. Now in the heart of the neighborhood, they continued to elicit suspicious stares from people peeking out from behind closed blinds or loading their cars. Mateo walked with a sense of purpose and a smile on his face, waving and acting like a friendly neighbor. He took Wanda's hand in his own, trying to project the illusion they were a couple.

For the first time since she encountered him, Wanda looked at Mateo as a man. He appeared to be in his mid-forties with deep blue eyes and a thick crop of brown wavy hair. Dark skinned and toned, he was fit but not muscular, and his face had a look of confidence born from experience. Wanda decided he was attractive in an understated way.

"Here, this is the one," he said. "Those two houses on the end of this cul-de-sac are empty. Behind these hedges there's an easement. That last house over there. We need to see if there's a car in the garage."

After making sure no one was watching, they darted behind a line of hedges that hid them from the street. The last house had only one real neighbor, and the garage bordered an easement. Mateo found a window and looked inside.

"There's a car in here, and the other stall is empty, so I don't think anyone is home." He picked up a rock and hit the window with just enough forced to knock out a small chunk, which exposed the latch. After waiting a few seconds to confirm that the sound of breaking glass hadn't attracted attention, Mateo opened the window, hoisted himself up, and crawled inside. Seconds later, the service door opened, and he gestured for Wanda to join him.

"The door to the kitchen is open. We need to find car keys and stock up on supplies. It'll be a long trip."

Chapter Nine

Lars sat with his head hung low, and his hands folded in front of him. The usual smug smile was absent, and his eyes were cast downward. Mr. Cox sat across from him with a look of disdain etched on his face.

"So, you had another opportunity to take care of this Suicide Society problem, yet you failed." The Benefactor tapped his nails on the hard wood of his desk. "And to make matters worse, you lost three more of our most lethal special forces people. You represent a bigger threat to our movement than the Suicide Society itself."

"I'm sorry... I didn't anticipate they would be so — capable."

"So, you felt their power firsthand, and they were able to penetrate your puny mental defenses, is that it?"

Lars nodded his head slowly. "They got into my mind. The pain and disruption was unbearable. It felt as though someone lit my brain on fire. My thoughts were jumbled and so very bleak. I still haven't recovered from this crushing headache that feels like someone drove railroad spikes through my eyes. I'm not sure I'll ever totally recover."

"Don't be so melodramatic. You should be thankful you have a mind left. What about the other survivor?"

"Jinks is recovering at your personal hospital. He's receiving the best care possible, but he's done nothing but scream and drool since I brought him back."

Mr. Cox sat back in his chair, folded over his fingers and inspected his perfectly manicured nails. "Let us stop tiptoeing around the subject, Lars. How did you find the Suicide Society? We have the best minds on this project, and no one has been able to locate them. You must possess resources that we do not have. I want you to reveal them to me."

"I'd prefer not to. It is important that I handle the apprehension."

Mr. Cox nodded. "I see…" As he looked directly at Lars, his eyes glowed in a deep crimson tinged by coal black. Mr. Cox unleashed a targeted filament of his darkest energy. As it pierced Lars' skull, it shredded his feeble mental defenses, which were still in tatters from his most recent conflict. He screamed in agony as he rose from the chair, stumbling around like some deranged version of Frankenstein's monster.

The veins on Lars' neck bulged as though they might rupture at any moment. His eyes bled and his tongue became swollen and thick. "Stop," he said with a pronounced lisp. "Stop, please. I'll tell you what you want to know."

Mr. Cox relieved the pressure slightly. He would allow Lars to reveal the information verbally for added humiliation, but he already knew the contents. "So, tell me what you know."

106

Lars fell back into his seat gasping for air and massaging his temples. His continuing agony was obvious. "I had advanced knowledge of the Suicide Society gathering in Portales, but somehow, they were warned of our arrival ahead of time. However, one of them left an envelope in an area they knew would be unaffected by the explosion. It contained a list of all their members."

"Tell me their names. I want to know everything about them." Mr. Cox leaned forward. *How could Lars have kept such information hidden from me?*

"Yes, here." He reached into his pocket and handed over a folded piece of paper.

Mr. Cox opened it hastily. "You were able to hide this from me. How is that possible?"

"I wiped the information from my brain to keep it secure. This is the only copy, so I suggest knowledge of its existence stays between you and I."

"Of course, but how did you acquire such a mind technique?"

"You know where I learned it, Mr. Cox. You know very well where I learned it," said Lars.

The Benefactor tilted his head slightly. "Who sent you?"

Lars shook his head slowly. "I don't know why I'm here. The information has been excised, but I used to know. I..." Lars paused as if he was on the verge of remembering something, but the moment passed. "My instructions and memories are only revealed when I need them. For now, I only know I am here to help you achieve your goals."

Externally, Mr. Cox remained calm, but internally, he was a raging caldron of conflicted anger. That Lars would defy him was bad enough, but the ability to erase his own memories was infuriating. He suspected he knew of Lars' origin, but who sent him and why? He decided to change the subject and revisit these troubling issues later.

"So, the Suicide Society escaped again, and we have no clues or theories?"

Lars reached into his pocket and pulled out a prescription bottle. He fished out two pills, paused for a moment, and grabbed two more. He swallowed all of them without water. "I have no idea. They were traveling in an SUV on I-17 in Arizona, I think. But I can't remember if they were heading north or south. They're doing a masterful job of remaining covert. I sense that like you, they're aware I present an asymmetrical threat."

"Do you have any positive news, Lars?"

"Yes, I do. Their leader's name is Jarad Anston."

"Yes, yes, I know his name," said Cox impatiently.

"He's dead."

Mr. Cox rarely expressed surprise, but he stopped inspecting his nails, and for a brief instant, his eyes widened. "*Dead?* The leader of the Suicide Society is dead, and you're only telling me now?"

"It's not as significant as it might first appear. I'm certain they're in disarray, but there are eight of them left. Perhaps, the one that takes his place might be even more dangerous."

"Zachery Randall, I presume."

"Exactly. I experienced his mental strength, and it was immense."

A small buzz from the door interrupted their conversation. Mr. Cox pushed a button, which unlocked a hydraulic mechanism. Hefe stepped in first.

"Alan is here to see you, boss," said Hefe.

Before Mr. Cox could answer, Ziminski pushed Hefe aside and walked through the door. "Little freak," he said loudly.

"You have no father, Alan," Hefe muttered as he waddled away.

Alan shuffled over and slumped down in the chair next to Lars. His yellow t-shirt was stained with some brown substance, and the arm pits were ringed with jagged lines of dried salt sweat. His face had the shine of someone who hadn't washed or bathed in quite some time. Ziminski opened his laptop and typed with a speed and ferocity that made it appear the keyboard was an extension of his hands.

"Alan, I asked you here to share the information you compiled on Zachery Randall."

"I have that Jarad Anston guy you asked about too," answered Alan.

"He's no longer relevant. He has been — eliminated."

Alan looked over at Lars and smiled. "Whoa, you smoked him, huh?"

Lars smiled weakly while massaging his temples. "Yes, he's dead."

"Okay, here's the thing," said Alan. "Zach Randall couldn't be more ordinary. He's a divorced accountant for Christ sakes, and he lives in a modest townhouse in Albuquerque. There's a mortgage that he'll be paying for the next twenty years, car payments and a balance on two credit cards. He hasn't had a traffic ticket in the last ten years. The guy is boring as hell."

"Except he has a very potent mind," said Mr. Cox.

109

"There is one thing, though. He has a daughter. I figured maybe we could grab her and threaten to kill her if he didn't give himself up."

Lars winced. "That's a really bad idea, Alan. We have no clue where Randall is, so there's no way to convey a ransom threat. Besides, he might be able to use that mind control stuff to find where we put her."

Alan shrugged. "Alright, I guess we'll keep it on the back burner."

Mr. Cox shook his head and stared at Ziminksi with a look of incredulity bordering on disgust. "Lars, I want you and Alan to work together to find the Suicide Society. Alan has certain — investigative talents that you might find useful as you pursue Randall and his associates." Then, after calling up his appointment calendar, he added, "I think that will be all for now."

Lars rose and took a few steps before stopping and turning back toward Mr. Cox. "I appreciate the help. I will consult with Alan when appropriate. Now, I've got a raging headache. Do I... Do I have the Benefactor's permission to leave?"

Mr. Cox smiled. "Of course, Lars. Of course."

The door closed, which left Ziminiski and Mr. Cox alone in the room. An awkward silence ensued as the Benefactor bent over his desk while looking at a report and scribbling notes. After several minutes, he shifted his eyes up without changing his posture.

"Is there anything else, Alan?"

"You said I had talents."

"And?"

"You praised me. You've never done that before. Does that mean you admit I'm your son? Do you — could you — love me?"

Mr. Cox dropped his pen and straightened up. "I stated a fact. In the scope of intelligence and data manipulation, you do have a talent. However, do not misconstrue my meaning. You are a perfect example of why humanity will likely not survive. You are repulsive physically; your personality is nauseating, and besides your exceptional coding knowledge, I don't believe you really have any redeeming qualities whatsoever."

Alan burst into tears and flung his laptop against a wall. He was almost out the door before Mr. Cox delivered the last of his stinging assessments.

"Beyond your computer skills, you have absolutely no value to me."

Alan turned and came back into the room. "Why do you hate me? I'm your son, and you've never shown me anything but hate. You know what? I hate *you*. I hate you too!" Alan pointed at Mr. Cox as the tears flowed freely. He pounded on the door, and his shrieks and wails could be heard throughout the entire floor as he walked toward the elevator.

Mr. Cox could only shake his head at Alan's unbridled display of emotion. He despised weak personalities, which mirrored a weak soul. The Benefactor would have none of it. Alan was a perpetual annoyance, and yet, he kept him around. There were several skilled computer people on his staff who could replace Ziminski, but he never got around to doing it. *Strange...*

Rising from his desk, Mr. Cox felt relief that the workday was finally ending. Preparing to rule over a world was exhausting. Fortunately, his walk was short, and he couldn't help but smile as he rode the elevator to his penthouse. As he entered his private quarters, he paused a moment to absorb the continuous flow of black energy emanating from the growing chaos below.

Already on the brink of anarchy, Detroit found itself in an abyss of hellish despair. Rapes, assaults and murders were all up over 180 percent year over year, exceeding all projections. With a loathing that brought great pleasure, Mr. Cox gazed out at the skyline through the full-length windows spanning the entire room. No matter where he looked, a panoramic view of misery, anguish and destruction played out before him in his new hometown, soon to be the capital of his global empire.

Walking over to his closet, he took off his leisure suit coat and dropped it to the floor. After undressing, he put on a silk robe and cashmere slippers and relaxed in his Human Touch ZeroG 4.0 Immersion Seating Massage Chair. With his eyes closed, he soaked in the bleak waves of hopelessness as they wafted up from below. The hatred, detestation and antipathy combined to form an appealing cocktail he soaked in greedily. Watts could handle the boring capitulations of nations; the Benefactor had far more important business to attend to.

When he opened his eyes, Mr. Cox occupied a space inside an inner-city Detroit home. He looked around the living room and smiled at the squalid living conditions. Rats ran across the floor with impunity, scurrying from one side of the room to the other while grabbing bits of rotten, discarded food the inhabitants left behind. The rancid smell wafted over from the kitchen, and as Mr. Cox looked in that direction, he saw stacks of plates, pans and glasses covered in spoiled food, mold, grease and other unidentifiable decaying solids.

A single doorway led to a bedroom, but it didn't appear to be occupied. In a far corner of the living room, a mother was huddled with two children pressed tightly against her bosom. All three of them stared ahead with eyes wide and full of terror. The children trembled, and the youngest had his thumb stuck firmly in his mouth. Their clothes were ragged, dirty and faded from years of wear far beyond their design life. Somewhere nearby, fresh feces off-gassed a vile pungent odor.

Following their eyes, Mr. Cox looked on the other side of the room, and as he expected, a despondent man sat on the floor with a rifle in his lap. He was covered in a black sludge of some sort. With the competing odors, it was hard to tell if this was human waste or auto grease, but it was smeared all over his face and arms. His shirt was wet with a perspiration usually symptomatic of a drug overdose, intense fear or mental illness. The man shifted his gaze rapidly around the room, flinching as though he was under assault by some invisible force.

Mr. Cox breathed deeply. The aromas were delightful, especially when they were saturated with hopelessness and misery.

"Adrian, you can't do this. Please. The children. You're scaring the children." The woman reached out her hand.

"Just shut up, Joyce. We got nuthin'. I got nuthin'. The kids are gonna have nuthin'."

The woman held out her hand. "It'll get better, Adrian. I promise."

113

"Bullshit! Look outside, Joyce. It ain't gettin' better. They're burnin' everyone out. It ain't gettin' better, and now I lost my job. How'm I gonna feed these kids? How'm I gonna pay for this place? They turned the water off and tomorrow it's the electric." He raised the rifle barrel towards his wife. She shuddered, whimpered and covered her face. The children screamed.

"No, Adrian, don't. I love you. Please. We can work it out."

"Daddy, no. I'm really scared, Dad." The girl, who looked to be about ten, placed her hands together and held them to her chest while the boy just continued to shake and suck his thumb.

Adrian lowered the weapon and reached for an open bottle of whiskey that sat next to him. He placed it to his lips and took a hearty pull. "Do you really think it could get better? Maybe if we moved to Atlanta. My brother's in Atlanta."

"Yes, Atlanta. Let's move away from here. We've got enough money for bus tickets, and maybe your brother will put us up while you look for a job."

"I'm not sure… Maybe." He put the gun on the floor and began to weep. "It wasn't supposed to be like this."

"It's okay, Adrian. Can I come over to you?" she asked. "Is it safe for me to come over there?"

He looked up as tears continued to stream down his face. "Are you sure we'll make it outa this? Are you *sure*?"

She nodded and leaned forward, pulling her feet under her as though she was about to get up. The children clutched her even tighter, but she gently pushed them away. "We'll make it, Adrian, I know we will." She turned to her daughter and said softly. "I have to go to your Daddy. He needs my help. You hold onto Keshaun while I go and talk to him."

Stepping from the shadows, Mr. Cox walked over to the broken man. "Bah, are you going to fall for this, you fool? She's lying and you know it. You're right; there's no hope. Look around yourself. You couldn't make it before it all started to fall apart. How can you possibly make it now?"

Adrian grabbed the gun and got to his feet in a single motion, pointing the weapon at Mr. Cox. "Who — who are you? How the hell did you get in here?" he asked while his nervous hands re-gripped the rifle repeatedly.

"Adrian, who are you talking to?" the woman asked as she looked at her husband and toward the empty space where he was pointing the weapon.

"What the hell do you mean, 'who am I talking to'?" he replied. "That guy over there in the black suit. He's smiling at me and just told me you were feeding me bullshit, Joyce. You see him. He's right there."

"Adrian, what are you talking about? Please, put the gun down. There's no one there."

In a swift, frantic motion he swung the weapon around and pointed it in her direction. The children shrieked and grabbed at their mother, almost causing her to lose her balance and fall back to the ground. "Please, please, don't shoot me. Please…" The last word tailed off as she backed up against the wall.

The man swung the gun back in Mr. Cox' direction. He had the look of a trapped animal: angry, frightened and desperate. The emotions bled through every pore of his body, and Mr. Cox inhaled the vapors.

"I wouldn't listen to her, Adrian. You'll be doing everyone a favor if you kill them all. They'll go to a better place. I mean, really, can it be any worse than this?" Mr. Cox gestured expansively across the room.

"Yeah, yeah, you're probably right. It ain't gonna get any better for penny-ante Adrian, is it?" He lowered the gun a few inches. "Are you an angel or something?"

"Adrian, please," said Joyce in a trembling voice. "There's no one there. For God's sake put the gun down, and we'll get you some help."

"Goddamn it, shut up, Joyce. Just shut the fuck up."

"Yes, you might consider me a kind of angel if you like," said Mr. Cox. "If you want my approval for killing your family, you have it my friend. I only came here to watch you do it. I imagine you're planning to blow out your own brains when you're done murdering them, right?"

"Well, yeah, I guess. I just wanted us to all be together. The kids'll go to heaven, maybe Joyce too. That's all I care about. Me, I don't matter."

"My, God, Adrian, you're really sick." She grabbed her children, each in one arm and began shuffling towards the front door, which happened to be where Mr. Cox was standing.

Adrian whipped the gun around and pointed it at her head. The children shrieked and pleaded in the high pitch reserved for those who instinctively know their lives are in mortal danger.

The woman began mumbling in a low, unnaturally calm voice. "Okay, Adrian, go ahead and kill me. But for the love of God, please let the children live."

Adrian grunted several times as his finger tightened on the trigger. Sweat poured off his forehead and temporarily blinded him as thick beads of oily perspiration ran into his eyes.

"Do it!" exclaimed Mr. Cox. "Go ahead and do it!" His face lit up with excitement, and he became intoxicated with the disconsolate emotions. Adrian's anger, Joyce's despair, the children's fear; the thick, black flow was as potent as mainlining pure white heroin.

"I'm gonna do it." Adrian's words sounded like they came from a man in the process of undergoing ritualistic torture. "I'm sorry, Joyce," he said.

"God, no," she whimpered while falling to her knees. "Our Father, who art in heaven..."

"Of course, Adrian," said Mr. Cox slowly. "There may be another way..."

Adrian let out a long breath and eased off the trigger. "What do you mean, another way?"

The gasp that escaped Joyce's lips was the sound of someone who had accepted her fate. With the children by her side, she remained completely still, unable to move from her kneeling position. A dark stain spread over the front of her tattered print dress as she soiled herself.

"Well, you can either blow them away, which is fine with me, by the way, or you can come and join me. If you agree, you and your family will be moved into my complex, which I think you would find far more preferable than your current living arrangements. You would enjoy a spacious apartment with a nice view of the city, and your children would have their own rooms. Food is served in the cafeteria every day, and of course, you would get a salary, although to be honest, I'm not sure if money will have any value soon."

Adrian lowered the rifle to his side. "Is this some kind of joke?"

Mr. Cox smiled. "Hardly. My company is just trying to help out unfortunate people like you who have been victimized by a corrupt system."

"What… what would my job be?"

"You would help us out wherever we needed it. Community organizing mostly. You seem to know a good deal about weaponry, and we can always use someone who isn't afraid to pull a trigger."

Adrian looked across at his wife and children before turning back toward Mr. Cox. "I—I got nuthin' ta lose. I'll do it. But if this ain't on the level…"

"Oh, I promise you it's on the level. I'm pleased to welcome you on board. Of course, I need you to understand we demand complete loyalty. All of our employees spend their entire careers with us. Do you understand, Adrian?"

"I understand. You'll have my complete loyalty, uh…"

"You can call me, Mr. Cox."

"Yes, sir. Thank you, Mr. Cox.

The Benefactor smiled as he turned and moved toward the open doorway. "Show up tomorrow in the main lobby of the Gehenna Corporation building at eight a.m. It used to be called the Renaissance Center before we purchased it. Go to the main lobby and check in. I'll make sure everything is arranged prior to your arrival. Once you're officially employed with us, you'll receive a $5000 bonus check."

118

"Yes, sir. I'll be there. Thank you. But if this is a joke…"

"If it's a joke, I'll just come back to watch you murder your family, which honestly would be a lot more fun for me, anyway." As he walked away, Mr. Cox turned back and said, "Oh, and give my best to the wife and kids."

Chapter Ten

The inside of the sanctuary at Sedona was immense to an extent it stunned the overseers upon entry. The lair in Portales paled in comparison to the expansiveness of this facility. Carved deep into the mountain, the main den covered almost half a football field. The rock was contoured and almost smooth as it gently arched upward and created a dome that peaked at forty feet above ground level.

As Zach gazed in awe at the dimensions of the place, he saw extraordinary carvings in bas-relief that looked like they came from 9th century Mesopotamian cultures. The soft lighting created an almost three-dimensional illusion, which mimicked the designs adorning the walls. The actual floor of the cavern was tiled in thick marble, which glistened and shined with an almost spit polish. From the floors to the glass cases that housed artifacts from ancient Egyptian, Sumerian and Greek cultures, everything appeared to be remarkably well maintained.

In the center of the room a magnificent waterfall flowed through a series of winding rock tributaries that converged at the bottom of the structure and emptied into a large natural pond. Multiple hallways connected to the main chamber and ran in numerous directions. Zach was having a hard time making sense of these surroundings. As he looked back at the group, they also seemed disoriented and confused.

He felt a light touch on his arm. Sarah smiled and whispered in his ear. "You're their leader now, Zach. They need direction."

Her words forced him to keep his attention in the moment, and he gathered the group in a small semicircle. "I don't know any more about this place than you do. I assume no one has been here before, so we're going to have to start exploring. Let's split up into groups…"

"That won't be necessary, Speaker Randall." The voice came from behind Zach, and the words were spoken in a perfect Received Pronunciation English accent. Zach turned to face a short, thin Hispanic man in his early forties dressed in a brightly colored tailcoat tuxedo. That he wore such an odd garment in the July Southwest heat would normally cause Zach to pause, but the surreal nature of the events over the last several days made him almost numb to surprises.

"Excuse me, sir," he said. "You have me at a disadvantage."

"Of course," the man said while bowing deeply. "My apologies. My name is Juan Gustavo Ricardo Pena the 17th. You may call me Pena. I am the caretaker of the facility. I would like to welcome you to the Suicide Society Sedona Sanctuary."

Zach looked back at his companions and then to the curator. "We have many questions. How did you know we were coming?"

121

"I have known for a very long time. Speaker Anston informed me you would be arriving many years ago."

"How could he have known? You're obviously unaware…"

"… Unaware that he's dead, Speaker Randall? I knew he was dead before you did."

"How is that possible?"

"I am a caretaker, Speaker Randall. I am the last in a long and distinguished lineage. Our purpose is to serve and protect the Suicide Society during its most challenging crises. Our abilities are similar to your own, but they are limited to sensing your thoughts and emotions and providing aid and comfort."

"You can read our minds?"

"No, it's more like we can understand your intent. Still, if you choose to block us, we won't experience anything."

"How many of you are there?" asked Jacques, who was still standing behind Zach.

"Sadly, I am the last, although I do hope to procreate someday. Once, there were many caretakers who watched over the numerous Suicide Society chapters. However, those days are long past. You are the last surviving chapter, and it is imperative that you endure."

"What happened to the other chapters?" asked Sasha.

"On several continents, the abilities of the group were exposed. The mob mentality can be vicious, especially when it encounters a phenomenon greater than itself. The chapter in Europe was hung in the 16th century, and the African chapter boiled in oil and their seared meat served to wild dogs.

"The time changes you are now aware of also took their toll. Since your minds are so complex and wired directly into the essence of the universe, you are all more susceptible to the effects of the changes, especially the major ones. I imagine you are unaware you lost three members in the last eleven years."

"What?"

"Yes, it is true. Changes in the timeline create new pathways and eliminate others. Two of the members never tried to commit suicide in the new reality, so they were not endowed with the 'gift'. Another was killed in an untimely accident. Unfortunately, it doesn't seem to work the other way. The changes never seemed to produce others with the gift."

"How do you know so much about the time changes?" Zach probed Pena subtly, but the caretaker didn't resist.

"I am aware of their existence, but I have no idea when they happen or how they relate to specific events. For that, you'll need to ask him." He nodded in Marshall's direction, and everyone looked that way.

"Marshall remembers time as it happened previously," continued Pena, "but even he does not perceive the volume of changes that have occurred. Some of his acquaintances experience the phenomenon, but the effects render most of them completely uncommunicative."

"Marshall shared the details of the time changes with Jarad and me," said Zach, "and later, he shared them with the entire group in Portales."

"*Details?*" said Rogelio. "I know we saw what was in his mind, but how do we know it's real? Maybe it was a hallucination or purposeful deception. Manipulation of time? Is that even possible?"

"I know you don't believe me, but it's very real," said Marshall as he stepped forward. "The fabric of time literally crumbled, periodically resetting a few moments backwards. A glitch occurred just as Speaker Anston revealed himself to Mr. Cox. "

"Marshall," said Sasha in a soothing voice, "I know you let us into your mind in Portales, but we need to understand your experiences on a deeper level. Would you be willing to open yourself to us again?"

Zach held out a hand. "I don't think that's a good idea right now. Remember, we may have a traitor in our midst. We can't afford to have such valuable information fall into the wrong hands."

Yasin balled his fist and flipped a thumb at Marshall. "How did he acquire his telepathic abilities, anyway? Did he come back from the dead as we all did?"

Marshall shook his head and ignored Yasin's aggression. "No, I never tried to kill myself, and I'm not sure where my ability comes from."

A long pause followed as several of the overseers exchanged troubled glances.

"I'm going to be honest here; I don't trust him," said Jacques. "The old man in Portales warned us of a traitor, and it almost seemed like he knew him."

"Now, wait a minute," said Sarah as she walked up to Marshall and put her arm around his shoulders. "There's not going to be any lynching here. Marshall hasn't done anything to anyone."

"Speaker Randall, we need to get into his mind." said Rogelio. "If he shares his thoughts and memories, we'll understand his intentions."

Zach shook his head slowly. "I said no. That can't happen, at least right now. As I told you, Marshall completely opened his mind to Speaker Anston and me. I'm convinced his story is authentic."

"But he is not like us," said Rogelio. "What if he can mask his thoughts?"

"That's nonsense and fear talking," said Zach.

Marshall took another step forward and spoke with surprising confidence. "Someone, or more than one person, has been trying to get into my mind since I first shared some of my experiences with you all. Since one of you may be a traitor, I'm not going to take a chance like that. You are all very powerful, and if I let you in, you could rewire my brain or something."

"You know," said Liu as he walked up so close to Marshall, the latter felt like he was being personally assaulted. "We could combine our thoughts and extract the information forcibly. I doubt you would be able to withstand an incursion from all of our combined energy."

Marshall gasped and pulled away from Liu as Sarah grabbed Zach's arm, "Do something. He's not prepared for this, and he doesn't understand."

Zach sensed two or three projections gently probing Marshall, but he was able to keep them at bay. Reacting quickly, he sent a chilling jolt of his own psychic energy back through the offending tendrils. The result was akin to a short shock from a wall socket. The streams withdrew immediately, and Liu, Rogelio and Jacques appeared momentarily stunned and unsettled.

"There will be none of that from this point forward. Marshall is not a suspect here. He saved my life and Jarad's life. If he was inclined to do us harm, he had every opportunity when we were in Desolation."

A short silence followed, ultimately broken by Pena. "Everyone, please remain calm. There is much to discuss, I understand that. But why don't you allow me to show you to your living quarters so you can freshen up."

Without a better alternative, no one objected, so Pena took the group down one of the corridors that led to a residence wing. Looking at the doors lining each side of the hallway, Zach imagined there were at least thirty rooms in just this section of the compound. Whoever constructed the facility must have anticipated a thriving population of transcendants living here. Instead, the eight that remained were in a battle for their very existence.

Pena seemed to have a specific order in mind when he escorted each of them to their rooms. He assigned the first to Jacques and put Aminah across from him. Sasha was given the room next to Jacques and across from Liu. Rogelio and Yasin took the next two rooms, which put Zach and Sarah across from each other. Marshall occupied the last room next to Zach, so he would be farthest away from the rest of the Suicide Society.

Once everyone had a chance to check out their new quarters, Pena called them back into the hallway.

"I'm certain the past several days have been exhausting, but I imagine you have many questions. In good time, you will receive the answers you seek.

For now, I think it best if you all relax and rest for a while."

"We need answers more than we need rest," said Zach.

Pena smiled. "It may seem that way. But when you do rest, you will find the recuperative powers in this habitat to be extraordinary. Personal conflict is very — unusual for this place."

Zach paused for a moment, then nodded and waved to the others. "I agree with Pena. Let's get some rest and address these issues later with a refreshed psyche and clear mind." Although there was some grumbling, everyone seemed to agree, and they left the hallway and started toward their rooms.

Once he was alone, Zach explored his spacious and lavish accommodations. The bed was Victorian style and replete with a full skirt and billowing canopy. He sat on the mattress and immediately wanted to lay down on it. The bathroom facilities were modern and clean. Two glass bowl washbasins sat on top of an oak cabinet. The shower was separate from the bath, which also served as a hot tub.

Inside an expansive walk-in closet, he found clothes for every season, pressed perfectly and spaced at a uniform distance to prevent wrinkling. He checked the sizes, and as expected, every item was a perfect fit. On the other side, he found an assortment of jackets, coats and bathrobes. When he walked out and opened the dresser, he wasn't surprised to find bedclothes and underwear in the exact style he preferred, stacked in a neat pile.

Sitting back down on the bed, the adrenaline that kept him fueled for the last week began to wane, and a deep sense of relaxation washed over him as the tension evaporated from his body. He wasn't consciously aware of it, but a feeling of serenity slowly enveloped him. Perhaps it was the thick stone walls that blocked out any sound, but he was confident nothing horrible would happen, at least not tonight.

Zach was just about to lay down when a soft knock at the door attracted his attention. After unlatching the bolt, he found Sarah standing outside in a nightgown and robe. Her hair was still wet from a recent shower, and she stood awkwardly looking at the floor.

"I just wanted to see — to see how you were," she said timidly.

"I'm fine. Please, come in." As she walked past, the pleasant smell of rose petals and jasmine drifted towards him. "I haven't had a chance to take a shower. I…"

She moved closer, and while he was still talking, she leaned up and kissed him lightly on the lips. He'd never felt such a kiss before, gentle, but full of passion. Almost as though an electric charge passed through him, Zach's entire body tingled, and he grabbed her close as they kissed with more urgency. Exploring with their tongues and fingers, tracing light pathways across the other's body, Zach's passions flared with desire for the beautiful woman he held in his arms.

"From the first time you entered my mind, I wanted to do that. I didn't even need to see you to know I loved you. Your gentleness and kindness overwhelmed me. I've never felt this way about anyone," she whispered in his ear.

"Sarah, I don't want to take advantage of you. You've suffered so much, and it will take time to sort it all out and heal."

She nodded. "I know I have a long road ahead of me. Maybe I'll never learn to deal with the despair, and the nightmares will never go away. But I know I love you, Zach Randall. Whatever else, I belong with you."

He pulled her close and kissed her again. "I love you too, Sarah. I fell in love with you the second I touched your mind. There's no explanation, but I knew it instantly. Come, lay with me, please?"

Together, they crawled into the luxurious bed. He lay on his back, and she moved in next to him, wrapping an arm around his chest and resting her head on his shoulder. They enjoyed the closeness of the moment and the shared intimacy. Neither felt any pressure to consummate their burgeoning relationship, so they fell into a deep sleep in each other's arms, happy and secure in the new reality they were creating.

Although he wouldn't remember the details, Zach floated out of a pleasant dream to the soothing rhythms of new age music. He looked over in the direction of the sound and saw a rectangular box sitting on a nightstand. The sleek looking device had a built-in display screen that read, "Dinner will be served at seven p.m. Please meet in the foyer, and you will be taken to the dining room." Almost anticipating his next request, the screen flashed the current time as 6:35 p.m.

Gently nudging Sarah, she woke with a yawn and smiled as soon as she saw his face. She reached up and put her hand behind his neck, drawing him close and kissing him before pulling the sheets back and getting up from the bed.

"We better hurry. Dinner is at seven. I need to take a shower and get dressed."

She nodded and began walking to the door. "I'm looking forward to it," she said. "I've never seen so many pretty clothes, and they're all my size."

"I'll come and pick you up at 6:55."

"Okay. But Zach, we should go down there with Marshall. I'm very worried about him."

Zach nodded as he took off his shirt. Once Sarah left, he finished undressing and ran the shower until it was steaming hot. He let the liquid cascade over his body, and it felt like he was washing away a lifetime of misery. The water had a rejuvenating effect on his soul and spirit, and by the time he started dressing, his mood was more upbeat and optimistic than he could recall in many years.

Choosing khaki pants and a blue polo-style shirt, Zach pulled out a pair of tan shoes that comfortably hugged his feet as though he had worn them before. He looked at his watch and realized it was time to meet Sarah, so he walked to her door and knocked only once. When she opened it, he could hardly believe he was looking at the same person. She wore a simple casual red dress with white shoes, accented by a red bow in her hair. Sarah had the type of face that required no makeup, but the light lipstick, blush and mascara accentuated her features and enhanced her natural beauty.

"You look amazing," he said with honest sincerity.

She blushed and then smiled broadly. "Thank you, sir. You look quite handsome yourself." They stood admiring each other for a few moments before she said, "We need to get Marshall."

Zach nodded, and they walked to the end of the hallway and knocked on Marshall's door. They waited about a minute, and when there was no answer, Zach knocked again with a bit more urgency.

"Marshall, it's time for dinner. Are you in there?"

Still no answer.

"C'mon, Marshall. You have to eat. It'll give you a chance to get to know everyone. Please, let's go."

After another couple minutes of silence, Sarah spoke. "Marshall, I want you to sit between us. We both want to talk to you because we like you."

The reply from behind the door was weak and clearly under duress. "They all hate me, and they want me dead, especially Liu and Jacques. They think I'm the traitor... Well, I'm not."

"We know you're not," said Sarah. "You saved us, Marshall. We haven't forgotten that. Please come with us."

Another long pause followed until the deadbolt clicked, and the door opened slowly. Marshall looked down and stared at his shoes. He was dressed in a brown shirt, black slacks and shiny white loafers. The ensemble screamed, "I'm an oddball."

"Well, don't you look nice." Sarah took his hand in hers. It felt uncomfortable for a minute, but then Marshall relaxed. He imagined it was Wanda holding his hand.

"I'll go, but I don't like this place. Something bad is going to happen here."

Chapter Eleven

Zach, Sarah and Marshall walked down the hallway into the expansive foyer while the rest of the group waited at the waterfall. An antique grandfather clock sitting next to a grand piano and oversized red velvet couch read 7:02 p.m.

"Our host is late," said Rogelio. "I value promptness."

"I do too," said Liu Wei. "But I must say, the accommodations are wonderful. My room is incredible." Murmurs and nods of agreement from the others followed.

"We still need to learn much more about this place and Mr. Pena," said Sasha. "I rarely find myself at a loss, but he knows far more about us than we know about him."

"That's true," continued Yasin. "One person can't possibly maintain this place. Who does the cooking, cleaning and repairs?"

Rogelio was about to speak when one of the hallways lit up with a cool white light. The sound of footsteps preceded the arrival of Juan Gustavo Ricardo Pena.

"Excuse my tardiness, my guests," said Pena while bowing. "There were some, ah, matters that needed to be addressed. Fortunately, my associates have resolved them. Please, follow me into the dining area."

As Zach expected, the main dining hall was as richly decorated as the other rooms. The table was ancient with thick dark wood and ornate carvings of neo-classic design. High-backed upholstered chairs carried so much weight Zach had to help Sarah move hers. Tiny age cracks ran through the priceless fine china. The Anna Weatherly flatware complimented the wine and water glasses that bore the first-generation Waterford mark.

Someone took the time to create placards with each name hand printed in Gothic calligraphic style, which alleviated seating arrangement awkwardness. The overseers took their appropriate places, and Pena gestured to the head of the table. "Speaker Randall, here is your seat."

Zach was uncomfortable leaving Marshall, but with some hesitation, he moved to the head of the table. Once he was seated, an older man who looked to be in his late seventies appeared with a bottle of Romaneée-Conti Grand Cru Pinot Noir, pausing to receive Zach's approval before filling each glass.

Meanwhile, a rotund, middle-aged woman with a lazy eye served a seafood soup while a third attendant brought out freshly baked bread in golden bowls. Once they finished serving the food, the staff quickly retreated to the kitchen. Everyone at the table looked at each other awkwardly, not knowing if they should eat or wait. Pena resolved the dilemma when he stood up with his wine glass in his hand.

"My friends, let us enjoy this exquisite Pinot. It is an extraordinary example of a fine aristocratic red wine. I make a toast to the Suicide Society: the last hope for humanity." He raised his glass high before he drank heartily.

All of Pena's guests raised their glasses and drank except Marshall, who had no taste for wine and didn't understand the toasting custom. He sat with his hands folded in his lap, looking down at his soup.

Once they finished sipping their wine and sampling shellfish appetizers, Pena and several of his guests indulged in a delicious Vichyssoise soup while Rogelio, Aminah and Wei ate salads with distinctly different dressings. After the second course plates were cleared, the meal progressed through a main course of salmon or chicken and desserts of chocolate mousse, strawberry cheesecake and Crème de Brulee. In every instance, the guests were served without any input, almost as though Pena already knew their food preferences.

When they finished the last bite of dessert, the servers came and cleared the table, offering coffee, tea or an after-dinner liqueur. Pena sipped Amaretto and looked across the table. Zach sensed it was time to deal with the awkward subjects conveniently avoided through polite dinner conversation.

"So, you have so many questions, my friends. Let me do my best to answer them." Out of respect, no one spoke as they deferred to Zach.

"Who built this place?" he asked. "Who funds it, and how does it remain viable with personnel and supplies?"

"Interesting first question, and not the one I would have expected," said Pena. "This facility was constructed in the late 16th century, about 200 years before this area was discovered by settlers. The work on the main hall was finished in 1597, and they constructed the sub-domains in phases around the turn of the century, right about the same time Jon Thompson arrived and founded Sedona."

"How could they build this complex three centuries before European settlers arrived?"

"The Suicide Society has existed for many centuries, Speaker Randall. The abilities of those living in the 16th century did not differ from your own. Previous generations of overseers defeated Genghis Khan at Bayad and recovered the first Orb of Gehenna.

"There was a compulsion that drew those people to this place. They braved the elements and nature to get here and persuaded the locals to help them build this sanctuary. It took hundreds of years to finish,"

"What is so special about Sedona that it drew Society members from thousands of miles away?"

Pena held up his arms, closed his eyes and breathed deeply. "Can you not sense it, Speaker Randall? I'm certain you can. I'm sure all of you can. Sedona is a special place where spiritual and psychic energy converge in five major vortexes. This has a protective and rejuvenating effect on those who are sensitive to the impacts of kinetic energy."

"I can't deny that I have felt refreshed, and more at peace than I have in a long time," said Zach.

"Almost like recharging a battery," added Sasha.

"Yes, something like that. For a millennium, native tribes understood and respected the healing power of the vortexes. They settled here and protected the land for centuries. Eventually, the shills arrived and exploited Sedona for commercial gain, but that never deterred those with true gifts from coming here. That is why the Society created this place long before the settlers arrived. They followed the trail of residual energy, and it led them here."

"As a group, we met several times with Speaker Anston when a crisis warranted, but never here," said Yasin. "How come?"

"This place is a sanctuary of last resort," said Pena. "Its existence must remain secret since discovery could lead to its ruin. Until this moment, only the Speakers knew of this place. Based on these extraordinary circumstances, Speaker Anston felt it was necessary to reveal it to you all."

"So, you and your predecessors kept it in a state of readiness for centuries just in case we needed it?" asked Rogelio. "That seems—impossible. Who maintains the facility? Where does the staff come from?"

"It is quite simple, Mr. Francisco. As I said, Sedona attracts many people with heightened sensory perception, but none of them have the capabilities of the Suicide Society. Caretakers can perceive deep emotions and thoughts, but we do not have the capacity to alter reality as you do. There are several levels of receptiveness that different people experience.

"When we encounter someone with any degree of this kind of ability, we contact them," he continued. "If they choose to join us at the sanctuary, we teach the skills they need to help us maintain the facility. Frankly, it isn't difficult to find people willing to help us."

136

"What if they want to leave?" asked Aminah.

Pena shrugged. "Well, naturally, we would allow them to do so. Of course, the Speaker would remove certain vital memories that could compromise our secrecy, but we would never force someone to stay if that is not what they desired. Interestingly, no one has ever wanted to leave."

"In 600 years, no one left?" asked Zach.

Pena shrugged. "No, Speaker, no one."

Zach grabbed his napkin and dabbed at his upper lip. "So, we are here. The most important question is *why?*"

"I imagine it is to provide a safe space to devise another plan to defeat the Dark One."

"And how would you recommend we go about that, Pena?" said Zach.

"I am not sensitive enough to know the answer, Speaker. Truthfully, you understand very little about the Dark One. I'm afraid only Marshall can help you."

Everyone turned toward the timid young man at the end of the table. Marshall sensed multiple probes that he fended off vigorously. He felt uncomfortable and afraid and no longer believed he was among friends. If they interrogated him, he would stop talking and demand to leave.

Zach ignored the negativity of the other transcendents and projected pure positive energy. *Marshall, I know you think you're alone and out of place here. The truth is, I don't really know the other overseers either. But we can do this together. We have to learn more about the time manipulation.*

Marshall continued staring at his plate. Sarah reached over and took his hand and squeezed. "It's okay, Marshall, really. Zach would never let anyone

137

hurt you." The squeeze was only mildly revolting, but Marshall also felt its calming effects. Finally, he nodded and looked up.

"Mr., uh, Speaker Randall, I've shared everything with you as it happened," he said. "You were in my mind and accessed my thoughts and memories. There is nothing more to tell."

"You told us everything you knew at the time we merged," said Zach. "Yet, I sense there may be something important you've learned that you haven't shared with us."

Marshall shook his head. "No, there is nothing…"

"Why did the old man in Portales say your name?" asked Yasin.

"… I don't know. I'm not sure it was my name at all."

Sasha leaned closer to the table. "Oh no, Marshall, he definitely called out your name and a number. What does that mean?"

"I don't know," said Marshall as he wrapped his arms around his chest. "Stop asking me all these questions. I've told you everything."

"This is absurd," said Jacques while shifting his body so his back was facing Marshall. "Why are we sitting here listening to his nonsense when we have a true crisis to deal with?"

Zach held out his hand as though he was stopping traffic. "No, I want to learn more."

Jacques looked at Zach, and his eyes narrowed. "I'm not even convinced you should be in charge here." Turning back to the table, he said, "Was Speaker Anston thinking rationally when he was dying? Who is Zach Randall anyway? None of us even know him, so how can he be trusted?"

"Stop it, Jacques. It wasn't only what Speaker Anston said; you felt the confirmation in your mind and spirit. I did, so I'm sure we all did," said Aminah.

"I won't listen to arguments about my leadership." Zach interrupted with a tone of authority and impatience. "The Speaker made his wishes known before his death, and that's the end of it. The spatial energy dictates who leads the group, and you have experienced its purity and unimpeded flow. The universe confirms that Speaker Anston's declaration was in harmony with its wishes."

A quiet fell over the group, and Zach allowed the strength of his statement and the solemnity he projected to verify his words. "Marshall, please continue."

"You already saw all this in my mind. Once my friends and I knew the time changes were occurring, we learned that one of our colleagues could actually remember the future." He paused and watched the various looks of disbelief and incredulity on the faces of his companions. "I guess it sounds absurd, but he really had that ability."

"This is silly. Why do we have to listen to more of his delusional fantasies?" Jacques poured himself another glass of wine as he spoke.

"I want to hear the whole story from Marshall's lips, not just reading his thoughts. His experience is critical to defeating Mr. Cox." Zach finished speaking and turned back to Marshall expectantly.

"After I saw my friend's list, I talked to Sixtus Maras, who was the time traveler I told you about. He revealed a future upheaval where a revolution played out between the existing leadership, known as the

139

Corporates, and an insurgent group. Apparently, two agents, one from either side, traveled back to the past with diametrically opposed versions of the future."

Marshall paused and took a sip of water. "Still, they both agreed that a single event would decide the fate of humanity, and that was the bomb in Chicago. Sixtus hated the Corporates, but he couldn't decide if deactivating the bomb or letting it explode would lead to the desired outcome. He was very conflicted."

"So, the Chicago detonation not only advanced the plans of the Dark One, it affected the future too, am I right?" said Zach

"Yes. The Chicago detonation was critical for those in the future.

"Where are these 'people from the future'?" asked Liu. "We need to speak to them to confirm your story."

"According to Sixtus, they're all dead except one."

"I want to hear more about Curtis Roberts. You say you were there when Jarad and I found him? asked Zach."

Marshall nodded. "We went to visit Curtis Roberts—his real name was Glendnar Raczor—at his trailer, and that's where we encountered you and Speaker Anston," said Marshall. "We arrived before you did, and we talked to him. Sixtus found out he was the oldest Time Sculptor in this era, and he was committed to maintaining the current timeline."

"How many Time Sculptors are, I mean, were there?" asked Zach.

"You already extracted all this from my mind."

"I know," said Zach. "But since everyone is shielding telepathically, we will have to talk through our problems."

Marshall nodded. "There were four. They arrive when they are twenty years old. Their missions run twenty years, which is the maximum level of trauma their brains can absorb from the changes. Once they complete their mission, they're allowed to stay in the past as long as they don't engage in any activity that could change the time line."

"Like?" asked Sasha.

"Like procreating, for example. A prodigy might become an influential politician or something."

"And there is only one of them left?" asked Aminah.

Marshall nodded. "Yes, only one. The second Time Sculptor remains hidden. The other three are dead."

"So, how did these 'time sculptors' affect our plans? I'm not making the connection," said Liu.

"The essence of time continued to break down. The massive number of overlapping changes caused it to 'glitch.' I can't find a better word, but you experienced the phenomenon as I did when you accessed my memories. At certain moments, time reset several seconds back into the past, and the replay forward was different. I experienced it, so I assume others with ASD experienced it as well, although it would not necessarily be symmetrical."

Marshall continued. "In the previous timeline, your associate, Detective Munoz, disarmed the bomb, and you rendered Mr. Cox impotent, as you planned. But then time glitched, and it rewound to a point before Speaker Anston's incursion into Mr. Cox' mind. He was ready for you the second time, which is why he was able to resist the assault. "

141

Gasps and grumblings of disbelief followed Marshall's words. Liu Wei and Jacques seemed particularly agitated.

"This is utterly ridiculous," said Jacques. "I know he thinks these memories are authentic, but he has no supporting evidence. Maybe it's just conjecture, or maybe he is powerful enough to deceive us," Liu nodded vigorously in agreement.

"You can believe what you want," said Marshall. "But it's all true. This reality is not the same as the last one. I have no idea how many times this loop has played out. I only know that originally, Mr. Cox was not supposed to succeed."

"And so, it was Sixtus Maras who intervened and stopped Jose Munoz from disarming the bomb?" asked Zach.

Marshall nodded. "Yes, I believe that's what happened. He must have allowed the detective to disarm the bomb. When the glitch occurred, I imagine he decided it was a sign he made a mistake, so he did whatever was necessary to ensure it would detonate."

A lengthy silence followed, broken only by the sound of silverware clattering against glassware and people clearing their throats. Finally, Zach leaned forward and looked at each member of the society. "I believe Marshall," he said. "We're facing something far bigger than we could have imagined. It's not just Mr. Cox, we're battling agents from the future."

Jacques rose and threw his napkin on the table. "This is total nonsense," he said. "Our attempt to subdue Mr. Cox failed; it's as simple as that. We must refocus our efforts on defeating the Dark One, and the rest of what he says should be disregarded."

"I agree," said Liu. "His story is preposterous. Unless he lets us into his mind again, I don't want to hear any more of this. He makes me — uncomfortable."

"Maybe Marshall will allow us to access his memories again to confirm what he is telling us," said Sasha. "We can dive deeper into his mind this time."

Aminah absently stirred her coffee far longer than needed. She laid the spoon on the saucer and looked up at Sasha. "Maybe you'll let him inside *your* mind, Sasha… No? I wonder why not? Perhaps he's afraid that one of us might damage him, as we're afraid of him damaging us. If we're honest, every one of us is protecting our space right now. So, let's not act like this is all about Marshall."

After exchanging worried glances and shifting in their chairs uncomfortably, Yasin pushed himself away from the table. "Well, I for one enjoyed dinner immensely, but I think it's time to retire."

Gustavo Pena smiled and gestured for Yasin to remain seated. "Please, sit my friend. There is still much for us to discuss. Your friend Aminah raises an interesting point. You are all shielding yourselves from the others. Why?"

Rogelio turned and said, "Because the man who showed up in Portales said there was a traitor in our midst."

"Ah yes, the traitor. What could be more dangerous than a conspirator inside the Suicide Society? I wonder how you will expose him — or her?" said Pena.

They sat in silence for some time. When Zach spoke, it was in a deliberate tone. "I don't know, but I sense that if we don't find out who it is, the consequences for the Suicide Society will be disastrous."

Chapter Twelve

Wanda stood in the living room, peeking through a slit in the blinds out to the street in front of the house. Several vehicles passed by at speeds far exceeding the posted limit. She saw people running back and forth on foot, but no one approached the home they had broken into. Mateo periodically looked out the peephole in the front door before returning to the search.

Feeling lightheaded, Wanda sat down on a drab green olive sofa and struggled to breathe. She was certain the police or the homeowners would burst through the door any second. Fifteen minutes seemed like an eternity when Mateo finally said, "Okay, we're ready to go."

"You found the keys?"

He nodded. "Yep. They left a spare set hidden in the master bedroom closet. I found them in a jar with a couple other keys. They took almost everything but left several cans of refried beans and spaghetti. We also have a few boxes of semi-perishables like cereal and crackers. There were a bunch of unopened liter soda bottles, so I emptied them and filled them up with water just in case.

"Do you think it'll be that bad out there, Mateo?"

"I don't know, but we should be as prepared as possible. The world was falling apart before the bombs went off. Who knows what's happening now."

"I can't take it all in. My friends are dead, and I'm not sure I can…" She looked at Mateo with tears in her eyes that started to run down her cheeks.

Mateo walked over and put an arm around her shoulders. "We'll make it, Wanda. We'll both make it home and find our loved ones."

"That's the problem," she said. "I'm not sure if I have any loved ones left."

He kept her close while walking back out to the garage. After opening the passenger's door, he set her down in the seat and finished loading the additional items. The Pinella family, which was the last name on the bills sitting on the counter, had forgotten to take several essentials, including toilet paper. They would no doubt realize their error soon enough, but if they returned home for it, they would find every single roll was missing. If this crisis really did dissolve into chaos, toilet paper would be a valuable barter item.

Mateo placed two suitcases full of clothes in the trunk along with the food, water, a competition bow, arrows and a hunting knife. He brought a pistol into the car and placed it in the armrest compartment. Wanda recoiled at the sight of the gun.

"Don't worry," he said. "It's a pellet gun. They took all the real weapons. But this thing looks enough like an authentic semi-automatic it might scare the rowdies away."

146

She nodded and fastened her seatbelt as he slid the key into the ignition. "Ok, Wanda, it's the moment of truth." He started the car and looked at the gas gauge.

"Half a tank. Ok, we're good. I was worried about that. I knew they would take as much gas as they could carry. I think Hyundai Sonatas have four cylinders, so we shouldn't have to refuel for at least 150 miles."

He pressed the garage opener on the visor, and the door rolled up slowly. Mateo pulled out and turned onto the street. Two doors down, a couple walked out to their porch and opened two folding chairs. They would be the grownups on the block, smugly laughing at the idiots who were fleeing their homes only to return a week later with their tails tucked between their legs. The couple would take every opportunity to remind their neighbors they told them the mass hysteria over the bomb would quickly fade. For now, they would monitor the neighborhood for unusual activity, and they were seeing some *very* unusual activity at the Pinella home.

"Shit!" said Mateo as they drove by the couple.

"What? What's wrong?"

"Those two on the porch weren't there when I scoped out the street. I can tell they know the family that lives here already left, so they'll suspect we've stolen this car. I imagine they'll call the police."

"Oh no, are we going to be arrested?" A look of abject fear crossed Wanda's face.

"Maybe, but I'm counting on the fact that the police are so overwhelmed, a car theft won't draw much attention."

As they turned the corner to exit the neighborhood, Mateo looked in the rear-view mirror. The couple had moved to the end of the driveway and we're looking toward the Pinella's car, talking and pointing in an animated way. The man pulled out a cell phone.

Mateo turned out onto Elk Grove Boulevard and drove a short distance before merging onto Arlington Heights Road. Although it was four lanes, the highway was clogged with slow-moving traffic. The arteries out of the suburbs closest to Chicago proper were jammed with people looking to flee. The congestion only got worse when local suburban motorists joined already heavy traffic.

Some were heading to mountain or rural areas where they had relatives or second homes. Others simply wanted to get away and would figure out their destination when they got there. The weather was hot and humid, and the resulting gridlock was unnerving, especially when the gas tank was only half-full.

Wanda looked out the passenger's window at the businesses locked down and boarded up. Hastily constructed handmade signs were abundant and repetitive. *Closed until further notice; sold out; no food or water*, and of course, *no gas*. Wanda could see the concern on Mateo's face as they passed the fourth closed-up gas station. His worry only elevated her anxiety.

She remembered when she used to self-medicate in stressful situations like this, but with the help of Marshall and the others, she quit taking the pills. Marshall told her a prerequisite for membership in the group was a clear mind, and she didn't need any more motivation than that. Everyone swore off the meds, including Korinth and Iglar. All things considered, learning to cope with reality without the haze of drugs improved her life.

They passed many vehicles stuffed with possessions and full of shocked and frightened passengers. Those who made eye contact expressed a combination of fear and suspicion. Twice, Wanda wondered if they would be ridden off the road by aggressive drivers, but Mateo deftly changed lanes or slowed down to avoid a confrontation.

After traveling for an hour on a journey that should have taken no more than twenty minutes, they turned off onto Route-14 and headed northwest. Mateo kept angling to get past the northern most boundaries of Chicago, figuring that moving further away would reduce traffic gridlock. Route-14 was also congested, and they inched forward before finally passing I-90. Traffic thinned out again in Crystal Lake, and they were finally able to hit the speed limit, but an hour trip still took almost two-and-a-half hours.

While traveling a little over thirty miles, the idling in traffic took its toll on their gas supply. At a shade over an eighth of a tank, Wanda knew they would have to fuel up soon. Yet, even as far out as Marengo, the gas stations were closed. Drivers topped off their tanks just in case they had to drive long distances with only a moment's notice, and the fear just created more panic.

"We're going to Rockford and get some gas," said Mateo. "We'll pick up the freeway and head south until we hit I-88 and then go due southwest until we reach Davenport."

"The anguish is unnerving, Mateo. The only people we see are leaving. There's no one in the supermarkets or shopping centers. These people aren't that close to Chicago, so why are they running away?"

"Some of them might be hunkered down in their homes. It's fear, Wanda. It's contagious. At our core, we're still animals. When something threatens us, we revert back to our primal instincts."

Mateo turned on the radio, but only static came from the speakers. He pushed the scan button, and the digital readout rolled through the numbers until the tuner stopped, and a somber voice filled the car

.... *cannot emphasize the importance of staying calm and not panicking as the President suggested. Anyone who doesn't have to leave their home should stay there. The United States military is on alert and ready to defend the country. The likelihood of another attack is small.*

Mateo pushed the button until the tuner reached the next station still broadcasting.

... *We're getting reports of rioting and chaos in cities across the country. A short-wave transmission from Baltimore indicated a mob dragged the mayor from his home and lynched him. Other mobs are congregating at government buildings in many cities and state capitals. Reports say a million people have gathered on Pennsylvania Avenue and at the Mall. They are angry, and many are armed. D.C. police seem overwhelmed, and the President has dispatched the National Guard to maintain order.*

Mateo reached over and snapped off the radio. "It's happening," he muttered under his breath.

"What, Mateo? What's happening?"

"Wanda, you don't look well. Why don't you try to get some sleep?"

"Don't treat me like a child, Mateo. I've been around death a lot lately. I can take it."

He sighed and looked out the driver's side window. "Okay. It doesn't look good. Every crisis has a tipping point, and we're getting there quickly. There may be no way back. The nukes in Istanbul and Mumbai started it, but the explosion in Chicago has taken on a life of its own. Other crisis situations are bubbling up all over the country, and before you know it, the trust that holds everything together evaporates."

"People are afraid of another bomb?"

"They're terrified. Everyone knew a nuke could go off someday, but I don't believe anyone thought it would actually happen. Now that it has, all over the world, they're afraid their city might be next. And they may be right."

"So, what do we do?" she asked.

"We try to get home. That's all we can do."

Mateo turned south on Rural Route-21, which was a two-lane road cut between several fields of orchards and undeveloped land.

"Where are we going?"

"I saw a sign for a service station a few miles from here. We might have a better chance to find gas somewhere off the beaten path."

Once they reached the town of Union, Mateo slowed the car as he approached a residential neighborhood. They passed several modest houses, but the only signs of life were the children's bicycles and toys that lay abandoned in the front yards. On both sides of the street, Wanda watched as frightened residents remained shrouded while slowly pulling back their curtains to see the passing car.

A pickup truck sat parked on the side of the road with four men in the bed chugging Pabst Blue Ribbon and tossing the cans over the side. The sound of the Sonata caught their attention, and they stopped talking and stared at the approaching vehicle. One of them stood up and adjusted his ball cap while another reached down into the bed of the truck and picked something up without bringing it into view.

"Wave at them, Wanda, and smile." Wanda did as Mateo asked and waved while grinning awkwardly. Three of the men did nothing except continue to stare, but one of them raised his arm and waved back once. Their friendly gesture was enough to get them past what appeared to be an impromptu guard.

They reached the Union Mart at the end of Main Street and pulled into the lot. Two cars were parked near the store, but no one was at the gas pump.

"No 'out of gas' signs. That's good news." Mateo pulled the car up to the pump and parked. He got out and removed the gas cap and ran his credit card through the slot. An error message appeared on the digital readout. He repeated the swipe and received the same response, so he leaned inside the open driver's door. "The gas pump isn't taking credit cards, so I need to go into the store. You stay here and keep the car locked."

Wanda ignored him and got out of the vehicle. "There's no way I'm staying here by myself. Besides, I have to use the restroom." Mateo sighed and nodded, and they walked tentatively through the parking lot until they reached the entrance. Breathing a sigh of relief, he pulled on the doors and entered the building. At least the Union Mart was open.

Wanda immediately noticed the bare shelves and non-food items scattered on the floor. Everything edible was gone, and the refrigerated coolers were just as barren. Throughout the store, the only items left for sale were nonessentials like lined paper, impulse products and tourist collectibles.

A heavyset man in dirty jeans and a wrinkled, faded t-shirt sat behind the counter and sipped a beer while reading a magazine. A radio blared in the background, reporting on the newest riots and other heinous crimes that were tightening their grip on the country. Almost like a self-fulfilling prophecy, the more destruction they reported, the worse the situation became.

"Ah, excuse me," said Mateo as he stepped up to the counter. "Do you have any gas?"

"Yep." The clerk muttered the words without looking up from the magazine.

"Great. Well, I'd like to buy some, but your credit card reader doesn't seem to be working."

"No credit cards. Not taken' 'em. The machine went out this morning, anyway."

"Okay then, cash. I'd like to fill it up. How much is it per gallon for regular?"

"It's twenty-five bucks a gallon."

Mateo smiled and let out a single laugh. "That's a good one. Twenty-five dollars. Great price if you can get it. Seriously, how much per gallon?"

The man put down his magazine and looked up at Mateo. "I said, twenty-five bucks a gallon in cash. It's not negotiable."

The smile quickly faded. "That's extortion."

Rising up from behind the counter, the man reached his full height, which Wanda imagined was somewhere around 6'6. "How about I don't sell you any gas?"

They stared at each other for a moment before Mateo shook his head in obvious disgust. He reached into his pocket, took out his wallet and counted the money inside while hiding the contents from the counterman. Ultimately, he pulled out a fifty-dollar bill, two twenties and a five. "I'll take four gallons," he said as he laid the money on the table.

The man behind the counter sat back down, grabbed the money and shoved it in his pocket. "Thank you, sir. Have a nice day."

"I need to use the bathroom," said Wanda. "Can I have the key, please?"

The counterman rolled his eyes. "Are you going to use the crapper? Because that costs five bucks." Without saying a word, Mateo walked toward the counter and slammed down another ten-dollar bill.

After using the facilities, they left the store, and Wanda looked over at the Sonata still sitting next to the gas pump. The pickup truck they passed earlier was now parked on the other side of the island. The driver was busy filling his tank while the other three lingered around the bed.

"Wanda, please go back into the store and wait until I'm done pumping the gas."

She looked at him and then scanned the parking lot. "No, I'm going with you." He appeared to sense her resolve because he didn't protest, and they walked together back to the car. Mateo unscrewed the gas cap without unlocking the doors, and Wanda stood near him as he inserted the nozzle into the fuel filler pipe and pressed the handle. She whispered, "Thank you," and looked to the heavens when she saw the dial spinning and heard the fuel being dispensed into the tank.

"We don't get visitors here much," said one of the men, who leaned on his straight arm resting against the roof of the car. He walked over casually and stood close to Wanda. "You got a boyfriend, hon?"

Wanda did her best to understand the situation. She felt threatened, so it wasn't unreasonable to believe this man had ill intent. He was also dirty and smelled of nicotine that leaked out his pores as his body tried to rid itself of the poison. His socioeconomic status and negligent upbringing were obvious.

"She's with me. Leave her alone," said Mateo.

"Hey, butt out," said one of the other men, who moved in closer. "My buddy's just tryin' to get to know the lady." He turned and looked at his friend, who inched up so he was less than a foot away from Wanda. "Go ahead, Dodie, this guy won't be interrupting you anymore."

Dodie smiled and tipped his cap. "Thanks, Kurt." He turned his attention back to Wanda. "Now, where were we? Oh yeah, I asked if you got a boyfriend?" He smiled to reveal yellow, rotted front teeth. "I'd like to be your boyfriend. I'm a nice guy most of the time."

"Yes, I've got a boyfriend," said Wanda in a near whisper.

"Not like me you don't."

The pump slowed as it delivered the last fifty cents of gas.

"I don't really like you," said Wanda. "You're rude, and I know what being rude looks like. I would never be your girlfriend."

Mateo put the nozzle back in the pump, screwed the cap back on the car, and hit the button on the fob to unlock the doors.

"Why you..." Dodie grabbed Wanda's arm just as she turned to walk away. He gruffly pulled her close. She could smell the alcohol and cigarettes on his breath. "C'mon, honey, how 'bout a lil kiss for ol' Dodie. The world's goin' ta hell in a hand basket, anyway. Let's have some fun."

Mateo started towards Wanda, but the one called Kurt grabbed his arm and spun him around. The third man approached from the side further blocking Mateo's path.

"Leave 'em alone, mister," warned Kurt. "Toby, you got 'em?"

"I'm ready, Kurt," said the friend.

"Listen, we don't want any trouble here. Just let us go. I've got money, and we've got other stuff," said Mateo.

"Oh, we're gonna take all that, don't worry," said Toby.

While they were talking, Wanda repositioned herself slightly. Dodie was busy trying to intimidate her by strengthening his grip on her arm and deepening his scowl, so he didn't notice her left thigh planted squarely between his legs just as she learned in a self-defense class. However, when the bone in her knee impacted with his genitals, Dodie immediately recognized what happened. He grimaced, growled and bent over as he clutched his testicles with both hands.

"Bitch," was all he could say before she brought a double clenched fist down on the back of his neck. Dodie crumpled to the ground and stopped moving. Only periodic low groans confirmed he was still conscious.

At the first sounds of distress, Kurt and his friend turned and peered down at Dodie, who was groaning and writhing as he cupped his genitals through his pants. "Holy shit," said Kurt. "Bitch, you laid out Dodie." He looked up at Wanda for a moment and then started to laugh.

Slowly at first, the hilarity grew into howls and chortles. Kurt slapped Toby in the stomach with an open hand, and his friend snickered and pointed at the prone form of their fallen mate. After a few more hearty laughs, Kurt turned to Mateo. "Go on, get the hell outta here. We don't wanna mess with your girlfriend."

They didn't need further prompting. Mateo and Wanda jumped in the car and sped off back toward the highway that would lead to Rockford. Periodically, Wanda glanced out the back window to see the men still laughing even as Dodie rose to his knees.

After five minutes of silence, Mateo said, "Damn, Wanda, you're one tough broad."

Not quite understanding his meaning, Wanda still took it as a compliment.

Chapter Thirteen

Mr. Cox looked at the clock and turned back to his computer screen. The President of Uruguay, Angel Martinez, had been sitting in Xavier Watts' office for over an hour. The trip from Uruguay to Detroit was long and arduous, and the President could only be annoyed they left him waiting alone inside the Detroit high rise. The Benefactor smiled and wondered if Martinez was still there. He pressed a kiosk button on a smooth digital screen set into the surface of his desk.

"Yes, boss?" Hefe's voice sounded full and realistic as it boomed through the sixteen-speaker surround sound system installed in the room. Mr. Cox reminded himself to play some death metal to test everything out once his schedule was clear.

"Tell Xavier to go to his office and begin the meeting with the President of Uruguay. I'll be there in a moment."

"Right, boss."

Mr. Cox expected the encounter would be relatively brief since there wasn't very much to discuss. As with other countries around the world, the HUGE conglomerate was squeezing smaller governments through a combination of extortion, force and coercion. Uruguay was a perfect example. In fact, the infiltration by his organization was so effective, Mr. Cox felt certain most of the people in the government worshiped him, and only a small minority remained loyal to the President. In a recent policy meeting with Watts and Delgado, Cox made it clear it was time to topple these governments to get them out of the way.

He rose from his desk and walked down the hallway, nodding to the attendant before he entered the elevator and rode it down to Watts' floor. Unlike his penthouse, which he reserved to himself exclusively, the lower floors in Building One were bustling with activity. He enjoyed seeing his employees carrying on the work of the organization, and if they stopped for a moment to bow or curtsy as they were taught, the Benefactor could live with the momentary loss of productivity.

Without any sense of urgency, he went into Watts' suite of offices and walked up to the receptionist counter. A pretty young woman looked up and did a double take, immediately recognizing the Benefactor.

"Hell—I—Hello, Benefactor," she stammered while awkwardly rising to her feet and curtsying. The girls on either side of her stopped in mid-sentence and followed suit.

"Please, please," said Mr. Cox while motioning for them to sit down. He noticed that all activity in the room had stopped, except for the multiple frequencies of computers and copy machine motors. "Please, don't let me distract you from your work."

Following orders, they did their best to look busy while stealing side glances at their leader. This included the girl Mr. Cox initially approached. "Not you, child. You can stand up."

The young woman rose so quickly her chair repelled backwards and hit the wall behind her with noticeable force.

"I'm sorry, sir," she said. "What can I do for you, sir."

"I'm going into Mr. Watts' office," he said. "I wanted to wait a moment to increase the drama if you know what I mean, Sandra. That is your name, right?"

"Yes, sir," she said with enthusiasm. Word around the office was that Mr. Cox could read minds, and she wondered if he had just read hers. Lost in the moment, she failed to notice him looking at the large nameplate attached to her workstation.

Mr. Cox gave her a friendly wave as he headed down the hallway towards Watts' office. He made a mental note to look in on her again when time permitted. Short of watching a suicide, there was nothing he enjoyed more than wooing the innocent and introducing them to the wicked underbelly of humanity.

He reached Watts' office and casually strode in to find the President of Uruguay on his feet gesturing animatedly and talking in Spanish. Two of his aides, who doubled as bodyguards, sat stiffly in plastic chairs at the back of the room. Watts rested comfortably in his overstuffed chair with his elbows perched on the desk and his eyebrows furrowed, creating deep creases in his forehead. The conversation stopped as Mr. Cox walked in.

"Gentlemen, please don't let me interrupt," he said in Spanish.

160

The President of Uruguay looked back uncomfortably. He was a robust man in his early 60s. His hair was jet black, likely dyed, and receding at the temples. He turned to Watts and said in English, "Who is this?"

Watts looked at Mr. Cox and then back at the President. "He sits on the Board of Directors. You may call him Mr. Cox."

"Please, Mr. President, have a seat," said the Benefactor as he gestured toward the closest chair. "We want to keep our discussions cordial. After all, we have the same goals for your people. You have traveled a great distance under difficult circumstances. Can I offer you an adult beverage?"

Angel Martinez looked over at the Exousia Gold water Watts provided. "Yes, I think I will. Perhaps a single malt Scotch? It was a difficult trip, indeed. As I explained to Mr. Watts, our airplane lost control tower contact three times. We had a near midair collision. With the turmoil on the streets of Montevideo, my nerves are frayed."

Mr. Cox motioned to Watts, who pushed a button on his kiosk, and less than five minutes later, a domestic employee entered the room with drinks for everyone except Martinez' body guards.

Mr. Cox sauntered over and sat in the chair next to Martinez and across from Xavier Watts. "So, Mr. President, you traveled all this way for a reason. Why did you contact us? We are just a corporate citizen, we aren't a government."

Martinez stroked his moustache as he chose his words. "Like much of the world, our society is falling apart. People are terrified that the next nuclear explosion will be in their city. We have open crime in the streets, and the police have abandoned their posts. I have lost control of the military. When I ask why this has happened, people continually reference an international conglomerate called HUGE. An internal investigation revealed that your people have infiltrated every part of our country from infrastructure to social services and especially the military."

Cox smiled and looked at Martinez. "It is unfortunate you have lost control, Mr. President, but let us be frank. You are a weak and ineffectual leader, and your people sense this. Our 'conglomerate,' as you call it, has simply filled a vacuum created by your lack of governance."

"I am still the President," said Martinez as he sat upright, and his back stiffened.

"Perhaps in name. But you know we effectively control your country. Mr. Watts need only give the word, and your government will topple."

"Who are you people? Where did you come from? How could you have done all this without our knowledge? You must have been planning this for years."

"I think you already know the answer to those questions. We are the Gehenna Global Corporation, and our mission, in cooperation with three other major international corporate citizens, is to serve humanity in this trying time," said Mr. Cox.

"For decades, your people cried out for food, clean water and decent shelter. Yet, your government never seemed to care much about those things, Mr. President. Instead, you cared much more about lining your greedy pockets with the money you stole from them."

162

"… What is it you want?"

"Mr. Watts is more familiar with your situation than I am. I'll let him explain."

Watts shifted his chair so he was facing Uruguay's President directly. He pulled out a tablet and poked at the screen several times with his index finger. After he called up the information he needed, he glanced at the device for several seconds before looking up at Martinez.

"Mr. President, you have serious issues to deal with. Your society has broken down. There is rampant looting in Montevideo, and almost 200 murders have been recorded in the last twenty-four hours. The police have virtually abandoned the city, and your military isn't following your orders. The people blame you and your government."

"Yes, yes, I'm aware of all these things," said Martinez. "Why do you think I travelled for over twenty-four hours and endured two layovers in Latin America? Our plane was almost overrun by hooligans in Panama City. I risked my life to get here."

"And why would you do such a thing, Mr. President?" asked Watts.

"You know why." Martinez slammed his hand on the arm of the chair. "Everywhere we look, the only assistance is coming from HUGE. Food, bottled water, clothing and shelter. Your facilities are safe and well protected. The people turn away from the government and toward your company. Yet, no one really knows who you are."

"Finally," Martinez said between gulps of his Glenfarclas 1955, "we were able to track the corporate registry to a very small town in Arizona that's not even on a map. It took great effort to find any useful information. This creation of yours is buried under layers of fictitious names and blind, irrevocable trusts. After months of work, our people finally identified Mr. Watts as a member of the Board of Directors for the Gehenna Corporation. When my office contacted him, he insisted that I come here personally if I wanted a meeting."

Mr. Cox shrugged. "So, you found out we incorporated in Arizona. Do you think you're clever?" His smile instantly disappeared, and he leaned over towards the President. "Again, what exactly is it you want from us?"

"I want to know why you're in my country, and what I can do to get you to leave. You and your organization are undermining our efforts to govern."

Mr. Cox' smile returned as he sat back and appeared to relax. "Let me make something clear, Mr. President. You're in no position to dictate anything to us."

"Who am I negotiating with, Watts? You or him?" The President flicked his thumb in the Benefactor's direction.

"Why, you are negotiating with Gehenna's President, of course," said Mr. Cox. "Excuse me for interrupting."

Martinez continued to look at Watts. "What is it you want?"

"We want you to dissolve your General Assembly and cede power to the HUGE Group," said Mr. Cox without looking in the President's direction.

Martinez' laugh sounded forced and hollow. "Impossible. You are a company not a political party. The idea is absurd."

"Perhaps," said Mr. Cox while licking his lips. "However, understand that when you return to Montevideo, you will be arrested and hanged for treason. A little matter of embezzling we've heard. We have your computer records, which provide evidence of your criminal acts."

Martinez rose from his chair, shaking with rage. His bodyguards in the back followed his lead. "I did no such thing! You are scoundrels."

"*Scoundrels?* Mr. Watts and I will take that as a compliment, Mr. President. Still, it changes nothing. Unless you agree to our terms, we will allow the citizens to revolt, and the military, which is under *our* control, will declare martial law. You will be returned to Montevideo, and I promise you will be killed in a very painful way, and your body will be dragged through the streets as the dogs chew your intestines. I imagine Mr. Watts will also have your family killed. He has little tolerance for fools. The choice is yours. Should we call General Ontiveros to substantiate my claim?"

"Ontiveros is a traitorous pig. Ever since his suicide attempt, he has been untrustworthy."

"I imagine he would not be happy to hear you say those words, Mr. President, so we'll act like we didn't hear them. Nevertheless, we need to know your intentions. As they say, commerce never sleeps."

Martinez stumbled back and fell into his chair. His head drooped, and he held it in his hands. "I must be given asylum," he mumbled.

"Agreed," said Mr. Cox as he stood up and clapped his hands together. "Now shake on the deal with Mr.

165

Watts. I have, ah, another engagement, so I will hand the meeting over to him so you two can work out the details." As he was leaving, he turned back at the door and said, "Oh, and fly safe, Mr. President. The skies are very dangerous."

Martinez smiled weakly and rose to accept Watts' handshake. Mr. Cox nodded at the two bodyguards who scowled at him as he left the room.

Once clear of Watts' office, he made his way back to his penthouse to make preparations for his own private celebration. Inside his apartment, the Benefactor took out his phone and pushed the lunch app icon developed specifically for him. He scrolled down the screen and ordered a light lunch of Pao Cai salad and Makizushito to be followed by a visit from his personal masseuse.

After finishing the order, Mr. Cox pulled up the interactive maps Alan prepared every morning that highlighted the most volatile areas in the world. In general, cities experiencing the worst levels of violence were the most receptive to listening to HUGE's proposals. Pushing the mouse over to a particular position on the map, he encircled and enlarged it. Apparently, the level of violence in Thailand had reached crisis levels, which was the perfect time for Mr. Cox to visit.

He sat in his chair and swiveled to look out over the city. Detroit was even more beautiful during the day, since the abundant acts of violence were more visible than at night. At any given time, he might see a high-speed chase, a looting, a gang shootout, an assault or any number of other heinous crimes. Even now, as he gazed over at East Jefferson, he watched a man with a knife raised high above his head standing over the prone form of another. The one on the ground leaned up on an elbow and raised his other arm defensively as he shook his head while pleading for mercy.

The Benefactor reached out and slipped into the mind of the aggressor, tapping into the man's complex feelings of hate, fear and anger that converged and melded into a psychotic rage. Cox drank deeply of the emotional intensity and allowed it to backflow into his own pleasure centers. He closed his eyes, gasped and shook with a kind of pleasure no worldly experience could duplicate. The purity of the energy was the absence of all color, which went well beyond mere black. He soaked it in fully like a parasite on a host.

Just as his euphoria peaked, he sensed the flow lightening. Somewhat agitated, he opened his eyes, feeling like someone interrupted a satisfying episode of coitus. He searched the man's mind and found the source; doubt crept into his psyche, and the fury subsided. Mr. Cox screamed out in frustration, and dove into the man's thought centers.

Kill him! He's just a gnat, and you want to show him who's boss in the street. It's the law of the jungle. Do you want to survive out here?

The flow grew darker...

Coward! You're a coward if you don't go through with it. Hate him! Kill him, I said, kill him, or kill yourself!

The man screamed as much from the physical pain as the emotional torment. He thrust the knife down in full force and stuck the blade deep into his victim's abdomen. Mr. Cox changed perspective and violated the wounded man's brain by plunging into it, sucking out the energy of intense mortified fear. At first, the victim couldn't fully comprehend he was stabbed until

167

he looked with disbelief at the growing blood stain on his white shirt. As the knife came down a second time, the reality of his situation flooded his consciousness.

"No, no—please, I don't want to die. Please, I want to live. Please—Aggh!"

The knife swung down again and again as the blood spattered onto the sidewalk and the clothes of the assailant. The wounded man screamed in a primal way, like an animal pulled from the herd by a pack of bloodthirsty wolves. Finally, the one with the crazed eyes and blood drops on his face pulled the knife out and looked down at the dying man on the ground, who reached out with a shaking hand and grabbed the killer's pant leg. He opened his mouth to say something, but no sound escaped his lips.

A small crowd gathered at the scene, but no one tried to apprehend the murderer or help the victim. Increasingly numbed by the daily violence, most people learned it was better to remain uninvolved and leave the scene as soon as possible. After his breathing slowed, the killer dropped the knife and stumbled away, drunk on adrenalin that coursed through his veins. People near him cleared a path, watching as he turned a corner and disappeared down Griswold Street.

The body lay on the sidewalk for several hours, creating a small stream of blood that flowed down from the concrete, over the curb and eventually into the sewer. People tried to pass by without acknowledging the body, but those with business at the Gehenna Center were forced to step over it to get into the building. Approximately four and a half hours later, an unmarked truck pulled up, and two men in soiled coveralls and used surgical masks stepped out. They moved with robotic efficiency as one of them grabbed the dead man's feet, and the other took hold of his shoulders. They walked a short distance, created a swinging motion with his body, and then threw him into the truck's bed.

Mr. Cox looked at his watch. Four hours to dispose of the body was still too fast. The violence was escalating, but he wouldn't be satisfied until the bodies decomposed in the street.

The intercom chimed, and Mr. Cox said, "Yes?" from across the room.

"Watts here, sir. I have someone from the FBI on the phone. Should I take the call?"

"Of course, Xavier, although I'm surprised the FBI still exists. Isn't Hagus running that organization?"

"Yes, he is, so I'm not particularly concerned," said Watts.

"It's probably nothing, but I want to be prepared. Take the call and patch me in. I want to listen. We're drawing close to our ultimatum, and this may be a perfect opening salvo."

Chapter Fourteen

"Are we sure a traitor even exits?" asked Jacques as the last of the dessert dishes were cleared away. "We're going on a witch hunt based on the ravings of some unknown person who penetrated our security in Portales?"

"I agree with Jacques," said Rogelio. "There's no reason to believe anyone has compromised our organization. There's no proof. Let's just leave it alone."

"Oh, there is plenty of reason to discuss it, my friend," said Pena. "Starting with a betrayal of Speaker Randall and Speaker Anston."

"What?" Rogelio's eyes widened and his voice conveyed astonishment.

"What do you mean, Pena? Explain," said Yasin.

"Speaker Randall, do you recall when you and Speaker Anston encountered Mr. Cox' agents at a restaurant in Las Vegas? You barely survived if Speaker Anston's recollection was correct."

Zach nodded. "I remember. We visited a woman named Maybel Downey."

"That's right. Did you ever wonder how they found you?"

Zach shrugged. "I never thought about it."

"Remember, Speaker Anston was always connected to the rest of the group. You were all exchanging information freely, so every overseer knew where you were during that time."

"So, you're suggesting someone alerted Mr. Cox?"

"I'm not sure. Yet, all through the journey Mr. Cox seemed one step ahead of you." Pena lifted his cup and sipped his lotus tea.

"These are serious charges," said Aminah. "Mr. Cox is an ecktosensor of the highest degree, and perhaps he could tap into the Speaker's consciousness."

"Perhaps, but I wonder. Isn't it just as likely someone inside this group has provided him with information?" Pena set his glass down and walked slowly around the table with his hands clasped behind his back.

"Speaker Anston complained frequently about an impurity in the flow. Apparently, the contamination was faint, but he could sense it occasionally. And what of this unexpected appearance of someone at Portales warning the group of a traitor? How can you ignore that?

Sasha looked up and met Pena's gaze. "I wonder how someone discovered us in Portales in the first place? Marshall's notion we are being tracked by people in the future seems... bizarre. Does it make sense to become so agitated simply because Jacques used his phone?"

"Because Marshall is the traitor. Can't you see how obvious it is," said Jacques as he threw up his arms. "Ever since he's arrived, there's been nothing but

171

catastrophe for us. And now, Speaker Anston is dead, and we hardly know the new Speaker."

"They are monitoring you from the future," blurted out Marshall. "You are all supposed to be smart and perceptive enough to figure it out. Mr. — Speaker Anston wasn't paying with cash to avoid the authorities, he was trying to keep the people in the future from learning our whereabouts."

"He's talking this nonsense again." said Liu. "I'm starting to wonder about his stability."

Marshall felt the familiar sensation of shame over a condition he never asked for. Sarah reached over and took his hand.

"It's all right, Marshall, please continue. They need to hear this." Then, turning toward Liu, she hissed, "I've had about enough of you attacking Marshall. He's a very gifted person, and he's trying to help us. You interrupt him again, and I swear I'll…"

"You'll what?" Jacques's eyes blazed as he stood up from the table.

"That's enough, Jacques," said Zach. "Sit down."

For a brief second, Zach wondered if Jacques might try to harm Sarah, but the admonishment from the Speaker was enough to jar his sensibility, and he quickly brought his rage under control.

Marshall continued in a shaky voice. "You don't understand. If it can be traced, they know everything the second you do it. When Mr. Jacques made that call, it created a cell phone record. Somewhere in the 24th century, that record pops up in a data base, and they send an agent in the past to that location."

"If they knew in advance, why didn't they send someone before we arrived and ambush us?" asked Aminah.

Marshall sighed to signal his impatience. These people may have extraordinary ability, but they obviously lacked a basic understanding of quantum physics. "In future cycles where time has looped and folded on itself, they will. But during the first cycle, they must obey the laws of space-time. The fact that they weren't waiting in ambush proves this was the first time Mr. Jacques made that call in this reality. It's called 'pristine time'."

"So, in essence, we're prisoners. We can't live a normal life because they would find out and come back to kill us," said Yasin.

"Essentially, that is correct, I'm afraid," said Pena.

"How did these 'Time Sculptors', as you call them, become interested in us in the first place?"

"The Event," said Marshall. "You played an integral role in the detonation of the Chicago bomb. They must see you all as a threat going forward."

"And what about the old man in Portales? How did he find us?"

"He wasn't just an old man. He was the one I spoke of from the future. His name is Sixtus Maras."

Zach's head jerked up. "How can that be, Marshall?"

"I don't know, Mr., ah, Speaker Randall. If the current timeline isn't altered, somehow Sixtus travels back from the future... again."

"For what purpose?"

Marshall shook his head. "I'm not sure. Clearly, he wanted to warn us and let us know that the present reality leads to horrible consequences in the future."

Another uncomfortable pause followed before Aminah spoke up. "I'm wondering if we're safe here. And what about our families?"

"Let me address that," said Pena. "You are all very safe here. The energy emitted by the five vortexes is very powerful, and it is virtually impenetrable for consciousness streams and thought probes. I am certain our location will remain a secret.

"However, your families are more problematic," he continued. "Whether it's Mr. Cox or these people from the future, we have to assume all your family members are under surveillance. I fear they will be left to their own devices…" His words trailed off.

"Is there any more?" asked Rogelio. "It's quite depressing, and I have heard enough. Let's at least be honest with one another. We are sharing nothing telepathically, and the emptiness is similar to separation by distance. Everyone is being guarded. I suggest we drop these barriers and merge once again. We're at our best when we're connected."

"I'm not sure that's a good idea," said Zach. "When we merge, we're all defenseless. If someone meant to do us harm in that vulnerable state, it could be very damaging if not fatal."

"Well, I want to see what's going on outside," said Liu. "When can we access the internet and TV?"

Pena nodded. "Every room has a connection and a workstation. Our internet infrastructure is all located here, so our proxy servers are secure. You can browse anonymously since there is no digital footprint that can be traced. However, all social media sites and email have been restricted for your own safety. You can read your email and the social media posts of others, but you won't be able to respond."

"That is outrageous," said Jacques. "I need to have access to my friends, family and business associates. You understand we all have lives outside of the Society."

"I wish it could be different," said Pena, "but we must maintain our secrecy, especially considering what Marshall and Speaker Anston told us. Only Speaker Randall can change those edicts."

"Well," said Jacques as he rose to his feet. "I want to leave here, right now. I'm going back to France to see my family. You cannot keep me here against my will."

Pena looked up and arched his eyebrows. "I understand your frustration, Mr. Franco. But it would be disastrous for you to leave. And besides, there are no flights scheduled to depart for France from any airport."

"What?"

"The scene outside has deteriorated significantly since you gathered in Portales. Monitors are available in your rooms. There are several stations still broadcasting for now. You should catch up on the news."

Jacques slumped back in his seat, and a disturbing quiet fell over the room. When they were together, the Suicide Society was always connected; it was the source of their strength. Yet here they sat, isolated and suspicious of one another since someone in the group was a traitor. This was the situation Zach inherited as the new Speaker.

"We've had a long day," he said. "I suggest we rest, and we'll meet up for a strategy session tomorrow morning at nine a.m." Turning to Pena, he said, "Juan Gustavo, I assume you have a meeting room here?"

"Of course," answered Pena. "Meet down in the foyer at 7:45 tomorrow morning for breakfast, and one of the attendants will escort you. Please reserve time tomorrow for more of a tour. I want to familiarize you with all the facilities. We are a truly self-contained community."

"I want to say one more thing," said Sasha. "Speaker Anston has died, and we can't even collectively mourn for him as we should. I have never felt so alone when I am disconnected from my brothers and sisters. My loneliness will make the grieving process that much more difficult. I despise the traitor, whoever you are."

The dinner guests rose together from their seats at the table and walked back toward the residence wing. Zach waited outside in the hallway, making it a point to say goodnight to everyone. Sarah waited outside with him, and he kissed her lightly on the lips.

"How do you think it went?" she whispered.

"Not well. They resent that I'm Speaker. I'm not even sure why Jarad bestowed that honor and burden on me, anyway."

"Your strength. You are much stronger than anyone else. They all sense it, although they may not want to admit it."

He nodded and kissed her again before she turned and moved slowly down the hallway. Once inside his own room, he closed the door and leaned against it. With head in hands, Zach wept. Silently at first, the sobs grew in intensity as his back arched and heaved. He hoped the walls were thick because he couldn't stifle the sounds of mourning for his best friend; a man so powerful, yet so simple.

Jarad was always there for him through his darkest moments, including his divorce, attempted suicide, work issues and family problems. His mentor did the heavy lifting while expecting nothing in return. They had years of friendship on the books before telepathy, energy streams, Mr. Cox or the Suicide Society became part of their shared experience. The Speaker hid his abilities and critical role as an overseer for years, and yet, he must have always known about Zach's emerging gifts.

After all they endured, Jarad Anston was dead. He imagined someone notified his wife by now, and she was trying to make sense out of why he was killed in the parking lot of a convenience store on an Arizona road in the middle of nowhere. Like Zach, she too would grieve alone.

After some time, the disconsolate feelings subsided, and a new emotion crawled through him and blossomed. The face of the demon, Mr. Cox, flashed across his mind's eye. The sickening smile, the pale lips and malevolent sneer. Mr. Cox killed his friend as sure as if he had pulled the trigger himself. Whatever the cost, Zach knew this madman must be stopped before the damage he was inflicting became irreversible.

Unsure of how long he stood at the door, Zach changed and eventually made his way to the bathroom. He had his choice of multiple toothbrushes, toothpastes, soaps and mouthwashes. Fine silk pajamas caressed his body, and he couldn't remember when he experienced such luxury.

Perhaps the vacation in Cancun with Carol on our honeymoon?

He walked over to the bed and settled in, wondering, no, hoping that Sarah would knock.

Something good was happening between them, and it seemed only a matter of time before their relationship blossomed into something more significant. Yes, she was badly damaged from a life controlled by a monster, but none of that mattered to Zach. When he was near her, he felt whole for the first time in years. The experience differed from his relationship with Carol where dependency was mistaken for love. Sarah gave him a sense of freedom he couldn't describe. He knew he loved her, and he could feel and sense her love for him.

Reluctantly accepting he was going to spend the night alone, Zach pulled the covers back and crawled into bed. He got comfortable and sighed while thinking about Jarad and reliving some of their shared experiences. Strangely, he found himself sitting at a counseling session, one of ten participants seated in a circle. Jarad was in the middle surrounded by people from all walks of life.

"Let's talk about the experiences that drove you to consider suicide," said Jarad in a strange lifeless voice. "Tabatha, why don't you tell us what happened to you."

A girl with auburn hair, acne and a large silver nose ring secured by a hole drilled through her septum shook her head. "I don't like to talk about it, okay? It's pretty personal. This guy; his name was Cappy. Well, he was my boyfriend. We were shooting some angel's dust, and he told me he didn't love me anymore. That was a real drag because I was pregnant, don't you see?"

"And how did that make you feel?"

"Like shit, how do you think it made me feel? I got no money, and this guy who used to say he loves me instead decides to leave me, and I'm pregnant."

"What did you do?"

178

"I – I waited till he left and I took a bunch of pills. If my sister hadn't shown up, and she wasn't supposed to come over, I would have died for sure."

"But you didn't die, did you?"

"No. My sister tried to give me CPR and called 9-1-1. If she hadn't been there…"

"Well, that's an unsettling story, indeed… Bobby, why don't you tell us what happened."

The muscular and handsome man shook his long hair back and sat up in the chair. "Not much to tell, really. My wife ran off with some guy and took my three kids. Life ended the minute she left. I mean, I had nothing except her and those kids, anyway. My life was wasted. Maybe I shouldn't have beat the shit out of her so often; I don't know. Anyway, I waited a couple of days and then got liquored up and put a quarter-inch hole in my forehead with some pistol my old man gave me."

"My, how unfortunate. Well, let's hear from someone more upbeat. Zach, tell us about your suicide attempt."

Zach shifted in his chair. "Well, I… My marriage was falling apart, and I was losing my wife. She threatened to take my daughter away from me. My life was an utter mess, and I decided to take a whole bottle of Percocets. I was clinically dead they told me later. And as I recovered, I found I had certain – abilities."

"Abilities? Don't you mean the ability to watch others commit suicide in real time? Whoa, that's quite a feat, Zach. Can you do it for us now?"

"No, I don't know when it will happen…"

"Well, what about your other abilities? Like the ability to mess with people's minds. You could have stopped that guy from killing me, couldn't you Zach? But you failed. You weren't strong enough."

"I tried, Jarad. Lord knows I tried."

"Not hard enough, Zach. And it will get you killed too. He knows he's stronger than you, and he's coming. The traitor is out there. If you don't find out who it is, Cox wins. I'm dead, and Cox wins."

Zach heard a knock on the door. He looked back at Jarad, but then he heard the rapping again this time with more urgency.

Zach woke with a start. The knocking at his door was loud and relentless.

"Mr. Randall. Please, open the door. It's Marshall. You have to open the door!"

Zach sat up in the bed and tried to gather himself. He blinked and turned on the lamp on the nightstand.

"Mr. Randall, please open the door. It's Marshall."

Zach pulled the covers back and swung his legs over the side of the bed. He put his feet into his slippers and rubbed his eyes as another round of pounding on the door jolted the last vestiges of sleep from his eyes. "Okay, okay. I'm coming," he managed.

Shuffling over to the source of the noise, he unlatched the deadbolt. For several seconds, he tried to process the scene as his visual senses sent information his brain had difficulty processing. Standing before him was Marshall Beiner, panting like he had just run a marathon. In one hand he held a long kitchen knife coated with blood that dripped from the shaft. Blood covered his hand, and a fresh, wet crimson stain discolored his light-blue nightshirt.

"Marshall, my God what happened?"

"Can I come in, Mr. Randall?"

Zach stepped back and gestured for him to enter. Marshall ambled over to the table and sat down, still gasping for breath while gripping the handle of the knife so hard his knuckles looked white.

"I didn't kill him, Mr. Randall. Please believe me."

"Killed who, Marshall. Who is it?"

"I'm not sure. Someone knocked at my door, and when I opened it, this knife was laying outside. I didn't kill anyone, Mr. Randall. I didn't do it. They're all going to think I killed someone. Please, help me."

Zach reached out and put his hand on Marshall's forearm. His skin was clammy, and small tremors wracked his slender body. "I'll try my best. But you have to tell me what happened as you remember it. Calm down. We don't even know if the blood is human."

Marshall slumped over and started to cry. "Why is this happening? I didn't ask to be involved with this. At first, they liked me, but ever since we came here, they all hate me. I sense it, and now they're going to think I killed someone. I just want to go home, Mr. Randall. I don't like it here anymore."

Zach stood up and paced the floor. If he had any doubt before, there was no question now. The Suicide Society did have a traitor in its midst.

Chapter Fifteen

When Wanda and Mateo arrived in Rockford, they took Business Route-20 to avoid the freeway and the anarchy that seemed to be affecting the bigger cities. Gas was an ever-present problem, so they were always looking for stations that were still open. Unfortunately, most were shut down, and the hammered-up plywood on the storefronts confirmed the progressive disintegration. Gangs tagged a majority of the buildings with graffiti and apocalyptic slogans like, *We're all Doomed,* and *God is punishing Sodom and Gomorrah.*

Up ahead, a large sign flashed on and off inviting patrons to Bubb's Grill. Since they only had a few cans of unappealing refried beans and spaghetti with them, Mateo pulled off the road into the parking lot where only two cars occupied spaces.

He reached into the console and pulled out the pellet gun, tucking it inside his belt buckle and pulling his shirt out of his pants to hide it. "Okay, Wanda, let's go. Say as little as possible about our past or future intentions. We want *them* to do the talking."

She nodded and got out of the car, walking through the parking lot toward the building amid the sound of multiple sirens wailing from different locations. The rise and fall of the shrill pitch was becoming indistinguishable from other persistent background noise.

Mateo opened the door, and Wanda stepped inside the small space with a row of booths near the front window and several tables to the right of the aisle. In the far-right corner, a breakfast bar was setup with old-style stools that swiveled in a 360-degree circle. The theme was a combination 1950s and 1980s, which reflected the owner's fascination with those decades. A James Dean caricature in neon hung next to an autographed photo of Madonna. A white glove allegedly signed by Michael Jackson sat in a trophy case next to a picture of Graceland and Elvis Presley.

Two tables were occupied but none of the booths. An elderly couple sat at the back table, two half-eaten hamburgers in front of them. A few tables over, a younger man kept watch over his two children. The kids slurped malted milks from fountain-style glasses while their father scanned the room for threats. Wanda walked over to a booth and sat down as Mateo followed close behind.

"Does this place have an emergency exit? I don't see one," asked Wanda as she leaned over and talked to Mateo in a hushed tone.

"What? What are you talking about?"

"An emergency exit. I don't see one. It's in the International Commercial Building Code. There has to be an emergency exit. And do you see a fire extinguisher anywhere? I want to check the inspection date."

The corners of Mateo's mouth turned up slightly, and his eyes moistened as he tried to stifle a laugh. "Wanda, this is just a greasy spoon restaurant. They're not big on building codes and such, especially during a crisis like this."

"Well, I want to make sure..." The approach of an elderly patron interrupted them. The man looked to be in his seventies, and he slouched at a twenty-degree angle as he walked.

"Excuse me," he said. "I don't want to intrude, but I suggest you two sit in the back at a table like we are. Sitting in front of glass... Well, there's been several hooligans driving by and shooting out the windows in town. Things are getting bad... really bad."

Mateo shook his head. "I never thought of that. Thank you. My name is Mateo, and this is Wanda."

"Pleased to make your acquaintance. My name is Todd Harmon, and that's my wife Irma. I'd like to invite you to join us if you'd care to."

"Thank you, but we're fine," blurted out Wanda.

Mateo looked at her with incredulity. "Please excuse my friend; she's had a couple days. Of course, we'd love to join you."

Mateo slid out of his seat and motioned for Wanda to follow. She was rarely in the mood to converse anyway, but this situation was far more stressful than normal.

Once they finished the introductions, Mateo and Wanda took the other two seats at the table. Mateo looked around and remarked, "Is there a waitress here?"

Todd nodded and yelled, "Hey Barb, you got two more customers." Turning back to the table, he said, "Sorry, but they haven't had much business, and you gotta let Barb know you're here." Just as he finished, a large woman with a worn white uniform ambled out from the kitchen with a notepad in her hand and an annoyed look on her face. She panted, and tiny beads of sweat populated her brow.

"I told ya a hundred times, Todd, don't yell at me. I gotta lotta stuff to do back there, and none of the help has showed up." She looked over at Wanda and said, "What'll you have, missy?"

Wanda hid her face inside the menu, and without closing or moving it, she said, "I'll have a grilled cheese lightly toasted on white bread. Please use no more than one tablespoon of butter when grilling the sandwich. Also, I would like to substitute cottage cheese instead of french fries. Do you have any data on the sodium content in your cottage cheese?"

The waitress continued to stare down at her order pad, but then she began to laugh. Small chuckles at first, but her obese body soon shook with laughter to the point that sweat balls flew off her forehead down to her notepad and onto the table itself. One of them landed on Wanda's arm, and she recoiled in disgust. Dropping the menu, she ran towards the restroom holding her arm out like the sweat was acid.

"What the hell is wrong with her?" The waitress said to no one in particular.

Mateo shook his head. "I'm not sure. She's perfectly normal most of the time, but she has certain— idiosyncrasies. Anyway, you have cottage cheese, right? Just give her a grilled cheese and a scoop of cottage cheese. I'll have a burger and fries, and we'll both have waters."

"Okay, that I can do," said Barb as she scribbled on the pad before returning to the kitchen.

Wanda came back to the table and sat down, still drying her arm after washing it in the restroom. "That bathroom was disgusting," she said. "It has one of those rotating cloth towels, and the whole thing was dirty. The paper towel dispenser is almost empty. Whoever the attendant is, someone should reprimand him."

The two elderly patrons looked at Wanda and then back at Mateo, who subtly raised his eyebrows. "Uh, Todd," he said, "Do you folks live in Rockford?"

"Yep, we've both lived here all our lives. We married out of high school. Everything was great until a few years ago. Then things started going downhill. I could feel it even though it happened gradually. People just became meaner and more selfish, especially the younger ones. Now they've become animals."

"We're afraid to even leave our house," added Irma as she looked at Wanda. "It's awful. Todd sleeps with a gun underneath his pillow for heaven sakes. And if that wasn't bad enough, now we've got these people coming from Chicago, and they're not all good people."

"What about the police? Aren't they keeping order?"

"They're overwhelmed just like everywhere else. And now a bunch of them have quit. I don't blame them."

"The bomb in Chicago has changed everything," said Mateo

"It's not just that," Todd said. "You heard about India and Pakistan, right?"

"No, we've been on the road and the radio had nothing but public service warnings, so I turned it off."

"They nuked each other this morning. India blamed the Mumbai nuclear bombing on Pakistan and retaliated by bombing a city called Multan, and Pakistan responded by launching one of their own nukes. Everyone expects India to respond with a full-scale invasion. It's a mess. The whole world is a mess."

"That's just unbelievable," said Mateo. "Tell me, Todd, what's the best way out of here? We're trying to get to Arizona."

"*Arizona?* Well good luck with that. Conventional wisdom says stay on the freeways because those are the only areas you'll still find cops and the National Guard."

"Don't go on the back roads," said Irma. "We hear there are bandits waiting to pick off stragglers."

"Wow," said Mateo as he stroked his chin. "There aren't any good options. I wonder when the military will arrive. They have to suspend Posse Comitatus. This is too big for the police and National Guard."

"Word on the street is the military is in disarray, and there's infighting within the ranks. I believe the troops on bases are locked down for some reason. Maybe they're waiting for orders from the President. Deploying the military to shoot civilians is a last resort."

"But there's panic in the streets." said Mateo.

"I know," said Todd. "Someone told me there's about a half million military personnel on active duty here in the states who are combat trained. We have 330 million citizens. That's about one soldier to control 700 people, and many of those civilians own guns as well."

"What about the Air Force?"

"Same story. They're locked down, but what are they supposed to do, bomb the cities?"

Mateo leaned back in his chair. "Well, they have to do something."

"I think they're trying. I've heard they're moving some personnel carriers and all-purpose vehicles into the big cities. Maybe that will help."

"I sure hope so," said Mateo.

"I've told Todd we have to face up to some realities," said Irma. "There's ugliness out there, and it's been festering for a long time. You can put a soldier on every corner, but if nobody wants to obey the law, there'll be no law."

"They're not crazy; people don't have any choice," said Wanda. "It's the time changes. So many different realities, and they all leave an imprint. The subconscious mind can't decide which one is real, and it rebels. Psychosis sets in."

Todd and Irma exchanged puzzled glances and then looked at Mateo. "I'm sorry," he said, "but as I told you, she's had a rough couple days."

The conversation reached an awkward lull, but Barb the waitress picked the perfect moment to bring out their food. She placed Wanda's grilled cheese and Mateo's hamburger in front of them and set the check down on the corner of the table.

"Uh, considering the times, I like customers to pay the bill as soon as they get their food. And cash only please."

Mateo reached into his pocket and pulled out his wallet, extracting two tens and a five. "Keep the change. And Barb..."

"Yeah?"

"Thanks for not gouging us."

She smiled as she took the money and tucked it into a pocket in her uniform. "I don't like what's going on out there. We're gonna try and keep the doors open as long as the food holds out or until somebody forces us to shut down."

She walked away as Mateo and Wanda began eating. She was hungry and wolfed down her sandwich in just a few bites before digging into the cottage cheese. Mateo was more discreet and ate his burger slowly. The Harmons were also eating their food, so the need to fill the awkward spaces with conversation diminished. About fifteen minutes later, Mateo finished the last French fry on his plate.

"Well, thank you for the company, but we need to be moving on," he said while laying his napkin on the table. "It's getting late, and we've got to find gas. Any idea where we can get some?"

Todd looked around suspiciously. "Every station in town is closed even though many of them have kept gas for their own use. I only know one place, and that's a private farm outside of town. We're friends with the owners, Elmore and Doris Shraeger. If you folks want to follow me out there, we can gas up together."

"That would be great, Todd. We sure would appreciate it," said Mateo.

After saying goodbye to Barb the waitress, they left the restaurant as a foursome. The older couple got into a Ford F-150 with multiple dents and chipped paint that told a story of hard work on a farm or ranch. After Mateo pulled up behind them, they made their way east on Route-20 and took several turns before reaching Westerfield Road.

They traveled much farther than Wanda anticipated, and she experienced claustrophobia as endless rows of corn created a confining path that made it seem like they were on a straight run in a maze. The setting sun added a greyish tint to the landscape that served as a reminder that nightfall would soon be upon them.

"I don't like this, Mateo," she said. "We're getting farther away from civilization."

"You're right, Wanda," he replied, "but there isn't much I can do. We need a full tank of gas, and we're just not finding any stations that are still open."

Unexpectedly, the pickup took a hard left turn onto a dirt road that could only accommodate one vehicle at a time. As Mateo turned to follow, a cloud of dust obscured the Harmon's pickup, and the steady *thwack* of cornstalks hitting the sides of their car was unnerving. Mercifully, Wanda saw a clearing up ahead, and the Harmons turned onto a paved driveway that ran through a series of maple trees lining both sides. The trees were full, thick and mature, and they created a canopy as their branches met high over the middle of the pathway, further obscuring the natural light to the point that Mateo switched on the headlights.

Wanda figured they must have traveled at least a quarter mile before the driveway curved in front of a large two-story house, which had a huge yard full of bright green grass and a variety of colorful flowers in several long and wide beds. Coming from Arizona, where the dirt was hard and dull red, the deep black color and rich composition of the soil was fascinating. The pickup stopped in front of the house, and Mateo pulled up right behind it. They got out of their vehicles and gathered together on a circular patch of grass framed by the driveway.

"This is a beautiful house," said Wanda as she continued to stare at the bright white paint, dark green shutters and white picket fence that outlined a small yard.

"Yes, it is beautiful, especially in the summer when everything blooms," said Irma. "You'll like Doris; she's as good as they come."

Wanda didn't quite understand what Irma meant, but she nodded and smiled, figuring it was the correct thing to do. Out of the corner of her eye, she watched as Todd started up the steps to the porch.

"Okay, let's go knock," he said with a wink.

They followed him up, and he took hold of the heavy brass doorknocker and rapped it several times. When that didn't seem to work, he pushed the doorbell.

"Hold on a minute." Todd held up a finger and then hurried around the side of the house toward the four-car garage. He returned a minute later shaking his head. "All the vehicles are here, so I know they're home."

"They're probably just afraid to open the door," said Irma.

Todd looked puzzled as he rapped harder with the knocker and pushed the doorbell repeatedly. They stood outside for some time, but no one answered.

"I'm worried," said Irma. "Todd, why don't you check around back."

"I'll go with you," said Mateo as he turned to walk with Todd. They stopped as an audible click sounded from behind the door. After a second deadbolt disengaged, the door opened about six or eight inches.

A woman looked out at the foursome as her brown eyes darted back and forth.

"Irma, Todd, it's so nice to see you. What a pleasant surprise."

"Hello, Doris. Sorry we didn't call, but the cell phone service is out," said Irma. "Our two friends are traveling to Arizona, and they're in desperate need of gasoline. All the stations are closed in town. We hoped…"

Doris raised her eyebrows and sighed. "I'm sorry, Irma. This is just a bad time. We can't help you right now."

Irma looked at Mateo and Wanda and then shrugged her shoulders. "Well, okay, I guess …"

"Wait a minute." Wanda pushed past Irma and approached the front door until she was only a couple inches away from the woman inside. "Look, we were almost at ground zero in Chicago when the bomb exploded. I lost my friend and watched his hair fall out and his face slide off his skull. Three of my other friends committed suicide. I want to get back to Arizona and see if my boyfriend might still be alive. We need gas, and you have it. We'll pay you for it, but we're not leaving without a full tank."

"You don't understand," said Doris from behind the door. "Just go away and leave us alone."

"No, we won't!" yelled Wanda as she raised her hand and pushed hard on the door, ripping it from Doris' hands and sending it swinging back until the stopper hit an adjacent wall. She started forward just before noticing the man off to the left behind Doris, who was obscured by the partially closed door. He was holding a shotgun pointed at Wanda.

"Get inside, you little bitch," he said with a snarl. His hair was short and looked like he used one of those home barber clippers. Dressed in black jeans and a plaid shirt, he wore a soiled ball cap that read *NASCAR* across the front. His eyes were dark brown, and thick scar tissue created lumps under each eyebrow, which drew attention away from his crooked nose. The intruder waved the gun at Wanda menacingly, motioning her to move inside, which she did.

"The rest of you get in here too," he said. Slowly and cautiously, the others shuffled through into the house. As soon as they were all inside, the intruder slammed the door and pushed Doris back into the living room just off the entry foyer.

"Get in there. Follow her."

Wanda stopped abruptly as she tried to understand what was happening. Another man sat on the couch watching TV and eating potato chips. A third older man was on the floor, bound with nylon tie straps and multiple layers of duct tape wrapped around his head. His eyes were wide with fear and panic.

"Elmore!" said Todd, and he rushed forward to help his friend. The one giving the orders raised the butt of the rifle and brought it down hard in the middle of Todd's back, sending him sprawling to the wood floor with a loud *oomph* where he remained motionless for some time. Irma gasped and hurried toward him.

"Don't," said the intruder with authority. "Go sit down on the couch. If you want to see tomorrow, you'll do exactly what we say."

Chapter Sixteen

"Well, Senator Chawsome," said Xavier Watts as he dabbed at a corner of his mouth with a napkin, "you certainly have a dilemma, don't you? When you lose the public's confidence, you've lost the ability to govern, wouldn't you agree?"

Senator Merl Chawsome was lost in thought as he looked outside at the colorful sign identifying *La Siere*. Decades ago, the famous French restaurant was regarded as one of the finest eateries in the downtown quarter of Detroit. Located about two blocks from the Renaissance Center, or the "Gehenna Center" as they now called it, La Siere was once a gathering place for Detroit's cultural elite.

Over time, numerous recessions, foreign auto manufacturers and self-driving cars eventually wore down a once proud city and brought it to its knees, including the famed culinary landmark. When the people in Detroit were trying to scrape together enough money to buy a hotdog, there wasn't much of a clientele for an expensive five-star French restaurant.

However, all of that changed when the Gehenna Group moved in. Out of nowhere, this small, privately owned corporation from some obscure rural town in Arizona began their occupation of Detroit. While free of scrutiny, the company engaged in a rapid series of mergers and acquisitions preceding their emergence onto the world stage. While abject poverty remained entrenched, fewer people died of starvation, disease and crime once Gehenna expanded into the city and began rebuilding certain parts of it. They even brought back the beloved La Siere.

Naturally, the uncertainty and fear that gripped the nation following the nuclear detonations in Turkey and India only helped Gehenna accelerate its activities as they worked through the HUGE conglomerate to pick up solid companies at rock-bottom prices. The recent Chicago detonation brought a deluge of business from CEOs willing to sell out of panicked desperation. Pennies on the dollar was almost too generous a description.

Normally, such unusual business activity would result in a slew of local, state and federal investigations, no matter that Gehenna was privately held. However, these were far from normal times, and the government was under a severe strain as it tried to maintain control over a populous that was nearing mass hysteria. Still, the emerging visibility of Gehenna and HUGE across a variety of landscapes attracted the attention of the Senator from Michigan.

"Yes, Mr. Watts, everyone faces enormous challenges... that is, everyone but you and your company. You're thriving, and I guess that's why I'm here, I—we would like to find out why."

The Senator reached down into his attaché case and pulled out a folder just as the waiter arrived. "Gentlemen, will there be anything else? Dessert perhaps? Can I clear these plates out of your way?"

"No dessert for me. Senator?"

"No, I'm fine thank you."

"I think we're finished eating. If you could just take away the plates."

"Of course, Mr. Watts." The waiter motioned for a busboy to help him clear the table, and he used a table crumber to remove any remaining debris.

"Thank you, gentlemen, and have a wonderful day." The waiter bowed deeply before leaving.

"The bill, Mr. Watts. Please, let me pay," said Chawsome as he reached for his wallet.

"Nonsense, Senator. When you're in Detroit, you're my guest."

"Ah, yes, well thank you." Chawsome took the folder he held on his lap and brought it to the table. "This is a classified report on your company, Mr. Watts. The National Security Agency compiled it. You probably know it as the NSA."

"I see. And what does the report reveal?"

"Almost nothing, and that's the problem. It appears you have global operations set up throughout the entire world. Your company, through the so-called 'HUGE conglomerate,' is devouring large corporations and smaller companies at an astonishing rate. It's difficult to understand how you could establish such a sophisticated global network in such a short time."

"How do you know it's been a short time, Senator? Has the United States participated in the growth and prosperity of Bhutan? We've been there for years helping the King develop a hydroelectric program that now comprises one-fifth of Bhutan's economy. What about Malawi or Tonga? Where has the United States been while we've been feeding people and creating peace?"

"There are 200 countries in the world, Mr. Watts. How many have Gehenna Group or HUGE offices in them?"

"To be exact, there are 197 countries if you count Taiwan. We are in 197 countries."

"China?"

"Of course."

"Iran?"

"I said all 197, Senator."

Chawsome did his best to hide obvious alarm. "What are your aims and goals, Mr. Watts?"

Watts shrugged and took his napkin from his lap and laid it carefully on the table. "We want to unite people, Senator. You must admit, the world needs that right now."

Chawsome paused and rubbed his jaw. "The bombs, Mr. Watts. I'm told by many that you have a relationship with those responsible for detonating the nuclear devices. Is that true?"

"We don't have a direct relationship if that's what you mean. Intermediaries do that for us. We only want to convey their intentions to protect the innocent."

"I see. And what are you hearing from your 'intermediaries'?"

Watts paused and seemed to carefully consider his answer. "Those responsible for the bombings hope to avoid detonating a fourth bomb, but apparently, several others are already in place."

"What is it you, uh, they, want, Mr. Watts?"

"Like most terrorist groups, they ultimately want peace, but they don't believe the world's major governments can achieve that. They want the world's leaders to step down."

The Senator chuckled and shook his head. He lifted his second dry martini and sipped the last of it. "Impossible and absurd. What would take its place?"

"I don't know, Senator. I'm only relaying what they have told me. Don't kill the messenger."

" … Who is the 'Benefactor', Mr. Watts?"

For just a moment, Watts' calm demeanor evaporated, and he appeared slightly unsettled. "I don't know who that is," he said after quickly regaining his composure. "Perhaps you can tell me."

"We don't know either," said the Senator as he shook his head and pursed his lips. "But that name comes up several times in the report. Never from anyone in government, mind you, but often from peasants and ordinary citizens in the countries where your company operates. They are terrified of this person, and it puzzles me."

"I wish I could help," said Watts with a smile and a small shrug.

Chawsome leaned in, and the tone of his voice went cold. "I'll get to the point, Mr. Watts. Some of us on Capitol Hill are very concerned about your company. In fact, I'm troubled enough to convene the Senate Intelligence Committee to look into your activities."

Watts' expression hardened, but the smile never left his lips. "That would be a terrible mistake, Senator. First, I'm not sure you could muster the resources to launch an investigation. Look around yourself. Angry mobs camp outside the Capitol building every day. Do you want to see those crowds grow bigger and more violent?"

"Are you threatening a United States Senator, Mr. Watts?"

"No," said Watts in a casual tone, "but I'm trying to give you an opportunity to see the folly of such an endeavor. The mobs won't go anywhere, and an investigation will only make things more—difficult for you and the government. Your time has passed, and with all due respect, you couldn't be so dull-witted that you've missed what's been happening for the last fifty years. The slow but steady erosion of your constituent's respect for their government. They don't care about you, Senator Chawsome. You're irrelevant."

The Senator's eyes narrowed, and he spoke through clenched teeth. "When you're visited by the FBI and indicted by the Justice Department, we'll see how irrelevant I've become."

Watts took his cell phone from his pocket and pressed a single key. He looked at the phone, and when he saw it connected, he said, "It's on." He put the phone away and rose from the table. "Senator, follow me, please. This will only take a second."

Watts walked toward a set of doors in the back of the restaurant that emptied onto a second-floor balcony. They stepped out into the sunshine but remained shaded by a canopy that covered most of the tables. The weather in Detroit was pleasant with a temperature in the low eighties accompanied by tolerable humidity. Wealthy customers sat outside and enjoyed outrageously expensive lunches and cocktails.

"Isn't it strange," said Watts as he looked over the balcony railing. "Look at those two floaters fighting over there." He pointed at two men in the back of an alley wrestling on the ground and throwing punches. "And at the end of the street; look at that guy defecating in the sewer feed." He paused for a moment and laughed. "And yet, here are these one-percenters sipping their twenty-dollar martinis and mai tais while trying to hold on to some vestige of their fading privileged lives."

"Why did you call me out here, Watts?" asked Senator Chawsome.

Watts looked down at his Cartier Rotonde. "Any second now… There, to the west." A small dot in the western sky grew in size and intensity as it approached. The swept wing F-35 descended as it moved closer, adjusting altitude and vector in a way that made it seem like the jet was on a collision course with a nearby building.

The rumbling grew louder until the glasses began to vibrate and the tables started to shake. The patrons stopped talking and looked up in the sky with concern as the noise level continued to rise.

"What's the meaning of this, Watts? What do you think you're doing?" The Senator raised his voice to be heard.

Watts only pointed to the jet again as it dipped even lower. Customers screamed and ran back inside the building. Traveling only a thousand feet off the ground, the fighter unleashed an AGM-170 hypersonic cruise missile that shrieked with Mach 10 energy until it slammed into a four-story office complex about five blocks away from the restaurant. An explosion shattered the windows of several nearby buildings and sent deadly debris flying in every direction. A fireball rose from the blast with such intensity the heat caused Senator Chawsome to shield his face with his hands.

The jet roared past the restaurant and streaked straight up in the afternoon sky, disappearing long before the roar of the engines dissipated. Chawsome stood panting like someone who just survived a murder attempt.

"You're insane!" he muttered.

"Senator, you and your cronies no longer control the military, do you understand? We are so much stronger than you could ever imagine. You start investigations and hearings, and I swear an F-35 will fire a missile into your house. Are we clear?"

The Senator nodded almost imperceptibly.

"Good, now let's move away from here. I think we're ruining the patron's enjoyment with our commotion."

Senator Chawsome walked woodenly back into the restaurant just as the people inside were coming out to watch the fire and smoke from the explosion. No one realized a U.S. fighter jet launched the missile, and the speculation and rumors bubbled up just as the sound of a fire department vehicle signaled its approach. Fortunately, pressure in the hydrants near the Gehenna Center was still over ninety percent of normal.

They descended the flight of stairs just as the Senator's single security escort was coming up. He looked relieved when he saw Chawsome was unharmed.

"Senator, are you alright? I have the car parked outside."

"Yes, yes Darryl, I'm fine. Please wait outside. I need to speak with Mr. Watts."

The bodyguard nodded and walked ahead of them until they reached the lounge on the ground floor. The Senator stepped into a short hallway that led to the coat rack room with Watts following. Once they were out of earshot, Chawsome looked at Watts as his jaw clenched tight.

"I wonder how many people died in that stunt of yours?"

Watts stroked his chin as he thought. "I don't know for sure. I imagine only a few. The building was old and scuttled from what I understand."

"What the hell are you trying to prove?"

Watts moved forward and grabbed the Senator by the lapels and shoved him against the wall. He leaned in so their faces were only a few inches apart. "I'll tell you what I'm trying to prove," he sneered. "Don't you dare fuck with us. We've worked for decades to infiltrate every facet of society, including the government. We *are* the deep state, and you have no clue how loyal and zealous our followers are. If you or anyone else tries to stop us, this demonstration will be nothing compared to what will happen."

"You're—you're threatening me!"

"Yes I am. This is a battle you can't win. I expect you to resign within the week. Go play with your grandchildren, and live out your life. We'll leave you alone if you do. But if you cross us, you won't live long enough to regret it. The choice is yours."

"Who *are* you people?"

Watts backed away, brushed off the shoulder of the Senator's suit coat and straightened his lapel. "Why Senator, we're just a company trying to be a responsible corporate citizen."

The personnel transport opered amid much gunfire, shouting and confusion. Muslim leader Caliph Naasar Gauhar ordered his troops to storm the western shores of the Bosporus River in Istanbul and attack the entrenched crusaders under Cardinal Anastasio Girodano.

The Cardinal rose from a bunker and faced the fast-approaching Middle Eastern horde. His eyes blazed with hatred and contempt for his enemies. He reached for a communication device that connected him with his generals. "The tenth Crusade has begun," he said. "Order a full-on attack. The day of our salvation is at hand." Girodono looked back at his impressive collection of troops. Religious zealots to a man, they foamed and frothed in anticipation of the bloodlust. Organizing the ten-thousand-man force had proven surprisingly easy. Religious hatred had been building for decades, and the evangelists were eager to join the Crusade as it provided a convenient way to satiate their growing need for violence.

From a hilltop less than a mile away from the battlefield, Mr. Cox set a picnic basket on a checkered blanket under a scorched, dead tree. Fortunately, it was an overcast day as the dust from the recent nuclear blast still hung in the air. The temperature was seventy-eight degrees without much humidity, but Cox didn't remove the red crushed velvet jacket that covered his white shirt. He sat down on the blanket and turned toward the unfolding battle below.

"Come sit my dear," he said while gesturing to the young woman standing near the tree. She wore a dazed expression and looked awkwardly at the ground. After continued coaxing, she walked slowly over to the

blanket and sat on the farthest edge, out of Mr. Cox'
reach.

"Look down there; the armies are ready to
engage each other. The time for battle is at hand.
Watch closely, my sweet. There's nothing more
vicious and barbaric than a religious conflict. Unlike
trained soldiers, these combatants don't kill with
lethal efficiency, so the fighting is crude and brutal."

"I don't know if I should be here," the girl
mumbled. "I'm supposed to be at work."

"Nonsense. I'm the boss, and I've given you the
day off, Sandra."

"I'm not sure…"

"Not sure of what? You were flirting with me
when I walked by your station on my way to Mr.
Watts' office, remember? You're not a little tease, are
you, Sandra? A girl that's willing to flaunt it should
expect the attention she asked for, am I right?"

"I — I was just trying to be nice… I think I want to
go home, sir."

"And spoil such a nice day. No, you'll come
closer — now."

She looked at his eyes and her expression
changed to one of fear and terror. Inching over
slowly, Mr. Cox reached out and pulled her close.
He grabbed her head with both hands and forced
her to look at the battle below, which was now
unfolding in all its splendid death and gore.

The bloodthirsty screams of the combatants
drifted up from the front lines, sounding like sweet
music to his ears. Within minutes, blood, limbs and
entrails covered the ground as dazed and wounded
warriors wandered like zombies, paralyzed by
shock and deep despair. The buzzards gathered on

the blackened limbs of dead trees in anticipation of the coming feast.

Mr. Cox pulled out sandwiches, potato salad and a fine merlot that he poured into plastic cups. "To us, and our first date," he said while smiling. He gulped at the wine and scowled at his new girlfriend while encouraging her to drink, which she did with some hesitation.

Down below, Cardinal Girodano emerged from his armored HMMWV, using field glasses to survey the landscape. As the fight continued to rage, a kind of stalemate spread across the battleground. The body count was rising, but neither side could gain the upper hand. From across the front lines, the Muslim leader, Caliph Naasar Gauhar, poked his head out of his MRAP, and brought a set of binoculars up to his eyes. From a distance, the two leaders located each other simultaneously. They shook their fists and exchanged verbal insults, but the shrieking of the wounded and sounds of clashing metal drowned them out.

Enraged, the Cardinal retreated to the interior of his armored vehicle. It lurched forward with a puff of smoke and headed toward Gauhar's MRAP. The Caliph ducked down into his fighting machine, and the treads churned as the engine whined under the strain of acceleration. From Mr. Cox' vantage point, the two religious leaders were on a collision course.

"Come close my dear," said the Benefactor as he grabbed the girl's arm and pulled her near him. He pawed at her breasts and pulled at her blouse.

"Benefactor, please," she pleaded. "I'm not—worldly in that way."

He smiled the smile of a lecherous man. "You soon will be. Now, disrobe."

She looked into his eyes, which smoldered and grew dark as burning coals. He sent streams of fetid energy that pierced her mind like a hot poker running through butter. The intrusive force burrowed past her weak mental defenses and tore down her resistance. She needed no further encouragement and began unbuttoning her blouse.

The two ground combat vehicles roared across the hard, scorched earth on the western side of the Bosporus in a classic game of chicken. Engines whined as the rotating treads pulled each of the moving armored fortresses over an endless collection of dead and wounded bodies, shredding raw flesh amid intermittent sprays of blood, pus, bile and other gore.

In the same manner as before, Mr. Cox planted a suggestion in Watts' executive assistant's mind, and she unbuckled his belt after removing her skirt. As they faced each other half-naked, he smirked and said, "I don't want you to report me to human resources, Sandra. I have your consent, to proceed, do I not?"

She starred into his fiery red eyes and nodded slowly. Mr. Cox laughed as he climbed on top of her while watching a man on the battlefield cackle insanely and gnaw at his own bloody intestines.

"Yes, yes, that's it," he said as he pried open her legs and roughly inserted himself. He pushed and pushed again, enjoying the anguish in her voice. She cried out as he bit hard into her shoulder and increased the pace of his thrusts just as the two vehicles slammed into each other head on. The sound was deafening. Steel twisted and warped while fluids and various engine parts hurtled out of the blast zone with extreme velocity. The damping and anti-explosive materials used to build military transports helped avoid an explosion and fire, but even with layers of forged iron protection, a massive pile of rubber and metal lay crumpled and smoldering.

Mr. Cox panted, stiffened and then released inside her. After some moments, he rolled off and lay on his back while she cried openly. A trickle of blood ran down her shoulder and discolored the plaid blanket. Bruises formed quickly on her breasts and other areas of her torso where Mr. Cox handled her roughly.

An eerie silence enveloped the battlefield, amid the wreckage of the vehicles. After some minutes, the creaking sound of a metal hinge cut through the stillness. A wisp of smoke escaped the interior of the armored Pit Bull as the personnel hatch opened. A blackened hand appeared first, followed by the head and torso of the driver as he climbed out unsteadily. Standing on top of the flaming rubble, a bloody and bruised Caliph Gauhar surveyed the scene on wobbly legs.

Because of the smoke, confusion and raucous cheering from the Muslim troops, the other vehicle's hatch opened unnoticed. Cardinal Girodano emerged to a deafening roar from the Christians, who raised the loud cacophony to feverish levels.

Girodano and Gauhar glared at one another from atop the fiery wreckage as a deathly silence again fell over the battlefield.

With a primal scream that pierced the unnerving calm, Giordano leapt across the charred metal as Gauhar sprinted to meet him. They slammed into each other amid growls, grunts, cursing and muttering, and their momentum carried them off the rubble and onto the hard ground. This served as a signal to the rest of the combatants, and the battlefield erupted into an even greater level of chaos and violence.

Mr. Cox stood up and walked to the edge of the hillside and looked down at the carnage below. Sandra was sitting up, trying to cover her breasts with her blouse, shaking and whimpering uncontrollably. Without turning back, he smiled and said, "What a wonderful first date, wouldn't you agree, Sandra?"

Chapter Seventeen

The sound of the commotion reverberated through the hallway, and all the occupied rooms in the wing opened as the overseers spilled out to find the source of the disturbance. When they reached Zach's room, the door was still open, but the scene unfolding in front of them caused everyone to stop at the threshold.

Marshall remained motionless, the bloody knife still wrapped tightly in his hand. His eyes darted back and forth in a fight or flight panic mode. Sarah came into the room and put her arm around his shoulders and tried to soothe him, but Marshall isolated himself mentally and emotionally.

Zach squatted down and held out his hand. "Marshall, look at me. Please give me the knife."

"Hey, he's got a knife," repeated Jacques as he pointed at Marshall.

"My God, look at all the blood," said Aminah, who covered her face with her hands.

"Don't you contaminate the evidence," said Jacques. "There are fingerprints and DNA on that knife we'll have to give to the police."

"But there won't be any police, Mr. Franco." The voice from behind the group was Pena's. "But you already know that, don't you?"

"What are you talking about? The man is holding a murder weapon." Jacques looked at Pena with incredulity.

"There was no body in the hallway," said Zach. "You have no idea if someone was murdered."

"I don't care," said Jacques. "We should still notify the police."

Pena walked into the room shaking his head. "The police wouldn't arrive here for days, weeks or maybe not at all, Mr. Franco. Obviously, you have not been watching your television or using your computer. In almost every jurisdiction, the police can't maintain order. Many departments have disbanded over personnel safety concerns. Every lawman from the Sedona police department is in Phoenix trying to help the local authorities quell the violence. Who would we file a report with when a crime may not have even been committed?"

"That's absurd." Jacques could hardly control his rage. "I insist on trying to call the local police."

"Again, I am sorry. Even if the local department was active, we can't risk revealing our location. A police report would create a paper trail that might lead the time traveling assassins right to us."

"If that story is even true," muttered Jacques.

They remained silent for a moment before Sasha stood up. "Well, none of this seems right; I know we all can sense it. I believe we have a murderer in our midst."

"It's him, obviously," replied Jacques while pointing a finger at Marshall. "He has a bloody knife in his hand for God's sake. Wake up!"

Marshall looked at Zach and pleaded. "It wasn't me. I didn't do anything." Almost as though he suddenly realized he was still holding the knife, he looked down and recoiled, tossing the weapon away as though it was toxic. It skittered across the tiled floor and landed at the feet of Pena.

"No," said Jacques as he watched Pena reach down and pick up the knife. "You're contaminating the evidence."

Pena pulled out a white handkerchief and carefully wrapped the table knife in it. "For you, Mr. Franco. In case we need the authorities... If they even exist anymore." Looking back at the group, he continued, "Let us return to our quarters and try to sleep. I'll post a monitor inside the hallway for your security."

"Wait a minute," said Rogelio as he stepped forward after looking down the hallway. "Where is Liu?" Everyone turned in different directions as though Liu could have somehow gotten lost in the hallway. Rogelio walked down to Liu's room and twisted the handle, but it was locked. He rapped several times, but no one answered.

"Pena, come over here and open his door," demanded Rogelio.

Pena nodded, and everyone except Marshall, Zach and Sarah gathered at Liu's suite. The caretaker reached inside his jacket and pulled out his universal room key and slid the strip through the reader, which caused the door mechanism to click open. Jacques and Rogelio aggressively pushed past Pena and walked inside the room with the rest of the group following. A hasty

211

search ensued through the bedroom, bathroom and closets, but Liu was nowhere to be found.

"He's not here," said Jacques. "He's not here at all."

Rogelio continued rifling through the closet. "Well, he *was* here. He left the clothes he wore earlier today."

"But he didn't change into nightclothes," Jacques called out. "Everything on the bed is still folded and undisturbed."

Sasha sat down in one of the chairs in the parlor. "I'm really worried," she said. "Where is he? And why did Marshall have a bloody knife?"

"I don't know, but I want answers," said Jacques. He left the scene and walked back to Zach's room, pounding on the door with urgency. When it opened, Zach stood in the threshold, blocking the view from behind.

"What do you want now?"

"I want to talk to him, Speaker Randall. We have to find out what he did to Liu."

"Marshall said he did nothing wrong. He didn't even see Liu tonight."

"I—we'd like to talk to him."

"And we want to search his room," said Rogelio from behind. The doorway was now crowded with overseers, and they pressed against Zach ever so slightly, but he gave no ground.

"He doesn't want to see anyone right now, Jacques. I'm sure you can understand that he's pretty upset."

"Yes, well, so are we. We want answers, and we need to question him." Several overseers voiced their agreement.

"No one is going to talk to Marshall until tomorrow," said Zach. "When he's ready, I'll speak to him, and as soon as I know anything, I'll call everyone together."

Based on the grumbling and angry crosstalk, it was clear the other overseers weren't satisfied with Zach's answer. "That's not acceptable," Jacques said on behalf of the group. "Marshall needs to explain himself right now."

Zach and Jacques stared at each other for some moments. The crush of people behind him pushed Jacques even closer to Zach so their chests were touching.

"I have given you my final word, and I speak for the group. Are you challenging my authority, Jacques?"

A short moment stretched into an eternity as a standoff ensued. Without warning, a single searing coil of aggressive mental energy targeted Zach, and he braced for the assault. Even if he didn't have the capacity to immobilize it, he doubted it would have done much damage. However, the extraordinary disrespect associated with the act had to be dealt with. Whoever it was hid within the anonymity of the group, so it was impossible for Zach to know exactly where it originated.

"You dishonor the Speaker by initiating an attack?" he said to the overseers at large. "Will the perpetrator at least have the courage to step out and issue a challenge?" No one said a word as an old grandfather clock ticked methodically in the hallway.

"Then I suggest you all back up before we find ourselves in an unprecedented conflict." Zach looked hard at Jacques and the rest of the transcendents. The forward pressure lessened, and Jacques backed away, creating space and easing the building tension.

"We will give you time to reason with him, Speaker," said Jacques, "but do not test our patience. We were a unified group before you arrived. One mind and one shared experience. Now we are fractured and isolated."

Zach nodded. "Perhaps. This is a dire situation, and no one could have anticipated the death of Speaker Anston. Still, he confirmed that I was to be the new Speaker before he died, and you all will respect that, do you understand?"

There was much muttering and feet shuffling. From the back came a weak voice. "I understand, Speaker Randall, and I humbly apologize for these deleterious actions and negative energy." Sasha turned and walked slowly towards her room. Aminah followed, and Yasin left shortly thereafter, which left only Jacques and Rogelio standing at the door.

"We will leave, Speaker," said Jacques, "but we'll expect to question Marshall tomorrow morning."

"We shall see." Zach stared hard at Jacques until he turned away.

"As for you," said Jacques to Pena. "We should start searching for Liu immediately. You will provide maps so we can explore all the potential places someone might hold him captive or hide his body. Let us get started immediately."

Pena shook his head. "That is impractical right now. You would only get in the way. Tomorrow, if my people haven't found him by then, we will allow you to help us in our search efforts."

"Unacceptable," said Jacques. "We should start searching for him right now."

"Yes," added Rogelio, "time is of the essence."

"You do not seem to understand," said Pena, "the search is already underway. As soon as we find something, we will report it to you."

Jacques pursed his lips and said, "Fine, I'll search for Liu myself." He pushed past Pena and walked toward the foyer. However, when he reached the end of the hallway, two men stepped out from the shadows and effectively blocked his exit.

Jacques turned back and glared at Pena. "What is the meaning of this? I want to search for Liu, and no one will stop me."

Pena raised his arms with palms stretched outward and shrugged. "I'm sorry, Mr. Franco. We can't allow it at this moment. You are unfamiliar with the facility, and you might inadvertently harm yourself. My two associates, Mr. Cheeves and Mr. Docker, will monitor this wing tonight. You can rest comfortably knowing you will be safe in your room."

"Perhaps you didn't hear me, Pena, I'm not asking. I intend to search for Liu right now."

Pena turned to Zach. "Speaker Randall, I ask you to intervene. I suspect Mr. Franco is preparing to influence my attendants telepathically. It is imperative we maintain order in the facility. We cannot have overseers instigating their own investigations. Our staff will handle this situation."

Zach nodded and turned to Jacques. "Pena makes sense to me. We haven't been here a full day, and we're unfamiliar with this enormous facility. We can't risk serious injury with such important business at hand."

Jacques stared at Zach without speaking. His eyes were wide, and he clenched and unclenched his fists as his jaw muscles tightened. For a brief moment, Zach wondered if a telepathic confrontation would break out, but the sensation passed quickly. Jacques snarled in frustration and stormed back to his room. He swiped his key card and slammed the door once he was inside.

Rogelio turned to Zach, but his demeanor was less confrontational. "Speaker Randall, I suggest we keep Marshall under surveillance tonight. I don't think it's wise to let him roam free under the circumstances."

"Yes, Rogelio, I understand and agree. He'll stay with me tonight, and we'll sort all this out in the morning."

"The sofa folds out, Speaker Randall," said Pena as he walked into the room and pointed at the couch. "I regret the inconvenience, Mr. Beiner. Should you have difficulty sleeping, please use the intercom to call an attendant." Marshall remained seated with his head hung low, but he nodded in acknowledgment.

Zach continued to stand in the doorway until Rogelio walked back to his room. Once they were alone, he turned to Pena.

"Something doesn't feel right about this place. The energy seems—compromised, but I can't trace the source. It shouldn't be this way in a location that's supposedly the epicenter for spiritual convergence."

"I understand," said Pena. "Frankly, I've noticed it too ever since your group arrived. We should be experiencing the antithesis of depression. It's as though someone has added a cup of spoiled milk to the batter. The sensation is sour."

Zach nodded. "Exactly. I am new to the Society, and I understand some of it might stem from the resentment to my leadership. Yet, it appears the antipathy has reached a near mutinous level. Such acts of defiance would have been unimaginable before today."

"It must be the traitor. It's the only explanation."

"Perhaps. If that's so, then finding him or her is our most pressing task, especially if Liu fails to show up unharmed. Where do you think he went?

"I do not know," said Pena while shaking his head. "I avoided saying this in front of your group, but there are areas in the facility that even I am unfamiliar with. It has a mysterious labyrinth of tunnels and rooms. Someone could stumble into an unexplored area and never return."

"Are you sure he didn't leave the facility?"

"It would be very unlikely. We have a sophisticated security system. If he tried to leave without a coded pass card, it would have tripped an alarm."

"What if one of your staff helped him? He could have manipulated someone into giving them their pass key."

"Every entry and exit is tightly controlled. Using a pass card leaves a data trail. I will check the log for an unauthorized exit. No one can leave the facility except to pick up supplies, and even that is rare. We are very self-sufficient. In any event, no unauthorized exits are allowed at night."

"Well, I suppose there's nothing more that can be done right now," said Zach. "What's tomorrow's itinerary?"

"We will meet in the dining hall for breakfast at seven a.m. A tour was planned, but now it appears it will be a search and rescue operation."

"Yes, regrettably, I agree. Goodnight, Pena."

"Goodnight, Speaker Randall.

Zach closed the door and walked over to Marshall, who had already removed the cushions from the sofa and pulled out the bed. He was underneath the covers still fully clothed. Sarah pulled up a chair next to him and gently stroked his hair.

"Marshall, can you tell me exactly what happened?"

Without shifting position or opening his eyes, Marshall said, "There isn't much to tell you. I was in the bathroom, ah, relieving myself," he nodded at the restroom. "Someone knocked on the door, so I answered it as soon as I could, but there was no one there."

"How long did it take you to answer?"

Marshall pondered the question a moment. "I'm not sure, since I was just finishing using the bathroom. Maybe ten seconds, I suppose."

"Marshall's room is down at the very end of the hallway. I doubt whoever dropped the knife could have made it out to the foyer before he opened the door."

"What are you getting at, Zach?" asked Sarah.

"I don't think whoever left the knife ran away. I think they went into one of the nearby rooms."

218

"My God," she said, "so you think it was someone from the Society?"

"It would seem that way, wouldn't it?" Turning his attention back to Marshall, he continued, "So, you looked down the hallway and didn't see anyone. Then what happened?"

"I glanced at the floor and saw the knife, and for some reason, I picked it up. I knew it was coated with fresh blood, but I was in such a panic. Blackness started closing in, and I thought I would faint. I don't know what I was thinking. Maybe if I just picked it up everything would go away. But then I started hyperventilating…"

"Is that when you came to my door?"

"Yes."

"Marshall, do you have any idea where Liu Wei is?"

"No, I swear I don't." Marshall pulled the covers over his head.

Zach looked at Sarah and said, "Well, we can't do anything tonight. Let's all try to go to sleep, and we'll deal with this in the morning."

"Zach, I…"

"It's alright, Sarah," said Zach with a smile. "You can stay here tonight. I think it will help Marshall to be among his friends."

***

Zach woke to a soothing symphony of birds chirping within the backdrop of a gentle running stream. The sound machine transmitted wavelengths designed to stimulate the hypothalamus and promote rejuvenation and serenity. When his eyes fluttered open, he was startled to see Marshall fully dressed and sitting in a chair opposite the bed. How long he sat and stared blankly at Zach and Sarah was anyone's guess.

"Marshall, how — how long have you been up?"

"Since one a.m. I showered and dressed at two a.m., and I've been sitting here ever since."

"Wha — what's going on?" Sarah sat up, stretched and rubbed the sleep from her eyes. The pajamas clung tightly, which highlighted her supple curves. Her left breast peeked out of her nightshirt as her body moved up while the fabric remained stationary. Zach was surprised and embarrassed at his partial arousal. He found an excuse to remain in bed for several minutes.

Sarah returned to her own room to shower, which meant Zach had the bathroom to himself. The experience was similar to a five-star resort, with all the exotic soaps, lotions and shampoos. The towels were thick and pliant, and it felt like he was drying himself with a pillow top. Once he finished grooming, he stepped into a set of boxer briefs, (the exact brand and style he preferred) and dressed in a pair of jeans and a blue t-shirt.

He walked out of the bedroom to find Marshall sitting at the table, a tablet computer in his hand. He was typing furiously and recording results in a spiral notebook.

"C'mon, Marshall, we should leave." Marshall powered down the tablet and they walked out into the hallway and knocked on Sarah's door. She was already waiting and gave Zach a peck on the cheek and patted Marshall's arm reassuringly. Together, they went to the dining hall and found the same seats they occupied last night. Over the next five minutes, the other overseers came in one at a time. When Rogelio arrived, the gathering was complete except for Liu Wei.

Pena walked in after everyone assembled. He appeared haggard, and his brow furrowed with a look of great concern. "I wish I had good news," he said, "but the efforts to locate Liu have been unsuccessful so far. We will eat breakfast and begin the tour as planned. Hopefully, our efforts, and the efforts of the staff, will help us find him in good health."

Zach looked around the table. Based on their expressions, Pena's explanation satisfied no one.

Chapter Eighteen

"Why are you doing this to us?" asked Wanda as she looked at the duct tape wrapped around the hands, feet and mouths of Mateo and Todd. They sat together wedged between a sofa and Elmore, who was bound and gagged in a corner of the living room.

"Shut up," said the intruder, whose face looked like he spent a fair amount of time in a boxing or MMA ring. "You want out? Persuade ol' Elmore here to tell us where he's hid the gold."

Elmore strained against the duct tape that covered his mouth, but all he could do is grunt.

"Hey, you ladies hurry up in that kitchen. Jason n' me is gettin' hungry," said the man on the couch who wore a pair of faded blue jeans, red t-shirt and a ball cap that said *Caterpillar* across the front.

"Goddamn it, you used my name," said the one with the scar tissue, who went by the name of Jason.

"So what? They're not gonna do nuthin'. You know as well as I do the police ain't gonna come way out here, anyway."

Two old west swinging saloon doors divided the breakfast nook and kitchen in the spacious farmhouse. Doris backed through them while carrying a large platter of fresh chicken she and the other women had prepared after killing one of the birds in the pen.

"Here's your fried chicken," she said tersely as she set the serving plate on the breakfast table in the nook. "Irma's bringing the mashed potatoes, and Wanda's got the biscuits."

"Fine," said scar-tissue Jason. "You better not of ate any either. I'll taste it on your breath."

"Don't worry," said Doris. "I won't eat as long as my husband doesn't eat."

"Hot damn," said the intruder in the Caterpillar hat as he popped off the couch and rubbed his hands together. "C'mon Jason, let's eat."

"Son of a bitch, Toby, I told you to quit using my real name."

"Yeah, and you just used mine, so I guess we're even, dumb ass."

They walked up to the table and grabbed a plate, piling the chicken and potatoes high and grabbing two biscuits each.

"Hey, bitch... yeah you," said Toby as he gestured to Wanda. "Butter my biscuits. Then, maybe I'll butter yours." He raised and lowered his eyebrows at Wanda several times, unaware she didn't understand his innuendo. She walked over, took the biscuits and smeared each with butter before returning them without replying.

The men took their food into the living room and set the plates on the coffee table while reclining on the sofa and watching the big screen TV. Toby walked over to the liquor cabinet and pulled out a bottle of sour mash bourbon. They already drank the Jack Daniels the night before.

"So, Elmore," said scar-tissue Jason between bites of chicken. "Almost two whole days without food or water. The food part you can do without, but no water? I'll bet you don't make it through tomorrow."

"Please," said Doris from the other room, "give him some water. I'm at the end of my rope, I can't take it anymore." Her voice cracked as she spoke.

Jason looked over at her and sneered. "You want him to have some water, Doris? Then get your fat ass over here." She shook her head and bit down on the knuckle of her forefinger.

"No? That's fine. We'll just leave him sit then. I told you two up front what we wanted. And now I'm raising the demand. We want the gold and all three women."

Doris turned to Irma, her face puffy from crying. "No," she whispered. "Please, please, no."

Irma took both of Doris's hands in her own. "Elmore needs some water, Doris. He's not a young man anymore, and we're in survival mode here. Do what you have to do to survive—to help Elmore survive."

"Hey, old hag. I said get your ugly ass in here if you want to give that old man water. I'd do it if I were you cause he's not lookin' too good." Toby laughed at his own wit.

Reluctantly, Doris pulled away from Irma and walked into the living room. She stopped in front of Toby with her head down and her hands crossed in front of her.

"Well, now that's better, honey. Sit down here next to ol' Toby. I'll pour you a lil drink." Toby grabbed a glass he used yesterday, licked the rim, and poured a generous portion of bourbon into it. "Here, sit down," he said and patted the seat next to him. Doris moved to the couch and sat down on the edge. She was careful to maintain a respectable distance.

Toby would have none of it. "Come closer, honey. You know you like the younger fellas, ya old broad." He reached out and drew her close. "C'mon, give Toby a lil kiss." She shuddered and resisted, which seemed to anger him. He scowled and used his strength to pull her close and licked the side of her face. "Here, drink this. You need to loosen up," he said while bringing the glass of bourbon up to her lips. He tipped it at such an angle that it caused her to gurgle, choke and gulp as the sour mash spilled out the sides of her mouth and ran down her face.

As soon as he was sure she swallowed most of it, he put the glass down and kissed her hard on the lips. She drew back and let out a short shriek. Toby's eyes grew dark as he watched her wipe his kiss off her lips, and he reached over and slapped her hard across the cheek. Elmore fought against his restraints and squealed like a wounded javelina.

"You do that again, and he's dead," said Toby while motioning to Elmore. "Now, come closer, and you better not purse your lips. He leaned over, and this time Doris didn't flinch as they kissed. Toby was an extremely unattractive man with a bulbous nose and eyes set much too far apart. For someone in his mid-thirties, his sexual experience was very limited, so even this sedate country woman in her sixties would do.

225

They continued to kiss, and he started to massage her breasts through her blouse. She recoiled but recovered in time to avoid another blow. He reached out and took her hand and placed it on his groin area, and now it was his turn to shudder. With her hand under his, he moved it slowly over his manhood. She grimaced and pulled away, but he repeated the lesson, and when he removed his hand this time, she continued the motion.

After some time, his hand inched up her skirt, and she drew back in horror. "No," she said firmly. "Nothing more until Elmore gets water and food."

Toby rolled his eyes and snarled. "All right, all right," he said as he stood up and walked over to Elmore, ripping the duct tape from the older man's face.

Tears were flowing freely down Elmore's cheeks, and he shook with rage. "You dirty bastard," he said. "I'll kill you, you dirty bastard."

"Aw, shut the fuck up, Elmore." Toby turned toward Doris. "Go get him some water and a piece of chicken. And be quick about it." Scar-tissue Jason looked away from the TV. He hardly noticed what was happening with Toby and Doris as he immersed himself in an old rerun of *Breaking Bad*. After pausing the show, he yelled, "Hey Doris, tell the other two to come out here."

Inside the kitchen, Irma and Wanda talked quietly.

"They took all the cutlery. Even the knife Doris used to cut the chicken," said Irma.

"Well, there must be some kind of weapon here. This is a big farm."

"I don't know," said Irma. "Maybe in the barn, but we'd never get there without them knowing. Plus, they have guns."

Wanda nodded as Doris came back into the kitchen. She smiled but wouldn't look directly at either of them. When she spoke, her words lacked inflection. "They want you both out there now," she said in a dull monotone while opening a cabinet and removing a large glass. She filled it to the brim with water and walked out with Irma and Wanda following.

When they returned to the living room, Doris walked up to Elmore, kneeled down and lifted the glass gently to his lips.

"I'm sorry," he blubbered. "I'm so sorry."

"Shhh," she whispered. "It's all right. Just drink, Elmore. You must drink."

He slurped and gulped at the water as his instinctive sense of survival took over. After swallowing every drop, he muttered, "More."

Doris looked over at Toby, who shook his head. "No way. Not until I get what I want. He's got water and some chicken. That's it for now."

Doris nodded and reached down to grab the chicken Toby tossed on the floor near Elmore. With her hands, she tore off little pieces of the thigh until her husband consumed every morsel. When he finished, she stood up and walked back to the couch, taking her place next to Toby.

This time, she didn't need coaxing, and they kissed and groped each other while Elmore sat and whimpered in the corner. Mateo shook his head and grunted through his duct tape gag while Todd lowered his head and refused to look. Wanda and Irma stood between the

227

dining room and the bedroom, stunned by the scene unfolding before them.

When Toby's hand once again snaked under Doris's skirt, she didn't stop him but breathlessly said, "We need to go upstairs, it's more comfortable."

"Wait, wait," yelled Elmore. "I'll give you everything I have. Just leave her alone."

"Don't, Elmore," said Doris. "It won't make any difference. They'll just take the money and do it, anyway."

"I can't watch this. I can't..." he said while shaking his head sadly.

"Where's the Goddamn money, Elmore," said Jason, scowling as he hit pause on the remote.

"Hey," said Toby, who reluctantly pulled away from Doris. "I was about to get lucky."

"If Elmore tells us where the money is, you'll get all the pussy you want, and it'll be young pussy too."

"It's in the barn in the back left corner," Elmore blurted out. "I made a hatchway look like the rest of the floor. Brush away the hay. The combination is 13-24-12-37." He finished talking and a large sob escaped his lips.

Jason got up and started walking to the back door. "Toby, get 'em all in the living room. You watch 'em close, you hear. I'm gonna duct tape ol' Elmore's face back up, and then I'm going to the barn."

"All right," said Toby with obvious disappointment. He pushed Doris off his lap and picked up the shotgun. She went to Elmore's side as Irma and Wanda walked over to Todd and Mateo.

228

"Don'cha all look so cute sittin' over there as couples," said Toby in a syrupy tone. "Y'all make me sick. I'd just as soon put a bullet in every one of you."

"Toby, tell me why?" said Doris. "We've always given you work, and we've never cheated you."

"Yeah, you gave me work. Shit work. Bailin' the damn husks, stalks and leaves for the livestock. Cleaning the pens, feedin' the cows... Shit work. And meantime, here you are livin' the fine life off the sweat of me n' Jason's back."

"Jason was our mechanic. He fixed the equipment, and we paid him handsomely to do it."

"Guess it wasn't enough," said Toby. He pointed the gun in Wanda's direction. "I know them two couples, but I don't know you. Where d'you come from, missy?"

Wanda's anxiety nearly overwhelmed her. She continued to fight against the black fog that pushed in from the sides of her peripheral vision, signaling a fainting spell was near. "I'm from Arizona; Mateo's from California. We were in Chicago, and we're just trying to get back home."

"Jeez, I hope you're not all radioactive and shit."

"We may have taken a lethal dose," she said. "Time will tell."

"Well, it won't matter, anyway. You ain't gettin' back to Arizona, I can promise you that. You ain't been listenin' to the news reports. It's every man for himself."

Wanda didn't know how to respond, so she shuffled her feet, twisted her hair and mumbled unintelligible sounds, which was something she did in times of severe stress. Toby furrowed his brow and looked at her like she was an alien. "What the hell is wrong with you?" he said just as the back door opened.

Jason walked in with a huge smile on his face. "I got it, Toby. I got it all. There's probably twenty big gold coins in this sack, all her jewelry and about ten grand in cash."

"Holy shit!" said Toby. "That's enough to get us the hell out of here."

"Damn straight," said Jason. "We have enough barter to get us to Cabo for sure. They say that's where the rich people are goin'. The livin' is supposed to still be good there. They catch the lobsters straight from the sea. I…"

"Let us go," said Doris. "You got what you wanted. Now, just leave."

"Wait a minute," said Toby as he looked at Doris and then at Jason. "She was just gettin' sweet on me. Don't tell me I can't have 'er, Jason."

Jason looked back at Elmore and then at Toby. "Okay, go ahead and have her. But don't take forever, understand? I want to get the hell out of here."

"No!" yelled Doris. "You promised." Elmore strained and groaned with such effort his eyes grew red and the veins in his neck looked like they would burst.

"Look," said Jason in a sinister voice, "me and Toby watched you two flauntin' your new cars and room additions and exotic trips for years while he was cleanin' up slop pens, and I was underneath the greasy hoods of your tractors. You may be rural, but your country club rural, and you're gettin' everything you deserve."

"No, I won't do it," Doris said. "You said if we gave you everything, you would leave us alone."

"I lied," said Jason. "Now, you make nice with Toby, or I'll put a bullet into each one of your heads. Things would be much easier for us if it happened that way. Police don't give a shit what we do now. Law of the jungle, lady, law of the jungle. Now get back over there... Now!"

Tears rolling down her cheek, Doris walked over and sat back down on Toby's lap. Within seconds, they were lipped locked, and Wanda could see their tongues dancing as Toby's hand once again slipped under her skirt.

After several minutes of lusty foreplay, she stood up, and without looking at Elmore, took Toby's hand and walked up the stairs as he trailed like a puppy in training. Once they were at the top of the landing, Doris turned left and led Toby into the master bedroom.

"Ok, bitches," said scar-tissue Jason. "It's your turn. You old bag, get your ass over here." Irma looked over at Todd, who screamed into the gag and strained against the restraints. Jason raised the handgun and pointed it at his head.

"Stay quiet, buddy. Me en your ol' hot mama gonna have some fun tonight." He grabbed Irma and pulled her close and kissed her despite her protestations.

"Please don't. Please..."

"Less talkin' and more smoochin', lady. You're lucky I'm gonna give you some lovin'. Now, act like you like it, or that fossil husband of yours is gonna get it right between the eyes."

He grabbed Irma and pulled her close, pressing his lips down on hers. She winced slightly, but he grabbed the back of her head and forced her into the embrace. The noise from the corner grew frenzied as the three bound men tried vainly to free themselves to help the

231

women. After some moments, scar-tissue Jason grabbed Irma's arm and dragged her up the stairs.

About three steps up, he looked back at Wanda and said, "Well, c'mon missy. Me 'en Toby gonna do these two, and then you're gonna get it from both of us."

Petrified, Wanda continued to stand in place, which only seemed to enrage him. "Goddamn it, you either move your ass and get upstairs, or your boyfriend gets it." Jason pointed the pistol at Mateo for emphasis. Somehow, Wanda looked down and made her leaden feet move toward the staircase and up the stairs, shuffling behind Irma as the miscreant led her into the guest bedroom.

When she reached the landing, Wanda hesitated for a moment. Eager to get on with the sexual assault, scar-tissue Jason pushed Irma onto the bed. He was on top of her in an instant, pulling off her clothing while she looked lifeless and in shock. She followed each of his instructions robotically, and soon he had almost all of her clothing and undergarments removed.

Turning in the other direction, Wanda looked inside the master bedroom. Toby was naked and lying on top of Doris while trying to spread her legs. He kept muttering and threatening her as she whimpered, pleaded and begged for help. Wanda could hear Toby talking, repeating the same line over and over.

"You want it, don'cha? Tell me you want it, or I'll slap the shit outta ya and kill your husband."

"I want it; I want it," she mumbled between sobs.

Wanda stood motionless when Jason called from the other room. "Hey missy. Get in here. You're gonna miss all the fun," She heard his voice, but her attention was focused elsewhere. No more than five feet away, Toby's shotgun sat propped up against the dresser directly across from the bed. Consumed with his violation of Doris, he foolishly left the weapon exposed and out of reach. Wanda saw his head turn away from the gun as he grunted and Doris let out a small whimper.

With no internal debate, Wanda charged into the room, the sound of her footsteps dampened by the thick carpeting. Before Toby knew what happened, she reached the gun and grabbed it, which finally gained his attention. For a moment, he lay still on top of Doris as Wanda backed up and pointed the weapon directly at his torso.

"Get off of her right now, or I'll shoot you," she said.

Toby twisted his body around to face her. "You put that gun down, you bitch, or I'll kill you."

"You get off of her, or I swear I'll pull the trigger." Wanda never handled a firearm in her life. She shouldered the weapon like she had seen on television and prayed the safety wasn't on because she had no idea how to switch it off.

"Jason!" yelled Toby. "This bitch has my gun. You need to come here quick." Scar-tissue Jason never replied, his voice drown out by Irma's loud sobs and cries for mercy.

After some seconds, Toby erupted in a maniacal rage. "Give me that goddamn gun," he said as he rolled over and planted his feet on the floor. He stood up and stalked Wanda with his hand extended. "Give me that fuckin' gun, you bitch."

Wanda wouldn't remember having a conscious thought as she pulled the trigger, but the barrel flashed and the shotgun recoiled so hard it sent her reeling backwards into the wall. Toby took the impact of the 2.75-inch buckshot right in the lower neck region, and it nearly tore his head clean off. He stumbled backward, his hand reflexively coming up to his neck as what remained of his head lolled to the side. Like a grade B horror movie victim, he stumbled forward as blood gushed from the open wound. Toby stopped, staggered and slumped against the back wall, falling over and hitting his shoulder on the side of the bed.

Wanda never heard Doris's shrieks and screams, but she instinctively turned in time to see Jason entering the bedroom buck naked with the pistol pointed in her direction. Before he could react, Wanda pulled the trigger on the semi-automatic again, and at such close range, the buckshot tore his abdomen open a good six inches. The pistol flew from his hand, and he stood a moment looking down at the hole in his stomach, as entrails and a thick chunk of bloody meat fell onto the carpet. He looked up at Wanda, mouthed something unintelligible, and collapsed to the floor, either dying or already dead.

Chapter Nineteen

Mr. Cox strolled down the hallway past Jarvier Delgado's suite to a smaller set of offices in the corner of the 71st floor. While very comfortable, this suite lacked the view and décor of the more senior members of Mr. Cox staff. Still, it was an extraordinary step up for its newest occupant, Sandy Bentenhouse.

After her first "date" with the Benefactor, Sandy learned she was being promoted to the new Assistant Vice-President of Security, which was only one level below Delgado in standing. Already, she sat in on several meetings to learn about the organization's methods and strategies for dealing with its enemies and traitors.

While the promotion of an insignificant clerk appeared to be a rags to riches story, those around her noticed a change in the twenty-one year old. From a perky, friendly blond with a kind word for everyone, Sandy, now referred to as *Sandra*, transformed herself into a moody introvert who treated her coworkers with contempt. The pinks and pastels gave way to blacks and grays as she replaced her entire wardrobe within days of her first encounter with Mr. Cox. The clothes she purchased were far from cheap, and included designer brands like Marc Jacobs, Fendi and Oscar de la Renta, all charged to the Benefactor's account.

Her accessories were as expensive as her clothing, including the fourteen-karat gold nose ring with the flawless one-third karat diamond in the center. *Sandra* cut off her shoulder-length blond hair in favor of a short-stacked bob dyed jet black. A new dragon tattoo with blazing red eyes ran from her shoulder down to the middle of her back. Several smaller tattoos of menacing demons and gargoyles marked both of her forearms.

Rumors she was the Benefactor's new girlfriend were confirmed when she received the surprising promotion and moved into an office only one floor lower than Xavier Watts'. Despite Sandy's recent good fortune, her former friends continued to whisper about her deteriorating physical appearance. Her skin grew ashen, and deep circles cut furrows under her sunken eyes. The transformation over several days was shocking.

In a session with her psychologist, she admitted memories of the trip to Istanbul with Mr. Cox were fragmented, and she couldn't even recall how they got there. The whole experience seemed almost hallucinatory, somewhere between the real and imagined. After Istanbul, every night she spent in Mr. Cox' bed was more depraved and vulgar than the one before, and Sandy retreated further into a deep, dark hole of despair.

"Good afternoon, Daphne. I hope you're having a pleasant day," said Mr. Cox as he passed by Sandra's assistant.

The grossly overweight woman with raging dandruff and crusty scabs beamed at the recognition. Rebuffed and ridiculed her whole life, Daphne found a home at the Gehenna Corporation.

"I am having a wonderful day, Benefactor. It is a privilege to serve you." She bowed her head in deference.

The Benefactor smiled. "It's the dedicated little people like you that serve as the backbone of our organization," he said while continuing on towards Sandra's office. Behind him, he heard Daphne gasp in a way that might have been mistaken for an orgasm.

Mr. Cox opened the office door and walked in unannounced. Sandra remained seated and hunched over a keyboard typing furiously without looking up.

"Good afternoon, my sweet," he said as he approached from behind and massaged her shoulders.

"Please, Benefactor, I—I have so much work to do."

"Ah, getting into your job; I like that. Delgado told me how pleased he is with your work ethic." Mr. Cox moved to the front of her desk and sat down in a guest chair. "So, are we still having dinner this evening?"

"Yes, of course," she said softly.

"What's the matter, my sweet? You seem disturbed."

She turned and looked up at him while arching her eyebrows. Her drawn face looked as if it had aged at least ten years since they first met. "I—I just don't know. Everything has happened so fast. I feel like something is taking over my mind and body. I used to be a positive person, but every day my thoughts become more—disturbed."

"In what way?"

"It's hard to explain. I find myself daydreaming about shooting or stabbing people just to watch them suffer. My new job requires me to assign field agents to kill the traitors and our enemies, who I hope die in horrible ways. And then there's the…"

"The *what* my dear?"

"The — the sex. Our sex. It's despicable and decadent. I never could have imagined doing things so horrible and disgusting. I dreamed of love, passion and gentleness. The first time we — we did it, I remember vomiting. But now I find myself almost…"

"… Looking forward to it?"

She hung her head and said in a whisper, "Yes."

Mr. Cox chuckled and tapped his forefingers together. "In fact, you can't wait to see what depths of debauchery I have in store for you tonight, can you?"

She paused for a long moment. "No."

"Excellent," he said as he rose from the chair. "You are coming along nicely, but you have so much more to learn from me. I look forward to seeing you tonight, my sweet." He walked over and pulled her to her feet. As he reached his hand inside her slacks, he was not disappointed. Her panties were soaking wet.

The Benefactor returned to the cylindrical reception desk in the middle of the open space and nodded to the numerous staff scurrying around as they completed various tasks. He walked into Delgado's office suite without knocking or allowing anyone to announce his arrival, which was his wont and privilege. During the renovation, Delgado positioned his office in a way that gave him a panoramic view of both the city and the Detroit River as it emptied into St. Clair Lake. Upon seeing Mr. Cox enter, Delgado rose and bowed. However, the man with the long blond hair and blue streak sitting in a chair opposite the security chief was slower to rise.

"Gentlemen, please be seated," said the Benefactor as he took Delgado's executive chair. For meetings that were strictly internal, it was customary for subordinates to give the best seat in the room to a superior. Delgado took one of the guest's chairs next to Lars.

Mr. Cox drummed his fingers on the table for a moment before turning to Delgado. "Where's Alan?" The words were no sooner out of his mouth when the door rattled as Ziminski entered. He was carrying a sweet coffee-based beverage he almost dropped as the computer bag slipped off his shoulder. Well aware he was late, Alan scurried over to an empty seat and slunk down in the chair without looking up.

"Sorry," he mumbled while unzipping the bag and pulling out his laptop.

"I value punctuality," said Mr. Cox.

"I know, but it's hard to be on time. This place is so fucking big. Maybe if you moved me out of that decrepit tower I'm in and brought me in here…"

"I've made sure your accommodations are more than adequate, Alan. Now, let's get to the crux of the matter." Cox leaned back in the chair and folded his hands. "The Suicide Society has disappeared; is that what I am to believe?"

Lars nodded his head. "It seems like it. My sources have no intel to offer. They've ghosted."

"*Intel*? The only *intel* you received came directly from me. I'm starting to suspect you're a good resume with little in the way of results to back it up, Lars. You infer you have—'special' contacts. Well, why are we still in the dark?"

Lars shifted in his chair uncomfortably. The insults seemed to affect him, and his jaw muscles strained against the flesh on his cheeks. "These people are different. I wasn't fully aware of their abilities. They're like mutants or some variant. They did a number on my head, and I'm still not right. Bosch has the brain of a six-year-old, and the others who survived are drooling vegetables."

"You appear to know some defensive mind shielding techniques, why didn't you use them?" asked Mr. Cox. "Did you think the assignment would be easy? I'm paying you handsomely, Lars. I expect results."

"They're too powerful. They somehow anticipate our next move before it happens. No one told me they have that ability."

"Well, I suggest you figure it out because you accepted employment with our organization. As I explained, our contracts last a lifetime."

Lars squirmed in his seat. "I know, I know. I'll continue to carry out the assignment to the best of my ability. However, as I said earlier, I have no leads. In fact, I have no staff. The Suicide Society killed them all or rendered them useless."

"Are you recruiting and training new men?" asked Delgado.

"Yes, but it's tough to find qualified people. They need an exceptional skill set. It's not like they walk down the street every day."

"Alan," said Delgado. "Search our employee data base and call up anyone with paramilitary experience. The more violent their past, the better."

"Excellent idea, Mr. Delgado," said the Benefactor. Alan began typing on the laptop.

"The last known location we have is Cordes Lakes. They disappeared without a trace. No historical data to follow. I've checked with my—sources. They've covered their tracks." said Lars.

"So, you have no idea where they are?" asked Mr. Cox.

"Unfortunately, I don't." Lars replied in almost a whisper.

"Here's the list," said Ziminski as a printer in the corner of the room came to life. "We have thousands of former special ops guys, but I narrowed the parameters to people with at least two tours who continued to use their skills once they returned to civilian life. I also only included vets with multiple confirmed kills, and there's eight of them."

"Good. Bring them to Detroit immediately," said Delgado.

"Already done," said Alan. "They have their instructions and will be here tomorrow on our jets, assuming they don't crash while they're flying." Ziminski let out a high-pitched cackle as he alone laughed at his attempt at a joke.

"We shouldn't have to worry about that," said Delgado. "We run the airports in all the major cities. We fly when we want to."

"Yeah, yeah, we're a big deal." Ziminski rolled his eyes.

"Enough, Alan," said the Benefactor. He shifted his gaze back to Lars. "Let us think this through. We know the Suicide Society was in Portales, New Mexico, and traveled to Cordes Lakes in Arizona... What direction did they head after that?"

241

Lars brought his hands up to his head and groaned. "It's so hard to remember that day... My memories are still faulty, but I'm almost certain they went—north."

"Are you sure?" asked the Benefactor. Lars paused before nodding.

After placing the index and forefinger of each hand on his temples, the Benefactor seemed to nod out for several moments. When his eyes reopened, a large smile spread across his thin lips. "Of course. Cordes Lakes is only an hour away from Sedona. I should have known that's where they would go to hide. I can sense it."

"Sedona? Why would they go there?" asked Lars.

"It is a most vile place awash in pure, positive psychic energy. It serves as the cosmic balance to Desolation and now Detroit. I tried to have a bomb placed there, but the agents lost their sanity when they encountered the power of the red rocks. It is a protected place, and its immense aura causes me great pain and distress. I believe the Suicide Society is hiding there and using the energy from the five vortexes to shield them."

"Vortexes?"

"They are energy sources. Some believe they tap directly into cosmic divinity, although I think that theory is rubbish."

Lars rubbed the back of his neck. "So, how am I to find them? They could be anywhere in the city or the surrounding mountains."

"Sedona is a small place, and you are supposed to be the expert, Lars. I have given you their probable location, and we'll repopulate your staff with experts in covert operations. Finding them is your responsibility."

"I'll have to assemble the team and train them in my techniques. It'll take time."

"We do not have that luxury," said Mr. Cox. "It shouldn't be difficult to plan the mission, so I expect you to be in Sedona within seventy-two hours."

"Seventy-two *hours*? That's impossible."

The Benefactor leaned over the desk. "Are you questioning me, Lars?"

Lars dropped his head and said quietly, "No, I understand. Seventy-two hours. We'll be in Sedona in seventy-two hours."

"Good. And this time, I suggest you plan carefully. I am running out of patience."

Mr. Cox rose and walked out from behind the desk. "Delgado will conduct the rest of the meeting. I am concerned about the insurrection in Japan. We partnered with the nationalists, and I believe they need our assistance. Tell the President of Korea we need air support. I want that government overthrown within a week."

"Yes, Benefactor," said Delgado. "We will contact President Kye and order the airstrikes."

Mr. Cox waved without turning back around.

***

He bathed in lilac water and drank Dom Perignon while tuning into the energy streams that linked everyone within the organization together. The blanket thickened, and the lack of tone or shade left a blackness that was no longer a color. Instead, it resembled an expansive void, lacking any sense of optimism, love or

243

compassion. Those plugged in and addicted to the energy stream were like heroin addicts given increasingly potent fentanyl strains. Whatever they took from the torrent, they returned tenfold in despair, envy, hate, jealousy and the other despondent emotions that intoxicated Mr. Cox.

The reports could not be more promising. Governments across the globe were collapsing under the weight of their own pomposity, arrogance and greed. They were teetering on the brink anyway, and he provided the small push that sent them over the edge. The floaters, his people, grew in number every day, and their venom was potent and lethal. He would visit many of the larger groups to provide inspiration and engorge himself of their hatred.

Yet, that must wait for another day. He rose from the tub and stood as Hefe wrapped a thick Abyss bath towel around him and dried his body and limbs. The small man removed every drop of moisture before he folded the towel and helped the Benefactor into his undergarments.

After removing the silk trousers from the hanger, Hefe held open each pant leg as Mr. Cox stepped inside. He brought over a stool and climbed on top, sliding the silk shirt over his master's scrawny shoulders, and then buttoning it up. Fetching the dark purple jacket from the hanger, Hefe again stood on the stool as the Benefactor slid his arms into the vestment. After retrieving a matching fedora, Hefe placed it strategically on Mr. Cox' head so that only one eye peered out.

Almost as if on cue, several screens lit up around the room. Sandra waited outside the door, and her escort stood next to her with his hands clasped behind his back.

"Hefe, answer that, and tell the server we'll have Fabiolas before dinner. I imagine we'll want to have the first course at seven-thirty."

"Of course, boss, Hefe will make sure it gets done." The little man waddled away, and Mr. Cox watched Sandra walk in on the security screen as her chaperon turned toward the elevator. He would wait down in the lobby until summoned to escort her back to her apartment.

Hefe came back into the expansive entertainment area with Sandra trailing. She looked around as though it was her first visit. In fact, she slept here every night since their initial encounter but had little time to take in the décor.

After dismissing his servant, Mr. Cox made a sweeping gesture toward the huge wrap-around couch. "Take a seat, my dear." He gazed at her, greedily running his eyes from head to toe. She dressed in a pair of skin-tight black leather slacks and a matching top that revealed her cleavage so the upper part of her areola showed.

Fresh graphic tattoos covered her shoulders, arms and abdomen to the point where her co-workers whispered and exchanged glances when she passed. The old Sandy would never have considered altering her body in such a way, but these days, she did everything she could to please Mr. Cox. For reasons she couldn't understand, when he wanted something, she soon found herself wanting the same thing.

The body modifications were a perfect example. Less than two weeks ago, she commented to her now ex-boyfriend that self-mutilation was repulsive and a sign

245

of lower class. Yet, here she was with a nose ring, two studs in her lower lip and matching curved barbells set into each eyebrow.

Her lipstick, mascara and eyeliner were all jet black. As she walked closer to Mr. Cox, she stopped to look at herself in a mirror. To her friends and coworkers, the transformation from the innocent girl with flowing blond hair in a yellow print dress to the personification of darkness and malevolence was stunning and disturbing.

Sandra appeared to suffer from a maddening psychological itch, and no amount of alcohol or pills could make it go away. For reasons she couldn't explain, the need for decadence and depravity saturated her mind and imagination. In fact, obsessive wantonness was all she really thought about. At work, at home, out shopping or in her new five-bedroom apartment in Building 4, it didn't matter. Her mind always wandered back to Mr. Cox, and the unimaginable licentious ecstasy he provided. Nothing she tried could duplicate the rush she felt in his presence.

He forced himself on her in Istanbul. While the stench of fresh blood saturated her nostrils, and the screams of butchered religious zealots filled the air, he penetrated and raped her. When he finished, she vomited and continued to retch and cry for hours afterward. Back in her own apartment, she couldn't get the shame off no matter how vigorously she scrubbed. And yet, she had no proof the event actually ever happened. Like a memory of a vivid dream, it skirted the boundaries of reality.

As Mr. Cox expected, her itch started to intensify almost immediately after he satisfied his lust. Small at first, he could sense the acorn-sized area between her stomach and heart as it pulsed with heated energy. He knew that every time she tapped into it, the heat grew in intensity and ignited a lust she could not explain. A desire to explore the dark side of life and all its depravity became an overwhelming obsession. At the heart of it all was the Benefactor. When she pictured him in her mind, the revolting rapist continued to fade, replaced by the sinewy presence who could satisfy her unbridled passion.

Mr. Cox tapped deeply into Sandra's psyche, and he looked at her with the wicked smile that defined him. She shifted uncomfortably, and he knew the heat was rising and traveling down between her legs. She sat on the sofa and waited for him to join her.

"We will have a wonderful meal, but first a Fabiola." As if on cue, a server entered carrying the drinks on a golden platter. After taking the beverages from the tray, Mr. Cox walked over to the Bugatti Grain Leather Sofa and sat down next to her. They toasted, and Sandra took a taste of her drink and then set it down on an end table. As Mr. Cox brought the glass up to his lips for a second sip, he almost spilled the contents as Sandra reached over and aggressively grabbed at the crotch of his silk pants. He set the glass on the coffee table without spilling as she unzipped him and reached her hand inside.

"Fuck me, Benefactor. I don't want dinner. I want you inside me. Hurt me, please. I can't think of anything else. You're in my head, and nothing can satisfy me. Do you like how I look?" She rambled as she undid the straps of her leather top while simultaneously trying to unbuckle his pants. "I did it for you. Tell me how you want me to look, and I'll do it."

247

"Yes, my sweet," Mr. Cox said as he leaned back. "You look ravishing. I love the change. Do you like your new job and office?"

"Yes," she said as she lowered her head in his lap. "I do like it, and I'm so appreciative," she said between licks and slurps on his rigid manhood. "But I want more."

"What do you mean," he asked as he closed his eyes and tapped into an energy she resonated that was so dark it almost startled him.

"I don't just want to *read* about the killings, I want to do them. Let me do them, please." Her entire body shuddered, and he sensed she had just orgasmed.

"Well, let me talk to Delgado. I'm…"

Mr. Cox didn't finish his sentence as a huge flash of light erupted from just inside his peripheral vision, followed by a massive explosion that shook the main tower and blew out two windows in his penthouse. Sandra recoiled and screamed as Mr. Cox looked out the shattered windows on the west side of the living room and saw countless pillars of flame erupting from several of the upper floors in Building 5. As he lay on his side blinking rapidly while trying to clear his eyes, he realized someone had just set off a bomb.

Chapter Twenty

After the Suicide Society gathered in the dining room, the attendants started serving breakfast. As Zach expected by now, the dishes were perfectly prepared and delicious. Somehow, Pena knew of each person's individual food preferences. Aminah enjoyed agidi joloff, Yasin ate Zater, white goat cheese and falafel, Jacques was served coffee and croissant while Zach enjoyed an omelet, potatoes and toast. The others were given prepared dishes that delighted their pallet and conformed to their native traditions.

What little was said at the table focused exclusively on finding Liu Wei, and Zach noted the other overseers continued to maintain a rigid telepathic shield around their thoughts and emotions. Everyone except Sarah of course, but considering her history, no one cared to intrude on her deeply personal and horrific experiences. As soon as they finished breakfast, the attendants cleared the plates, and Pena stood up and motioned for silence.

"Please, please, can I have your attention," he said. "Mr. Cheeves and Mr. Docker are continuing to look for Liu Wei, but unfortunately, they have not been successful. Let us start the tour so you can familiarize yourselves with the facility, and hopefully, we will find Liu Wei along the way. My assistants will pass out copies of the layout. I suggest you keep it with you in case you get lost or can't remember the location of a feature."

Two different attendants, clothed in the same black apparel their co-workers wore last night, stepped forward and handed out the maps. They were both big and muscular, and Zach wondered how many of these physically intimidating employees were on the staff.

Once everyone finished their breakfast, Pena turned and walked toward an exit on the far side of the dining room as the others followed. They entered a long hallway cut through the rock. Multiple side corridors branched off periodically, and Zach wondered why a facility that needed to house a dozen people could accommodate hundreds, perhaps thousands? This sanctuary held a multitude of mysteries, but they could wait until later.

The group stopped and entered an expansive library, which was well stocked with everything from current fiction titles to classics and reference material. Computer terminals lined the walls of the room, ready to access the secure internet connection.

"This is our main library, but we have several smaller satellites throughout the facility. I highlighted these archives on your map in blue. You can access the internet anonymously or use our private intranet, which has information unavailable to the public. We have many original editions of classic books, and combined with other resources, virtually everything ever written is available to you." Pena turned as a woman in an understated off-white business suit joined him and nodded while smiling pleasantly.

"This is Ms. Pland, the head librarian. Seek her out if you have any questions."

Ms. Pland nodded curtly and moved forward to address the gathering. "I am a certified professional master librarian. I am well versed in all bibliographic classification systems, including Dewey, Library of Congress and Superintendent of Documents." She paused and wrung her hands. "I—I hope you visit the library often. It gets lonely sometimes…"

"Ah, yes, thank you Ms. Pland," said Pena while quickly ushering her back over to her desk as she mumbled to herself. Returning to the group, he said, "We must be moving on. There is much to cover today."

Zach couldn't imagine the boredom of running such a large library for essentially an empty fortress. The more he learned about this place, the more puzzled he became.

Pena left the library and led the group over to a huge workout room. The equipment looked unused, and included ellipticals, recumbent bikes, treadmills, stack gyms, stretch trainers, stationary bikes and other state-of-the-art exercise machines. A tanned, toned and muscular man stepped out of an office and stood next to Pena.

"Marcus is a certified trainer skilled at yoga, Tai Chi, Pilates and a variety of workout disciplines. He will help you develop a personalized regimen to keep you in top condition so you have the stamina to face the challenges you may encounter in the future."

Marcus smiled, bowed and waved. "I'm here most of the day, so I encourage you to consult with me at any time. I'm number seven on your intercom, or you can access me on the intranet."

Pena thanked Marcus, and after surveying the other areas in the gym, they left and continued the tour. In succession, the group moved to an indoor Olympic-size swimming pool, a large recreation room, a basketball court, a reading room, a conference center, an observatory, a full-size movie theater and an ice-skating rink.

The overseers exchanged curious glances along the way, amazed at the array of entertainment, cultural and sporting options. Every door had signage identifying the purpose of the room with specialized diverse activities like stained glass and fusing, pottery, foreign languages, chess, meditation, philosophy and woodworking.

As Zach tracked their path on his map, he noted they were entering the deep recesses of the facility and approaching its center, outlined by a large circle without a description. Pena stopped in front of a nondescript door that punctuated a slick curved wall stretching several stories to the top of the cave enclosure. "For those of you who have been following the map, you see we're at the center of the complex. This is actually my favorite place. He pushed on the bar, which disengaged the latch, and the door opened.

The bright sunlight caused Zach and the others to shield their eyes, and it took several moments to adjust to the sudden change in lighting. He stepped into the open outdoor area while holding Sarah's hand, and they walked on a lush carpet of green grass that spanned several acres. On the other side, rows of corn, wheat and other crops dotted the landscape for as far as the eye could see.

The red rock sandstone face of the sheer mountain walls towered over them and seemed to stretch directly up to the sun itself. Huge cumulous clouds billowed overhead, slowly moving through an impossibly deep blue sky. The view in every direction was spectacular, and Sarah tightened her grip as they walked slowly behind the rest of the group.

Picnic tables, lounge chairs and patios were placed at comfortable distances throughout the grassy area, and a wide cobblestone walkway created a path that took them from the grass to a large secluded rock formation with a forty-foot waterfall cascading down into a small lake. The lakefront was surrounded by Arizona Ash and Sycamore trees that made the setting secluded and intimate.

"This is remarkable," said Zach. Everyone who was not busy gawking nodded their head in agreement. "Who could have built all of this?"

"The Suicide Society has a long history, and it is important that it survives," said Pena. "Sympathetic patrons donated vast sums of money in precious metals, gold, jewels and real estate centuries ago. The gains are significant, so funding was never an issue."

"But the size. This place appears endless, and the horizon is infinite. According to the map, it should only be a couple acres in diameter. The map can't be to scale."

Pena shrugged. "No one knows why perception distorts distance here. Numerous surveyors agree the size of the plot is 2.8 acres. Yet, when you are inside, it seems like it is vast and boundless. I have no explanation."

253

"I—I have experienced nothing like this," said Zach.

Pena motioned for the group to follow, and he led them directly to the waterfall. The action of the water crashing down on the rocks displayed the infinite power of nature and its ability to captivate the human imagination. Pools of pristine, ice blue water danced and shifted rhythmically with each surge from the falls. If Zach had a blanket and some privacy, he would be making love to Sarah right now.

They strolled down the cobblestones past the waterfall into a large gathering of trees that blocked the view to the other side. The vegetation grew increasingly dense as they moved further into the thick of the forest, and the large indigenous White Oaks, Emery Oaks and Ponderosa Pines nearly blotted out the sun as their branches created an opaque canopy high above.

Zach gripped Sarah's hand tighter and made sure Marshall was within arm's reach. The lack of light cast a strange shade of gray over the landscape. A heavy fog rose up and drifted across the floor of the forest, further obscuring visibility. From somewhere slightly up ahead, Zach heard Sasha's voice.

"Where are all of you? I can't see through these branches, leaves and fog."

"I'm lost too," Another voice came from the left of Sasha. Zach thought it sounded like Rogelio.

Pena stopped suddenly, and Jacques almost stumbled into him, which set off a chain reaction that caused Marshall to bump hard into Jacques, and they both tumbled to the ground.

"*Espece d'idiot!*" yelled Jacques as he regained his feet. "I ought to teach you a lesson."

Marshall cowered and brought his arms up over his head just as Zach stepped forward and grabbed Jacques by the shirt. "Leave him alone, do you understand me? I've had it with your confrontational attitude. This is not what the Suicide Society is about. We're supposed to work together."

"And what would you know about the Suicide Society? You came here a few days ago, and everything's gone to hell since. I don't think you're our leader." Jacques eyes bulged, and he seethed with rage.

Zach paused a moment as Rogelio and Sasha rejoined the group. Off in the distance, a crow cried, *caaawww, caaawww* in a harsh, raucous voice. The wind whistled ominously through the trees, and the rushing water in the distance sounded angry, but the silence in the ten-foot square area where they stood was deafening.

"Jacques! The breach of protocol... Insulting the speaker. This is all unheard of. What is happening to us?" said Sasha.

This is it. If I lose this one, I'll lose control of the entire group.

Zach moved closer. "Are you challenging my authority here, Jacques? I won't ask the question again. If you don't believe I'm the rightful leader of the overseers, you need to tell me, and we can settle that issue once and for all."

Jacques continued to stare at Zach with scorn, and he clenched his fists and leaned forward. His energy signature was blistering hot, and contempt leaked from every pore in his body as he amassed a concentrated pool of kinetic plasma. Zach braced for the onslaught

255

and hoped he could weather the assault. This was perhaps the most serious internal confrontation in the deep history of the Suicide Society. Jacques shook with anger, and the release of his temporal weaponry seemed imminent.

How could this be happening? Especially here of all places where we're supposed to experience total spiritual cleansing and complete harmony.

"Oh, God no! Help me, someone help me!" The voice was high and shrill, and Zach estimated the cries came from about thirty or forty yards up ahead and off to the right.

"Help me, for God's sake, help me." Pena and the others already were following the sound of the voice before they heard the second plea, and they plunged into the thick of the deep woods. With a last look that communicated a promise to finish their business later, Zach and Jacques took off after the rest of the group but had trouble keeping them in sight because of the darkness and fog.

Zach expected that once they arrived, whoever called out would already be rescued and comforted, but instead, the screaming intensified, and now several other voices joined in. He could hear Pena talking excitedly amidst what sounded like mass confusion.

When he pushed through the last stand of trees, Zach immediately discovered the cause of the frenzy. He focused on Aminah, who continued screaming while looking up at the underside of a huge tree. Zach followed her line of sight until it reached a thick, low-hanging White Oak branch. One end of a rope was attached to the limb and the other end was fashioned into a noose wrapped tightly around the broken neck of Lui Wei. His body hung limp and swayed from side to side in the wind. The flesh on his face appeared grossly discolored, and Zach couldn't tell if the bruising was from natural suffocation or a brutal beating.

On his naked torso, the signs were much more obvious. A large stab wound directly under his solar plexus left a long trail of dried blood down the length of his body and left leg. Large purple and blue contusions covered most of his trunk and extremities. Liu's neck stretched grotesquely from the weight of his body so it appeared almost cartoonish. His head slumped to the side, and the wind started twisting him in circles as though he was on display in an open-air market.

"For God's sake, someone cut him down," said Rogelio as Pena's assistants ran towards the body. Zach, Jacques and Rogelio also went over, poised to help. Unfortunately, the branch with the rope draped over it was higher than any of them could reach. They moved around frantically, but no one could figure out how to get Liu down.

Finally, Sasha walked up and said, "Someone give me a knife."

As everyone looked at each other, one of the attendants pulled out a multi-tool and handed it to her. Sasha quickly shimmied up the tree, and once she crawled out on the branch, she opened the knife, leaned over, and cut into the rope. After a maddeningly long period of ripping and slashing at the thick fibers, the line finally snapped, and the body fell into the waiting arms of an attendant.

Even though Liu was slight, rigor mortis had set in, and the body was stiff and rigid, which caused the attendant to stumble around before regaining his balance. He gently set Liu down on top of a soft bed of humus, leaves and pine needles. Everyone stood quietly for several minutes in the descending darkness as the sound of wind gusts tearing through the trees grew deafening. Ominous dark clouds pushed the fluffy cumulous varieties out of the way, which only made the forest seem gloomier and foreboding. To Zach, it reminded him more of twilight in the dead of winter than a July summer morning.

Pena seemed particularly shaken, although it was difficult to read his emotions without the benefit of using telepathy. He ran his hand repeatedly through his hair and turned around several times as if he was looking for someone. When he spoke, his words came out dry and raspy.

"I—I hardly know what to say. Nothing like this has ever happened to the Suicide Society before. We have no precedent, especially in this place."

"*Precedent?* Who cares about any of that? Someone murdered Liu," said Jacques, "and we need to find who did it."

"We should protect ourselves first," said Sasha, who climbed down from the tree and had her arm around a still shaken Aminah.

"Pena, do you have a morgue here?" said Zach.

Pena nodded. "Yes, of course. Since we can accommodate many people, we had to plan for end-of-life circumstances. The medical facilities, including the crematorium, were part of the tour. In fact, we were going there next."

"I'm afraid the tour is over," said Zach. "Can you have Liu's body taken to the morgue, please?

We need personal space and time to recover right now."

"Yes, yes of course. LeBlanc, please take Mr. Liu's body to the morgue." The attendant nodded and grabbed Liu under the armpits while the other attendant lifted him by the feet. The overseers stood silently and watched as the pair retreated from the forest until they vanished into the shadowy darkness.

"Well," said Pena, "as Speaker Randall suggested, I think we should go…"

"Wait a minute," said Rogelio as he looked around frantically. "Where is Yasin?"

"Yasin? Where is Sarah?" said Jacques as his angry gaze found Zach. "And more importantly, where the hell is Marshall?"

Zach turned and looked around frantically. He swiveled his head in multiple directions as he tried to locate Marshall and Sarah, but they had disappeared. He looked at Pena, who only shrugged and shook his head.

"Where are they, Speaker Randall," said Jacques contemptuously as he moved aggressively forward. He stopped and stood with his face about six inches away from Zach's. "I told you it was that *putain d'idiot*. You wouldn't listen, and now Liu is dead and probably Yasin and Sarah too."

"Back off, Jacques. I'm in no mood for this. We're wasting valuable time, so let's start looking for them."

"I told you about him," Jacques continued. "You caused Liu's death, and now you might have killed your girlfriend too."

Zach looked at Jacques, who was shaking with rage as his face contorted into a mask of anger and fury. For a moment, Zach considered tearing into Jacques' psyche, but the outcome was unpredictable. Zach might be the most potent telepath since Mwimbi Adoula from the Congo, who led the group in the late 900s, but he was not a popular leader, especially since the pain from their beloved Speaker Anston's death was still fresh. With Liu Wei gone, Zach had no way of knowing if the others might come to Franco's defense.

As the split second passed, he decided to address this situation in an unexpected manner. In one swift motion, he drew his arm back and swung directly at Jacques' face. The other man reacted to the punch just in time to pull away slightly, and the blow landed on his lower jaw instead of his nose where Zach intended.

Jacques staggered backward and grabbed at his jaw while looking at Zach incredulously. "Are you kidding me?" he asked. "Seriously? You punched me on the jaw?"

Zach nodded. "Yes, and I'll do it again if you say anything more about Sarah, Marshall or Yasin."

A cold chill rode in on a gust of wind, and Pena looked up and shuddered.

"Please, there is no time for this foolishness. You must all follow me," he said over the shrill sound of the keening wind.

"We have to find Sarah, Marshall and Yasin first," said Zach.

"If they went back to the facility with LeBlanc and Toseman, they are safe. If they went farther into the woods, we must look for them. Besides, there is something I must show you there, anyway."

Without waiting for an answer, Pena turned and walked back into the thick of the forest. For an instant, no one moved, and he turned back impatiently and waved them on. Sasha, Rogelio and Aminah looked to Zach for guidance as Jacques continued to rub his jaw. Randall nodded and followed Pena while the others, including Jacques, slogged along at a distance.

They weaved their way through trees crowded together so tightly there was no way to walk in a straight line. The dense pack of leaves and branches blocked out the sun completely, so Pena turned on a lantern and called to the others to track the beam. The muted light from the torch grew weaker as they moved deeper into the woods.

As he walked, Zach saw odd shapes slipping through the trees, and the branches appeared animated as though they were reaching out to grab at his ankles and legs. *I feel insects crawling all over me and nipping at my flesh. Do I hear a snake hissing in the background? I — must be hallucinating.*

A series of short shrieks caused him to stop in his tracks. "Aminah? Sasha?"

"It's me, Zach. Sasha. I feel like — like bugs are crawling on my skin and the trees are grabbing at me."

From some distance in the opposite direction, Aminah said, "I feel them too, and it's creepy."

Branches snapped, and the wind howled, distorting the third voice. "The energy here is incredibly strong. My head is throbbing. Does anyone else feel it?" Rogelio's voice sounded hollow and distant.

Zach felt relieved when he heard Jacques' call out, "Something is wrong here. I'm so afraid and nervous."

At least the others are still alive. "I know," Zach replied, "and it's growing stronger... Almost overwhelming."

261

"Just a few more steps," yelled Pena as he swept the light back and forth to help the others locate him.

Trudging through the thick underbrush and almost impenetrable vegetation, Zach finally saw a clearing up ahead. He forced his way through the last of the branches and entered an area covered in a finely manicured carpet of Japanese Spurge. Within seconds, Aminah, Jacques, Rogelio and Sasha emerged from the forest. They stood within several feet of each other, but their attention focused on the middle of the clearing where a huge, flawless pure quartz crystal radiated a swirling, penetrating focused beam of gray energy up into the hazy cloud cover. The rays from the boulder-sized gemstone bathed everyone in a flat monotone color, making them look drab and lifeless.

Zach reached out and touched the energy stream with his mind, but it had an odor of rot and a taste of spoil. Overcome with severe sadness and depression, he looked over to see Sasha sobbing and Aminah holding her face in her hands while droning, "I'm so sorry, I'm so sorry," over and over again. Jacques fell to his knees, his face contorted in pain as he started praying. Rogelio stood next to a large tree, slamming his head into it repeatedly while mumbling incoherently.

Pena stumbled toward Zach, tears streaming down his face. "This is horrific. The pristine energy was always the deepest sapphire blue here, and this place offered extraordinary rejuvenation and spiritual healing. Yet, I have never felt such despair before. If we don't leave here immediately, I fear I am going to kill myself."

Chapter Twenty-One

Wanda dropped the rifle and stared blankly at scar-tissue Jason as his body twitched and bled. Behind her, Toby lay half decapitated in a quantity of blood that spread and ran toward an opposite corner of the room. Doris was sitting in the bed with her knees bent and the sheet pulled up to her chin. Eyes wide and glazed over, she whimpered softly as she tried to process the dreadful ordeal.

Irma walked into the room semi-naked with a bedsheet wrapped around her. She slipped on Jason's slick blood and fell to the floor. The liquid gore crawled up the bedsheet, and when she finally got back to her feet, she looked like a survivor from a slasher movie. Besides the bedsheet, both her palms were covered with blood, and one side of her face showed a deep crimson smear where her cheek hit the wet floor. Irma staggered over to Wanda and grabbed her by the shoulders.

"Wanda, Wanda, it's ok now. You saved us, Wanda. You saved us." Wanda continued to stare straight ahead, blinking occasionally but too traumatized to talk.

Irma moved on to Doris, who trembled as she stared blankly at the nearly headless corpse. "Listen to me.

You've got to pull yourself together!" Irma shook her, but Doris only moaned and started clawing at imaginary attackers. Finally, Irma slapped her hard across the cheek twice. The second blow seemed to bring Doris out of her stupor. When the carnage and bloodshed finally registered, she let out a blood-curdling scream, which further agitated the bound and gagged men downstairs. From the floor below, the women heard muffled high-pitched shrieks.

"C'mon Doris, we have to hurry. Get dressed while I wash this blood off. We must get Wanda out of here and go free the men."

Doris looked at Irma and shook her head as she curled her lips downward in a pitiful frown. "I can't face Elmore, Irma. I just can't. That man—Toby, he—he…"

"I know, Doris. The other one was getting ready to rape me when he heard the first shot. Thank God for Wanda."

"No, no, you don't understand…"

Irma cut her off. "Stop it, Doris. You mustn't tell Elmore anything about what happened. Now, get up, get dressed and clean yourself up if you have to." She grabbed Doris by the elbow and pulled her to her feet. Gently nudging her forward, they went into the bathroom, leaving bloody footprints behind. Irma turned on the shower while Doris sat on the toilet, shaking her head and continuing to cry.

Irma let the water cascade over her for several minutes, and she seemed more alert and purposeful once she finished. After pulling Doris inside and thoroughly scrubbing her, Irma helped her friend get into a pair of sweat pants and tee-shirt she found hanging in an adjacent closet. Irma rifled through the clothing until she found a similar set of sweats and put them on.

Back in the bedroom, Wanda continued to stand motionless in the same spot where Irma left her.

"Should we slap her like you did to me?" asked Doris as she waved a hand in front of the girl's blank eyes.

"I don't think so," said Irma. "Her psychological wounds are very deep, and this isn't the time. Let's see if we can get her to walk downstairs." They stood to either side of Wanda, and each held an arm as they guided her forward. Wanda complied without resistance, and the threesome walked in tandem from the bedroom to the landing and then down the stairs. When they reached the bottom floor, Irma led Wanda into the living room while Doris ran over to Elmore.

"Oh, Lord, Elmore. Where's a knife? Where's a damn *knife*?" She half sprinted to the other side of the living room where the thugs had gathered all the sharp kitchen utensils and returned with a large Santoku knife and a pair of scissors. She snipped off the wraps of duct tape and then cut the nylon zip ties with the knife. Elmore sat in a daze for several seconds as he rubbed his wrists and worked his jaw muscles. Meanwhile, Irma led Wanda to a couch and helped her sit down before freeing both her husband and Mateo.

"My God," said Todd as soon as he was able to speak, "what the hell happened up there?"

"Wanda saved us all. She got ahold of their rifle and shot both of them."

"Are they—dead?"

"Yes, both of those monsters are dead, thank God."

265

"What's wrong with her?" asked Mateo as he nodded toward Wanda who sat motionless on the couch.

"I think she's in shock," said Irma while drawing a pitcher of water from the kitchen sink. In a louder voice, she said, "I don't think it's a good idea to do anything to her right now. You can really mess someone up by trying to bring them out of it too soon."

Sitting up against a wall with his head tilted backwards, Elmore watched as his wife massaged his raw and bleeding ankles. "Doris," he said softly. "Nothing happened up there, did it?"

She stiffened and her hands stopped the massage. Without looking directly at her husband, she replied. "No, nothing happened. Wanda shot him before he could do anything to me."

"That better be true," he replied, "because I don't think I could deal with knowing another man violated you."

Irma interrupted the tense moment and handed Elmore a glass of water before sitting down next to Todd and gently stroking his hair. She noticed everyone was looking at her, and she leaned back and brought her hand up to her chest. "What? Nothing happened. He was going to hurt me but heard the gunshot and ran out. Wanda had such courage."

Mateo stood up and tried to increase the circulation to his legs by moving stiffly around the living room. He shook his arms as he walked. "Well, there's two dead guys up there," he said. "We have to call the police immediately."

266

"I'm not sure that's such a good idea," said Todd. "They may not believe us. Shootings have consequences, and the investigation could drag on for months. This won't be one inconvenient day and we're done."

"We need to see the bodies," said Elmore. He got unsteadily to his feet while looking at Doris. She met his gaze for a moment and then turned away, which caused him to freeze. After forty-two years of marriage, there wasn't much a couple could hide from one another.

"I'm calling the police. We can't act like nothing's happened here. There's a reasonable explanation for the killings, and it's the truth. It was self-defense. There's no reason to feel ashamed about anything. Those brutal thugs had it coming." Mateo walked over to a phone mounted on a wall that separated the kitchen from the living room.

"Don't do it, Mateo," said Todd from behind. "I can't let you involve the women after what they've been through."

"That's right, Mateo, back off. We can handle this ourselves," added Elmore.

Mateo ignored them and took the phone off the hook. "Are you both crazy?" he asked. "The women are the main reason we should call the police. What if they were violated?"

"I wasn't violated," said Doris in an almost desperate tone. "Stop saying that. I wasn't. Everything is fine." She laid her head on the arm of the sofa and covered her face with her hand.

"Well, Irma. Are you sure nothing happened?" Todd desperately needed his wife's affirmation.

Irma couldn't hide her obvious anguish. "No… nothing happened. I've already said it several times. Why does everyone keep asking me that?"

Mateo looked at the two men and shook his head. "Alright, that's enough. All three of them need to have a doctor's evaluation."

"They don't need any damned evaluation," said Elmore. "We can't draw anyone else into our nightmare. What would people in town say…"

Mateo shook his head while turning away in disgust. "You don't want the shame of having your wife raped, isn't that it, Elmore?"

Elmore took two steps forward and shook his fist. "Goddamn you, who the hell do you think you are? I don't even know you. My wife says they didn't have sex, and that's the end of it. You bring it up again and so help me God, I'll tear into you."

"I wasn't raped," screamed Doris. "He didn't lay his filthy hands on me. Stop saying it. Elmore, make him stop for God's sake."

Mateo grabbed the phone and dialed 9-1-1. As he waited impatiently for the call to engage, he realized the line was dead. Not busy, but dead. He pushed the buttons again with the same result. He put the handset into the cradle and sighed.

"There's no answer at 9-1-1," he said in a dull monotone. "The line is dead."

"Oh my God. Maybe they cut the phone lines," said Todd.

"Those worthless deadbeats weren't smart enough to cut the lines," said Elmore. "Most of these young ones don't even know land line phones exist."

268

Mateo pulled out his cell phone. "Damn it, no signal."

"For 9-1-1 emergencies, your phone will access any available network. If you're so dad blame insistent, go ahead and try it," said Todd.

Mateo pushed the 9-1-1 keys on the phone and then hit enter. He put the device to his ear and heard a steady busy signal. Two more calls ended the same way, and he slammed the phone down on an end table in frustration,

"It's hopeless. Rockford PD isn't answering. I imagine they're so overbooked they can't accept any more phone calls until they can address the backlog."

"Well, I'm taking this as a sign from God," said Todd. "We mustn't involve the police. Let's go upstairs, wrap up these bodies in plastic, and drive them out to the middle of the fields and bury them."

"It doesn't seem right," said Mateo.

"Doesn't seem *right*?" asked Elmore as he got to his feet. "These vermin almost raped our women and killed all of us. I don't care what happens to their bodies. Like Todd said, let's just get rid of them."

Reluctantly, Mateo nodded and followed the two men out into the hallway. Elmore left through a side door and went to the garage and fetched a box of lawn-size trash bags. Once he returned, the threesome walked cautiously up the staircase. Irma and Doris watched from behind and exchanged worried glances.

"He's going to figure out what happened," said Doris in a whisper. "They're all going to know." Her eyes filled with tears again, and large droplets rolled down her cheek.

"They might not," said Irma without conviction. "As long as there's no—evidence, you can deny it."

269

Elmore walked into his master bedroom, looked around, and promptly vomited. Todd took in the scene before stumbling back out in into the hallway. Only Mateo seemed unaffected. He pulled out several of the trash bags and split them open at the seams, laying them next to one another and taping them together. After several minutes, Elmore came out of the bathroom after rinsing his mouth out and helped Mateo fashion the bags so they were double layered and big enough to hold human bodies.

Once they finished cutting and taping, Mateo grabbed the side of Toby's partially decapitated head and tried to push it back into place. Fortunately, the blood was thickening at the source of the gaping wound, so it was easier to put several wraps of tape around his neck to keep the remaining tendons and skin from tearing away. He motioned for Elmore to help, and each man lifted Toby from under an arm and dragged him over to the bags. A wide blood smear followed the trail of the body, but they were able to lay him in the center and pull up the sides of the plastic so they met in the middle.

Mateo wrapped the tape while Elmore lifted the body each time he passed underneath. Satisfied the corpse was bound tight, Mateo called to Todd, who was still out in the hallway. When he didn't answer, Mateo went out to get him, and that gave Elmore an opportunity to walk over to the bed. Mateo came back in the room and saw Elmore staring down at the mattress.

"They had sex," Elmore said without turning around. "I can tell. The sheets and blankets are all pushed around. I can smell him. She fucked him."

"For God's sake, Elmore, if anything happened, it was rape," said Mateo. "There's a huge difference. She'll need a lot of sympathy to deal with this, not condemnation. Besides, I don't see any body fluids. Wanda may have killed him before he could do anything."

"I can't believe it," said Elmore as he fought back tears. "My wife had sex with another man. Forty-three years of marriage."

Todd looked out the door into the other bedroom. "I wonder if Irma…"

"No!" said Mateo as he grabbed Todd's arm. "You're not going in there. Leave it alone… I can't believe you guys."

Todd pulled his arm away gruffly. "She said it didn't happen, but I need to know." He glared at Mateo until the other man shrugged and let go of his arm.

As Todd left the room, Mateo turned back just as Elmore kicked Toby's dead body. "You dirty bastard," he yelled. "You rotten, dirty bastard. Die, die, die!" Elmore's voice cracked and wavered, and he eventually stopped kicking the corpse and sprawled on the bed, his body racked with emotion.

Mateo put a comforting hand on his shoulder. "C'mon, Elmore, we should move him out of here. It'll be all right, but we've got to deal with this." Elmore rose to his feet, wiped away the tears and walked back over to the plastic-sheathed corpse. He reached down and lifted the feet, waiting for Mateo to grab the arms. They maneuvered the dead weight through the doorway, and Elmore backed down the stairs just as Todd emerged from the guest bedroom.

271

"Nothin'," he said with more hope than conviction. "There was nothin' on the bed. That means they didn't do it, right?"

"Sure, that's good news," said Mateo. "Now get your ass over here and help us move this piece of shit."

They eventually got the body down the stairs and into the foyer. Still sitting in the living room, the women watched without saying a word. Doris looked at Elmore, hardly able to hide her shame, but he refused to look back. Irma reached over and gently took hold of her arm for support.

After throwing the first body into the bed of the pickup truck, they went back upstairs and repeated the process with scar-tissue Jason. Once both of the plastic-wrapped bodies were in the truck, the men returned to the house. Doris walked over to Elmore and touched his shoulder, but he turned away.

"We need to clean the upstairs bedrooms, and it will take a fair amount of work," said Elmore. "All the blood needs to be washed away, and anything with blood on it should be burned in the incinerator out back. That room needs to look spotless before we're done. If it means we have to paint the walls, that's what we'll do. It can't look like anything happened here tonight."

After gathering buckets, mops, gloves and an array of cleaning supplies, Mateo, Todd, Elmore and Irma walked upstairs and began the arduous process of scrubbing a crime scene. Doris stayed downstairs, ostensibly to comfort Wanda, but the reality was she couldn't return to her own bedroom.

The cleaning process took hours, and fortunately, the slugs Wanda fired were embedded in the bodies, so there was no damage to the drywall. After much scrubbing, mopping and bleaching, there was no obvious visible evidence two shootings occurred just hours before.

The sun was beginning to rise as the three men jumped in the pickup truck. Elmore drove them to a remote part of his land, covered in tall stalks of ripening corn. Hidden by the vegetation, Elmore used his backhoe to dig a single deep grave, and they tossed the bodies and the weapons inside. After throwing the last shovel full of dirt in the hole, they spread the displaced soil and drove the truck back through the field.

In ordinary times, killings like this would have drawn enormous scrutiny. But under the circumstances, it would be unlikely if anyone ever found Toby and Jason or even bothered to look for them.

Once they returned to the old farmhouse, the group gathered outside on the front porch. The awkwardness was palpable and the conversation forced. Elmore made sure that both Todd and Mateo received plenty of food and water and as much gas as they could carry. As they shuffled around and avoided eye contact, it became clear that goodbyes would be difficult.

Elmore came out of the house with a rifle, handgun and several boxes of shells. "Here, take these. I have an arsenal inside. It's dangerous out there."

Mateo took the weapons and ammunition and clapped Elmore on the shoulder. He maneuvered Wanda over to the Sonata and carefully set her in the passenger's seat before walking around to the driver's side. He paused with one foot on the rocker panel and looked back at the foursome still on the porch.

"I think I can find my way back to the main road," he said. "The car has a GPS. Elmore, thank you for the gas, food and protection. And—and I'm sorry. I don't know what else to say."

Irma and Todd hugged Doris and Elmore before walking over to their truck. "Follow us, and we'll make sure you make it to the road, okay?" said Todd as he closed the door to the pickup.

As both vehicles moved away from the house, Elmore and Doris watched until they reached a bend that took them out of sight. For a long time after, they continued to stare at the dust clouds rising up from the dirt road. It would be a very long time before they would look each other in the eye again.

Chapter Twenty-Two

The concussion from the explosion was so severe it pushed Sandra back against an exterior wall where she hit her head on a bookshelf and collapsed. Mr. Cox couldn't understand why his vision was so clouded until he rubbed his eyes and saw blood on his hands. A shard of glass had sliced through his forehead, and he would wear a scar to remind him of the incident for the rest of his life.

The Benefactor struggled to his feet, trying to regain a sense of balance and coherence, and he staggered over to Sandra to see if she was still alive. He leaned down and checked her pulse, which was weak but steady.

A concussion more than likely.

The glow from the fiercely burning fire illuminated the dark penthouse in various shades of orange and yellow as flames licked the sides of the structure and spread through the damaged floors on Building 5. Among the many jumbled thoughts that ran through his brain, Mr. Cox wondered why the emergency lights hadn't turned on yet.

The answer became clear as he heard gunfire outside his apartment. The piercing sound of a power saw cutting through the plate steel on the door warned him of an impending breach. In the fire's light, he could see sparks as the blade peaked through the hole it created in the metal. The loud shrieking grew deafening as shards splintered while the opening grew wider.

Mr. Cox knew the intruders would soon be inside, and he struggled mightily to reset his intensely complex brain circuitry. Without his full faculties, he would just be another mortal with vulnerabilities that his enemies could easily exploit. He was thin, frail and physically no match for anyone but the elderly.

The door panels split open, and the Benefactor could see the bottom of a boot kicking at the slivers of jagged metal clinging to the edge of the hole. He could barely make out the outlines of several people as they came into the apartment in a stack formation with automatic weapons raised, swinging them from side to side in a manner that suggested paramilitary training.

The point man wore the kind of battle gear reserved for elite tactical units. His helmet and visor obscured his face, and a Kevlar vest covered the entirety of his torso. He sported an AR-15 with a laser scope, and the beam swept across the room. A second beam danced with the first, and then a third and fourth followed.

Mr. Cox retreated to his study and crouched down behind his desk. He felt his brain slowly begin to normalize as the circuits reconnected one by one. Almost like a reboot, but he needed more time.

"I found a girl." He heard one of the intruders talking softly into the headset. "No, I don't have ID on her." The helmet's embedded communication system helped eliminate sound leakage that might compromise the soldier's position. "She has a good pulse, so I don't think she's in any danger, but we should get her to Medevac just to be safe."

Mr. Cox took note. A Medevac unit confirmed a military action of some sort. They had the audacity to challenge him. As he huddled under his desk, he vowed the conspirators would pay dearly for their transgressions.

Out in the living area, a second voice said, "Let's get this operation over quickly. He's in here somewhere but not in the living room or kitchen."

"Check the sub-domains. You take bedroom number four; I'll take the den."

"Roger that…"

Mr. Cox tried to slow his breathing as he heard footsteps approaching slowly. He saw the red dot of the laser scope as it danced on the walls. The footfalls slowed until they were barely perceptible, and the special forces operative disappeared. The room was quiet except for the soft hum of an electric clock.

"I know you're in here." The voice was loud and commanding. "There's no point in trying to drag this out. You can either come out, or I'm going to smoke your ass. Your call."

Mr. Cox didn't doubt the soldier's resolve, so he crawled out on his knees and slowly stood up. He squinted as the red laser light crossed his retinas and highlighted the blood that flowed from the wound on his forehead. A charred purple jacket hung loosely off his frame, dirty and tattered from the explosion. Still, despite the disheveled appearance, his thin lips twisted up in a sardonic smile, revealing teeth so white they were unnerving.

"What in holy hell are you?" the soldier asked.

"You can call me Mr. Cox or the Benefactor if you prefer."

"How about if I call you *asshole*, asshole?" The soldier waved the gun toward the door. "We have little time. I'm instructed to take you back alive if possible. But if you don't want to cooperate…" The soldier shrugged his shoulders and leaned toward the radio on his shoulder. "Gold Dust Two this is Gold Dust One. I've got the package."

"Roger that Gold Dust One. We'll reconnoiter at your location. Gotta move cuz they'll be coming soon."

Within thirty seconds, the entire four-man squad was in the den sizing up Mr. Cox. The gun barrels were all trained on him, and the soldiers seemed to have a sense of fear mixed with awe as they regarded him cautiously. The Benefactor suspected a rogue department from a dying government sent these men. In truth, these so-called "leaders" were only now beginning to understand they had little relevance and few mechanisms to deal with the threat he posed.

"C'mon, Cox, we have to go. Hurry!" The one known as Gold Dust One waved the gun menacingly as the Benefactor moved out from behind the desk with his hands in the air. The fog continued to cloud his brain, but he still contemplated whether he should test his mental prowess, ultimately deciding against it. In his weakened condition, there was a good chance one of them might squeeze off a round before Mr. Cox

278

could melt his brain. Besides, he was mildly curious to find out who was behind the explosion and his abduction.

Once the Benefactor was close enough, Gold Dust One moved behind him and placed a palm in the small of his back. With a hard push, he said, "Get going."

"You have made a terrible decision," said Mr. Cox as he moved forward under the prodding. "Who may I ask is responsible for this act of terrorism?"

"Shut your mouth, you piece of shit," the Benefactor winced as the butt of the attacker's assault rifle slammed into his left shoulder blade.

"Ooooo, you nasty man. That just bought you even more pain."

The other operatives stood in the middle of the living room waiting for their leader to join them. They reconnoitered the entire suite, until it was time to initiate the final part of their well-crafted plan.

The second in command grabbed the squad leader by the shoulder as soon as he was within earshot. Natural gas explosions in Building 5 continued at regular intervals, and combined with the blaring sirens, it made hearing speech difficult even though they were only a couple feet away. Though it looked silly, they used the radios to avoid confusion.

"The girl. What should we do with her?"

"We're out of time, so we'll have to leave her," replied the squad leader. "The Medevac is on its way, so she's got a shot. She was out before we got here, so she won't have any details to give them... If she even lives."

His second nodded and gave thumbs up.

"C'mon, let's go." The barrel in the small of Mr. Cox' back urged him to move faster.

They moved from the penthouse to the fire stairwell, and once inside the concrete structure, one of the men pulled out a long chain. He wrapped one end around the bar on the door and attached the other to a nearby sprinkler system riser. This would make it more difficult for anyone to follow them, at least from this floor.

The squad cautiously climbed a flight of stairs, and the squad leader pushed open the door that led to the roof. He stepped outside and swung his gun around just as a MH-60G Pave Hawk Air Force helicopter circling overhead began its descent. Mr. Cox found it somewhat ironic that the Air Force wasn't even trying to hide its role in the operation. The Gehenna Group had many followers, moles, plants and spies within the military. While some were devout, others were coerced with threats or bribery. This action tonight represented a fundamental breakdown, and it was not acceptable. Within his own operation, Cox vowed heads would roll… literally.

As soon as the chopper touched down, the soldiers ran towards it, ducking to avoid the rotating blades and air wash. They pushed and prodded Mr. Cox until he was onboard. The Pave Hawk rose quickly and then disappeared into the dark night sky, illuminated only by the raging fire from Building 5 below. Mr. Cox watched the receding flames at a distance as they burned hot and lit up the night clouds in orange and red hues. The image would become a memory the Benefactor would not soon forget.

Lars burst through the door of Mr. Cox' penthouse with four of his new men in close pursuit. He was mainlining cocaine in his apartment in Building 2 when he felt the explosion and immediately expected the worst. Except for Delgado, no one would take more blame for the egregious security breach.

His senses were on a razor's edge as he flashed his weapon and came up on the prone body of the Benefactor's new girlfriend. Her skin was pallid, and Lars stooped down and took her pulse. She was alive, but her breathing was erratic, and she twitched as small tremors ran down her extremities. Lars ran to the kitchen, opened the refrigerator and returned with a bottle of water. He prodded her gently until he got a response.

Sandra's eyes fluttered and opened momentarily. She looked up and spent several seconds trying to work through the confusion. "What? How did I?"

Lars made a shushing sound and brought the bottle to her lips. She drank, choked, and then drank some more. "There was a massive explosion in Building 5. The concussion blew out windows in the other buildings and knocked you unconscious."

She nodded her head. "Yes—the explosion. I…" She sat up with a start. "The Benefactor? Where is he? Is he all right?"

"We don't know. We're searching the penthouse, and if we don't find him, we'll tear apart the entire complex until we do." Lars helped her up just as two of his men returned from their search. "Negative," said the one named Agusto. "We've checked all the rooms, and no one is here."

281

"Goddamn it," said Lars as he shook his head. "We've got to find him. Take the girl to the infirmary. The rest of us will rendezvous in the lobby in five minutes. And get our other three men out of bed and off their asses. I want everyone involved in the search, including the Benefactor's personal security detail."

Agusto stubbed out a cigarette, nodded and moved away, as Lars turned back to Sandra. "We need to get you to a doctor." Despite her protests, he took her by the arm and walked toward the door just as Hefe was entering and almost took a knee to the head.

"Where is the boss?" asked Hefe. His eyes were red and swollen. "Hefe is scared he is dead"

"I'm not sure, Hefe," said Lars. "But this is a crime scene, and I need you to leave."

Hefe's head dropped, but he turned on his heel and slunk out of the room. Even with the din of the sirens blotting out local sounds, Lars could hear Hefe crying.

***

The meeting took place in Xavier Watts' office on the floor just below Mr. Cox' penthouse. Building 5 still smoldered across the courtyard, and the cascade of flashing lights from the fire trucks that surrounded the disaster area overpowered the light from the fire.

Watts convened the meeting in a robe and slippers. Jarred from a light slumber by the explosion, a security detail rushed in and locked down his apartment. As soon as he learned of Mr.

Cox' abduction, Watts was quick to convene the senior members of the Benefactor's staff. In a matter of minutes, Delgado, Ziminski, Lars and a still rattled Sandra assembled inside his office.

He looked around the table at the stunned and groggy participants. This kind of catastrophe would have been unthinkable just a few hours ago. That someone could have kidnapped the Benefactor was beyond comprehension.

"Let's get to the point," said Watts addressing no one in particular. "How could this have happened? How could a breach of this magnitude been *allowed* to happen?"

"Nothing is foolproof," said Delgado. "We have safeguards built into the system, but we never expected to experience such a coordinated and sophisticated assault. They used the bombing of Building 5 as a diversion."

"Where was the Benefactor's personal security detail? Why weren't they able to foil the kidnapping?"

Delgado shrugged. "They were, uh, sent away by the Benefactor once Ms. Bentenhouse arrived at his apartment. Then they went to help with the evacuation efforts in Building 5."

"If they left their post, I want them executed," said Watts. Delgado bristled at the suggestion but reluctantly nodded in agreement.

"Sandra," said Watts as he turned his attention to the Benefactor's companion. "What do you remember?"

She leaned into the table and massaged her temples. "I remember almost nothing. A flash; the windows blew out, and the force knocked me against a wall. After that, everything is blank."

"I see," said Watts. "Lars, have your men picked up any clues from the scene?"

Lars paused to sip a Perrier. "Nothing yet, but we know they were professionals. I think it was an American government operation. All the signs are there. Sophisticated training and equipment and well-coordinated logistics. They escaped unnoticed."

"Nearly unnoticed, but not entirely," said Ziminski as he kept his eyes trained on the computer screen in front of him. "They were sloppy and missed taking out one of the surveillance cameras in the hallway. Like Lars said, these guys are professionals, but they made a few mistakes. Don't worry, I'll find out who did it."

"Act quickly, Alan. We already strongly suspect the Defense Intelligence Agency conducted the operation," said Delgado. "The DIA is the only agency where we're not well-represented. We only have one person embedded there. Her name is Tammera Sondulson, and she runs the Directorate for Science and Technology. She's one of the suicide survivors, so her loyalty is beyond reproach."

"If she's so fuckin' loyal, why didn't she tell us about this when it was being planned?" asked Ziminski.

"She didn't know," said Delgado with the slightest hint of contempt. "When she found out about the plot, she reported it immediately. Rumors travel fast, and we have enough people in lower levels to confirm it."

"So, Lars, what do you have in mind?" asked Watts. "A rescue operation?"

"Yes, at the appropriate time," said Lars. "For right now, intelligence is the key. I suspect wherever they have the Benefactor detained, several high-ranking government officials will be nearby. I suggest we kidnap a few of them for future barter."

"What? Is that—is that even possible?" Watts was suddenly very attentive.

"Yes, it's very possible," said Lars. "It's about time we show these people who's in charge. According to Delgado, we control the Joint Chiefs, and we control seventy percent of the active military units. Our people have infiltrated every department in the executive branch."

"Wouldn't such an action endanger the Benefactor's life?" asked Sandra.

"It might actually save his life," said Watts. "There's no chance they would harm him if we have some of their deep-state autocrats. We might even attract the attention of the President."

"It might work unless the blast incapacitated the Benefactor... or worse," said Sandra.

Watts nodded. "Yes, I've thought of that. There is blood in his penthouse, so he might have been hurt or—killed."

"Nope," said Ziminski. "The camera shows him walking out on his own."

"Thank goodness," said Delgado. "Alan, have you established the identities of the kidnappers?" asked Delgado.

"Just one came back so far. His name is Dowd McDowell, and he's one nasty son of a bitch. We caught his face on camera, and the resolution was clear enough that the facial recognition software I designed made the match. Here's some hot off the press news. He's out of Joint Base Acosta–Ballman in Washington D.C."

"DIA. I knew it. How can we get in there?" asked Watts.

"They'll give us a goddamned key if we tell them to," said Delgado. "Naval support is also there, and we own them. We have enough on the Secretary of the Navy to put him away for life. There's a woman who claims he raped her in college. He apparently extorted money from a superior and embezzled from the survivor benefit program. John Leeds has a checkered history, so he'd admit to killing Kennedy if we told him to."

"Good, then draw up the plans. Lars, when we free the Benefactor, I agree we should try to capture a few of their influential people in the process. And find out who the hell ordered the bombing in Building 5 and the abduction of Mr. Cox in the first place. Whoever it is will wish he burned alive in the fire before we're done with him," said Delgado.

Staring out the window, Watts brought his attention back to the meeting and pounded the conference table. "Wait a minute…. Goddamn it, I know who's behind it. I should have thought of this earlier."

"Well?" said Delgado as the others looked on.

"It has to be Merl Chawsome from the Senate Intelligence Committee… Well, I'll be goddamned." Watts rubbed the back of his neck as he looked back out at Building 5 while several smaller fires still blazed.

"Will someone call the fire chief and tell him to get every unit in the city over here? I don't care if Detroit burns down. I want that fire put out now!"

Chapter Twenty-Three

Zach slumped over and fell to the ground as waves of sorrow and self-loathing washed over him. The source of the energy was so powerful he felt puny and insignificant. In a state of severe paranoia and despair, he was certain that without his protective mental shield, he would kill himself instantly.

The others were doing even worse. Pena howled like a dog and scratched at his face, which was raw and red from the skin he tore away. Sasha whimpered as she tried to crawl but kept tumbling over in a disoriented fog, grabbing her hair and clawing at her breasts. Aminah rolled around on the ground, hitting herself in the head as she endlessly cried, "No, no, no…"

Jacques looked about suspiciously with wide, maniacal eyes as he stumbled around while biting and chewing on his own forearm. The louder he screamed, the harder he bit into his arm, and the blood dripped down in thick droplets, mysteriously swallowed up by the hard-packed dirt when they hit the ground. Rogelio smashed his head into a tree with such force that he split his forehead open, and blood splattered in multiple directions with each impact.

Zach tried to fight the overwhelming anguish and rise to his feet, but he collapsed again under the weight of his misery. His psyche was dark and bleak, and he couldn't fight through the feelings. With his perception of time distorted, he felt trapped in a conscious nightmare without end. Hours, days or months might have passed as he wallowed in infinite torment.

At the point of capitulation, he covered his head with his hands and allowed the suffocating depression to descend even further when he felt a gentle touch on his shoulder. A moment later, someone started pulling him to his feet, and he turned around to see Sarah looking down at him.

"Zach, you have to get up. You need to leave this place."

"I can't," he replied through tears that streamed down his face, "It's too bleak. I just want to die."

She moved behind him, reaching underneath his armpits as she tried to pull him away from the center of the vortex. While she struggled mightily, each tug moved him another couple feet. As they got farther away from the pull of the maelstrom, the feelings of despair receded until Zach could stand on his own. He leaned on Sarah as she kept walking, until finally, he stopped and faced her.

"You came back for me," he said. "I – I think I'll be alright now, but I'm very weak. Help the others. Please hurry!"

Sarah nodded and hugged Zach before running back into the area immediately surrounding the vortex. She stopped and looked around until her eyes locked on Pena. His face was a bloody mask, and if he hadn't succeeded in gouging out his own eyes yet, he was very close.

She maneuvered behind the smallish man, and a strong shove moved him away from the source of the foul energy. Unable to see, he swung his arms wildly, but Sarah changed positions repeatedly and kept pushing him from different angles. He screamed, cried and howled, but his protestations diminished as the distance from the vortex continued to increase. Once he was beyond the boundary of influence, Pena wiped the blood from his eyes and looked down at his hands.

"My eyes. My face. What have I done to myself?" he asked while lightly touching the deep gashes he inflicted on his own countenance. "I don't understand. Why would I..."

Sarah patted him on the shoulder reassuringly and then turned back toward the vortex. Aminah and Sasha were lighter than the men, and both were ambulatory. She drove them out of the area by locking arms and guiding them to safety as they continued to scream, sob and moan in bone-chilling agony.

Rogelio fell into a state of shock so deep he didn't notice Sarah's presence. She called to him several times, but he was preoccupied with trying to stab himself in the abdomen with a stout tree branch while mumbling and cursing under his breath. Sarah approached cautiously and reached out until her hands rested on his arms. Carefully turning him around, she took advantage of the catatonic emptiness in his eyes and took the branch away before gently pushing him forward.

With only passive resistance, Rogelio walked stiffly and jerked his empty hand as though he still was stabbing himself. Outside the vortex's perimeter, Sarah passed him off to Zach, who grabbed his rogue limb and pulled the struggling man further from the source of the spoiled energy.

When Sarah returned for Jacques, she regarded him for a moment and then moved into his line of sight. Their eyes met, and Jacques momentarily stopped biting into his arm and stared at her with malice. He growled and snapped his jaws, snarling in a low tone with a raised upper lip. Sarah stood her ground, glaring at him as he moved tentatively toward her.

"You pathetic excuse for a human being," she said while slowly backing away. "You can't even hurt yourself with dignity. Look at you, chewing on your own arm like some wild animal. You disgust me."

Jacques walked toward her as though he was stalking prey, continuing to growl and bark.

"You're a pitiful excuse for a wolf, all growl and no bite. I bet you..."

The taunting was enough to enrage Jacques to the point where he stopped and crouched low, an obvious sign he was ready to pounce. Sarah turned and ran from the vortex as fast as she could, but Jacques was faster and stronger, especially with the massive release of adrenaline flooding through his body.

He covered the twenty yards between them in mere seconds and jumped on Sarah's back. They tumbled to the ground as his jaws snapped and teeth gnashed. The struggle continued for only a few moments until he gained control and flipped her around so they were face to face. Sitting on her stomach with both hands pinned, Jacques leaned in closer, focusing on the fleshy portion of her long, thin neck. His nose lightly touched her skin as he deeply inhaled her scent, and his lips curled back in a bellicose snarl. With both hands he throttled her neck and tightened his iron grip as Sarah sputtered, gasped and tried desperately to dislodge his fingers.

"No, please," she whimpered.

Jacques stiffened for just a moment and pulled back slightly. He looked at her and eased the pressure on her neck. Appearing confused, his growls became less pronounced, and the intervals between them grew longer.

"Sarah?" he said as his head cocked to one side. "What the... What the hell?" Finally aware of his surroundings, he let go of her completely and dismounted, appearing dazed and disoriented.

"Thank God," said Sarah as she wiggled backward away from him. "I counted on getting you far enough from the vortex so you could escape its influence, but you ran so fast, I wasn't sure if you were still under its control when you jumped on me."

Jacques continued to back away as though he couldn't process what he had done. He glanced down at the shredded bloody flesh on his arm and then looked back at Sarah. "I—don't know what to say. What could have possessed me? I experienced such hopelessness. I wanted to kill you all and then kill myself."

Sarah nodded. "Everyone had the same kind of delusions, but you're safe now."

"Thank you for saving me, Sarah. I—I hope I didn't hurt you."

Sarah rubbed her neck, which was red and raw from Jacques's chokehold, but she still managed a smile. "No, I'm fine. Let's go to the others."

She led him through the thick strand of trees, making sure they kept a respectable distance from the vortex. It didn't take long before they reached the clearing where Zach, Aminah, Sasha and Pena were sitting on large boulders and fallen trees that created a ring around an open grassy area.

"Jacques," said Sasha as she lifted her head from her folded arms, "What happened to you? Are you alright?"

"Yes," he said as he tried to hide his injured forearm. "Sarah saved me, even though I was — violent. If she hadn't been so quick thinking, I would probably be dead by now."

"Pena, what happened here?" Zach stood up unsteadily in the midst of a crushing headache.

Even though he wiped most of the blood away, the deep scratches on Pena's face were unsettling to look at. "The energy is corrupted, but I don't know why. As I said, this has never happened before."

"The Benefactor?" said Zach.

"Perhaps. I can't think of another plausible explanation."

"How could he find us here? We're so isolated."

Pena continued to dab at the wounds on his face as he spoke. "I have no idea, unless he is using the traitor as an intermediary to influence the energy here."

"So, what can we do about it?" said Zach

"First," said Pena as he turned away from the vortex, "we need to get back into the facility. The walls, glass and distance will provide additional protection, and our thoughts will be much clearer than they are here. Besides, several of us need medical attention."

Rogelio shook his head. "Even though I have a skull-crushing migraine, I'm not going anywhere until we find Yasin."

"Yasin and Marshall. They're both still gone," said Jacques while flashing an angry look in Zach's direction. "Where are they? And for that matter, where was Sarah before she rescued us?"

Pena purposely stepped between them. For the first time, Zach saw a trace of anger in his eyes. "Please," he implored, "we have no time for this foolishness."

Zach nodded and signaled to the other overseers for silence. Without further discussion, Pena tucked the bloody handkerchief in his pocket, and retraced his steps back to the facility as the others followed. It didn't take long to reach the cobblestone pathway, and they moved quickly past the waterfall, red rocks and grass pasture before finally reaching the exit.

Once they were safely back inside the facility, Pena moved back down the corridor until it intersected with a smaller hallway that led to one of the recreation rooms. After taking a bottled water from the refrigerator and inviting the others to do the same, he sat down at a large gaming table and motioned for everyone to join him.

Pena breathed deeply and looked like he was struggling to collect his thoughts. "The vortex has been compromised, that much is clear. It only happened twice before during the reigns of Kahn and Hitler."

"What does it mean?" asked Zach

"It is terrible, Speaker Randall. As I explained earlier, this entire region is the primary source of the planet's positive spiritual and psychokinetic energy. The five vortexes keep the world in balance, and they act like a giant spiritual heatsink, absorbing massive quantities of negative energy that emanates from the ugly side of the human race."

Zach glanced at Pena's hands. They were clasped together but still shaking as he tried to hide them under the table. "The purity of the energy here acts as a protectant that allows us to remain safe from those who would do us harm. If the energy is fouled, we will be open to any kind of attack, and humanity will descend deeper into the abyss."

"How could the energy have become so polluted?" asked Rogelio.

Pena pondered the question for a moment. "Is the Dark One working through the traitor? I don't know."

"Marshall," hissed Jacques. "It explains everything. He killed Liu, and now he's disappeared. Let us pray he hasn't killed Yasin too."

"We don't know if Marshall has done anything," Zach snapped back. "Stop jumping to conclusions."

"Then where is he?" asked Jacques. "And where is Yasin?"

"They both disappeared during the commotion when we found Liu's body," said Pena. "And Sarah, you were missing too. While we are grateful to you for saving us, there are questions…"

Sarah stared at the floor and only lifted her head slightly when she spoke. "I saw Marshall leave, and I tried to follow him. But just before he reentered the facility, I heard your screams from a distance and decided to return."

"Why wasn't she affected like we were?" asked Aminah.

"It's quite simple. Sarah doesn't experience the psychic flow as the overseers do." Pena made a

294

sweeping gesture to the group. "I am also not as sensitive as you, but I do have a higher perception, and I am aware of the energy. The feelings of despair were overwhelming to me. I can only imagine the mental and emotional torture you all endured."

"So, Sarah is immune?" said Zach.

"I didn't say that. She has the same sensitivity as the general population. While it may take longer, even those with the lowest level of sensitivity are beginning to feel a heightened sense of hopelessness, depression and despair. Unless the vortexes are restored, it will only get worse."

"The perfect recruiting tool for Mr. Cox," said Zach.

"Indeed," replied Pena.

"I'm more concerned about finding Yasin," said Jacques. "That should be our number one priority. Then finding Marshall and getting the truth out of him. Once we're done with both of those things, we can finally mourn the loss of Liu Wei."

Zach turned to Pena. "Jacques makes some sense here. We need to find Yasin and Marshall. Can we organize a search party?"

"Yes, but it will be small and limited, and we'll have to cover a lot of area. Since this is a place of peace, we only have four security attendants at the facility. Obviously, we could not have anticipated such a situation. The Suicide Society has always been the paramount example of unity. To have a murder..." Pena shook his head as tears filled his eyes, "It is unthinkable."

"Still, we've had one," said Zach. "So, I suggest we go in pairs for safety. That means we have four search parties. Pena, you stay near the foyer in case Yasin or Marshall returns to that area. We'll also need to coordinate communications. Since no one will remove their mental shielding, we'll have to use physical devices."

"We have those," said Pena. "They are in my office just outside the foyer. We can go back there, get them, and map out the search area responsibilities…"

"I'm sorry," interrupted Rogelio as he pointed to the gash on his forehead, "but I'm still bleeding profusely, and I may have a concussion. I need medical attention and some time to rest."

Zach looked around at his battered colleagues, and they all nodded in agreement. Even Jacques stared down at his arm as he gently touched the torn muscle and flesh.

"I—I suppose I should get this disinfected and bandaged up before we begin the search," he said.

Zach pondered the suggestion for just a moment. "Agreed. Let's meet here in two hours. That should give everyone time to dress their wounds and freshen up."

After they had their showers, snacks, antiseptic, bandages and medical exams, the overseers gathered back at Pena's office exactly two hours after they split up. With the exception of Jacques's arm, which required eleven stitches, all of the wounds proved to be superficial, including Rogelio, who tested negative for a concussion.

Pena distributed handheld transceivers and printed out several copies of a more detailed map of the facility. The Spaniard used colored lines to define individual search assignments. When he finished, he handed the maps to Zach, who studied them carefully.

"Okay, Pena's men will cover the blue and purple zones. Rogelio, you go with Aminah to the red area. Jacques, you and Sasha cover the yellow area, and Sarah and I will take the green zone."

As he distributed the maps, he continued, "Keep those walkie-talkies on, and once you're finished searching your zone, return to Pena's office." They nodded to each other in agreement just as the security attendants arrived to pick up their assignments.

Zach and Sarah traversed a long, isolated hallway before descending two flights of metal-grated stairs and entering a basement lined with thick concrete walls. The mechanical room housed the equipment that produced the facility's power, water and electricity. Single bulbs spaced exactly three meters apart illuminated a short hallway with white directional lines painted on the walls. The passage was adequately lit except for a small space between each bulb where unnerving shadows grew and faded as they walked.

Eventually, they came upon a room with a large sign stenciled over the door that read, *Chillers*. A smaller *Authorized Personnel Only* directive was fastened underneath the larger one. The cooling towers were located somewhere outside, probably on top of the building, but the actual water-chilled equipment for the vapor compression process was inside this room. Sarah held Zach's arm as they moved past an endless series of insulated pipes while the motors on the units emitted a steady drone that made it difficult to talk.

Zach turned to Sarah and motioned for her to follow a walkway lined with yellow caution tape that would take her in the opposite direction of where he planned to explore. She nodded, kissed him on the cheek, and went over to a large control unit with buttons lit in a variety of different colors. Zach walked up and down a series of long corridors, checking behind large machines, tool chests, pumps and vessels. The process-generated heat was oppressive, and he wiped his brow several times. Slowly scanning the perimeter of the room, he looked behind every platform, riser and junction box, but there was no sign of either Marshall or Yasin.

Sarah continued to search near the back of the room, but after an hour passed, she finally glanced over and shook her head and gave him an "all clear" sign. Zach didn't want to spend another moment in the uncomfortable heat and fetid air of the equipment room, and once outside, he breathed deep and wiped his brow.

"We need to go through every one of these rooms," he said to Sarah as she joined him out in the cool air of the main building. "They're all going to be loud and hot. If you want, you can leave. I'll finish this myself."

"There's no way I'm going to leave you do this alone. Let's get to the next one," she said.

They walked over to an adjacent door with a sign that read *Air Handlers*. Repeating the search, they moved through several more of the equipment rooms that housed the heat exchangers, sprinklers, electrical generators and water pumps respectively. The boiler room was the last place they needed to search, and it turned out to be the largest, hottest and dirtiest of the mechanical rooms.

Five huge cylinders positioned on a high platform generated processed water used for everything from bathing to forced-air heating in the winter. Summer lightened the load, but the hum of the pumps was an ever-present reminder that hot water was a year-round necessity, even in the middle of July in Arizona.

By now, Zach had tired of the search, and Sarah also seemed exhausted. So far, the day proved to be extremely trying, and with no evidence of foul play, he wanted to finish up so they could return to their rooms to relax and shower. The temperature inside the boiler room was unbearable, and Zach sensed his pores opening to release perspiration in a futile attempt to cool down. He leaned over and almost shouted in Sarah's ear. "Let's get this one done quickly. It's hotter than hell in here."

They split up, and Zach moved between the myriad of motors, pumps and controls. The roar of the equipment was deafening, so when he heard Sarah's shriek over the din, he knew something was terribly wrong. He ran toward her screams, turning a corner and almost falling as his knee hit a metal railing along a designated pathway near one of the huge boilers at the end of the line.

When he saw Sarah, his heart sank. She was on her knees with a hand balled into a fist pressed against her mouth. Zach stopped and walked slowly toward her. Against his will, he looked up until his eyes reached the naked form of Yasin pinned against a scalding high-pressure steam pipe attached to the boiler. The insulation was torn away, exposing his back to the 400-degree piping.

Raw meat still bubbled and sizzled where it contacted the scalding iron, but most of the flesh had burned away some time ago. Zach approached the body, and as he grew closer, he could see a visible blunt force wound on the forehead just above the left eye.

Perhaps the bludgeoning hadn't been enough to kill Yasin, but exposure to the scorching boiler outlet pipe had cooked his insides.

Zach tried to pry him off the pipes, but Yasin's meat, flesh and other unidentifiable internal substances stuck to the metal and continued to broil, creating an odor Zach would never forget. The scene was so gruesome he stumbled back and fought rising nausea.

My God, what kind of psychopath could do such a thing?

Chapter Twenty-Four

Interstate-39 was far less congested than the freeway near Chicago, and by the time they reached I-55, traffic was almost nonexistent. Wanda didn't appear to listen, but Mateo explained his plan to take I-40 over to I-17 and drop down into Phoenix. That way, they would only have to bypass St. Louis, Oklahoma City and Albuquerque.

They drove through the day and into the night, and Mateo snacked on sandwiches, chips and Doris's homemade cookies, but Wanda continued to stare straight ahead. He tried to engage her in conversation several times, but he was met with only silence. Besides periodically using the restroom, she sat quietly in the passenger's seat without changing position or moving a muscle.

The essence of Wanda retreated to an obscure corner of her subconscious mind she hadn't visited for many years. As a child, she often crawled under the bed in her room after a day of teasing at school or a severe scolding from her impatient father. Peering out of the darkness through the small sliver of light between the bed skirt and the floor, Wanda felt safe, invisible and immune to the cruelty she endured growing up.

After traveling hundreds of miles in complete silence, Mateo jerked the wheel and pulled over to the side of the road. Several minutes passed without either of them saying a word. Finally, he shut off the engine, pulled the keys out of the ignition and laid them in Wanda's lap.

"I'm leaving, Wanda," he said without looking at her. "You can have the car. I'll hitch a ride with someone, but I can't travel all the way to Phoenix with you like this. I understand you've been through hell, but so have a lot of people. I wish you the best, but you'll never survive if you're going to be permanently tuned out."

He waited for a reply, but her face remained expressionless and empty. After reaching into the basket and grabbing two waters and a cookie, Mateo opened the door to the vehicle, hesitated, then reached over and kissed Wanda on the cheek. "Goodbye sweetheart." The door closed gently as he walked down the shoulder of the road, his hands thrust in the pocket of his wrinkled and soiled suit coat.

Dusk retreated as night fell over the barren landscape, and the headlights created a growing shadow as he moved farther away from the car. He was almost swallowed up by the descending darkness when he heard a frantic voice call from behind.

"Mateo!"

He paused but didn't turn around.

"Mateo, I can't make it without you. Please don't leave me." Wanda sounded frightened and desperate.

A small smile crossed his lips, and he turned around and started back toward her. They met half way, and she wrapped her arms around him, crying on his shoulder as he held her tightly.

"It's ok, we'll get through this," he said while gently guiding her back to the car. "Wanda, please get in. We have a lot to talk about." She nodded, and soon they were back on the road heading south on I-55.

"Let's get this out in the open," he said tentatively. "Tell me what happened at the Shraeger's place."

She spoke in a whisper. "That filthy man was raping Doris. He—he was trying to put his thing in her; I know that. The gun was just sitting there, and when the other one went into the second bedroom with Irma, I picked it up. I—hated them for what they were doing to us. I wanted to kill them, Mateo. When the chance came, I *wanted* to kill them... I feel so ashamed."

"Listen to me, Wanda," he said. "You saved everyone in that house. It's as simple as that. If you hadn't shot them, no one would have survived. We're living in a jungle now, and people aren't playing by rules anymore. You have nothing to feel guilty about. In fact, you're my hero."

She blushed and wiped the tears from her eyes but kept looking out the window.

Finally, she said, "Do you think the others will ever forgive me? Do you think God will forgive me?"

"*Forgive* you? They owe you their lives, and they wanted to tell you that," he replied. "Your courage prevented six innocent people from being murdered, Wanda. You're a fucking hero, do you understand me?

And don't worry about God; he knows what happened."

Almost imperceptibly, Wanda nodded. "Mateo, I still want to talk, but please, not about that anymore. Tell me something about yourself. I don't care what you say; I just need to hear your voice."

"Well… There's nothing extraordinary about me," he said while reaching into a bag of potato chips. "I'm just a salesman from San Diego."

"What exactly is it you sell?"

"Okay, are you ready for this? I sell commercial site furnishings."

"What?"

"Commercial site furnishings. Like the metal benches in parks, or the trash receptacles. The stuff vandals or animals can't destroy."

"Oh, I see," said Wanda. "I never stopped to think about it, but I guess someone has to make and sell park equipment. Is it interesting work?"

"Well, it's a living, I guess," he said. "What about you, Wanda? What do you do?"

"I'm a forensic statistician. I also dabble in particle physics and quantum theory."

"Wow," said Mateo as his eyes widened. "Well, as if I didn't feel inadequate before, I certainly do now."

Wanda looked over at him with alarm. "Oh no, Mateo, you mustn't think that way. Every job is important if it's work you love."

"You know, I always wanted to be an artist. Maybe I'll get to show you my paintings someday."

Wanda smiled. "I'd like that very much. I'm sure they're wonderful."

The miles rolled by without incident as they continued to talk. Several abandoned cars lined the roadside, and groups of people, mostly men, stood near the overpasses in the light of the street lamps, glaring at the Sonata as it drove by. Their bodies were slick with July sweat, and they had the look of suspicion, anger and desperation in their eyes.

"Don't make eye contact with them, Wanda. That incenses them."

"Why are they in the middle of nowhere? Why aren't they working?" she asked.

Mateo remained stoic as he spoke. "These things snowball fast. Sales for nonessential products come to a screeching halt, and those people get laid off. They have no money to buy anything, but they have to feed their families. Stores get looted and close up, which means there are even fewer jobs, but now more people need food so the looting gets worse. The bomb added the element of terror to the mix."

"This is so frightening," said Wanda.

"It takes centuries to build a society but only a few weeks to tear it down."

"It's so depressing," she said. "Where does it end?"

"I don't know. Most will stay inside as long as they have food, water and electricity. I'm counting on getting you to Arizona before the really bad stuff starts."

"If this isn't the bad stuff…" Wanda's voice trailed off.

Mateo looked over and sensed she was becoming sad and sullen again. "So, who's in Arizona anyway, Wanda? Is your family there?"

"Yes. My mother and father live there, but they're divorced. I see my mother a lot, but I really don't see my father very often."

305

"Brothers and sisters?"

"I have two brothers, but I never see them either."

"Why is that? Your father and brothers, I mean. Why don't you see them?"

"They — I think they're ashamed of me."

"Ashamed? You're a scientist for God's sake. What do your brothers do?"

"One is a chef, and the other is a mechanic."

Mateo let out a hearty laugh, and Wanda looked over and frowned. "Why is that funny?"

"C'mon, Wanda, you must see the irony. You're a scientist, and they're chefs and mechanics? You have more going for you than either of them."

"But I'm... autistic. I say the wrong thing sometimes and get emotional at the wrong times. I've embarrassed them a lot..." Her voice trailed off. "The funny thing is I usually don't even know when I've done or said something wrong."

Mateo looked at her and smiled. "So, you mean you're human like the rest of us. Because what you've just told me are things we've all done. If your family doesn't love you for the wonderful, talented person you are, fuck 'em. Uh, excuse me, I shouldn't swear."

For the first time since the incident at the farmhouse, Wanda actually laughed. "Mateo, you're incorrigible."

"What about your love interest, Wanda? Tell me about your significant other."

Wanda looked down and folded her hands in her lap. "Well, I'm in love with him, but I'm not sure how he feels about me."

"It sounds complicated."

"It is. He's very cautious with his feelings. But sometimes he lets his guard down, and he's just wonderful."

"Pretty easy to see you're in love. I'm kinda jealous. I guess there's no chance for you and me."

Wanda blushed and her smile widened. "Don't be silly, Mateo. I'm sure you have someone."

"I have an ex-wife and two kids in San Diego," he said. "The ex-wife hates me, and the boys don't really think of me as their dad." Wanda noticed Mateo's grip tighten on the wheel. "They reserve that title for Drew."

"Who's Drew?"

"Their step-dad." The words were brittle and tinged with bitterness. "He's taken my place for all intents and purposes. I get to see the kids twice a month, but Marilyn, that's my ex-wife, does everything she can to mess that up for me."

Wanda reached over and gently touched his arm. "That's awful, Mateo. Why would she do that?"

"She hates me. Maybe I deserve it. I was into my work, and I wasn't home that much when the kids were young. I missed a lot of birthdays. When we got divorced, she said I should be happy. I could shed the façade of being a father, and I was free to pursue my other interests without the burden of a family."

"So, *were* you happy? It sounds like you really didn't enjoy being around your family."

Mateo looked puzzled but then smiled. "Sometimes your bluntness is refreshing," he said. "I guess I wasn't happy at all. In hindsight, I was massively depressed. It took something that harsh to make me realize it."

"Well, you still have time, Mateo."

"I suppose I do. I look forward to my kids becoming adults so they can visit me without their mother's approval." He stared straight ahead in deep thought. Finally, he said, "Would you like to start a family someday, Wanda?"

The question made her shift in her seat uneasily. "I—I never really thought about it. But I guess I would. But only with Marshall."

"That's your boyfriend's name?"

"Yes, well, I hope he's my boyfriend. He's complex, and we were just beginning to address the relationship."

"*Address the relationship.* You make it sound so clinical."

"You don't know Marshall. He's a very analytical person."

They passed the small town of Hamel, which was just outside of St. Louis. The sky was pitch dark as they approached the city, and the pungent smell of burning rubber saturated the vehicle's cab. Traffic increased exponentially as they neared the downtown area, so Mateo plotted a course to stay outside the city proper.

The dashboard light monitoring their fuel flashed amber, so they looked for gas station signs near exit ramps that didn't have many people loitering near them. They headed west, which would hopefully keep them far enough north of the city to avoid any violence.

"I'm having trouble breathing, Mateo," said Wanda as the smoke from the downtown fires wafted directly at them, aided by a heavy northeasterly breeze.

"It's thick, but the smoke should clear soon," he said. "It seems like the whole city is on fire." Just as he finished his sentence, a fire truck approached from the rear with its sirens blaring and loud horn honking.

No sooner had it passed than another car pulled up beside them. A young woman in her early twenties sat in the passenger's seat. She rolled down the window and leaned out, revealing her purplish hair, black eye shadow and face tattoo. "You got gas?" she yelled.

"No," replied Mateo. "We're running on fumes. Any idea where we can get some?"

"Fuck!" she said loudly before leaning over and saying something to the driver. She came back and shouted, "Good luck finding any; the whole city's a mess. You're lucky you don't have some. I'd have wasted your ass to get it." The car sped off, and she put her arm out the window and flipped them off.

Mateo's jaw clenched. "*Necesitamos unas gasolina.* We're almost on empty," he muttered.

They continued skirting the edge of the city on I-270, missing the worst of the chaos and anarchy. Traffic slowed at Florissant as looters walked over a footbridge carrying a variety of power tools, televisions and other high-ticket items stolen from big-box retailers in a nearby strip mall. Several people climbed down the embankment onto the freeway, their arms filled with pilfered merchandise.

A fight ensued as the overpass dwellers battled the looters for possession of their plunder. Mateo and the other drivers stalled as the drama unfolded without any law enforcement officials in sight. He alternated his gaze between the gas gauge and the violent confrontation up ahead. The Sonata was in a line of cars in the right lane, and some of them were jumping off the freeway onto the exit ramp. Mateo pulled over to the shoulder in order to block the vehicles coming from behind. Horns blared as impatient motorists tried to get him to move.

The driver in the car directly behind them was out of his mind with rage. Wanda turned around and saw him pushing on the horn, beating the steering wheel and screaming so loudly the veins in his neck bulged. The line of cars moved slowly up the off ramp, their progress impeded by the dead stoplights at the intersection. Fortunately, most of the vehicles were able to get through the clog and back on the on-ramp, bypassing the bridge violence.

Mateo finally reached the intersection at the top of the overpass and proceeded slowly. Horns kept honking and brakes screeched amid the sound of shattering glass and twisted metal as another accident stopped traffic. Wanda hid her face in her hands while Mateo muttered in Spanish, ignoring the threatening charge of cars coming from the opposite direction.

Seemingly out of nowhere, an older man who looked to be in his seventies walked laboriously in front of the Sonata carrying a stereo. He appeared frightened and made eye contact with Wanda just as a much younger man in a brown bombers jacket ran up from behind and stuck a knife in his back. The older man stiffened, dropped the stereo and staggered past the car, clutching his back with both hands. The thug in the bombers jacket picked up the stereo, looked around, and ran, pushing the older man to the pavement as he moved past.

Wanda gasped and yelled, "Oh no, he's hurt, we have to stop."

Mateo kept his hands locked on the wheel and stared straight ahead. "I'm sorry, but we can't."

Wanda waited for someone to get out and help the old man, but they were all like Mateo and didn't want to get involved. "Look at the poor man. He's writhing on the ground in the middle of the road. Someone's going to run over him."

"Goddamn it, Wanda, we can't stop. We have no gas, and the crazies would jump us to get our car. Just don't look."

Wanda never experienced Mateo's anger before, and the sudden outburst frightened her. She twirled her hair and struggled to breathe as she pushed up against the door panel. A loud wail escaped her lips, which signaled a severe panic attack was in progress.

The combination of the blaring horns, angry motorists, the wounded man in the street and now Wanda's moans created a stressful situation that only got worse when one of the cars tried to maneuver through a small gap between an SUV and a Volkswagen. The Dodge veered sharply to avoid a collision and inadvertently hit the old man, spinning him like a top until he fell hard to the pavement. His arms flailed, and he tried to get up, but the impact broke one of his legs. Another car followed and ran him over a second time. With his torso crushed, the septuagenarian regurgitated a significant quantity of hemorrhaged abdominal blood through his mouth and nose.

Wanda screamed again, this time even louder, and Mateo clutched the wheel tighter. Looking at the anger in his eyes as his jawbone worked and teeth clenched created even more fear and panic. Wanda grew silent, which seemed to settle Mateo a bit. He had no way of knowing this was a troubling barometer of Wanda's fragile mental state.

Mercifully, they were able to reenter the freeway past the violence and drove in silence as the two-seventy turned south. Mateo searched the GPS for gas stations while Wanda cried, letting out an audible sob every so often.

When they reached the Manchester exit, he pulled off and headed east. A cluster of stations were up ahead, and they drove slowly past each of them, hoping to find someone who was still open. After seeing the first *No Gas* sign, it seemed the effort would be futile. Four stations in a row all had handwritten signs on pieces of cardboard telling desperate motorists there wasn't any gas at the pumps. Just as they were about to give up hope, Mateo spotted a lit sign at *Wingers Full Service*, which was the last station before the developed area ended.

"That sign is lit up, and I think I saw someone in there," he said. "He might have gas or know someone who does."

They pulled into the parking lot and got out of the Sonata, walking into the store where a man in a uniform with the name *Ed* sewed on his shirt stood up from behind the counter. He kept both arms out of sight. "What can I do for you, bud?" he asked with a strong note of suspicion.

"Gas, I need some," said Mateo.

Ed shook his head. "Ran out the day after the bomb in Chicago blew up. Not sure when we're getting more. Some say tomorrow, but they'll ration it, that's for sure."

"Do you know anyone who has gas?"

"It's like a moving target, really. Some stations acted like they sold out but kept some in reserve. The prices are crazy. People tell me some owners are charging $500 per gallon."

Mateo hung his head. "Jesus, I don't know what to do. We're traveling to Arizona, and somehow, we have to get gas."

Ed eyed Mateo for a minute. "You got anything to trade?"

Mateo lifted his head, and his eyes lit up. "Yeah, we got some canned goods, toilet paper and some other stuff."

"I don't need any canned goods, but I'll take all the butt wipe ya got. I'll give you a quarter gallon per roll."

"That isn't going to do it. We only have ten rolls, and I need a full tank."

"I'll tell you what," said Ed. "I'll give you two gallons for six rolls. And I'll throw in this." He reached under the counter and pulled out a five-foot section of half inch irrigation tubing and tossed it to Mateo, who looked at the hose and then back at Ed.

"What's this for?"

"To syphon the gas you're gonna steal. Because that's the only way you're gonna make it to Arizona."

Mateo took the hose and nodded to the clerk. "Thank you. I suppose it'll come in handy. One more thing. Do you mind if we stay parked here for a few hours? We really need some sleep."

Ed the clerk started walking back into the storeroom. "Knock yourself out. But I'd keep the windows rolled up if I were you."

Chapter Twenty-Five

Two one-ton trucks with covered beds drove down Capitol Street Southwest until they reached the South Gate of the Acosta-Ballman Joint Base at MacDill Boulevard Southwest. Lars drove the lead vehicle with Delgado in the passenger's seat and Ziminski positioned uncomfortably between them. The effort to locate Mr. Cox was swift and effective since the long reach of the Gehenna Corporation extended deep into the military. This included the Joint Base Vice-Commander, Air Force Captain, Shane Egan. He ranked one step below the Base Commander, who was sleeping soundly in his quarters.

Lars pulled the truck up to the gate and presented the security guard with a legitimate ID issued through a high-ranking loyalist at the Department of Defense. The guard walked into the shack and ran the credentials through the IMESA system, which verified their authenticity. He walked back while continuing to look at the ID before finally returning it.

"Apparently, you're meeting the Vice Commander at the DIA building, is that right?"

Lars nodded his head. "Yes, that's where he told us to go."

"And you have computer supplies in the back of those trucks?"

"Yes, that's right. Critical supplies," said Lars.

"You know, there's a service entrance for that," said the guard while leaning through the window and looking around.

"Service entrance my ass," offered Ziminski. "We've got first-class merchandise for the General himself."

The guard looked at Ziminski oddly, but his expression hardened as he turned back to Lars. "Is there something wrong here?"

Delgado leaned over and looked at the guard directly. "Pay no attention to our friend. Maybe too many tours in Afghanistan, if you know what I mean. They told us to go to the DIA with this stuff. Direct orders from Vice-Commander Egan."

The guard nodded. "I assume you also have a DOD ID?"

Delgado reached into his pocket and took out his own official identification. The guard nodded and backed off a few steps while motioning the trucks through. Lars maneuvered up the street and turned on Laward James Boulevard, which took him to the rear of the targeted building. He turned off the headlights and pulled into the unloading dock.

Meticulous planning and coordination among the organization's sympathizers within the DIA ensured that the roll up door was left open. They rigged the cameras to play on a loop, so the guards in the security center never saw the ten men dressed in black fatigues

315

jump out of the truck beds and move quickly into the warehouse.

Once everyone was inside, Lars closed the door softly and gathered the masked squad around him as they assembled their automatic weapons and screwed on the silencers. A woman waiting behind a large steel rack stepped out from the shadows, glancing suspiciously to her right and left as she approached. The men looked at her casually, but continued their preparations.

When she reached Lars, they made eye contact but didn't exchange greetings. "We will disrupt the power at twenty-three hundred hours. A thousand people work here during the day, but only a few hundred are here this late at night. There's a staircase right over there. Once you reach the basement, you'll find the target behind the third door on the left side of the hallway. There will be four guards outside, and they'll see you come out of the stairwell, so I'd be prepared to take aggressive action."

"Thank you," said Lars without mentioning her name. He wouldn't identify the Directorate for Science and Technology, Tammera Sondulson, to the rest of the squad. "We'll take it from here."

She nodded. "You'll have maybe ten minutes before they get the power and backup systems back online. I've assembled a force of our people who will defend the Benefactor with their lives, but it would be better if that wasn't necessary."

"Understood," said Lars. He looked down at his watch. "We have less than five minutes before the power is cut. We need to go."

"Roger Wilco," said Ziminski, which only elicited irritated looks and scowls from the hardened mercenaries. Alan insisted on taking part in the mission to rescue the Benefactor and pleaded with Watts to allow him to tag along. He went so far as to threaten to crash Gehenna's entire IT infrastructure if they left him behind. Watts finally relented because he couldn't take a chance that Alan might actually carry out the threat.

Lars fixed his night vision goggles over his eyes, and the rest of the squadron followed his lead. They hurried to the stairwell and quietly opened the door as Delgado, Ziminski and the rest of the group followed them in. Once they reached the bottom of the metal grated stairs, Lars glanced at his atomic chromatic watch that read 10:59:27. At five seconds before the hour, he raised his hand and started the countdown by closing one digit at a time.

At exactly eleven o'clock, the lights in the stairwell went dead, and Lars quietly pushed the door open. He looked down the hallway and saw four military personnel stumbling around, their hands instinctively resting on their side arms. One pulled out a flashlight and nervously cast the beam around in different directions. By now, the insurgents had entered the narrow passage, their weapons trained on the disoriented MPs. The night vision goggles gave them a decided advantage.

Lars, Delgado and five others moved toward the four-man security detail, and by the time one of them illuminated the group with his flashlight, multiple laser tags covered his uniform and those of his three companions. Lars pulled out a handgun and pointed it at them.

317

"I can hit you with the tranquilizer gun, or I can kill you; it's your choice. If you want to live, stay quiet and pull your side arms out slowly, place them on the ground, and kick them over in my direction."

In tandem, the soldiers complied, and four guns skittered across the cement floor. Before they stopped sliding, Lars already fired tranquilizer darts at each of the four men. They immediately grabbed at the site of their wounds, but the drug was already coursing through their bodies. The sedative worked quickly, but it took about three minutes for them to totally lose consciousness. While time consuming, this method avoided weapons fire and preserved the element of surprise.

Once the last guard nodded out, all four were bound and gagged and dragged into an adjacent room. Lars and Delgado gathered close to the door and listened for any sounds coming from inside. Unfortunately, Tammara Sondulson couldn't secure a passkey, and none of the guards had one either. If they wanted to get in, Lars knew they would have to do it the old-fashioned way.

He motioned for Tray Houseman, a demolitions expert with two tours in Mosul and Rouandi. When he returned to the U.S., Houseman's depression was so severe it led to a suicide attempt. He survived the first one but wouldn't have lived through the second if Mr. Cox hadn't shown up. Tray was fiercely loyal, and he handled explosives as though he was swaddling a baby in soft blankets.

"This is a double lock," he whispered.

"What the hell does that mean?" asked Alan.

Houseman rolled his eyes. "Locks on both sides of the door. The low-yield explosive I've used should take care of both of them. Move away and turn your back. Tell me when."

"Just do it," said Lars, "we're running out of time."

Almost as soon as the words were out of his mouth, Houseman pushed an icon on his phone, and two muted pops accompanied by small bright flashes signaled the explosives had detonated. Lars stood to the side, grabbed the knob, and yanked the door open. A barrage of bullets came through the opening and slammed into the opposite wall. As soon as the volley ended, Lars peered in and saw a frenzy of disorganized activity through the green tint of his night vision goggles. Several men were down on one knee, their guns pointed blindly toward the entrance.

The small doorway limited his field of view, so Lars had difficulty locating the Benefactor. He motioned for five of his men to shoulder their arms. On his signal, they moved low and swift through the opening, peeling off to either side and focusing on the un-cleared sectors. The precision afforded by assault weapons and night vision equipment allowed them to eliminate five hostiles after a short firefight. The first two men in the stack took slugs from small caliber fire, but their vests prevented penetration, and they were able to continue on with the mission.

As the weapons fire ceased, Lars tried to enter the room, but someone from the rear pushed him out of the way and ran through the doorway. Several shots from a handgun rang out, followed shortly by a burst of muted automatic weapons fire. By the time Lars gained his bearings, the enemy's remaining armed personnel had been taken out.

He walked up to the overly ambitious commando, who stood over a fallen member of the base security detail. The wounded man lay on his back with his arms raised over his head, a large bloodstain spreading through his uniform. "Please, please help me. I'm hurt. I need a doctor."

Lars' soldier remained standing with the gun pointed at the security guard's head. Without hesitation, a single shot blew off a significant part of the man's skull.

Clapping his hand on his crewman's shoulder, Lars said, "Nicely done."

The combatant turned around and removed a pair of night goggles and black mask. Looking straight at Lars, she said, "Someone had to have the balls to make the charge, Lars."

"Sandra!" He took a step back as his mouth opened, but he didn't utter another word.

A low-level light illuminated the room as one of the fighters fired up a battery-powered lantern. A second increased visibility so that the entire interior was lit up. Over in a corner, several people huddled together, obvious fear in their faces.

A single chair sat in the center of the room. The occupant had his back to the squad. His hands were tied behind him, and his head tilted to the side but straightened as his liberators approached.

"It's about time you got here, Mr. Delgado. I don't know how much longer I could restrain myself from lobotomizing these fools."

"Benefactor!" said Delgado as he rushed over to the wooden chair Mr. Cox occupied. He fumbled with the restraints. "His hands are cuffed. Find the goddamned key." The assault team searched the dead bodies until the handcuff keys were found.

Delgado ripped them away from one of his men and freed the Benefactor's arms and legs.

Mr. Cox turned around and faced his loyalists, and a thin smile spread over his lips as he surveyed the group. "Sandra," he said. "Was that you who burst into the room with reckless disregard?"

Smiling smugly with a lit cigarette in her mouth, she said, "I didn't want to spend another night alone, Benefactor."

"I'm here too," said Ziminski as he stepped through the crowd. "I'm part of it. Ask Lars or Delgado. I was one of the first through the door, right?" Lars rolled his eyes, and Delgado looked at his shoes and shook his head without replying.

Mr. Cox' smile widened. "We will discuss the unacceptable breach of security later, but for now, I think we'll all be happy with our spoils. Cowering in the corner is our friend, Senator Merl Chawsome. We also have the Director of the CIA, Tomas Fuentes, and the White House Chief of Staff, Pam Runyun. The Director of the DIA and the Foreign Services Attaché were also here, but sadly, I'm afraid Sandra killed them."

"Ah, we have less than two minutes until the power comes back on, so we better go quickly," said Lars.

"Lars?" said Mr. Cox with incredulity. "Aren't you supposed to be in Sedona exterminating the Suicide Society?"

Lars backed up a step and raised his eyebrows. "You're kidding, right? Under the circumstances I thought I should be here."

"Considering your gross dereliction of duty, I suppose you're right," replied Mr. Cox with a voice that conveyed his sarcasm.

Already a group of five loyalists had gathered around Senator Chawsome and the others. Prodded by weapons poking at them, the hostages rose unsteadily to their feet and made their way over to the door. The Benefactor rubbed his wrists and shook his arms as he walked. He made sure he was standing near the Senator as they shoved him forward roughly.

"Senator Chawsome, isn't it ironic. Less than ten minutes ago you were blowing cigar smoke in my face and subjecting me to that delightful waterboarding technique. You seemed to enjoy it too. Well, now you'll be *my* guest, and I imagine we'll have even more fun."

"You're a freak," said Chawsome as the spittle flew from the corners of his mouth. "And you're about to bring the entire U.S. government down on you."

"Oh, I think quite the contrary, Senator. How do you think my people got in here so easily? Over half the military personnel on this base answer to us, especially the commanders. But don't worry, you'll see soon enough."

The close proximity of the interrogation room to the loading dock proved fortuitous, and they ascended the stairs out of the basement and went back up to the main level of the building. As they rehearsed, Lars, Delgado and the second driver changed into civilian clothes and got into their respective trucks, so the engines were running by the time the balance of the squad arrived. Sandra pushed Senator Chawsome into the back of the first truck along with his accomplices. Lars instructed his men to keep the captives silent and restrained with the threat of instant death if they attempted to alert anyone or escape.

Once everyone was loaded into the trucks, they drove slowly back to the main gate. By now, several emergency vehicles converged, and squadrons were dispatched to seal the perimeter. It was impossible to tell how many of the soldiers were loyal to the Benefactor, so the trucks approached the civilian business exit cautiously. As Lars expected, one of the security force guards flagged them down.

"Excuse me, sir," said the Military Police Corporal as he approached the truck. "The base is on lockdown due to the power outage. No one is allowed in or out until further notice."

Lars reached out of the cab and handed the guard a piece of folded paper. "That doesn't apply to us," he said. "The Joint Base Vice-Commander issued an exemption. Our business is of vital importance, and we can't afford a delay. Besides, you can see the lights just came back on."

The guard inspected the document, crafted in advance and signed by Vice-Commander Egan. As though he couldn't believe its authenticity, he kept alternating his gaze between the document and Lars.

"I need to verify these orders," he said while rubbing the back of his neck.

"Fine," said Lars with obvious impatience. "but I'm sure the Vice Commander has nothing better to do in the middle of a crisis than to verify orders that will delay a critical deployment."

The guard tapped the orders into his palm as he thought through his dilemma. Verifying orders that were issued by a Vice Commander might take hours, if someone could even find Egan at this time of night.

After some consideration, the MP puffed out his cheeks, shook his head and handed the paper back to Lars. "Alright, go ahead." He stepped back and waved them on as the gate opened.

Once they were back on South Capitol, the trucks belched diesel smoke and maneuvered through the heavily fortified DC streets until they reached I-295. Military units patrolled the freeway in heavy numbers, policing the area and protecting the transportation department as it worked to clear the thoroughfare of debris, garbage, manmade barricades and dead bodies. Humvees lined both sides of the road in regular intervals throughout the Capitol area, and soldiers stood near the protective panels of their vehicles with weapons at the ready.

Lars traveled south on the two-ninety-five to avoid the ultra-intense military presence around the White House and Capitol Building. This route would take them about fifteen minutes longer, but they would face a lot less scrutiny. Out of fear or anger, floaters from across the country were vigilant in their relentless protests against the impotence of the government. The President remained silent since the Chicago bombing, but the clamoring for his impeachment grew louder by the day.

As the trucks exited I-295 and entered Rosile Island, Lars headset cackled with momentary static.

"Lars, we've got company." It was Swede Henderson, the driver in the second truck. Swede had the most combat experience in extreme situations, so he drew the assignment of getting the Benefactor to the corporate jet intact.

"Hostiles?"

"It looks that way. Three Humvees flying like bats out of hell weaving through traffic. The gunner's taking aim with an M2 Browning."

"Go evasive, Swede."

"Roger that."

Lars hit the accelerator, and the Ram truck picked up speed. He looked out the side mirror and confirmed the Swede's observation. Two Humvees were dodging back and forth as they fought through traffic and debris that covered the roadway. The trucks were well into the passage over the Woodrow Wilson Memorial Bridge when the Humvees opened fire from behind. Bullets whizzed past the cab of the first truck, and Lars saw the Swede swerving to the Ram's extreme tolerance to avoid the volleys.

"Swede," Lars yelled into the headset, "I'm dropping back; you take the lead. I'll shield you. The Benefactor is the only one who matters."

"Roger that."

Lars switched lanes, let his foot off the accelerator and braked, which allowed the Swede's truck to lurch ahead. Once he was past, Lars slipped in behind him and sped up. A second volley of slugs slammed into the truck causing chaos in the bed. About three quarters of the way through the bridge crossing, he realized they wouldn't make it to the other side. Multiple army vehicles joined the pursuit, and the convoy quickly gained ground. Since they couldn't outrun their pursuers, Lars considered pulling off to the short shoulder on the bridge and making a stand.

He pushed the transmit button and opened his mouth to speak, but his words were drowned out by the sound of a massive explosion behind him. The concussion hit their truck, and it lurched forward like it had been struck from behind by a runaway train. Lars fought for control as the vehicle lurched up on two wheels. Time seemed to slow, and he could see the Swede's truck teetering on the opposite side.

The cab shuddered violently as it slammed back to the pavement, and for a long moment, Lars wondered if he would lose control. He turned sharply into the skid and did it a second time before the tail end straightened out. By that time, the Swede's vehicle was already picking up speed.

When Lars looked in the side mirror, he could see several military vehicles falling off the ragged edge of the shattered bridge into the Potomac River below. The fortunate ones swerved and skidded to the brink. The rising dust and debris became so thick it blotted out the other side of the road.

From inside the cab of the lead truck, the Benefactor started to laugh. "Fools!" he bellowed. "They think they can stop me? Their suffering has just begun."

"Uh oh," said the Swede while pointing ahead, "here come more military vehicles. We're not going to make it."

The Benefactor smiled and watched as the drab green jeeps, Humvees and Joint Light Tactical Vehicles pulled in front and behind the two trucks.

"You are mistaken, Mr. Henderson," said the Benefactor. "They are not here to harm us; they're here to escort us back home."

Chapter Twenty-Six

"Please, get him off there, Zach. I can't bear to see him like that." Sarah slid down against a large air handler and covered her face.

Zach nodded and placed his hands on Yasin's viscous body, grimacing as his fingers penetrated the dead man's mushy skin. The sound of blood sizzling and the nauseating smell of burning flesh was overpowering, and he fought against his gag reflex. He tried tugging on Yasin's arm, but large areas of the disfigured body fused with the scalding iron surface and wouldn't give. Zach pulled with increasing force until he heard Yasin's flesh finally begin to peel away from the pipe.

Once the dead overseer was clear of the scalding vessel, Zach carefully laid him on the floor. He made sure the body was face up so that Sarah wouldn't see the raw, angry red fissures in the places where Yasin's trapezius and latissimus muscles used to be.

"We need to let the others know what's going on," said Zach as he pulled out his communicator and pushed the send button. "This is Speaker Randall to anyone who's listening. We've found Yasin. Please respond." Zach released the stud, but only static cackled out of the small speaker. He tried again, and then a third time, but still didn't receive a reply.

"There's too much interference from the machinery and concrete walls," he yelled to Sarah as a pump turned on, raising the background sound level even more. "I need to go and get help."

"Yes, you go get the others. I'll stay here with Yasin."

"Are you sure? I understand how upsetting this is to you."

Sarah's head dropped. "Zach, I know death all too well. I grieve for Yasin, but I have seen much worse."

Zach leaned over and kissed her on the forehead and left the equipment room at a moderate sprint. In his current state, he had difficulty remembering exactly how to get back to the foyer.

Slow your breathing, stay in control. Zach used skills he developed to cope with the visions and maintain his composure. He turned left and walked down the corridor, working his way through the labyrinth of hallways and sub-domains that led past the areas Sasha, Jacques and Rogelio were searching. As he made a final turn down one of the main feeder passages, he saw Pena in the distance sitting at his desk.

"Pena!" Zach shouted the proprietor's name before running toward his office. By the time he reached it, he was out of breath and panting. Pena's face appeared drawn and weary, and his expression conveyed an obvious sense of dread.

He got up and opened the office door, motioning for Zach to take a seat. "What is it? Have you found Yasin?"

"Yes, and he's dead... Someone stabbed him and then discarded his body. We found him pressed up against a large pipe that was so hot it burned away his skin and muscle. Utterly gruesome."

"That is heartbreaking, Speaker Randall," said Pena as he rubbed his face with his hands. "I'll contact my attendants to secure the body. Where is he located exactly?"

"The boiler room. I'm not sure how long he was there, but I believe the crime scene is relatively new. We need to get him out of there quickly."

Pena was already on the walkie-talkie before Zach finished his sentence. In short order, Cheeves and Docker left their sector and returned to the foyer. Together, they followed Zach and Pena back down the path that led them to the boiler room. Zach felt nauseous when he heard the sounds of the motors and once again smelled the distinctive odor of burnt flesh. Sarah was still standing near the body with her head in her hands. When she saw Zach, she rushed toward him, and he wrapped his arms around her tightly.

The two burly attendants unfolded a body bag and laid it out on the floor. Despite their best efforts to gently lift Yasin, several strings of jellied muscle and fat stretched from the ground up to the body before eventually snapping. They lay Yasin in the bag, zipped it up and carried him out of the room, presumably to the same place they had taken Liu Wei.

"I called the others before we left and told them to meet us in the foyer," said Pena as he held the door open for Zach and Sarah. The walk back was painfully slow and oddly exhausting. Once they reached the foyer, they found the other overseers waiting.

No sooner had Zach stepped into Pena's office when Jacques confronted him. "Another dead Suicide Society member, *Speaker* Randall'? We're getting picked off one by one. And where is Marshall, the one you've been protecting?"

"Can we have a few minutes to grieve, Jacques," asked Sasha while dabbing her eyes with a tissue.

"No, Jacques is right," said Rogelio. "Where *is* Marshall? We can't sit around waiting for him to kill each of us like this."

Pena started to speak, thought better of it, and pursed his lips.

"What is it, Pena? You were about to say something. Tell us what you know," said Jacques.

Pena shifted uncomfortably in his chair. "Marshall has left the facility."

Everyone looked at Pena with varying degrees of incredulity. "What?" said Rogelio. "How was he able to leave, especially without your knowledge?"

Pena shrugged. "It is a sanctuary not a prison, Mr. Franco. Anyone can leave, although I do not recommend it."

"We're in the middle of nowhere. Where would he go? Could he make it to Sedona by foot?" asked Aminah.

"The terrain is difficult, but it is not far to 260," said Pena. "Once he gets there, he might find someone to pick him up. He could even make it to the city on foot if he took some water with him."

"And no one saw him?" asked Jacques. "I find that very hard to believe."

"This is an elusive person, Mr. Franco. Our attendants have limited security access to preserve our guest's privacy. Somehow, he was able to disengage the entryway alarm."

"Well, at least we know who the murderer is. We have to go after him," said Rogelio.

"I would advise against it, Mr. Francisco." Pena waggled his finger and shook his head.

Sasha turned to Zach. "The Speaker will decide what we do from here, and we will follow his direction."

Zach nodded to express his appreciation at her show of respect. "Of course, we have to find him. There isn't any choice." Turning to Pena, he continued. "We'll need a vehicle. Please get one prepared as quickly as possible."

"Speaker Randall, I do not think that is wise," said Pena.

"I'm in no mood for my directives to be questioned. Please get the vehicle ready."

"Of course, Speaker," said Pena while bowing in deference.

Zach dismissed the group and sent them to their rooms to change into clothing more compatible with the desert heat. They planned to reconvene in half an hour, so he hurriedly changed into quarter-length khakis and a sun-resistant light cotton shirt. After lacing his shoes and stopping to unwrap a protein bar, he heard a knock at the door. *It's Sarah. Do I know her so well I recognize the sound of her knock?*

"Okay, Zach I'm ready," she said as she walked past him into the room. Even in a pair of shorts and a women's polo shirt, she was beautiful. The absence of the intense fear she experienced her entire life, combined with a healthy diet, breathed vitality into her lithe body. Her hair was glistening, and Zach noticed she began to use some light makeup. Like a butterfly emerging from a cocoon, Sarah was transforming into a truly stunning woman.

Reluctantly, he broke the mood. "I'm sorry, Sarah, you can't come with us on this one."

She turned abruptly, and for a moment, he saw anger flash across her face. "What? I have to go. Besides you, I'm the only one Marshall trusts."

"No, Sarah. He has the gift, and if we're wrong, and he's a traitor, I can't take the chance he would attack you to get to me. You've experienced the power of mind control and what it can make you do to yourself."

She turned away and spoke in a small voice. "I can help, Zach. Don't leave me here. You don't understand. I can't be alone…"

He walked up behind her and put his arms around her shoulders. "I'm sorry, but I won't put you in danger that way." He turned her around and looked into her soulful brown eyes for a moment. Without hesitation, he leaned down and kissed her.

"Sarah, I think I'm falling in love with you."

She sighed in a way that was so full of emotion her breath caught in her throat. "I love you too, Zach. With all my heart." They kissed once again, and when he left the room, Sarah lay down on the bed and cried.

Once he reached the foyer, Zach joined the assembled team and followed Pena over to the garage area. A Toyota Highlander was sitting just outside a high roll-up door, and Cheeves stood near the vehicle holding a set of keys.

As Zach walked over to the driver's door, Pena approached while wringing his hands. "Speaker Randall, I ask you not to do this thing. There is so much danger on the outside, and it is only getting worse. There may be phenomenon you encounter that we couldn't have imagined."

"That's a chance we have to take, Pena. Whether Marshall is innocent or guilty, we can't have him wandering around out there by himself." He reassuringly patted the smaller man on the arm and climbed into the driver's seat.

"At least let one of the attendants accompany you."

Zach shook his head. "We have to do this on our own. Please, take care of Sarah."

After everyone got into the vehicle, Zach pushed the start button, and the Highlander's V-6 engine roared to life. He pulled out onto the rocky terrain that camouflaged the location of the facility. Clouds of gritty dust kicked up behind them as they moved slowly out to Dry Creek Road and eventually 89A.

Once they reached the pavement, Rogelio looked around and then back toward the facility. "You know, the sanctuary isn't that far from the highway. Marshall really might have walked. It's only a few miles to 89A and only five miles into Sedona. I'm not saying it would be fun on a hot July day, but it's very possible."

"We have to assume he's done it, so we'll have to make sure he hasn't left Sedona," said Zach. "He had a head start, but with the heat and terrain, it would take him at least two or three hours. We might catch him walking down this road, so stay alert."

"Unless he got a ride," said Sasha. "Then he's probably long gone."

"Well, he lives in Phoenix, and I would imagine that's where he'll go. So, if he isn't in Sedona, we'll try there." Zach paused a moment and looked in the rear-view mirror at Sasha and the others. "Does anyone want to meld? We would find him much easier if we used our collective capabilities."

They exchanged nervous glances before Sasha looked down, Rogelio twirled his fingers and Aminah peered out the window. Finally, Jacques spoke for the group. "I don't think so, Speaker Randall. Frankly, we can't be sure *you're* not the traitor."

Zach looked at Jacques and shook his head. "You know, I could make the request a directive," he said.

"Please don't do that, Speaker. It wouldn't be wise."

"Is that another threat, Jacques? The Suicide Society has always existed in perfect harmony and symmetry, according to Speaker Anston, so I've been patient. But…"

"I don't want to interrupt, but I'm feeling a bit queasy. Is everyone else all right?" asked Aminah as she leaned forward and grabbed the passenger's seat headrest.

"Actually, I'm not feeling so well myself," said Rogelio. "I'm getting clouded by something. It's pressing on me like an approaching suicide vision, but it's different."

The overseers were especially sensitive to attempted suicide. Through visions, they watched those in the act of taking their own lives. These advanced abilities allowed them to project their essence directly into the moment and interact with the victim. Sometimes, they saved a life, and the families were spared the horror of losing a loved one in such a dreadful manner.

"It's more than one vision," said Sasha as she brought her hand up to her head. "It feels like — many."

"They're growing stronger as we approach the city," said Jacques. "I'm seeing a man with a gun, a woman slitting her throat.... Someone — someone hanging themselves on a door frame. I..."

Zach also felt the pull of the visions. As they grew closer to Sedona, the urgency and number of suicide windows increased exponentially. With practice, Zach had become far more disciplined when the visions forced their way into his psyche. He exerted a small degree of resistance and kept them at a manageable distance, but the sensation was increasingly uncomfortable.

The Highlander passed Airport Road when Aminah screamed and doubled over in pain. "I can't take it," she shrieked. "They're in my head. Hundreds of them all pushing in. They're killing themselves in overwhelming numbers. I can't keep them out."

Zach looked over his shoulder at Rogelio, who slumped down in the seat as his body shook with tremors. His eyes rolled in the back of his head, and a trickle of blood flowed down his left nostril.

"Speaker — Randall, we can't absorb this. The misery is overwhelming; it's breaking down my will. I can't hold it off much longer," said Sasha. "I'm being pulled apart. These visions are dissecting me, and I can't escape them."

Jacques started moaning as he put his head between his legs and vomited on the floor. "Can't fight them," he mumbled. "So many guns pointing at their own heads. Some are pulling the trigger, taking the pills. Blood...

bile… vomit… They all need my help, but I can't take it."

Zach slammed on the brakes and steered over to the shoulder. The visions came from so many sources, even he found it nearly impossible to fend them off. Each desperate soul grabbed, tore and pulled at his psyche for attention. The torment was indescribable as he focused on maintaining control over the increasingly vivid and desperate apparitions. Zach's hold was tenuous, but his composure remained intact.

"Sasha." As he looked over, she cried and trembled. "Sasha!" This time he said it more forcefully, and it seemed to momentarily pull her back from the brink.

"Get out and come to the driver's side. The closer we get to Sedona, the worse the visions are becoming. I can only imagine what it must be like in the big cities. We haven't prepared for this, and we'll be shattered mentally. You must take them back to the sanctuary."

She stared at him blankly. Zach fell out of the vehicle and stumbled to the back door. He opened it and pulled Sasha out, but her body was limp, and she struggled to stand on her own. After steadying her, Zach pushed her into the driver's seat and closed the door. "Sasha!" When she didn't respond, he reached inside the cabin and slapped her hard. Her eyes widened, and she grabbed her cheek.

"Speaker Randall. Why did you do that?"

"Drive back, Sasha. Drive back now."

She nodded, put the car in gear, and made a sweeping, jagged U-turn until the SUV pointed back toward the facility. She stopped and rolled down the window. "Speaker, I can't leave you. These relentless visions will destroy you. "

"Get the hell out of here, right now!" he said gruffly as he pounded on the hood of the vehicle. She hit the accelerator, and a spray of rocks and dirt flew up from the rear wheel.

Zach turned and plodded forward, focusing on a single purpose. The visions clouded his eyesight, and sweat leaked from his pores. Summoning all the mental veracity he could muster, he started walking the last mile to Sedona.

Once he reached Airport Road, he felt the malign intrusion of dark energy emanating from a funnel somewhere off to his left. He remembered Pena's map showing the five vortexes. To the south of 89A, the Airport Vortex emitted thick waves of black exuviated energy now free of its deceptively innocuous shroud. Whether this was due to the influence of Mr. Cox or the presence of a telepathic terrorist, he didn't know, but the black energy enveloping him was an ominous sign.

Fighting both the draw of the vortex and the punishing impact of the suicide visions, Zach found it increasingly difficult to move, and he lifted each leg with an extraordinary strength of will as he continued toward Sedona proper. Sweat poured off his body, and he trembled from the relentless bombardment on his psyche.

He simultaneously watched an old woman pull a knife across her wrists as a young man jumped in front of a moving truck, his head exploding like a crushed melon. A sobbing non-binary person swallowed an entire bottle of pills as a man slammed his car into a cement pylon. The visions played endlessly like a maniacal cinematographer's demented version of a spliced trailer.

Panting as his heavy footsteps brought him closer to the city limits, Zach finally reached the juncture of 89A and one-seventy-nine. The visions eased a bit, and the blackness of the surrounding energy slowly dissipated. He straightened up, and the nausea abated as he moved forward. This was the vicinity of the Sedona Sutra vortex, which was much larger than the others and served as the primary telepathic and telekinetic energy source for the entire planet.

Zach followed the dynamic signature of white purity, and he instantly noticed its cleansing and protective effects as he approached. The infinite harmonics cut through the spiritual sludge that clogged his psychokinetic pathways and cleansed his mind. The crushing depression lifted in stages, and Zach sensed purity and light. His senses sharpened, and shortly thereafter, he became keenly aware there was another transcendent nearby.

A winding pathway led up a small hill until it emptied into a shrine constructed just outside the entrance to the vortex. A flight of stone steps passed through a set of arches, but when he entered the zone of influence, the entire area was deserted. In light of the growing chaos that consumed the attention of the populace, the regular tourists, healers and seekers were absent, and the area around the vortex was eerily silent.

Zach stopped and looked directly into the brilliant effulgence. White light of a purity that exceeded human perception erupted in an ebullient plume and rose straight to the heavens with the tight continuity of a fine-tuned laser. Small particles of effervescent light danced and interacted as though they were alive and playful. The luminescence reached out and embraced Zach as a feeling of utter calm and tranquility washed over him.

Without looking in any specific direction, he knew the identity of the other transcendent occupying the space.

Hello, Marshall, he said without making a sound. *I want to communicate with you. I'm not here to cause you distress or bring you harm.*

With no answer forthcoming, he plunged his consciousness into the center of the vortex. How much time passed was anyone's guess. Perhaps it was a second, or it might have been an eternity, but he stood silently and absorbed the soothing and healing waves of unfettered energy.

I didn't do it, Zach, I swear I didn't kill anyone.

I believe you, Marshall. I always have.

I — I know who did kill them. I know.

Who, Marshall? Tell me who the traitor is.

I can't, Zach. I just can't.

Marshall, I need you to tell me. Please.

The conversation ended with a single thought transferred across a quiet eternity into Zach's tuned consciousness.

It's Sarah. She is the traitor...

Chapter Twenty-Seven

Mateo listened to the advice of the man at the filling station. Traveling became an exercise in scavenging and horse-trading, and as the miles passed, both he and Wanda perfected the craft. When she developed a horrific migraine in Mount Vernon, they traded one of Doris's apple pies for some aspirin. Later on in Sarcoxie, they gave up half the bottle of aspirin for two convenience store sandwiches and a liter of cola.

In Vinita, Mateo cruised through the neighborhood, aware of the multitude of shades and curtains that pulled back as he passed. After locating an abandoned car in the high school parking lot, he struck with speed honed from experience and siphoned ten gallons, which translated into more than 200 miles on the highway.

For large stretches, the images along the roadside seemed pseudo-apocalyptic. The initial chaos from the Chicago nuke never really subsided, and instead, morphed into primal fear and an overwhelming sense of dread. With rumors of road bandits running rampant, few dared to travel farther than the local grocery store, although even that trip proved futile due to empty shelves, closed banks and boarded-up storefronts.

Most of the commercial radio stations were off the air by now, and Mateo hit the scan button to find the local emergency broadcast frequency. The transmissions continued without interruption, and the somber announcers provided updates on local, regional and national efforts to restore order. The anchors went to great lengths to avoid creating panic, but their efforts were ineffective and far too late.

They bypassed Tulsa after hearing a local report about a riot that blocked I-44 at the juncture with I-294. The detour added another thirty minutes to the trip but helped them avoid a five-hour delay and the danger the violence presented. The situation in Oklahoma City was even worse, and like many of his colleagues, the Governor declared a state of emergency. Reports in the few remaining roadside cafes and grocery stores that were still open focused on the mounting anarchy as civilians died in growing numbers at the hands of emboldened gangs and hordes of floaters. Military units skirmished against one another amidst massive defections.

Finding a suitable bypass around major cities was challenging and unnerving. Law enforcement and the National Guard were completely absent, and a mechanical breakdown might prove fatal. Mateo exited off I-44 onto State Route 62 and reconnected with I-44 around Chickasha. The stretch of road was long and desolate, and they didn't see a single vehicle or occupied building for hundreds of miles until they came upon a minivan on the side of the road with its hazard lights blinking.

As they moved closer, Wanda noticed a woman, who was already some distance from the vehicle, walking along the shoulder. Clearly unprepared for the potential challenges up ahead, she inexplicably opted for fashion over practicality. Her skirt and high heels loudly stated she was not going to accept the savage new reality. As the Sonata grew closer, she turned around and stumbled, almost falling to the ground at one point.

"Mateo, we have to stop for her," said Wanda as she moved up on the seat.

He regarded her for a moment before answering. "You can't keep doing this. We have no food to share, and this might be a set up. She could have someone waiting inside that van to jump us. It's too much of a risk."

"But look at her, Mateo. She's staggering around like there's something wrong. We need to help her."

"No. It's a bad idea."

"Mateo, stop the car... damn it!"

Mateo looked over at Wanda and back at the road several times. "What makes this one different? We've seen breakdowns and people who obviously needed help everywhere, and we just drove away."

"I know," she said as she laced her fingers together. "And each time I left a part of me with them. I understand the reality here, Mateo, but I want to help someone. Please, stop the car just this once. I can't explain it, but I have a feeling..."

Mateo grimaced, shook his head, and then braked as he pulled the car over to the shoulder. The woman raised her arm and then ran toward them as best she could, considering her impractical footwear. By the time she reached the car, Mateo was already tempted to speed away.

"Oh, thank God, thank God," she said as she leaned through the window. "There hasn't been a car through here all day. And the heat and humidity…"

"Are you all right?" asked Wanda.

"Why are you dressed that way?" said Mateo.

She looked at both of them as though she was debating who was in charge. "It's a workday. I'm a school teacher in Middleburg. We're down to three days a week, but we're trying to keep some semblance of normalcy for the kids."

"Middleburg is back the other way," said Mateo.

"I wasn't going to the school. I was heading out of town when the van acted up. There's a diesel repair shop up ahead, and I know the mechanic. I figured they could fix it for me."

"What's wrong with it?" asked Mateo.

"I don't know. It was idling poorly and then a rattling sound before it just quit. I've been sitting out here for hours."

"So, I ask you again," said Wanda, "are you alright?"

The woman placed a dirty hand on Wanda's arm and smiled. "No, I'm not all right, but thank you for asking. My situation is the worst. I have two kids in a locked van back there and an abusive husband at home who's been stoned since all this began… I don't know what to do." She quickly stifled a brief sob as emotions overwhelmed her.

"You weren't going to school today. You only dressed like that so your husband would think you were going to work, isn't that right?" said Wanda.

The woman nodded.

"Okay," said Mateo. "Get in. We can't leave your kids back there. They'll die in that closed up van."

The woman climbed into the back seat and breathed a sigh of relief as the cool air from the air conditioner washed over her. Mateo turned around and drove back a few hundred feet and pulled up in front of her minivan. As soon as the car stopped, she got out and ran over to the vehicle. Wanda followed, but Mateo lagged behind. He waited until they were out of his line of sight and then reached inside the center console and tucked the handgun Elmore gave him into his waistband.

By the time he reached the van, the two children were standing by the roadside. Wanda reached out and offered them a candy bar, which the boy snatched and broke in half so he and his sister would get an equal share.

Using the candy to gain their confidence, Wanda leaned down and spoke to the children in reassuring tones. The boy appeared to be around ten and the girl about eight. They looked emaciated, and each had the kind of deep, dark circles under their eyes that children develop when they're subjected to prolonged periods of fear, anxiety and sleep deprivation. While Wanda tended to them, Mateo turned his attention to the mother.

"Do you have any food in there?"

"No. We ran out of food before all this happened."

Mateo sighed. "Any water?"

She shook her head. "No."

"Any gas?"

She immediately perked up. "Why yes. I filled the tank before the Chicago bomb exploded, and everything went crazy. I think there's still over three quarters of a tank."

Mateo's face lit up, and he clasped his hands while turning to the heavens. He walked over to Wanda and whispered. "I should know better than to question your instincts. We'll probably have enough gas to make it to Amarillo."

Once Mateo transferred the fuel, they piled into the Sonata with the mother and kids crowded together in back. Wanda knew the initial awkwardness of these situations was always the worst, and her own discomfort didn't make it any easier. Across the globe, people were dealing with the uncomfortable reality their cell phone service might be out for a very long time, and they would actually need to talk directly to each other.

Fortunately, Mateo sensed the uneasiness and jumped right in. "So, why don't we start out with our names? I'm Mateo, and this is Wanda." Exchanging last names was becoming irrelevant in the new reality.

The woman looked up as though she was deep in thought. "Wha? Oh, I'm sorry. My name is Lotus, like the flower. These are my children, Coy and Missy."

"Well, it's nice to meet you." Mateo nodded at Wanda, who didn't grasp the cue. "So, where are you heading?"

Lotus stared absently out the window. "I don't know. I guess wherever you're going. We don't want to be alone."

"Are you afraid your husband will find you? What did he do to you?" Wanda's bluntness made everyone pause.

"... I'll be afraid until we're past Texas," Lotus said. "He'll come after us, but he won't know we're with you.

It's such a blessing. He—he hit us. All of us. I tried to protect the children, but he's much stronger."

"Mama got the worst whippins'," said Coy. "You should see her back. The whip marks just never go away."

"Coy, that's enough."

"He hit you with a whip?" asked Wanda.

Lotus's eyes teared up, and she nodded her head. "He beat me with a belt and hit me with his fists. Bart hated me, but for some reason, he would never let me leave."

Wanda watched Mateo check the rear-view mirror frequently until they reached I-40. She wasn't aware how relentless these obsessed, abusive men could be, but she sensed how much it worried him. Mateo didn't relax and sit back in his seat until he finally saw the Amarillo city limits sign.

Places like Amarillo weren't big enough to justify sending military units, especially since there was no active base nearby. Yet, with 250,000 people, the city had its fair share of gangs, ruffians and vagrants emboldened by the lack of order. Like most mid-American cities, local law enforcement was overwhelmed, and without a deterrent, the floaters controlled the streets.

Even on the lightly traveled thre-thirty-five, abandoned cars littered the road with doors flung open and contents scattered haphazardly, telling a silent story of passengers pulled out unexpectedly and violently. Purses, hats, empty wallets and other personal possessions littered the shoulder of the road, the discarded remnants of the gangs and scavengers. The environment was deteriorating, and the roar of two F-22 fighter jets screaming overhead at low altitude reminded them that the string that held civilized society together was fraying badly.

They traveled over 300 miles since they picked up Lotus, and practical matters emerged as Mateo motioned to Wanda they once again needed fuel. He pulled off the road into a residential neighborhood just outside of Amarillo where the GPS identified a nearby elementary school.

Throughout the trip, schools had proven to be a fertile ground for harvesting gasoline. Syphoning gas out of an abandoned car left in a deserted school parking lot was considerably less dangerous than trying to take it from a vehicle parked in someone's driveway.

After several turns, Mateo pulled into the Gordon Howe Magnet School. Dusk was descending, which provided cover as he drove up to a parked car in front of the building. Unfortunately, no one inside the Sonata noticed two other cars sitting alone at the far end of the third row, hidden behind a cluster of thick trees on a large patch of dirt between the end of the parking lot and the road.

Wanda, Lotus and the children got out to stretch their legs as Mateo crept over to the vehicle he targeted. Shortly thereafter, the sound of voices drifted over from the isolated area where the other two cars were parked.

"Don't do it, please. We've given you everything we have." A woman's voice trembled, and she choked on the words.

"Don't hurt us; just don't hurt us." A second high-pitched voice sounded weak and pleading.

As her eyes adjusted to the dim lighting, Wanda could make out two women on their hands and knees. A man and a third woman were standing, and the man had a gun pointed down at the two who were prostrated on the ground. The Sonata's arrival drew everyone's attention, and the man looked at Wanda and pointed with his free hand.

"Hey, you all need to get back in your fuckin' car and get outta here." The receding gray light grew darker by the minute. Wanda couldn't see their faces very well, but the man had a medium build, while the woman was much shorter, with long hair that hung down to the middle of her back.

"What are you doing to these people?" Wanda shouted without understanding the potential danger of the situation.

"Bitch, I said shut the fuck up and get back in your car." From a distance, the man took several steps forward, using his body language to convey aggression.

"Please, help us," cried the woman closest to Wanda as she raised her head from the pavement. The small woman with the long hair reached out and slammed the heel of her boot into the side of the captive's head. "Get your fuckin' face back on the ground," she yelled menacingly.

"Hey, leave those people alone," Wanda yelled back.

"Fuck it," said the man as he took the lead in handling this new threat. "I was gonna let you go, but you had to stick your goddamned nose where it don't belong. Now I'm gonna come over there and beat your ass, bitch." He walked with purpose, and as he came closer, Wanda realized she was dealing with a filthy street thug. The man's nose was grotesquely bent out of shape, and he had a horrible case of acne. From her back pocket, his girlfriend pulled out her own gun and trained it on their hostages.

Lotus and the children retreated back into the car, but Wanda stood her ground. When they were about twenty feet apart, the man pointed his pistol at her. Instantly terror struck, she let out a small squeak and covered her head with her arms.

"You just couldn't leave it alone, could you? Now I'm gonna have to waste you too. Can't mind your fuckin' business." He aimed the pistol at Wanda's head. They were now only about five feet apart.

The sudden crack of the Baretta PX4 pierced the night air. From the corner of her eye, Wanda saw a bright flash before she was drawn back to the man in front of her. He twirled in a 360-degree circle like a marionette as he dropped his gun, clutching his chest and falling to the pavement.

"You shot me. You bitch, you shot me. *Oh, mama, voy a morir*... He groaned and whimpered in Spanish, a language Wanda was fluent in.

In the distance, one of the prone women took advantage of the ensuing confusion, and she rose up and barreled into the much smaller kidnapper. The victim grabbed the arm that held the gun while repeatedly slapping and punching the stunned antagonist's face with her free hand. The petite assailant was ravaged by drug use and wasn't able to put up much of a fight. With a definite advantage, the younger, stronger woman clubbed her assailant with a series of roundhouse punches to her ears and nose. Finally, she reached down and grabbed the gun after it fell to the pavement.

"You worthless, skinny piece of shit! I'm going to kill you for threatening my family."

"No, Theresa, you can't do this." The other woman, who was still kneeling, finally stood up and grabbed her companion's arms tightly.

The taller woman went limp as the adrenaline abated. "Lara, they took everything from us. They made our children watch as they humiliated us. We gave them all we had, and they still demanded that we take them to your parents' house so they could rob them too. She deserves to die."

"This isn't you," said the one named Lara. "We're supposed to get married next week. Theresa, please…"

"Married… Yeah, right. Thugs like these two robbed the church and beat the pastor senseless, Lara. We're not getting married next week. No one is getting married anymore. It's all over."

The thin girl got to her knees with one hand over her bloody nose and the other raised high over her head. "Please. It was all Pedro's idea."

"I don't care. You let him do it… You let him humiliate and terrorize us."

"Please, lady, don't kill me…"

"Theresa, no!"

Another shot rang out, and the skinny girl toppled over backwards with a gaping hole through the center of her face.

Wanda glanced at Mateo for a moment and then walked over toward the couple. As she approached, the woman named Lara ran up and hugged her tightly as tears streamed down her cheeks. They lingered for some time, exchanging few words as Theresa dropped the gun and quietly thanked Wanda and Mateo for intervening.

"They broke into our house," said Theresa as she held Lara closely. "They tied us up, including my kids. They forced my fiancé and me to play Russian roulette while my kids watched. We gave them money, our valuables — everything. But they wanted more, and they demanded we go to her parent's house so they could rob them too. When they realized we took them to the wrong address they... Well, that's when you showed up."

Mateo shook his head and clapped Theresa lightly on the shoulder. They stood awkwardly in the darkness, but what could be said under such macabre circumstances? After some time, Wanda leaned in and hugged both Lara and Theresa as Mateo said goodbye and returned back to the car to finish syphoning the gas.

"You can come with us," Wanda said. "Maybe a fresh start somewhere else..."

Theresa shook her head. "This is our home. My children wouldn't understand."

"So, what... We're just leaving them here?" asked Lara as she pulled away from her fiancé's arms and pointed at the dead bodies.

"We'll never say anything, and I doubt anyone will even ask. Things are — different now," said Wanda.

Theresa nodded and walked back over to the gun she used to kill the accomplice. After wiping it clean with a tail of her blouse, she set it back on the ground. "C'mon Lara, we need to get out of here."

Lara hugged Wanda a last time and then got into their car. Wanda watched as the taillights receded down the side street before she returned to the Sonata to find Mateo pouring the last few drops of gas into the tank.

"Mateo, are you... are you okay? You saved my life again."

He set the gas can down and looked away. "Vermin, Wanda. It's starting to feel like killing people is no different than killing rats."

Everyone was quiet as they drove down a deserted highway in pitch darkness. Nothing from the encounter would be retained except the emotional scars. Lotus huddled with the kids in the backseat, comforting them in low, soothing tones. The children ate potato chips and a burrito Lara gave them, and everyone shared a liter of water as the hum of the engine and noise from the tires were the only sounds that interrupted the silence.

Just outside of Albuquerque, Mateo passed an army cargo truck sitting on the side of the road as bright orange flames flashed from the engine compartment, sending thick black plumes of smoke into the air. Empty cardboard boxes littered the highway along with a number of crushed containers of MRE rations. Farther off the road in the bottom of a ditch, the bodies of two soldiers were lit up by their truck's dying headlights. Dried blood splattered on exposed flesh showed as a black stain on their fatigues.

"My God," said Mateo as they slowed, "they're killing soldiers now."

"Should we... Should we try to help?" said Wanda.

"No," said Mateo emphatically. "It's getting worse out here, and we don't know who's waiting in those high weeds to ambush us. Phoenix is only about five hours away. We won't even need to make another stop."

Wanda looked off in the distance for a moment. When she spoke, her voice was firm but calm.

"We're not going to Phoenix, Mateo. We're going to Sedona."

"What?" He turned his head sharply.

"Sedona. That's where we're supposed to go. I've known it for a while, and the feeling keeps getting stronger as we get closer."

"I don't understand. Do you have family there? Why are you changing your plans?"

In a small voice from the backseat, Missy said, "Yes, Mateo, you must listen to Wanda. We have to go to Sedona."

"Missy!" said her mother in a voice that had a slight note of alarm.

"No, mother, Missy is right," said Coy. "We *are* supposed to go to Sedona."

Chapter Twenty-Eight

Senator Chawsome sat in an uncomfortable wooden chair in his underwear staring straight ahead with a landline handset pressed up to his ear. His eyes were blank, and he blinked robotically like someone who was in a coma.

The Senator would not remember the last twenty-four-hours fondly if he remembered them at all. Upon arriving back in Detroit as the Benefactor's "guest" aboard his private plane, Chawsome found himself thrust into a number of situations that could be generously termed uncomfortable. Lars and Alan were both pushing for outright torture, but the Benefactor found that too primitive and barbaric. Instead, he remained in Chawsome's mind like a diluted acid on the skin. Instead of unleashing a torrent that would leave the Senator's brain a molten lump of melted tissue, he continued to stimulate his pain centers and irritate his pleasure receptors.

This led to bouts of intense sobbing followed by unimaginable depression and despair. Mr. Cox placed false memories into his hippocampus so Chawsome believed he murdered his wife and children. Naturally, it didn't take long for the interrogation to yield results. The disheveled politician begged for a merciful death before the Benefactor allowed him some relief.

Delgado and Sandra laughed and mocked the Senator as Chawsome's head lolled from side to side. "I don't know if I can... very confused. I feel so horrible... just want to die. Cox, why won't you kill me? I'm so afraid. Please, make it stop. Please."

"It will stop when he arrives, Senator Chawsome. Hopefully, you still have enough influence that he took your call seriously."

Just as the Benefactor finished speaking, Delgado's phone lit up. He turned away and answered, pressing one finger to his ear. He walked to a corner of the room and nodded while speaking in low tones. When the call was finished, he slipped the phone into his pocket, walked over to the Benefactor, and whispered in his ear.

Mr. Cox smiled, and he turned to Chawsome as Delgado moved away. "Well, Senator, being the Chairman of the Intelligence Committee actually does carry some weight after all. You're very fortunate. The President has just arrived and is being escorted to our conference suite. With any luck, you'll get to die soon."

Turning to the attendants, he added, "Make sure we have a nice spread laid out. I want fine wine and cheese. After all, he is the president." The servants nodded and scurried away to complete their appointed tasks.

"Okay, I did what you asked," said Chawsome as he shifted his naked legs uncomfortably. "Now please, release me from this torment and kill me. I can't take these feelings anymore. It's so hopeless. My family... My God, how could I have killed them?" The Senator hung his head and resumed sobbing.

"I need you to remain cognizant just a little longer, Senator." A sudden knock at the door diverted their attention.

Delgado walked over and welcomed the guests in. A small contingent of secret service people entered first and surveyed the premises. The Benefactor's security detail stepped to the forefront, subtly asserting its authority. Once a thorough sweep of the room was completed, a pair of security people returned to the doorway and covered either side. Shortly thereafter, the President of the United States walked in with panache, flanked by two additional protectors and another man dressed in a fine Italian suit and perfectly cropped hair.

Xavier Watts rose from behind his desk and went to greet the president with his hand extended. "Mr. President, it is an honor to make your acquaintance. Please, have a seat." The president refused to shake Watts' hand but followed him over to a nondescript upholstered executive chair. Delgado pushed over another chair for his well-dressed aide. After everyone was seated, two secret service men took a position to either side as the president glanced over at Senator Chawsome, who was still in his underwear shackled and chained.

Watts cleared his throat before speaking. "President Halderson, thank you for visiting us during this difficult time. I hope we can have a productive discussion."

The president stared at Watts with contempt, ignoring the salutation. "I'm Richard Halderson. This is my chief advisor, Michael Sanchez. I'm here because of the disturbing phone call I received from Merl Chawsome." The president glanced over the

356

Senator, who drooled on a bulge of greasy belly fat that hung over the band of his white briefs. "How are you, Merl?"

Without looking at the president, he replied, "He's put death in my brain. I can't describe it. He burrows into your mind. Please, kill me." Chawsome brought his face up to his hands and continued crying.

"Senator Chawsome brought this on himself," said Watts. "He organized a terrorist act that destroyed several floors in one of our buildings and killed thirty-seven people. A key employee was kidnapped, which is entirely unacceptable. Naturally, we had to liberate him and make those who were responsible pay for their crimes."

"I want to see Tom Fuentes and Pam Runyun immediately."

"I'm sorry, Mr. President. Fuentes and Runyun are, how shall I say it, nonessential. They're in another room in the facility being—rehabilitated."

The president leaned forward in his seat and stared at Watts. "I'm not talking about this with you. I want to speak with the one who's in charge of this so-called 'company'. Based on the descriptions I've received, I assume that's you." He turned and pointed to the Benefactor who mockingly thrust his thumb into his chest and silently mouthed, *Who… Me*? He looked back at the president with a wide smile.

"I'm just a lowly corporate employee, Mr. President. Although I may have some pull with the CEO."

Halderson looked over at Mr. Cox with disdain. "I wasn't personally involved with the plan Senator Chawsome and the DIA devised. But based on the reports I've received, you should be arrested. Using a

357

rogue fighter jet to blow up a city block in Detroit? You'll be lucky if I don't have you hung for treason."

"*Treason?* Well, that's quite a severe punishment, don't you think?" The Benefactor paused and scratched his chin. "And yet, you're here Mr. President. In the midst of a global meltdown, you traveled incognito from Washington to an office complex in Detroit just to talk to me. Who could hold such power that the president would risk his own safety to leave the White House and fly to Detroit?"

"Let's get down to business," said Halderson. "What is it you want?"

"I want your resignation," said Mr. Cox. "We have forty-seven states that will approve of an amendment to the Constitution we've drawn up. It's a very simple document, Mr. President. It dissolves the Constitution and replaces it with corporate governance."

"I've heard about that nonsense. Are you out of your mind?" The president ran his hand through his hair and shook his head. "I mean seriously, are you deranged?"

Mr. Cox' smile widened. "*Deranged,* Mr. President? I'm the most mentally balanced person in the room. I'm not sure you understand the gravity of your situation. We control the media, or what's left of it. We control the streets, and we control the people. Most importantly, we now control the military."

"You don't control the military. *I* control the military, dammit!"

"Mr. Watts," said the Benefactor while still looking at the president, "Get the Secretaries of the Navy, Air Force and Army on the line."

"Certainly." Watts picked up a phone and gave instructions to the person on the other end.

"You see, Mr. President, while you and the rest of your crooked colleagues spent your time figuring out how to enrich yourselves at the expense of your constituents, we were out in the streets, going into the ghettoes to give food, medicine, money and hope to the people your government despises."

"I resent that characterization. I've spent a lifetime in public service..."

"Bah," said Mr. Cox dismissively. "You've spent a lifetime serving yourself, Mr. President. But your ruse is over, isn't it."

"Ah, Mr. Cox, all of the secretaries are on the line."

"Speaker," said Mr. Cox.

Watts punched several buttons on the phone and nodded to his superior.

"Gentlemen, I am here with the president, please say hello."

A silence followed, punctuated by one man clearing his throat, another sighing and a third mumbling something under his breath.

"All right, let's not all talk at once. Secretary of the Army, Donald Smalls, say hello to the president."

"Ah... Mr. President, I, uh, it's good to talk to you."

"Smalls, is it really you? How could you betray your country like this? You're a disgrace."

"I'm sorry, Mr. President, it's you who has abdicated your responsibility to the country. Have you looked around? The cities are on fire, the streets are filled with people who hate the government. Mr. Cox can bring order…"

"You fool!" said Halderson.

"My, my," said the Benefactor, "all this sanctimonious babble is making me nauseous. Mr. President, you entered politics flat broke, yet you're now worth over 25 million dollars, and you never made more than $250,000 a year. I wonder how you were able to do that? At least Secretary Smalls is more transparent. He has a little gambling problem we took care of for him, isn't that right, Mr. Secretary?"

"Well, I, um…"

"Say 'hi' to the president, Secretary Nigel and Secretary Leeds."

"Hello, Mr. President," said Nigel.

"Yes, hello, sir," added Leeds.

"I want each of you to give the president an assessment of the state of the military. In other words, tell him who controls the assets." Cox spoke while staring at Halderson.

"Sir, this is Secretary Smalls. Operatives loyal to the HUGE conglomerate control seventy-eight percent of our command personnel, and that, ah, includes me. I answer to the Benefactor, and I will give orders to the troops reflecting his will."

"Nigel here. You have very little control over air assets, Mr. President. I would imagine it's fewer than twenty percent. A couple squadrons at Vandenberg, but other than that, we fly to protect the Benefactor,"

"You too, Leeds?" The president's voice sounded desperate.

"Ah… I'm afraid so, sir."

"What about Warren? I still control the ICBMs," said Halderson.

"No sir, The Twentieth Air Force is under the Benefactor's control," said Nigel.

"The army is almost completely loyal to HUGE," added Secretary Smalls. "If a conflict broke out, your forces wouldn't last more than a week, and there would be horrible carnage. Over the past several years, I have replaced all of my commanding officers with personnel loyal to our cause."

The president turned to Sanchez, who sat quietly next to him. "The codes."

Sanchez reached down and picked up a large metal Zero Halliburton briefcase and placed it on his knees. He snapped the latches open and pulled out a card he handed to the President.

"The authentication codes won't work, Mr. President." The Benefactor reached down into his pocket and pulled out another card that looked identical to the President's. "These are the new launch codes. Do you care to play a game of nuclear chicken to see who has the right ones?"

Halderson looked at Mr. Cox with incredulity before his shoulders slumped, and he shook his head sadly. "How could this have happened? A silent coup right under our noses." He looked back up in a moment of desperation. "Terrance, have you given this man the nuclear codes?"

"We all did," answered Nigel. "It was the right thing to do. We need clarity and strong leadership, and you haven't provided either. He has access to Milstar and control over NORAD and the National Military Command Center."

361

"Don't act so surprised, Halderson," said Mr. Cox. "If you couldn't have seen this coming, you are horribly naïve. Distrust and resentment towards the government has been festering and rising for six decades. We just helped it along a little bit."

"What is it you want exactly?"

Mr. Cox shrugged. "I told you, I want your resignation. Earlier today, we effectively assumed control in Russia and fourteen other countries without a violent confrontation, although we were handsomely prepared for one. China is experiencing a massive revolt, and the government is being overthrown as we speak. But who knows, they might nuke themselves before it's all over. That would really mess up my plans, but I have to admit it would be fun to watch." The Benefactor's eyes lit up at the prospect of China in a nuclear winter.

"The rest of the world will capitulate when they see you have ceded control. This is especially important for Europe. Those Brits are stubborn to their own detriment."

"I won't do it. I…"

"Then many people will die. The terrorist group we are negotiating with will detonate another nuke in a major city every twelve hours starting at midnight tonight, and we'll announce to the world it's because you won't step down. I'm sure you recognize the consequences if that happens. What is left of society will evaporate, and brothers will kill each other in the streets to survive. And, of course, we will kill you and your family in a horrible and gruesome way, just because."

The Benefactor paused to allow the president to consider his words. "Is that what you want? If you resign and support our Article Five amendment, you'll have my word your family will remain safe, and you can live out the rest of your life in luxury in a large estate anywhere outside the country."

"I can't believe it has come to this." Halderson slumped over as though he was going to be sick.

"Face it, Mr. President, they hate you, but you can take solace in knowing they hate the entire rotten system. We offer clarity; it's just that simple. Our demands on the populace may not always please them, but we will provide the discipline they so desperately crave."

"Merl, what do you think of all this?"

The Senator continued to stare straight ahead, and he spoke without moving. "I never understood how powerful this person is. It's like he's rubbing a steel wool pad on my brain. He controls my thoughts and emotions and muddles my memories. We can't fight this, Richard. While we were consumed with the pursuit of money, he was slowly and deliberately amassing this enormous multinational organization right in front of us. The people support him and want to lynch us."

Turning back to the Benefactor, the president said, "How long do I have to decide?"

"Regrettably, you don't have any time. One of our buildings was blown up, and that is a sign of vulnerability that may embolden our enemies. I can't take the chance there will be another attempt to silence us."

Richard Halderson remained slumped over as he grabbed the sides of his head with his hands. "How can this be happening?" he said to no one in particular.

"As I said earlier, forty-seven legislatures have authorized a Constitutional Convention. With your endorsement and resignation, these bodies will convene tomorrow to vote for the dissolution of the Constitution. Mr. Watts, as the representative for HUGE, will assume control of the government. Believe me, this is for the best." Mr. Cox let the last sentence roll off his tongue to maximize the sarcasm.

Watts stood up and walked out from behind his desk with two sheets of paper and a pen in his hand. He handed them to the president, who took the documents and laid them on a small, round table next to his chair. He continued to sit quietly, hunched over and staring at the floor.

"Please, Mr. President," said Senator Chawsome as he started to furiously scratch at his naked torso. "My skin suddenly feels like it is being bitten by a thousand mosquitos. The itching is unbearable. For the love of God, sign the document. There is no other way."

With a shaking hand, the president reached over and picked up the pen. He used his other hand to move the first paper closer to his chair. Reaching down, he used the pressure on the pen to steady his hand while signing his name to the proclamation that endorsed the Constitutional Convention. He moved it aside and looked at the second document for some time. The president froze as the pen remained on the signature line without moving.

Executive Office of the President

Notice of Presidential Resignation and Dissolution of the Constitution of the United States

Effective: Immediately

I, Richard Halderson, hereby resign the office of the Presidency of the United States. I accept the dissolution of the Constitution under Article Five and endorse

Congress's recommendation that Humans United for Global Equality (HUGE), an international conglomerate, assume stewardship of the government of the United States until a more permanent solution can be found.

FR Doc. 2021-05171

When he looked up, President Halderson's eyes were red and watering. "... You did say my family's safety is guaranteed."

"Yes, yes," said Mr. Cox impatiently. "Just sign it and look into the camera over there as you're doing it. Remember, this is historically significant.'"

"Yes, sign the goddamn resignation!" said Senator Chawsome, who was now pulling violently against the restraints while scratching down through the layers of his epidermis until he created wounds that bled freely. "I can't stand this itching. Sign it and tell them to kill me, please!"

President Halderson looked like he was hyperventilating as he hastily scribbled his signature across the paper and pushed it away. Watts picked up the documents and walked back to his desk.

"Are we done here?" asked the president. "Can I leave to get back to my family? How long will I have before you move into the White House?"

"You'll have twenty-four hours to vacate the White House," said Mr. Cox. "Demolition will begin in forty-eight hours, The Capitol Building, the Supreme Court Building and all the national monuments that honor racist slave owners are scheduled to be destroyed."

"But... But why would you do such a thing? It's our history. What will happen when there are no governments and no courts?"

"The people hate the government, and they hate the courts. They've watched a court system that allows rich influential people to get away with murder while poor minorities spend their lives in prison for crimes they didn't commit. No, you don't understand, Mr. President. The people will cheer the destruction of this poisonous document and these shrines to an imperial, hegemonic country responsible for so many deaths."

"That's not the country I know…"

"It's irrelevant what you think, Mr. Halderson. You are now just a footnote in humanity's history. However, before you fade away in Aruba or Belize, you're going to do a televised press conference with Mr. Watts. You'll read a statement prepared for you, and you'll wear a shirt we had made especially for you. Oh, and we'll give you a haircut so you'll look your best."

The former president sunk even lower in the chair and began to weep.

"Gentlemen," said Mr. Cox while looking at the president's secret service escort. "You now are officially in the employ of the Gehenna Corporation, a subsidiary of the HUGE conglomerate. You will all receive a raise and report directly to Lars, our head of field operations. Please escort the president to the next room so he can get ready for the press conference."

Recognizing the futility of their situation, the secret service men looked at one another and then over at Halderson. The larger of the two tapped him on the shoulder. "Uh, sir, I guess you need to get ready to address the nation."

Getting to his feet, the president shuffled out to the hallway, escorted by his former secret service agents, his assistant and five of the Benefactor's security detail. They entered a well-appointed dressing room where those featured in Gehenna's promotional and propaganda materials received wardrobe and makeup assistance.

Once inside, they gruffly shoved the president into a chair, and the makeup artist applied a thick coating of black eye liner, mascara and a deep shade of orange foundation that made him look garish and slightly malevolent. An overzealous hair stylist ran a set of electric clippers over his head so that his scalp showed through a slight stubble.

Someone in wardrobe removed Halderson's jacket, shirt and tie and pulled a t-shirt over his head emblazoned with the phrase, *HUGE for a Better Tomorrow*. The president stared blankly at his reflection in the mirror while several Gehenna employees stifled giggles behind him. His former secret service agents grabbed him under each armpit and helped him to his feet. Two of the Benefactor's men motioned for them to follow, and they pushed the president forward and moved to the elevator. After riding down to the floor that housed Gehenna's media wing, they led the former President through a long hallway and brought him into a dedicated broadcast studio.

At one time, the room had been part of the "Prince and Princess" package offered by the Renaissance Center and reserved for affluent newlyweds willing to pay $1300 per night for pampering from personal servants, masseuses, and a master chef. However, it was re-purposed as a broadcast studio used to produce the multitude of promotional and propaganda films Gehenna and HUGE ran on the internet and global TV networks.

367

Halderson sat on the long side of a conference table. He looked around at the bank of cameras pointing in his direction. A production assistant walked over and pushed a script in front of him.

"This is what you will read when we go live, Mr. Halderson." She smiled and walked away just as Xavier Watts, exquisitely groomed and wearing a classic cut Brioni suit, pulled up a chair next to the president. He looked over at the sullen former leader of the free world and adjusted the microphone directly in front of him while trying to stifle a laugh.

The producer waved his hand to gain their attention, and a digital clock counted down from five. When the red light engaged, Halderson looked down and began reading off the paper in a robotic monotone. The image of his semi-bald head, pancake makeup and HUGE t-shirt transmitted across every public and cable network still broadcasting as Ziminski pirated international signals and broke into their regular programming.

"My fellow Americans, I have good news. I, Richard Halderson, hereby resign the Office of the President, effective immediately. Prior to my resignation, I authorized and endorsed the creation of a Constitutional Convention according to Article Five. The sole purpose of the Convention is to renounce the Constitution itself in order to dissolve the Union in its entirety, something people on both sides of the political spectrum have wanted for decades. Thus, the twenty-eighth amendment has already been passed by forty-seven state legislatures as required, so it is officially the law." Halderson paused and wiped tears from his eyes before continuing.

"As you know, our government is utterly corrupt, dishonest and immoral. You have known this for years. We—we dirty, scum politicians have cheated and robbed the people for our own profit. We deserve our fate.

"To ensure a smooth transition, I am handing over responsibility for governing the United States to the international conglomerate known as Humans United for Global Equality, or HUGE as they are known throughout the world. HUGE will form a universal government based on fairness, equality, diversity, inclusion and multiculturalism. They are the only global entity with the resources to govern effectively. Even as we speak, countries all over the world are ceding control to HUGE." Halderson paused and cleared his throat. When he continued speaking, his voice was dry and raspy.

"That is all I have to say. I—I apologize for being a dirty, filthy, slimy, conniving shitbag politician and beg for your forgiveness..." The last words were barely a whisper and tailed off into silence.

After the cameras were turned off, the people in the room began to clap before the escorts led the president out to a Gehenna aircraft where his wife and children were already waiting. The plane took off for Barbuda in the Caribbean while Sandra put a bullet in Merl Chawsome's head.

The Benefactor always kept his word.

Chapter Twenty-Nine

Marshall walked out from behind a small stand of trees and circled the perimeter of the vortex until he was standing next to Zach, who continued to look absently into the brilliance of the white, healing light. They stood together without talking for some moments before Marshall made a gesture with his hands but spoke no words.

I'm telling the truth.

I know, Marshall. I — I'm having trouble wrapping my mind around it.

"I couldn't believe it either." Marshall broke the mental link and spoke to Zach directly. "The first night, when Liu disappeared, I thought I heard her door close right after someone knocked on mine. The sound was very subtle, just a small click of the lock, but I have superb hearing."

"So, you heard Sarah's door close, and when you opened yours, the bloody knife was just outside."

Marshall nodded. "But Sarah was so kind to me I knew I must be mistaken, so I said nothing. Then, when everyone succumbed to the negative energy from the vortex in the courtyard forest, Yasin ran

370

away, but I knew he was crazed. I saw Sarah leave and follow him, so I decided to see where they were going. Yasin went back into the facility and ran through the corridors shouting and screaming like an insane person. He was out of his mind. I saw him crashing into walls and trying to harm himself."

"What was Sarah doing?"

"She was careful to keep her distance, but she never let him out of her sight or helped him. When he went into that room with the heavy machines, she followed him in. I was afraid one of them would see me if I went in there, so I stayed outside. A few minutes later, she came out carrying a big wrench like they use on those huge pipes, and the large end was covered with blood. She went into the next machine room and must have hid the wrench there. After that, she went back out into the courtyard."

"And you didn't know what to do, so you ran."

"Yes. Rogelio and Jacques would never believe me, and I would have been blamed again. I was afraid, and so I tricked one of the attendants into opening the facility and then started walking to Sedona. Once I reached the main road, someone gave me a ride to the city. I guess it was the power of the Sutra Vortex that drew me here since it's the only one that's still untainted by the dark energy. I had no idea where I was going from here."

"We need to go back, Marshall."

"Oh no, I don't want to go back." Marshall shook his head vigorously. "No one will believe me. And what about Sarah? You're—involved with her."

"My relationship with Sarah doesn't matter right now. She won't be able to lie to me, Marshall. You've got to trust me. Now c'mon, we need to go."

371

Zach started walking back toward the vortex monument when he realized Marshall wasn't following. He turned around and raised his eyebrow. "Let's *go*, Marshall. There's no running from this."

Marshall looked toward the vortex and lost himself in the enormity of the infinite transcendent energy that gushed from its epicenter. He allowed the purity of the flow to envelope him, and the warmth and serenity felt like an inviting blanket that calmed and soothed his frayed nerves. Reluctantly, he pulled himself away and started walking towards Zach, who waited for him at the monument.

What choice do I have? Since all my friends are gone, where would I go? Wanda is gone. I might as well face this. At least I have the Speaker's support.

As they walked down Airport Road, the noise and buzzing in Zach's head returned. The visions of countless people taking their own lives burned in his mind and beseeched him to intervene. The sheer volume of the visions was unnerving and depressing on a level that might have pulled an overseer with less capability into the abyss. Every fiber in his body worked in unison to hold the visions at bay so he could maintain his focus.

Marshall continued to walk in silence, looking largely unaffected. Zach glanced in his direction several times before realizing his companion was not exhibiting the same signs of stress the other overseers suffered when exposed to the unsettling mental imagery.

"Marshall, are you seeing these visions?"

"Visions of what?" Marshall looked over as his eyebrows furrowed.

"The visions of people committing suicide. It's a common denominator with all of us. We can see those who are ending their lives. Sometimes, we can help them."

"I don't know what you're talking about." The tone of his voice was such that Zach suspected he was telling the truth.

"Then where does your ability come from? We all received the 'gift' when we tried to take our own lives, but we survived a near death experience…"

"I'm not sure," said Marshall. "I told you I thought about suicide when Mr. Cox visited me, but I never tried to kill myself, at least as far as I know."

"That's very curious," said Zach. "You're different from the rest of us in some ways, but you still have the gift."

"I've always been different," said Marshall. "It's nothing new."

At the junction of Airport Road and 89A, an old Toyota Tundra approached cautiously from behind before slowing down and pulling over to the side of the road.

"Where you headed, and what happened to your car?" said an older man in leather boots, Wrangler jeans and a Stetson with several dried sweat stains running around the band of his hat.

"We gave our ride to our friends. They had an emergency." said Zach. He and Marshall remained motionless, not wanting to present a threat.

"Where you headin'?" the cowboy asked.

"To Dry Creek Road. We have a campsite set up in the area."

The man pulled out a red handkerchief and mopped his brow and the back of his neck. "Goddamn. I'm prolly gonna regret this, but get in."

Zach and Marshall accepted the ride, and after expressing their gratitude, they climbed into the rear bed of the vehicle. The driver looked back at them several times with some curiosity as the truck moved slowly down the highway. When they reached Dry Creek Road, he stopped long enough so they could jump out.

Zach waved at him, and from inside the cab, the old man waved back, but it was obvious he never felt at ease. He drove off without asking any questions, probably fearing the answers. After all, what would two people be doing in the middle of nowhere in the July heat anyway?

After walking for nearly an hour, they came to the dirt pathway that would lead back to the facility. Finding the entrance was much easier now that Zach knew its location, and once they reached the vehicle storage and maintenance garage, he entered the security code that activated the doors.

With Marshall just a step behind, Zach led him through the auto service department, past the mechanical rooms and finally into the foyer. Nothing was out of place, but the whole area was completely deserted.

"There's something wrong here, Speaker Randall. I have a suffocating sense of dread. An inexplicable wickedness is inside this place.

"I know," said Zach as he looked around. "While we haven't been connected, I always sense the presence of an overseer, but that space in my psyche

374

is empty. Something terrible has happened here. We have to find Sarah and the others."

He signaled to Marshall, and they moved toward Pena's office. At first glance, it looked like the room was empty, since no one sat behind the massive array of monitors. But as Zach drew closer, he noticed a pair of arms lying across the console on either side of the main screen.

"Pena, I'm back, and Marshall is with me. We need to convene a meeting of the overseers immediately."

No one answered, so Zach walked cautiously towards the computers, but as he made his way to the other side of the station, he was greeted by the sight of a man slumped over the keyboard. His head lay on its side facing away, but sticky matted black hair only partially covered a large jagged hole in the back of his skull.

"Pena!" yelled Zach as he moved close to the corpse.

The murder weapon was still at the scene. A heavy pipe fitter wrench covered with blood lay near the body. The lifeless head rested on the "m" key, applying constant pressure so the monitor displayed endless lines of monotonous text.

Almost against his will, Zach reached down and turned the man's head around. "It's not Pena," he said with some relief as he looked up at Marshall. "It's Docker, one of his assistants."

"Why would someone kill him? It couldn't have been..."

Zach lowered his head and whispered, "Yes, Sarah..."

"She's gone completely berserk," said Marshall.

"We have to find her, but I don't think we should split up." Zach checked for a pulse, but Docker was cold and dead.

"Oh no, we can't split up. I'm not going through this place by myself." Marshall shook his head vigorously.

Zach regarded his companion for a moment before nodding. "Ok, Marshall, I understand. These horrid feelings get worse with each passing second. Let's check Sarah's room first. I imagine she locked the door, so we'll have to get a passkey or find someone who can get us into the room. You look through Pena's drawers while I try to figure out the communications."

Marshall said nothing but started rifling through the contents of the desk and filing cabinets that lined the walls of the office. Zach leaned over Docker and looked at the touch screens. The one on the left was dedicated to communications, and he pushed the main menu icon and scrolled through different options until he reached the key labeled, *personnel*. After opening the directory, he found the master list of the employees in the facility that would be wired up. Inside the folder for the maintenance department, Zach clicked on the first name he came across, which happened to be someone named *Fantasia Alvarez*.

He opened a new page that revealed an extensive amount of information on the employee. At the bottom of the screen before the fold, he found her personal employee communications ID. Without hesitation, Zach grabbed the headset lying next to Docker's body and punched in the number. An icon on the screen turned green, which indicated he was connected.

"Ah, I'm looking for Fantasia Alvarez. Is she there?" The line appeared dead as there was no sound to confirm an active connection. After waiting a few moments, he tried again. "I need to find Fantasia Alvarez. It's an urgent matter."

More silence, but Zach thought he heard the distinct click of a send button. A tap on his shoulder caused Zach to stiffen, but it was only Marshall. "I've looked everywhere. There's nothing here unless it's in that safe, and I don't have the combination."

"Great. I..." the radio clicked, which meant someone was pressing the send button.

Just as he was ready to abandon the effort, a woman started talking in a whisper. "I'm Fantasia Alvarez. Who is this?"

"I'm Zach—I mean I'm Speaker Randall."

The voice on the other end spoke in a whisper, but he could sense she was clearly agitated. "Speaker Randall, you've got to help us. There are seven of us here in the rec area. We're hiding in an equipment closet. There's someone out there, and they're killing people. Even the overseers are in great danger."

"Do you know who it is or where they're at?"

"No, but we've heard screaming down the hall in the main cafeteria."

"Fantasia, stay hidden and don't move. I'll be there in a moment."

"Okay. Please hurry, Speaker Randall."

Having listened to the entire conversation, Marshall sat down and shook his head. "How are we going to stop her? There are no weapons here."

"We'll figure out a way. C'mon, let's go.

Zach let off the button and headed out of Pena's office while motioning for Marshall to follow. They furtively moved down the corridor towards the cafeteria, crouching behind furniture and fixtures as they tried to maintain some semblance of stealth. They checked inside the meditation chamber first, but the lights were out. Zach was about to leave when Marshall grabbed his shoulder and pointed to the floor. Two red smears covered about twelve inches of the tile and disappeared under the cut of the door.

Zach turned the knob and cautiously walked inside, feeling along the wall for a light switch. Marshall slipped in behind him and let out a ragged breath that caught in his throat. The shades were drawn, and it took several moments to adjust to the shallow light leaking into the room through the gaps around the windows. Zach found the switch and flipped it on, but the brightness only intensified the shock of the carnage in its unfiltered brutality.

In the middle of the room, Aminah lay sprawled on the floor, her throat slit from ear to ear. The front of her peach-colored agbada was stained in dark crimson, a sign she bled out some time ago. Zach couldn't stop staring at her eyes, bulging wide and etched with a look of fear and terror. With arms extended straight out, her hands were frozen in claw shapes, another indication Aminah had been desperately fighting for her life.

Closer to the door, one of Pena's attendants, Toseman, lay propped up against an interior wall. His face was split open from the forehead down to his jaw. Blood and bone protruded through a wound inflicted by an axe or some similar melee weapon.

Since the security attendants were prohibited from carrying armaments, Toseman's size and strength were neutralized by the attacker's hardware.

Zach wiped tears from his eyes as he stooped down and touched Aminah. The pain of the loss of another overseer was intense and overwhelming. His insides seized as though he lost a limb or a vital organ. Each of these murders prompted a kind of necrosis in his soul. He leaned down, closed her eyes and softly stroked her cheek.

Without turning around, Zach said in a low monotone, "Come with me, Marshall, we have to stop this."

After several seconds without an answer, Zach turned around and found Marshall stooped over in a corner retching uncontrollably. He stood up and walked over to his companion, taking his arm and leading him away from the room.

"It couldn't be Sarah," said Marshall as he wiped the spew from his mouth with his shirt. "There's no way she would do this."

"I'm afraid it's true," said Zach, "and I think I know exactly how and why she's killed the overseers with such violence."

They left the meditation hall and moved past the deprivation chamber and the recreation room. Marshall detected low murmurings and some movement coming from inside the cafeteria. He whispered to Zach, and they approached the entrance, standing outside for several seconds to ensure they remained undetected. Zach turned to Marshall and brought his mouth close to his companion's ear and spoke in a soft whisper.

"I'm going in alone. If Sarah will listen to anyone, it's me."

Marshall nodded, and Zach slowly pushed the door open and stepped inside. The first sight that greeted him was another one of Pena's attendants stooping over the prone form of Jacques, whose hands clutched the shaft of a knife stuck deep into his abdomen. Jacques was gasping for breath, and blood bubbles expanded and popped from his nose and mouth every time he took a breath.

Perception of time seemed slow and distorted, and as Zach turned his head, he watched in disbelief as Rogelio writhed on the floor clutching his face as blood and another yellowish liquid oozed through the spaces between his fingers. Occasionally, he would remove his hands, and Zach could see yawning gashes cut into his forehead and both eye sockets, as though someone struck him in the face with a heavy, bladed object. Somewhere between Rogelio and Jacques, several of the cafeteria attendants lie prone on the floor, either dead or nursing mortal wounds.

Somewhere in the background, a television anchor droned on with a nonsensical commentary, which made the setting even more surreal. Peering out through the lens of shock and trepidation, Zach continued to shift his gaze until he found the person he had hoped wouldn't be in the room. Sarah stood up against the serving table with wide bloodshot eyes that maniacally shifted in all directions. Her clothes clung to her body, saturated with the gore from ravaged bodies and ruptured organs. In one hand she grasped a six-inch knife, and the other held a fire axe she must have pulled from an emergency glass case.

As she scanned the room, her eyes locked with Zach's for a moment. He used the opportunity to send an explosive stream of energy directly into her cerebral cortex. A combination of anesthetic and inquisition, the strength and force of the probe snapped her head backwards, and she stumbled a few steps before recovering.

"Zach," she uttered his name in a sad way before a smile spread across her lips, revealing blood and raw meat on her teeth.

Was she chewing on someone?

He tried to calm her, but his powerful probe returned nothing, and he encountered enormous interference and obstruction from a source he could not identify. Sarah displayed no sense of free will, so it was likely that some alien influence was manipulating her thoughts and actions. An impenetrable barrier shrouded her aura, which explained why the other overseers weren't able to protect themselves through telepathic projection.

"Sarah, why are you doing this?"

She hesitated and opened her mouth but said nothing. Shaking her head, she took two tentative steps forward. "I—I had to do this, Zach. There is no choice. You know it had to happen this way."

"No, I don't, Sarah. You've killed some wonderful people. Tell me *why*?"

She took two more steps toward him. Zach conveyed a strong command for her to stop, but she took another step almost in defiance. "You're trying to stop me, but it won't work, Zach. I think you understand that now." She continued to tentatively move forward; her face contorted into a mask of hatred as her eyes darkened and skin grew sallow and ashen.

381

An overpowering malevolent power radiated from her and washed over him like a foul psychokinetic tsunami.

Sarah was not from the darkness, but the energy she released was the deepest shade of ventablack. Clearly, she was the one who polluted the vortex streams. Murky emotive sludge gushed out of her pores and contaminated everything within her sphere of influence. A malign force appropriated her essence, and the Society unwittingly invited this evil creature into their most guarded sanctuary.

How could I have missed the obvious? She deceived the entire Suicide Society.

Sarah took two more steps and was now within striking distance. A pungent odor rolled off her body and offended Zach's olfactory senses, causing him to gag. He pushed back at the encroaching blanket of darkness but could only hold it at bay. Whatever had control of Sarah was extremely powerful.

"Who is behind this, Sarah? Is it Mr. Cox?"

Sarah's smile widened. "Mr. Cox? Of course not, Zach. I am acting on my own free will. It's obvious that what you're doing here is very wrong. We should be among the people trying to help them instead of hiding in this ivory tower. They all needed to see, and by blinding them, I gave them sight."

Sarah raised the axe above her head and brought it down with a sweeping motion. It grazed Zach's shoulder as it sliced through the air with a distinctive *whoosh*. He looked at the blood seeping from the fresh wound and turned back toward Sarah. This time, he released a torrent of aggressive energy designed to hurt and incapacitate. The perceptual shield that protected her deflected much of it, but some of the energy pierced the veil and penetrated into the pain centers in her brain.

Instinctively, she dropped the axe and cried out in agony. "Ohhhh... You're much stronger than the others. Please stop, Zach. You're hurting me."

An emotive response to her obvious discomfort affected Zach's resolve, and he lowered the threshold of his assault. As the pain passed, Sarah reacted instantaneously. She raised the knife, shrieked, and ran directly at him. Burdened with confused emotions, Zach didn't react in time, and as his mind calculated the intangibles, he realized he couldn't avoid the thrust of the knife from cutting deeply into the vital arteries of his neck.

As Sarah started to swing the blade on its downward arc, she seemed to momentarily lose coordination and staggered backwards as the weapon fell to her side. Zach instantly reentered her mind, but he felt another presence already there. He turned around to find Marshall standing just inside the door looking directly at them with a fierce intensity in his eyes. Sarah hadn't anticipated a second intrusion, and Marshall's unexpected arrival disrupted her momentarily.

Taking advantage of Sarah's disorientation, Zach cut through the static and dense neural fog to trace a path to her hippocampus where he discovered the delayed sensory trojan horse Mr. Cox had placed in her mind. As he hid behind Marshall's mental energy, Zach penetrated the membrane of the ethereal trip wire to learn its purpose and potency. The forensic was nearly instantaneous but revealed troves of information.

Without her knowledge, Sarah was programmed months ago to integrate and destroy the Suicide Society, and once the instructions were activated, the embedded code created an insatiable desire to kill.

Apparently recognizing the ruse was foiled, Sarah looked at Zach and smiled. When she spoke, the tone and inflections in her voice sounded eerily similar to Mr. Cox.

"If you're hearing my voice, it means you've discovered my little deception, *Speaker* Randall. Hopefully, the damage the whore has caused is extensive and has hurt you. When we meet again, and we *will* meet again, I plan on eliminating your annoying organization once and for all."

Together, Marshall and Zach reentered her mind and defused the psychokinetic weapon, and eradicated any remnants of Mr. Cox from Sarah's psyche. There was no way to easily assess the degree of permanent damage she may have suffered. Once freed from the Benefactor's control, she collapsed to the floor in shock and exhaustion. Zach kneeled down, cradling her head in his hands.

"Zach, I'm... I'm so sorry," she muttered while fading in and out of consciousness. "What happened to me? What have I done? Oh my God, tell me..."

"It's not your fault, Sarah," he said while rocking her tenderly. "You had no way to stop him."

Marshall turned around. "Sarah isn't our only problem, Zach. Look." He pointed up at a TV mounted to the wall. A baritone voice from the wall monitor reverberated across the empty room. Zach stood up and moved closer.

... President Halderson announced that forty-seven states have agreed to rescind the Constitution, and a Constitutional Convention will take place on the twenty-ninth of this month in Detroit. At that time, it appears every state legislature will simultaneously pass an amendment assigning governmental authority over to the global conglomerate known as Humans United for Global Equality, or HUGE. Led by the Gehenna Group, the consortium consists of four major corporations that give HUGE a presence in every country across the world.

It is thought by many that these multi-national corporations are in the best position to provide essential services to those disenfranchised by the structural breakdown most areas of the world are experiencing. Numerous other countries including Russia, Japan, France and Brazil have dissolved their governments and awarded governing authority to the HUGE Consortium.

We expect a global announcement from Gehenna's headquarters in Detroit in the near future. We're told CEO Xavier Watts, will speak to us within the next twenty-four hours.

"My God," Marshall said as he grabbed Zach's arm. "Sixtus was wrong. Havas Zir was the agent working for the Corporates. Daxtar Liss was telling the truth. Sixtus thought the glitch was a sign he should stop your friend Munoz and ensure the bomb exploded, but he was wrong. In fact, he unwittingly created the pathway to totalitarian control. This HUGE conglomerate will eventually become known as 'The Corporates'. The future will remain unaltered, and billions will suffer at the hands of these despots."

Zach shook his head. "Xavier Watts is a surrogate for Mr. Cox. We must get to Detroit and try to stop him. Watts can lead us to Cox."

"Yes," said Marshall, "but there is something you must know. I have suspected it for some time, but now I'm certain. Mr. Cox is the second time sculptor."

"Marshall, are you sure?" said Zach as his eyes widened. "If it's true, it would make him almost invincible."

"Yes, I'm sure of it. The old man in Portales was Sixtus Maras. He was trying to warn me of... Zach, it's Sarah!"

Zach whirled around and saw Sarah grabbing the knife she dropped on the floor. She had it extended out to the side of her own head.

"I'm sorry, Zach. I can't live with what I've done," she said as she started to swing the heavy blade at her own neck.

Chapter Thirty

Before she could strike herself with the knife, Zach flooded Sarah's primary motor cortex with a command that temporarily paralyzed her. She dropped the weapon after it nicked the flesh on her neck, drawing only a single drop of blood. Her entire body went limp, and she fell to the floor and started to shake with violent convulsive spasms.

"Please, let me die." Sarah slurred her words in a way that resembled someone in the midst of a stroke. "I can't live with this, Zach. For God's sake let me die. Who knows what else he put into my brain?"

Zach kneeled down and tried to comfort her. "Listen to me. There's nothing else, Sarah. Marshall and I made sure of that. None of this was your fault. If anyone is responsible, it's me because I should have anticipated that bastard would find a way to use you. He robbed you of your free will."

"It doesn't matter; no one will believe it. I couldn't live with it if I…" She grabbed his arm and looked deeply into his eyes. "Zach, did I… did I kill anyone? Tell me I didn't kill Yasin and Liu Wei."

Zach paused before mumbling softly, "No, Sarah, you didn't kill anyone. But Mr. Cox killed many people."

"Oh, God…No…," she screamed the words in a way that was so raw and tortured it sliced through Zach like a thousand cuts from the edge of a fresh razor blade.

"He's right, Sarah," said Marshall. "This wasn't your fault, and if I believe it, others will too."

Zach stood up and looked at Marshall. "I have to check for survivors. Take her to her room and stay there until I get back. Make sure she remains calm and sedated."

Marshall nodded, and together they helped Sarah to her feet. Still unsteady from the assault on her motor skills, she draped one arm around each of them. Once they got into the hallway, she regained some coordination, and Zach gave her a long hug before passing her off to Marshall.

"Remember," he said. "Cox did this, not you. You're as much a victim of his cruelty as everyone he murdered." He squeezed her a little tighter and said, "Don't you dare give up, I need you." At the sound of his words, she once again broke into tears.

"Zach, there's something I need to tell you," Sarah said as Marshall tried to usher her away.

"What is it?"

"Privately." Zach moved closer and leaned down, and she cupped her hand while bringing her lips close to his ear. Whispering softly, his eyes widened and back stiffened. He pulled away, nodded, and then watched as she walked with Marshall down the hallway toward her room.

Zach turned and retraced his path back to the recreation hall. He knew there were survivors there, including Fantasia Alvarez, who he talked to on the radio earlier. Pulling the doors open, he walked inside an empty room with the lights out.

"If anyone is in here, it's all clear now," he said loudly. "It's safe to come out." No one replied, so he walked over to an equipment storage room off to the side in a far corner. He tried to open the door, but it was locked.

"Is anyone in there? Fantasia? This is Speaker Randall. I talked to you on the radio. It's safe to come out now."

He heard movement and the sound of the deadbolt twisting. The door opened slowly, and Pena appeared first, looking ragged and disheveled, his usually perfectly groomed hair a tangled mess. Several other people followed him out, and Zach later learned that one of them was Fantasia Alvarez.

When it seemed the storage room was clear, he started to close the door but felt pressure from the other side. As he pulled it back open, Sasha was standing there motionless. He smiled and tried to embrace her, but she pushed him away and walked over to a far wall, sliding down until she was sitting on the floor, away from everyone else.

Zach waited a moment and then followed. He stood in front of her and said, "Sasha, tell me what you're feeling."

She looked at him with eyes that were heavy, and the whites streaked with deep red. Sasha's complexion was normally flawless, but worry lines creased her forehead, and her lips trembled as she tried to speak.

"They're all dead. I can feel it. Speaker Anston, Jacques, Rogelio, Aminah, Lieu and Yasin. I have a huge hole in my spirit. It's as though a large part of me died with them. I am totally numb."

Zach sat down and held her in his arms. "Our confrontation with Mr. Cox has been devastating. Speaker Anston knew his power was so potent that the chances for success were small. Regrettably, it seems we have failed."

"Sarah… How could she do such a horrible thing? We tried to stop her, but it was as though she was immune to our telepathic suggestions. She exhibited extraordinary physical and mental strength and tossed Pena's security people around like they were rag dolls."

"Sarah was under Mr. Cox' influence for over two decades, and he planted a mind control suggestion deep within the recesses of her psyche. It was well hidden, but like a delayed bomb, it triggered when she found herself in our midst. The embedded instructions turned her into a killing machine." Zach paused and sighed deeply. "Right now, she's suicidal and needs our total support, or I fear she won't make it."

"Everything went wrong when Marshall showed up."

Zach shook his head. "No, Marshall saved us again. He's the only one who experienced the time changes first hand. He gave us insight into the time reset and explained how and why we were living in a new reality where the bomb in Chicago detonated and Cox escaped our trap. No one is more important to us going forward."

"He has the gift but didn't try to take his own life. Jacques and Rogelio never trusted him."

"I know." Zach nodded his head. "I can't explain his gift yet, but we need him, and you've got to accept him as one of us. You know, Sasha, the Suicide Society only has three members now."

She sat silently for a moment before hastily arranging her hair. The somber, depressed expression remained, but she got to her feet. "You're right. We'll have to move on somehow. I'll mourn for my soulmates and then turn to the business at hand, Speaker Randall."

Zach grabbed her and squeezed her tight. "You have no idea how much it means to me that you survived." In that moment, they both dropped the mental shielding held in place since they arrived in the facility. Their minds intermingled, and their auras coalesced, and Zach felt the closeness only two overseers could share. He shared her enormous sense of loss, and she felt his, and the collective experience provided a foundation for healing.

Will we ever find another overseer, Speaker Randall?

If you and I acquired the gift, then others will as well. The Suicide Society is not finished as long as there is one member who remains…

They opened their eyes simultaneously and exchanged knowledge and appreciation that soothed and created a bond so deep it would prove unbreakable. At least for now, they were the last of a remarkable lineage.

"Speaker Randall," Zach focused his attention back to the group. Pena was standing next to him with a look of surprise, alarm and joyfulness. "We must return to the foyer, the first group is arriving."

"The first group? What are you talking about?"

"Come, you will see. It is as it was prophesized."

The survivors left the rec room and made their way back to the foyer. Along the way, they searched for survivors and the dead. Once they reached Pena's control room, he issued an "all clear" signal through the intercom system. The recovery began immediately, Zach would learn later that thirteen people died in Sarah's berserker assault, including five members of the Suicide Society.

"Look," said Pena as he pointed at one of the monitors. Outside the facility, a group of five people stood and stared at the sheer face of the mountain that housed the sanctuary. In spite of reaching what looked like a dead end, they didn't appear to be confused or concerned even if they were only vaguely aware of why they had made the pilgrimage to this place. Several sets of hands felt along the red rock as though they were searching for an entrance.

"Who are these people?" asked Zach.

"They are the enlightened ones," replied Pena. "While they do not have your gift, or even mine, they have a heightened sense of consciousness. They are the artisans, the meek, the protectors of Ghia, the philosophers, the academians, the inventors, the bold thinkers and those sensitive to the multi-dimensional consciousness all around us."

Pena paused as though he was having difficulty expressing the concept in words. "While they may not understand it yet, they thirst for authentic power and reject the quest for external power that has driven humankind since the beginning of our existence. In this time of horrible crisis, they were attracted to the energy of the vortexes." Pena turned and faced Zach directly. "They have been drawn to the overseers and especially to you, Speaker Randall."

Zach looked at the screen as several more people arrived. "Let them in," he said. "I now understand why the facility was built to accommodate a thousand people. The energy of the five vortexes is purified again, and it has intensified considerably since we arrived. This place is impervious to any assault from the realm of evil."

Pena nodded. He reached for his communicator and gave the order to open the secured entryway. "Excuse me, Speaker Randall, but I should go meet them. There is much we must do and much to explain."

Zach nodded. For now, he needed to tend to Sarah and begin to make arrangements to commit the lifeless bodies of his friends to the winds of the vast universe.

***

Wanda's eyes fluttered, and a small smile spread across her lips as they passed the Sedona city limits sign. By the time they reached Dry Creek Road, Coy and Missy were pointing in the direction of a large rock formation due north. Mateo followed Wanda's instructions and turned off on Vultee Arch, and when the pavement ran out, he stopped the car.

"We can't drive any further; we'll bottom out," he said. "Only a four-wheel drive can make it over those boulders. See those two other cars up ahead? They look like they were abandoned."

"It's okay," said Wanda. "We need to go that way, so I guess we'll have to walk."

"And where is it we're going?" he asked in a small voice.

Wanda patted his arm reassuringly and looked into his eyes. "You can't come with us, Mateo. It's time for you to go back to your children in San Diego."

"But... there's nothing up there but rocks and dirt."

She shook her head and smiled. "This place has called me... I can't explain it, but I'm sure our new home is just up over that rock cropping in the distance. The children and I must go there."

Lotus leaned over from the back seat and grabbed Wanda's shoulder. "Now you wait a minute. You're not taking my children."

"Mama, it's all right, we're supposed to go," said Coy. "This is a special place. Missy and I both can feel it. It's what told Wanda to stop and pick us up in Oklahoma. We need to go with her."

"No," Lotus said while shaking her head vigorously. "No one is taking my children. No one."

Wanda gently grasped the frightened mother's hand. "This is where they belong, Lotus. I'm not sure why, but the attraction of this place is like nothing I've ever experienced. It's as though I have a deep spiritual thirst that can only be quenched here."

"But—but they're my babies. I don't even know you."

"I understand," said Wanda. "but where will you take them, and how will you keep them safe? You've seen what the world is out there, and it's only going to get worse. Is that what you want for your children? Constant fear, violence and starvation?

"Over there," said Wanda as she pointed behind her, "is something extraordinary. I can't visualize the details, but I sense the children's gifts will be nurtured and developed. They will be safe and well educated. Most importantly, they'll be happy.

Lotus sat back and looked at Wanda for several seconds. "Fine," she said, "but I want to go with you." Then, more desperately, "*Please*, let me come with you."

Wanda shook her head slowly. "If you can't hear the call, this place wasn't meant for you, at least right now. I know that's hard to understand, but it's the way it must be."

Wanda got out of the car and walked into a small clearing just off the side of the road. The others followed and stood silently, searching for words that might lessen the sadness and tension. Lotus reached into her purse and pulled out a cigarette. Her hands were shaking badly as she struck a match, but Wanda came up and helped steady her. Missy and Coy ran up to their mother and hugged her from either side as Lotus puffed deeply on her cigarette.

After a few moments, she crushed it out and bent down so she was on the same level as Missy and Coy. "What do you two think of all this?" she asked. "Do you want to go with Wanda?"

"We have to go with her, Mama," said Coy. "They need us."

"How do you know?" Lotus's voice quivered.

"Because the mountains told us," said Missy. "Can't you hear them, Mama? The mountains are calling to us. We have to go now." Just as she finished talking, two more people came walking up the dirt road. They stopped and smiled at Mateo and Lotus and then moved over to Wanda and the children.

"We sense you three hear the call. Would you like to go on together?" said a man who looked to be in his early twenties. "We want to get there as soon as possible."

"Yes," said his companion, an older woman in her mid-fifties. "They're waiting for us, and there's so much to learn."

Wanda nodded her head, looked at Mateo, and shrugged her shoulders. Taking a child under each arm, they started climbing up the rocky embankment along with the two people they just met. From a distance, she heard Mateo's grief-stricken voice.

"We're going to wait here awhile, Wanda. If there's nothing there, please come back." Lotus was already in the car overcome with sorrow. After watching the threesome disappear over the first foothill, she waited with Mateo for over two hours before they realized Wanda and the children weren't coming back.

***

Once they moved past the camouflage of the rocky embankment, Wanda discovered a well-hidden path constructed with intelligent design. Holding hands with both of the children, she followed the couple in front as they walked around a berm before reaching a clearing that led to a sheer-faced red rock cliff.

About ten people were already standing in front of the mountain using their hands to touch the surface features of the rough, jagged sandstone. She heard many of them talking, and they were all drawn to this exact spot.

396

Wanda knew they were in the right place, and there was no fear or uncertainty as she waited patiently for whatever would happen next. She never experienced such a feeling of inner peace, security and complete sense of belonging. With her eyes closed, Wanda raised her face to the sun and enjoyed the sensation of its warmth and energy. The temperature was probably in the nineties, but she felt no discomfort. Lost in a meditative state, she hardly noticed the sound of the mountain wall sliding open.

Following those in front of her, Wanda held both children closely as they walked into the interior of an enormous complex carved into the mountain itself. She tightened her grip on Coy and Missy and moved cautiously forward, awestruck by the magnificence of this place and the overwhelming peacefulness she felt inside.

I knew it. This is where we're supposed to be.

A man and a woman in nondescript uniforms smiled and directed them to a spot in the middle of a large foyer near a natural waterfall. The stream cascaded down from the side of a craggy rock wall onto a large outcropping and ultimately into a crystal-clear pond. The action of the swirling waters cleansed the air and left the room with a sweet smell of bee blossoms and desert lavender.

Like the others, Wanda continued to look in wide-eyed wonder at the extraordinary features of this incredible place. For the first time in her life, she understood her purpose. This was home; the place of comfort and tranquility she had searched for her entire life. "Wanda, is this heaven?" asked Missy.

"I don't know, sweetheart, but it's the most wonderful place I've ever seen." Immersed in deep thought, it took Wanda several seconds to realize someone was talking.

"… name is Pena, and I will be your host here at the sanctuary. I am sure you have many questions, and I will do my best to answer the most urgent ones. There will be many gaps in our explanation, and we will fill them in as time permits." Wanda watched as Pena paced across a small elevated platform built high enough that he was visible to everyone as he spoke.

"Let us explore you're most pressing question: Why were you compelled to come here? The answer is both complicated and quite simple. You are all gifted in ways that separate you from the others. Many of you never quite fit in with any peer group. You may have an unusual creativity, deep empathy or an ability to experience certain realities that transcend the five senses."

Pena paused and sipped from a glass of water. "This place called you. There are five distinct vortexes of spiritual energy in and around Sedona. In fact, one of them is in the center of this facility. Over time, you will become familiar with the sensation.

"The energy in the rocks and soil serve to heal, inspire and protect those who are sensitive to it. All of you have that capacity. We knew the energy intensified recently, and you heard its call. You all represent the next reality that will rise up and usher in a new spirit of enlightenment so that people and all the other living beings on earth can live in harmony as the universe intended."

Strangers in the group exchanged reassuring glances, smiles and a growing sense of shared purpose. No one scoffed or questioned Pena. Instead, they looked at him intently, eager for more information.

"There will be much to learn before you are ready to return to the outside world. You are the first to arrive, but there will be many others. Every resident in this sanctuary will have the benefit of learning from outstanding scholars. The most gifted of all of us are the overseers, part of a group known as *The Suicide Society*, which has protected the earth and its inhabitants for centuries.

Pena smiled and looked back toward three people standing in the shadows. "The overseers have the ability to project transcendent energy in a way that can alter thoughts, actions and events. They are extremely powerful but entirely benevolent. I am honored to present their leader to you. Speaker Randall, can you please come and say hello to our newest residents?"

As he emerged from the shadows, Wanda felt an immediate sense of trust and loyalty for this man, whose smile was genuine and warm. He waved to the group, and they enthusiastically waved back.

"I am honored to meet you all today," he said. "This is an extraordinary time, and we are privileged to be a part of this evolution of the human experience." He paused and raised his hands outward. "In this place, you will perfect your skills and learn ways to bring peace, security, tranquility and illumination to our fellow humans throughout the world. We are honored and humbled to help you in your journey. I would like to introduce you to our two most senior guides... Marshall and Sasha, please step forward.

Wanda wouldn't remember the exact moment she realized the person walking up onto the stage was *her* Marshall. A series of flashing lights and wavy lines suddenly appeared in her peripheral vision and spread inward. She wobbled unsteadily before fainting.

Chapter Thirty-One

Mr. Cox looked out at the crowd of filthy vagrants gathered on the streets of the Bridgeport-Stamford-Norwalk corridor. They came from roads and highways that connected poor cities like Ansonia, New Britain and Hartford to the multimillion-dollar homes that lined the shores of East Connecticut.

Outside a massive colonial mansion in Bridgeport's Black Rock neighborhood, a mob of angry floaters shook the gates that kept them at bay. They used discarded rebar and other makeshift tools to pound at the lock until it gave. Streaming onto the grounds, they hurled rocks at the banks of triple-pane windows, and the cascading sound of broken glass drowned out the angry chorus of profanity and demands for killing.

Mr. Cox took up a position in a neighboring yard where he could watch the action of the waves crashing against a sea wall at the same time he saw the crowd drag one of the homeowners out onto the front lawn. The man screamed and begged for his life, but that seemed to only further agitate the mob. A floater in a dirty yellow cap and stained winter coat kicked the man unmercifully, and others held him down by grabbing his legs and putting pressure on each shoulder.

Someone opened a bottle and poured the contents in the incapacitated man's mouth. He screamed, gurgled and shook his head from side to side, but a good portion of the liquid found its way down his throat. Shortly thereafter, he began to spasm and froth just as the mob hauled his naked wife out of the home as she cried and begged for her life. She watched the foaming blood pouring from her husband's mouth and nose as his body lurched in violent convulsions.

"No!" she screamed in a tone that would curdle the blood of anyone with a semblance of compassion, but Mr. Cox only shivered with delight and moved up closer to see what they planned next for her. While they held her down, a woman with long, unwashed gray hair stepped forward and ground her heel into the victim's face. The victim screamed again, but Mr. Cox couldn't tell if it was because of the heel digging into her skin or another floater who stooped down and bit into her leg, ripping away a large chunk of flesh.

The shaken woman writhed and squirmed under the assault, but the crowd grew weary of her whining and begging. Someone pushed through the mass gathering carrying a large decorative lawn boulder, and he lifted it over his head before throwing it with force at her face. A noise like a head of lettuce being chopped in half followed, and her screaming and pleading ceased.

A small group of vagrants brought two children out of the house and pushed them into the interior of the murderous mob. Mr. Cox strained to see what the frenzied throng was going to do to them, but his view was obscured by a large overhanging oak tree and the crowd itself.

After ransacking the house and setting it on fire, the floaters turned their attention to the neighbor's home. Mr. Cox wanted to stay and watch more of the plunder and slaughter of innocents, but there were so many other places he wanted to visit. Like a child with an endless array of Christmas presents, he hardly knew which one to open next.

Eventually, after traveling to see the aftermath of a bombing in Japan and a mass slaughter in Brussels, he returned to Detroit to attend a meeting he scheduled with his closest advisors. As he waited for them to file in, he stood looking out the window of his penthouse suite at the large crowd pushed up against barricades at the corner of Jefferson and Randolph. The sea of humanity stretched as far as the eye could see, and they were all there to give the Benefactor his due respect. The seeds of lust, greed, treachery, deceit and hatred had sprouted into a fine crop of utterly wretched souls. He tapped into their negative energy and drank deeply.

For the first time in many years, people united around a common cause, which centered on inflicting pain on others whose opinion or social status differed from their own. The rich were the most obvious targets. The definition of "rich" became fluid as the people with the highest incomes and most possessions were burned out and killed off first. With the announcement that the Constitution was rescinded, and the Union dissolved, massive numbers of floaters celebrated by targeting the affluent and torturing, beating and burning them alive.

Just like Bridgeport, uncontrolled angry, hateful mobs eager for revenge and looking for an avenue to vent their pent-up frustrations invaded neighborhoods and dragged people from their homes, killing them in increasingly gruesome ways. Lawlessness reigned as the police and military either dissolved or disengaged as the carnage raged on unabated for days on end.

Firmly entrenched as the leader of the new world order, Xavier Watts, under direction from Mr. Cox, issued a proclamation confirming the HUGE consortium's support for the "People's Fairness Movement," which essentially licensed murder and theft for targets who attained "unfair" levels of wealth and prestige.

Gehenna issued special permits to many key executives from the other three corporations who were part of the HUGE conglomerate. Watts deployed military assets to safeguard those people and their families, and Gehenna offered protection for a price to smaller companies and lesser-known administrators hoping to stay alive.

Mr. Cox turned toward his conference table and looked at the participants. They were beaming and with good reason. Lars, Delgado, Watts, Alan and Sandra waited for him to take his place at the head of the table. Mr. Cox was on the verge of assuming sovereign control over the entire world, and the power was intoxicating for those close to him.

"My friends," he began, "our reports indicate that except for isolated pockets of resistance, we, or our surrogates, now control virtually every continent in the world. We have the capacity to crush anyone who defies us. Finally, humanity is close to being united under one world government. I have succeeded where Caesar, Kahn, Alexander and Hitler failed.

"Along with our corporate partners, we will ensure that everyone is treated equally. While the people may interpret the meaning incorrectly, they will adapt to serving us and thank us for whatever we choose to provide." He paused, and Sandra began to clap. The others followed, although Lars and Alan clapped with less enthusiasm.

"I've entrusted my confidant in this journey, Xavier Watts, with the role of CEO of Gehenna and Chairman of HUGE. He will be in charge, and I expect you will follow his direction without exception." Cox's eyes blazed red for a moment, which expressed the seriousness of his directive.

"I've also decided that Sandra Bentenhouse will replace Jarvier Delgado as Head of Security." Delgado dropped his pen and looked up in disbelief. Xavier Watts lowered his head and stifled a laugh. Sandra smiled and winked at the Benefactor and then looked at Delgado with contempt.

"But Benefactor, I've been in charge of security for many years," said Delgado.

"I'm aware of that. But the breach that resulted in the destruction of Building 5 and allowed for my abduction was unacceptable. Frankly, it is only your years of service that spared you from a very painful death, Delgado. My understanding is that Sandra has assigned you to the Middle East security sector starting immediately. Your plane leaves in less than an hour, so I suggest you pack, unless, of course, you choose to leave our organization entirely…"

405

"Holy shit, that's harsh, dude," said Alan. "Harsh, but funny."

Delgado trembled as he grasped his briefcase and shoved his papers, notepad and pen inside. He opened his mouth to speak but thought better of it. Without a salutation, he turned and staggered to the door, wiping sweat from his brow and muttering under his breath as it closed behind him.

"Now that we are governing, some things will change," said Mr. Cox. "From this point forward, I want you all to carry on as though I wasn't here to guide you." Now he had their full attention, and their faces displayed a mixture of puzzlement and deep concern.

"Our only adversary is the Suicide Society, or whatever is left of it. Unfortunately, our disappointing intelligence hasn't been able to locate them, and our agent in their midst has been... deactivated. Rest assured, wherever they are in seclusion, they will continue their effort to disrupt our plans and topple our global governance. Above all else, every vestige of that organization must be destroyed. Ultimately, they will reveal themselves, and we must be ready. Hopefully, our new Minster of Defense will prove more imaginative than the old one." Mr. Cox smiled at Sandra, who returned his gaze and licked her lips.

"I'm turning the meeting over to Mr. Watts, who will bring in the CEOs from our corporate partners. There is much work to be done in terms of logistics and restructuring. As most of you know, I find these policy meetings quite boring." He paused for a long moment, and his smile disappeared.

"And so, I will say my goodbyes to you now." Mr. Cox stood up and stepped away from the table, raising his hand and waving just before he left the room. The Board of Directors watched him depart, but his absence created an unsettling sense of discomfort. The temperature dropped suddenly, and a chill ran through everyone still seated at the conference table. Something just didn't feel right.

***

Once they made eye contact, Marshall jumped from the stage and rushed toward Wanda. An attendant got to her before he did and revived her with some water before creating space so she could breathe. Marshall stopped about five feet away and just stared at her. She was sitting up and sipping water when she saw him standing in front of her. His smile was wide and genuine, and he didn't have to say a word. In that instant, even as the tears flowed freely, Wanda understood she had found her soulmate.

"How did you know I was here?" he asked.

"I didn't. I was — called here. All these people were called to this place. Is it true, Marshall? Are we gifted in some way? Are *you* part of this 'Suicide Society'?"

He nodded. "Yes, I am, and I'll explain it all to you later. We'll have as much time as we need to work everything out, but right now I have to get back up to the stage. Speaker Randall is talking again." He leaned over and kissed her full on the lips.

"I don't understand any of this, but I know I love you, Marshall Beiner," she said.

"I love you too, Wanda." There was no hesitation in Marshall's reply. "I can't imagine what you've gone

407

through to get here, but you'll have my undivided attention soon." He hugged her before returning to the stage just as Zach resumed talking to the group.

"I'm so pleased you found this wonderful place of healing, renewal and spiritual growth. Every day, new residents will complete the pilgrimage to our sanctuary. For the foreseeable future, all of you will remain safe while you're learning and expanding your capabilities." Zach paced the stage as he talked.

"You came here because something bigger than any of us compelled you. Call it a spirit, intuition or God; it hardly matters. The laws of the universe are immutable, and they tell us that light triumphs over darkness; good triumphs over evil, and we experience authentic power when we act from love instead of fear." Zach paused and allowed the words to filter into the receptive minds of the gifted new arrivals.

"Pena and his staff will provide you with everything you need. The facility is self-sustaining and includes recreational facilities, cafeterias, exercise rooms, swimming pools, meditation chambers, libraries and classrooms. Listen and learn from your guides. They will be your mentors. You will grow mentally, physically and spiritually. When it is time, you will graduate from this place and become the salvation of humanity."

Zach waved to the gathering and walked over toward Pena, who was standing off to the side of the makeshift stage. As they spoke, the caretaker appeared agitated, and his gestures were increasingly animated. After some time, Zach clasped him on the shoulder and went into the residence wing while Pena returned to the stage and began to discuss living arrangements with the recent arrivals. With hundreds of new residents expected shortly, it was time to implement procedures that were crafted centuries ago and updated as required.

Zach looked across the stage and motioned for Marshall and Sasha to join him. When they arrived, he playfully cuffed Marshall on the shoulder.

"Well, is that your significant other?" he asked while grinning.

Marshall shook his head without embarrassment. "Yes, that's Wanda. I just can't believe she's here. She's so strong and a survivor. Isn't she — beautiful?"

"Yes, Marshall, she is very beautiful. Don't let her go or ever take her for granted." Zach looked at the remaining overseers with a hint of sadness in his eyes. "You two are all that stands between humanity and anarchy. These people need your patience, guidance and leadership. No matter what happens, the Suicide Society must endure."

"What are you saying, Speaker Randall?" said Sasha. "You're not leaving us?"

"I have to leave the sanctuary for a time. If by some chance I'm unable to return, I want you both to understand how important it is that you survive and find others with the gift'"

"I don't care for the sound of this, Speaker Randall," said Marshall. "Your leadership is vital. I'm not confident enough to guide these people."

"No, Speaker Randall," said Sasha. "I agree with Marshall. We need you in this time of crisis. You can't leave us."

Zach shook his head and smiled. "I'm sorry. There really isn't any choice. You've got to work with Pena to make sure these gifted people reach their full potential.

The way we prevail in this struggle is to start on the smallest level.

"You must help prepare them to integrate back into society and bring enlightenment to those around them. The vortex has done its job by drawing them here. Now, you must do your job. Know that I believe in you both." Zach reached out and placed a hand on each of their shoulders.

"You haven't told us where you're going," said Marshall.

"I'm sorry, but I can't. It might jeopardize both of you and this place. I'll return shortly if it's possible, but if I'm not back within a day or two, it probably means I won't be coming back at all."

He hugged them both, and Sasha buried her head in his chest and cried openly. Marshall returned his embrace, and they exchanged traces of energy that would bind them together with the same feelings a father might have for a son.

"Look at them," said Zach as he pointed at a new group of people entering the foyer. "Within the next few weeks, they'll arrive from around the world, and this facility will become full. Take your rightful places next to Pena." He paused and nodded to them reassuringly. "I have to go talk to Sarah now. Please take care of her while I'm gone."

They stood awkwardly for a moment before Zach broke away and walked down one of the facility's residential wings. Pena moved Sarah to a different apartment to help alleviate some of the depression and anxiety she experienced every time she looked at the rooms where Liu, Aminah, Rogelio and Jacques had stayed. Two assistants sat to either side of her door, and two more were inside the

410

room, taking turns on a twenty-four-hour suicide watch.

As Zach entered, he saw Sarah lying on the bed with her head buried under two pillows. When she heard the door close, she moved the pillows and slowly sat upright, looking at him with a sense of sorrow and sadness so deep it took his breath away. Zach sat down next to her, and she grabbed on to him. The flood of tears started all over again.

Without Sarah's knowledge, Zach entered her mind and began to subtly smooth and caress the raw and inflamed portions of her psyche that caused the intense feelings of guilt and remorse. In his absence, the responsibility for propping Sarah up emotionally would fall to Marshall and Sasha. Even though she understood her destructive actions were rooted in the powerful hidden suggestions Mr. Cox placed in her mind, she still couldn't forgive herself.

"You're leaving," she whispered as she held him tight.

"I have to, and you know why."

"The message I gave you. I wish I hadn't told you." She slipped her hand underneath his shirt to feel the warmth of his skin.

"I'll come back, and we'll be together forever. I promise."

"Please, stay with me tonight."

"Of course." He nodded and turned to the attendants. "I'll watch over Sarah. You can come back at daybreak."

"Yes, Speaker Randall," said Cheeves while signaling to the other attendant.

Once he was sure they were gone, Zach pulled her close, and they kissed as passion flowed freely from his

411

body and mind, which helped further the healing process. He pushed her down onto the bed and kissed her again.

"I love you," he said. She smiled, stroked his hair and looked at him like there was still a reason to live.

***

Zach stepped from the car and walked the short distance to the front of the abandoned building in Desolation. To remain untraceable, he drove from Sedona, and as he looked around at the deserted streets, he absently wondered where the townspeople had gone. He suspected that some of them left with the Benefactor while others fled or died.

Walking inside the former town hall, Zach noted the dirt, dust and disrepair that crept through the building since his last visit. He moved to the elevator and pressed the button, which lit up instantaneously. Once he stepped inside the cab, the doors closed, and the downward plunge began.

Zach cautiously crept through the underground compound Mr. Cox used to devise and implement his malevolent plans. He followed the trail of rotted, rancid energy that grew in strength as he came closer to his destination. Fighting growing nausea, he looked over at the cage that once held Sarah and the library where Marshall hid. A visit to Desolation was always unsettling, but it was even more eerie when deserted.

At the end of the room, he noticed the back of an executive chair positioned under a single lit bulb next to an end table. He stopped and watched as Mr.

Cox spun the chair around and faced him directly. The Benefactor's eyes were shut, but his grin was oversized and spread from ear to ear. Dressed in a pinstriped suit that looked more appropriate for the 1920s gangster era, he breathed deep and clasped his hands together. The end table was clear except for a small metal box sitting just in front of his right hand.

"Ah, Mr. Randall. How good it is to see you again," he said. Mr. Cox' eyes fluttered open, and Zach could see the inflamed reddish-orange of molten lava burning just below the surface of his irises. "Apparently, you received my message. I take it Sarah is well?"

"She's recovering from your monstrous subliminal suggestions if that's what you mean."

"She was always so impressionable. The girl will do anything if you prod her a little. And I mean... anything."

Zach's nostrils flared as he clenched his jaw.

"Oh wait; I'm sorry. I forgot you two are... an item, right?"

"What do you want?" Zach ignored the provocation. "Why did you ask me to come here?"

The smile instantly evaporated. "The Suicide Society. Where in Sedona are they hiding? I'm familiar with every inch of that dreadful town, but I can't pinpoint their exact location. As you know, those vile vortexes are shielding them."

Zach smirked. "As if I would tell you that. We will remain hidden until we're ready to undo the damage you've inflicted on humanity. Remember, we have the advantage since we know where you are. How do you like Detroit?"

The Benefactor's smile returned. "Ah, yes, Detroit. The new capital of the world. Everything has proceeded

413

as expected, but I can't allow your irritating band of rebels to continue to disrupt my plans. I will find where you have them hidden."

"You are the second Time Sculptor, aren't you?" The question seemed to catch Mr. Cox off balance, and he paused as his ever-present smile disappeared for just a moment.

"Who told you that?"

"I figured it out myself with the help of someone I imagine you expected would not survive."

"Sixtus Maras could not have lived through the explosion, and I'm certain he was there to facilitate the detonation of the third nuclear device. It must be someone else who told you."

"So, you *are* the elusive second Time Sculptor."

"I am not here to answer your questions, Mr. Randall. I am here to *receive* answers. Tell me where you have hidden the Suicide Society." Simultaneously, Mr. Cox unleashed a hot torrent of black energy, which only surprised Zach with its intensity. He shielded himself from the assault but was certain Cox had gained some peripheral information.

"There's only *three* of you left," the Benefactor exclaimed as his eyes widened. "Sarah became the berserker and killed the rest. Wonderful!"

Zach didn't reply and instead attacked the pre-frontal cortex in Cox' diseased brain, looking for clues as to his origins and intentions. The Benefactor deflected the attack, but Zach modulated the incursion and used alternate pathways to send a mock tendril as a diversion. This caused Mr. Cox to defend his hypothalamus instead of his temporal lobe, the area that contained long-term memories.

By the time he was able to repel the attack, Zach recovered shards of important information.

"So, that's it," he said. "All along you were intent on preserving the future, not changing it."

Mr. Cox reached over and opened the small metal box that sat on the table. A translucent yellow light leapt out and crackled with intense energy, bathing every corner of the room in dazzling color so bright Zach had to cover his eyes.

No matter where you go, I will find you and your surviving Suicide Society brethren, Mr. Randall, and I will kill them.

Zach tried to shield himself from the intensity of the luminance, but it cut through him like a strong wind on a cold day. The light started pulsing and slowly turned from yellow into a deep blood red. Zach reached out telepathically to locate Mr. Cox, but every solid object in the room transformed into malleable energy that flowed and converged until nothing was separate or distinguishable. The pulsing increased in intensity until the light became so oppressive that Zach fell to the floor and screamed in agony. Somewhere in the background he heard Mr. Cox' distinctive laugh.

Goodbye, Mr. Randall, I'll say hello to Sixtus Maras for you if I happen to see him.

Reality became elastic in that moment, and it pulled and pushed against the bonds of matter until the shredded subatomic quarks and leptons created a hole in the fabric of space-time.

***

The man sat huddled in a corner of the state institution in Phoenix, a blanket over his legs and a

415

steaming cup of tea in his hand. The doctor approached and pulled up a chair across from him.

"Thomas, is it you? Is it you? The man carefully placed the cup on the table next to him and reached over to feel the face of the doctor. "Yes, yes it is you," he said.

"How are you feeling today, John? Any recollections yet?"

"No, only the ones I've told you about many times. I know I fought with an evil man with great mental powers. I have great mental powers myself, you know."

"Yes, so you have said. But you still can't remember who you are?"

"No, I'm sorry, I can't—can't remember my name."

"Or where you're from?"

"No, I can't remember that either."

"Okay, John. We'll try again tomorrow."

"Doctor, what about my eyes? When will I be able to see again… soon?"

The doctor stood up and looked at his patient. He ran his hand through his hair and sighed. "Your retinas are badly burned, John. We found you screaming in a strip mall parking lot in Mesa, and no one knows how you got there. The ophthalmologist is doing everything he can, but he says he's never seen burns like these. Hopefully, we'll know in time."

John Doe nodded, reached over and carefully picked up his tea. He sipped the warm liquid, swirled it around in his mouth and openly wept.

The End

416

Sign up to my email list:
https://authorwbk.com/contact/

Visit my website: www.authorwbk.com

Facebook:
https://www.facebook.com/WilliamBrennanKnight

Twitter: https://twitter.com/Williambrennank

Instagram:
https://www.instagram.com/wbkauthor/

Books in the Suicide Society Series:

Prequel: Desolation (novella)
Book One: The Suicide Society
Book Two: Rational Insanity
Book Three: Kill it to Death
Book Four: Resurrection of Death

If You Liked the Book, Please Leave a Review

If you enjoyed this book, would you mind taking a few minutes to leave a review on Amazon? The process is very easy. Scroll down on the book page until you see the reviews section. On the left side, underneath the ratings, you'll see a button that says, "Write a Review." Simply click the button and a box will pop up where you can leave your review. If you're uncomfortable with writing, not to worry. Most review readers are just looking for your general impressions and how much you liked the book.

About the Author

William Brennan Knight is originally from Chicago and settled in Arizona in the 1980s. In his life, he has been a father, musician, salesman and business owner. His passion for writing began early in his childhood and flourished as he grew older. He enjoys reading horror, thriller and science fiction as well as memoirs and biographies.

Knight currently lives in Southern Arizona and spends most of the summer in Ruidoso, New Mexico.